Mason

Rebel Wayfarers MC
Book #6

MariaLisa deMora

Edited by Hot Tree Editing

Updated cover design: Debera Kuntz

Original cover: Melissa Gill @ MGBookcovers and Designs

Front cover image: Gridiron Records and Kyle Turley

Back cover image: Motorcycle and Super Car Photography by Frank J. Bott, a Frank J. Bott & Eli Whipple Visual Production Company

Copyright © 2015 MariaLisa deMora

First Published 2015

ISBN 13: 978-0-9863562-4-7

DEDICATION

When a man is denied the right to live the life he believes in, he has no choice but to become an outlaw. – Nelsen Mandela

This book, more so than all the others, is dedicated to the readers who never stopped pushing for more of our favorite outlaw.

Contents

ACKNOWLEDGMENTS

This book is for every reader who demanded to know Davis Mason's story, every reader who fell in love with this dynamic and dangerous character. His voice is prominent in each Rebel Wayfarers MC story, his perspective influencing every milestone event encountered. Strong, loyal, steadfast, intelligent, and passionate, I believe Mason resonates so strongly with readers because he is the father, friend, hero, and lover we all want in our lives.

He snuck into my life slowly. As a support character, when Mason first entered my dreams of Mica, I was not certain if he would be hero or villain. While we know which end of the spectrum he now inhabits, what about his younger years? Has he always been the hero? Will you, the reader, still love him if that's not the case?

Get ready to meet a more nuanced Mason, one who is perhaps more vulnerable, who internally questions his decisions and agonizes over mistakes. Especially when those mistakes cost the people he cares about, the ones for whom he bears responsibility.

Fans of the Rebel Wayfarers have been asking why Mason's book isn't the last one in the series. How, if he is such a keystone character, his story can be told now, in the middle of everything? You all want to know what comes next. My answer? More Rebels, at least for a time.

Think of these books as a saga, beginning with *Mica*. *Mason* settles into the center of the series because, as always, Prez is in the big middle of everything! There are many other characters woven in and around him as he enters their timeline, and so many of them have something to say. Right now, I have another four books planned for this series, so get comfy, we have a bit of time together still.

The 'thank yous' for this book are many. From alpha readers and listeners, to editors, and famous folks who gave me a green light on the project, I have much for which to be thankful. And, I cannot forget the readers and fans. Because of you and your willingness to enter this world with me, because of your support for these stories, we have the chance to continue the journey together. Thank you.

The cover is one of my favorites. Absolutely stunning, the image captures the essence of Mason in a way that makes words unnecessary. Kyle Turley, former NFL star and current country rock sensation, I was honored to work with you for the cover image, and I still get goosebumps every time I look at the picture. In so many ways you **are** the Mason I see in my head. Frank Bott, hot bike photographer extraordinaire, you were willing to entertain a crazy idea from this unknown author, and worked hard to make sure it happened. You guys rock hard and I am forever grateful to you!

Kayla, Becky, and the HTE betas, thank you for your work and feedback. As always, you make these stories better.

Hollie – you listened through more hours than was reasonable of my 'read aloud' edit for *Mason*. Your reactions as I delivered dialog and read scenes were critical to the creation of this final version. To my fabulous alpha readers: Kristen, LeeAnn, Kay, Kori, and the bold MirandaPanda, your feedback made the story better. Never doubt your part in this process. Thank you.

Last, but never least, to my personal motorcycle men, members of clubs in Michigan, Indiana, Ohio, Texas, and New Mexico. Your patience with me is beyond expectation. Love you all so hard. I am blessed and highly favored.

~ML

1. Call me Mason

1988

"Davy, hon, you don't have to do this." DeeDee's soft voice came from behind him, but he ignored her. As he stared at the man who stood across the rude ring from him, he knew she was wrong. He did. He had to do this, because he couldn't keep going the way he was...the way things were now. He needed to get off the streets, and this was the fastest way for him to accomplish his goal.

Deacon, the club president, had been clear: Beat a member in a no-holds-barred fight or accept a beating with unyielding strength and courage, and he would win the right to a place in the Rebel Fiends. He rolled his shoulders, pushing her words away with his actions, silently communicating he needed her to shut her mouth and stop undermining his determination. He needed this, needed it to move away from the brink of barely surviving. He had to do this, had to beat the club's champion, had to become a member, had to...

In his escape from Kentucky, he had stayed two months in Fort Wayne with his cousin and her old man, Winger, but Chicago was where he needed to be; he knew it in his gut. So he headed up here weeks ago, only to find less of a welcome than he had naively expected. He had managed to endure so far, but only narrowly, always sleeping with one

1

eye open, whether it was in shelters when he could find an open bed, or under bridges when he couldn't. Surviving. Clothes dirty, pants ripped, belly empty. Alive and breathing, barely existing. But not living.

Drawn to the bikers gathered in bars and homes he had seen around since his first day free, he found himself lusting after the machines they straddled as they rode down the streets. Drifting closer to the fringes where their lives bordered on the rest of the world, he found the idea of the clubs to be a gripping attraction, luring him in. Winger had introduced him to the compelling culture shared with his men in Fort Wayne, and he recognized the bond the men in that club had between them, the tight brotherhood, and Davy hungered for the connection nearly as much as the bikes themselves.

Sauntering into the uneven space that had opened between the two men, Deacon looked first at the member selected to face Davy, a man about five years older than him called Ripper, who nodded, and then at him. Setting his jaw, he dipped his head once sharply and, taking a deep breath, settled himself more firmly into a ready stance. He hadn't grown up wrestling the boys in the family compound without learning a few things; this kind of harsh competition sat firmly in his wheelhouse. He was born for this. His daddy told him so frequently as he pocketed the earnings from Davy's bouts. As he shifted his gaze from Deacon to his opponent, he easily recognized the bunching and shifting play of muscles under the other man's skin, a glaring signal the man was expecting to come at him explosively, trying to take him off guard.

Outwardly, he didn't react, but inwardly, he snorted, because, clear as if he were holding a flashing sign, the man was telegraphing his intentions. *I'll have to teach him how to handle himself better.* He had time for the thought before Deacon's hand came down in a sharp knife movement, signaling the start of the fight. Ripper's head went down and he charged across the ring, arms pumping to give him greater speed. Davy sidestepped the rush, turning with him and hitting him three times over his left kidney, hard but quick, each fisted blow finding its mark. Twisting aside, he danced away and across the open circle of men to the other side before Ripper could slow and turn.

His opponent went down heavily on one knee, a pained and surprised sound bursting from his lips. With his size advantage, he probably wasn't accustomed to taking the brunt of the punishment in a fight. Davy stilled, but didn't shift his focus. If the fight were over, someone would let him know, but he couldn't afford to be taken by surprise because he was distracted or overconfident.

Surging to his feet with a grunt, Ripper approached him more guardedly this time, reaching out a long arm to try and grab one of Davy's hands. Scowling, because the man was taller than him by four inches and had a longer reach, Davy batted away his hand three...four times, patiently waiting for the moment when the big man would overreach, be off-balance...*now*.

He seized Ripper's wrist and pulled him close, bringing up his other fist and battering at his ribs until the man bent over, reflexively trying to protect himself. Davy saw an opportunity and seized it, shifting his hands up, grabbing onto the sides of Ripper's head. With a roar, the only sound he had made during the fight, he brought the man's face down onto a bare, bony knee as he lifted it, inwardly wincing when he felt the distinctive crunch of nose cartilage.

Releasing the suddenly lax body, letting it slump down, he backed to the edge of the circle again. Settling into his waiting and ready pose, he kept his focus solely on the man lying motionless on the floor. It didn't escape him that he was unmarked from the fight. The only time Davy had allowed Ripper's flesh to touch his had been when he was taking a punch from Davy's knuckles, or on the man's face, when brought down onto his knee. He knew simply dominating and controlling the fight didn't imply his rival wasn't still a threat. It also didn't signify he wasn't still in danger. These were men living a life bound only by their own rules. While honorable in their own way, it didn't mean they wouldn't jack him if it mattered to them.

"Jesus *fuck*, boy." Winger muttered the curse in awe from behind him. Huffing out a short breath, he was more secure with the reminder his friend was at his back as he flexed his fists and relaxed minutely, watching as avidly as the spectators as Ripper lay there, still unmoving.

Deacon spoke from across the circle. "Damn it. Ripper, you just cost me fifty dollars. Gonna take a bill from your next envelope, boy." He pulled out his wallet, twisted the chain attaching it to his belt out of the way, and dragged out a small wad of bills, handing them to the man next to him. "Under a minute, too, goddammit. Too fast to even be entertaining. Jackson, you motherfucker, how the hell did you know the boy could fight like that?"

Grinning, Jackson accepted the money, folding and tucking it into the front pocket of his jeans. "You're a city boy, Deacon. Y'all get raised a lil different from us country folk. I took a chance he'd be a tough bastard. Didn't know the boy'd whup ass like he did, though. Owned the fight, man. Flat out *owned* it. That's purely a bonus, a joy to watch." He looked down at Ripper, beginning to stir on the floor. "Not a joy for Rip, though. Mother*fuck,* our boy took a lickin'."

Taking several deep breaths, Davy rolled his shoulders and watched Deacon through narrowed eyes. No one had addressed him directly yet, and he was beginning to wonder if the fight was a set-up for their entertainment, rather than initiation into the club. DeeDee's palm settled onto his spine, the small patch of warmth silently telling him she had his back, too. He gave an inward snort again, because there wasn't a fat lotta good her support would do him. She was a woman, and he knew women only had one place in this rough world, and it wasn't in a fight ring defending a man's back. She was only here on sufferance, because when Winger set the match up, he had vouched for her presence, promised she wouldn't interfere.

Deacon finally met his eyes, and Davy raised his chin, giving the man his full attention. Being the singular focus of his stare made some men nervous, but it brought a grin to Deacon's face. "All right, boy, you've earned your chance to be a member. Get a vest and we'll give you a prospect patch. What'll we call you?"

"Mason," the sixteen-year-old boy said curtly and nodded. "Call me Mason. Much obliged, Deacon."

2. Monaco

1989

Stepping backwards, he set his shoulders and leaned against a wall inside the house the Rebel Fiends owned in town. Mason tucked his thumbs into the front pockets of his jeans, watching the members as they ramped up for what promised to be a typically epic Saturday night party. He heard his name called and raised his gaze, finding Ripper standing in a doorway across the room. He lifted his chin, watching his friend walk across to where he was standing.

He didn't give much attention to the woman tucked under Ripper's arm, because, like the rest of the women in the room, she was disposable. House mouse or club whore, either way, the pussy would be here this week, gone the next. The club didn't let women hang around for long, mostly because the women didn't want to stay, but Deacon explained in his experience men got possessive, and then bitches came between brothers. He thought about his cousin and her husband down in Fort Wayne, but didn't care enough to argue the point with his president.

At six months in and still a prospect, he was even now trying to figure out how best to keep his head down and not attract unwanted attention. Adapting himself into what the club expected had come quickly to him. The dynamics in this male-led group were not much different from the compound in Kentucky ruled by his father. Strength and pure-assed meanness were traits of the top dogs in both situations. Here, it was their president, Deacon, who held top dog position, and it was a mistake to get on his bad side, as Mason learned. It helped that the rules here were easy to remember: club first, individuals last; protect your brothers at any cost. Everything else was up for discussion...when you could find someone sober enough to discuss, that was.

"Mason." Ripper greeted him, and he nodded. "You hear what Deacon's planned for tonight?"

Shaking his head, Mason asked, "Do I even wanna know?" Half the time, it seemed Deacon's plans resulted in trouble, most often trickling straight down to him. He had earned a reputation around town, known to the gangs and clubs in Chicago as the man to beat in a fight, which meant Deacon was constantly fielding offers for matches. If the money was right, he would accept, sometimes not even telling Mason something was up until they were nearly in the middle of the event. It was an effective intimidation tactic against the other clubs, because if someone as young as Mason could repeatedly win against their well-seasoned men, it came across as a toughness on all sides of the entire club. The assumption would be a lie, but he sure as fuck wasn't going to tell anyone.

He snorted, glancing around the room. Besides him and Ripper, the only straight person in the room was John, who had a chick bent over the back of a chair. Head thrown back, his hands were on her hips, and he was powerfully punching into her from behind, fucking her. Mason watched dispassionately as another member sitting in the chair stood, staggering a little when he took his dick out, and shoved it into the woman's mouth. After a couple minutes, the man cursed and staggered again, his hands tugging at her hair, moving his hips in counterpoint.

Outwardly, Mason didn't react when the man pulled his now soft cock out of her mouth before hitting her with an open hand, but inwardly he winced at the blood that ran from her nose and mouth. Most likely, it was booze or dope that caused the man's dick to go limp before he got off and not her performance, but she took the punishment stoically anyway. Not arguing, in fact, not even moving except to cup her hands, catching her blood in her palms until John finished.

Slapping her on the ass as he tucked his dick into his pants, John turned and strolled across the room towards him and Ripper. Mason watched over John's shoulder as the woman stooped and pulled up her shorts, turning to go to the bathroom. He shook his head because he didn't understand the bitches. He had seen this particular woman around before. Deacon had used a knife on her pants one night at a local pool hall, cutting a hole in the front of the crotch, careless of the skin behind the fabric. Directing her to stand at one corner of the pool table when his opponent was shooting, he hoped the blonde's curly hair peeking out through the opening would distract the man. It worked, and Deacon had won several hundred dollars, laughing about holding the man by the short and curlies in more than one way. The woman had gotten fucked from behind that night, too, bent over the pool table she had recently been decorating.

John walked up, the three of them clustering in their usual three-pointed configuration as he asked, "What's going on tonight?" Looking at Ripper, he raised one eyebrow, glancing down at the woman tucked against his side. Ripper shook his head and thrust her away, and John swatted her ass, telling her, "Get us some beers." After she had taken several steps away from the group, he repeated his first question, "What's going down?"

"Deacon wants to take over the Monaco. We were doing protection for the joint until a couple weeks ago, when the owner started paying the Dominos instead. It's going to be bloody." Ripper held out his hand for a wrist clasp from each man, saying, "Brothers, I got your back."

Mason nodded, echoing the words. Questioning a rumor he recently tracked down, he asked, "John, you hear anything about the Skeptics getting restless where they are?"

"Fuck you, Mason. Call me Diamond. I've told you a dozen fucking times. Diamond." John scowled at him.

Mason laughed. "You don't get to name yourself, motherfucker. You know how this shit works. We just ain't found a real name for you yet." He had lucked out when he found John already a member of the club here in Chicago. Although they had never met before that day, John was his half-brother and knew his name as well as he had known John's. His brother...blood brother, had been a member of the Fiends for nearly two years. He helped ease the way for Mason in part, and Mason found he liked knowing he had blood close by.

John had been back and forth to California several times in the six months Mason had known him. He would go home to San Diego, where his father was president of a club, hang out there for a while, and then come back with new ideas for Deacon to try. Everyone expected him to take over the Cali club at some point, especially since it was also where his wife and daughter were, along with an illegitimate son. Mason shook his head, remembering the story John told one night, half drunk, about how the bitch had hidden his boy from him, denying the child's parentage. Mason couldn't imagine having kids, much less having one you didn't even know about for five years. *What a fuck-up John was sometimes.*

Loud shouts rang from the front of the building, and the three men raised their heads, all tensing as they looked towards the doorway. Hand going to the middle of his back where he kept his gun tucked into the waistband of his jeans, Mason waited with the others to discover what would come through the door. They all partially relaxed when Deacon came in, his gaze sweeping the room to stop on their group. "Monaco," he said with a sneer. "I want you to get your asses to the fucking Monaco and explain to the bastard running it that he ain't running it anymore." He laughed and turned then twisted his head back, dark eyes boring into Mason. "Terminal fucking situation if he argues, you got me?"

"Got you, I got you, man. Fucking hate Tilly, arrogant bastard. Will be good to give him what he deserves. I got you, Prez," John responded immediately, brown-nosing as usual, but Deacon ignored his run of words, eyes locked on Mason until he received a single short nod in response. He knew Mason was friendly with the owners of the bar, Merry and Tilly, and knew what the statement would do to him.

"Boy, you hung onto your response a mite long," Deacon said, and Mason felt John and Ripper easing away, giving him room. *Fuck*, he thought, taking a deep breath. This would be a repeat of a scene acted out many times since he joined the club. Deacon was determined to break him, make him bow, and Mason was exactly as determined never to give any man that kind of power over him again. He had vowed his father would be the last man to beat this type of response out of him. And, even if he didn't know it, Deacon's level of discipline fell far short of his father's anyway, lacking the arrogance and conviction that came from believing oneself God's mouthpiece.

He stood, waiting, watching Deacon saunter across the room. "I believe I just said I want you to get your fucking ass to the fucking Monaco." He swept his hand out, indicating the room. "And yet, I note you're still here in front of me, standing in my goddamn clubhouse."

"Our clubhouse," Mason said before he could clamp his lips closed. *Fuck*, he thought, *there's the gasoline*. He was the match; anyone could see how his presence lit Deacon up like a bonfire. These days, any excuse was enough for the man, and with this fuel, now everyone in shouting distance would get to witness the fucking inferno blaze high and hot. Before he could even settle his feet into a bracing stance, Deacon was on him, fist punching the side of his head hard.

He learned early on that fighting back wasn't an option. You didn't hit your president and expect to keep breathing air. Deacon quickly hit him again, fist to his temple. Dazed, Mason stumbled and fell to one knee then climbed back up, fists clenched at his sides, gaze locked on Deacon's eyes. "My fucking clubhouse." Deacon grunted, coming at him again, taking his time knocking Mason to his hands and knees. He shook his head hard before standing again, hot blood welling in his mouth. They had repeated this dance a dozen times before Deacon stepped back, breathing hard and glaring as Mason staggered to his feet once again. He swallowed the mouthful of blood, clenching his jaw, waiting.

"Get your fucking ass to the Monaco. You got me?" Deacon leaned forward, putting his fleshy lips next to Mason's ear as he said, "You ain't gonna ever learn. My fucking club, my fucking clubhouse, and you're my fucking pussy if I want it that way. And, boy…you sure the fuck won't fight me back. Will you, pussy boy?"

"I got you, Prez," he gritted out, ignoring the rest, and waited. Waited to discover if this was over, waited to determine if he could hold himself in check once again. Waited to see if today would be the day one of them would die.

Deacon pulled back, his gaze scanning Mason up and down, and then without another word, he turned and stalked out of the room. Mason clenched his eyes closed, tightly clamping a lid on the pain, ears still ringing from the blows he had taken.

"Fuck," Ripper said, pressing a bandana into Mason's hand. "He fucked you up, Mason."

"You like pushing the old man's buttons, don't you?" John laughed shrilly, excitement evident in his voice at the promise of more action. "Clean up. Let's get rolling."

"I'm still fucking standing, ain't I?" Mason asked, wiping the blood from his face and neck, feeling a slow trickle still coming from his nose. He swallowed the blood in his mouth again, the bright taste of copper making him sick. Reaching up, he poked at his split lip with one finger, wincing at the pain. "Still standing." He gave Ripper a chin lift. "I'm good, brother. Let's go."

"We gotta fucking do this." John led them out to the lot, yelling and pumping his fist into the air, with a shouted, "Let's *do this*."

Mason followed him, sighing as he walked up beside his bike, the engine finally turning over after several hard kicks. He sat and waited for the other two to start their bikes, and then pulled out in the lead, knowing they would fall into formation behind him. On the ride over, he rolled sample scenarios around in his mind, trying to plan for every contingency, knowing it was a futile exercise, because he couldn't know all the players ahead of time. Frustrated at his apparent inability to change the path before him, when they pulled into the lot of the Monaco, he didn't wait for the other two men to park, simply standing up off his bike and heading for the door.

Glancing around as he walked, he saw a few other bikes in the lot already, and it twisted a knife in his gut when most of them were far better quality than what he and the rest of the Fiends rode. His brothers deserved better than what Deacon was providing, but he didn't know how to change it any more than he knew how to change what he was walking into right now.

Reaching the door, he flung it open, scarcely stepping over the threshold. Standing for a moment with widespread legs, he knew his figure was backlit by the sunlight streaming in through the doorway. The glare flowing into the room lessened, elongating shadows appearing alongside his, and he knew his brothers were now at his back. He took another step inside, giving them room to enter.

A table of bikers near the pool tables moved as if to stand and Mason slowly shook his head at them. Receiving an acknowledging nod in response, it came from a heavily tattooed member of the Skeptics he had seen around before. Looking towards the bar, a sigh slipped past his lips when both Tilly and Merry were present. He knew his wild hopes there would be hired help today had been slim, because Tilly owned the place, and both he and his wife worked behind the bar most days.

Merry's voice held a full quota of fear when she questioningly called, "Boys?" She knew, he realized, thinking, *She has to know.* From the blood and bruising written right there on his face, she had to know what was coming.

Ignoring her, he quickly walked around the end of the bar and held his hand out, palm down, the action halting Tilly's reach for the scattergun mounted beneath the bar. "Tilly," he began to speak, but John shouted over him. "Fiends own the bar now, mother*fucker.*" Mason tensed, hearing the scrape of chairs from behind them. As if in slow motion, Tilly's hand moved again, fingers scrabbling at the stock of the gun, catching in the trigger guard, and then grabbing and pulling the weapon out. Mason drew his gun from his waistband, feeling the catch and scrape of the metal against his skin.

The shotgun was still pointed harmlessly downward, and he was shouting at Tilly not to be stupid, when there was a loud boom beside him. Liquid splattered on the wall, spray covering Merry's bare arm, speckling her face and neck with bright red dots. Everything froze in place for what seemed like drawn out minutes, and he had time to think, *Oh, good Goddamn, that went sideways bad and fast.* The shotgun fell, the steel barrels ringing as they hit the floor, catapulting the gun sideways to where it settled alongside the base of the bar. Reaching out to catch Tilly as the man's knees unhinged, awkwardly still holding his gun in one hand, Mason lowered him gently to the ground. *Fuck.* Merry didn't move from where she stood, her eyes locked on her husband lying bleeding on the floor.

In the aftermath of the shot, a still and silent vacuum settled around Mason, and he knelt next to Tilly, looking him over. With a shudder, he saw the gaping chest wound and imagined the wet sounds of the sucking breaths the man was dragging in, his mouth yawning wide with each straining effort. There was no way Tilly would last until an ambulance got there, much less through a ride to the hospital. *Fuck*. Shifting his gaze up, he saw John's pale, sweaty face peering over the bar, and he snarled instructions at him, his own voice sounding like it came from blocks away. "Lock the fucking door. Clear the onlookers. Let them know *nicely* if they talk, we will own them. Get the Skeptics out, too. Respect, man, show them respect and hold it together. You screwed the pooch on this one, brother. Screwed the goddamned, *fucking* pooch."

His ears were still ringing, but sound was beginning to return, so even as John stood there unmoving, staring down, when Mason heard footsteps shuffling away, he knew Ripper had listened at least. He could also hear Tilly now, a weak keening sound coming from the man's mouth, liquid bubbling, coming from his chest.

Mason twisted to look up at Merry and she returned his gaze, her eyes wide and frightened. In a quiet, commanding voice, he calmly said, "Merry, sweetheart. Get me a towel, okay? Get me a wet towel." With a gasp and a jerk, she nodded and turned to go through the door behind the bar, and he pulled her to a stop with a sharply spoken, "No." More softly, he explained, "Don't go through the door, okay? I need you to stay in this room, sweetheart. Get a bar towel. Stay where I can see you."

Looking at him over her shoulder, she nodded, moving erratically towards the sink, coming back with a dampened cotton towel, approaching step by slow step. He motioned to the floor, telling her, "Come down here by Tilly." He watched her as she slowly knelt, one knee at a time, coming to rest beside her husband, who was already unconscious from shock and blood loss. The sound of his rasping, bubbling breaths filled the air as Mason took the towel from her. With shaking hands, he carefully cleaned the blood and flesh splatter off her face, neck, and arm, tugging on her hand until he could press her palm to Tilly's forehead. "I'm sorry, Merry," he said as she gasped in shock at the chill already settling into her husband's body.

Standing, he looked down at the not-quite middle-aged couple and shook his head, suddenly and overwhelmingly enraged. He knew there could have been a better outcome. *Goddammit. Fucking John. Shooting first, thinking second.* The thought was still running through his brain just as there was another gunshot, this from the front of the bar. He flinched and spun, reacting in time to see John go down to the floor on one knee, cradling a hand to his chest. One of the Skeptics who had been sitting at the table when they walked in was now standing over John, his tattooed hand holding a gun against the back of the kneeling man's head.

"Hey," Mason shouted. "What the fuck do you think you're doing?" He pulled his gun again, training it on the biker, trying desperately to keep the weapon from wavering back and forth.

Without looking at him, the man spoke to Mason, never taking his focus from John. "Fucktard called me trash. Touched me with his hand. I decided it was time the shooter became the shot, embraced the pain of his own actions." He paused and then in a softer voice said, "I liked Tilly."

Mason shook his head, asking, "You gonna shoot him in the head next?" *Shooter*, he thought. *Right there is John's club name.*

"Only if he doesn't stop thinking stupid thoughts. He clears his little mind, we're all gonna be just fine." The absurd rhyming response made Mason grin, even in the midst of everything.

"Shooter, you gonna be stupid or smart?" he called across the bar and watched John flinch at the name, knowing it would forever be a reminder of what went down today. Maybe he would take the time to contemplate what it meant to be named after such a bloody act, and by a man who held you in such contempt as this man did. "Talk to me, brother."

"Smart. I'm gonna be smart. Get the fucking gun away from me. I'm gonna be smart." John spoke in a low tone, trying to shift his head away from the barrel of the gun, but it closely followed his movements and he subsided, stilling.

"Okay, Poet, he says he's gonna be smart. So why don't you back the fuck off him, put up your fucking piece, and assure me you're gonna keep your fucking mouth shut about this." Mason took several steps towards them, pausing when the man promptly moved back from John.

"Bones," he said absurdly, and Mason shook his head, holding his palm out in a questioning motion. The Skeptic frowned and responded, saying, "My name is Bones, not Poet."

"What the fuck ever," Mason growled. "Jesus. Fucking cluster. Shooter, you good to ride? I need you to head back, bring Deacon here. Don't want to use the bar's phone to call the clubhouse."

"Yeah, I'm good," John lied, looking down at his blood-slicked hand. The bullet had passed through his palm between his pinky and ring finger, and when Mason realized he still held the towel covered in Tilly's blood, he tossed it to Shooter, who used the sodden rag to wrap his bleeding hand tightly.

"Then get the fuck up and get gone," Mason said, turning on his heel to face Bones. Putting Shooter from his mind, he focused on the Skeptic standing in front of him. "Assure me, man. Convince me." He heard Shooter climb to his feet and then the sound of receding footsteps. In a moment, the soft creak of the lock disengaging sounded through the room, and then the outside door opened and closed.

"I can find no reason to rile the Fiends, man. My president would not be pleased if I took that route, so I believe I would rather avoid the detour which would ensue. This is your business, in any way you would like to take the statement." He looked past Mason at the rest of the men who had been sitting with him. "Skeptics will vacate now. We shall leave you to it, man."

"Mason," he said briefly, shoving his hand out at the man, who took it then shifted to a forearm grip.

"Oh, yes, I know who you are. The name Mason is already widely known and respected," Bones said and nodded, holding fast to him for a moment, their eyes meeting in a surprisingly friendly stare. Quietly, for Mason's ears alone, he continued, "Something I cannot say is true for your president." They stood like that for another moment, and then Mason lifted his chin, breaking the spell and dropping his hand. "Skeptics ride," Bones called in a low, commanding tone, and led his men out the door, leaving Ripper to relock it behind them.

Standing in the middle of a suddenly empty and silent bar, he took several deep breaths and then gagged a little as the stench of gut perforated by gunshot registered. He had smelled the same many times growing up, so this was not a new thing, but knowing this was human and not deer made it seem different, so much worse. "Ripper, make some coffee. Pour Merry a cup, and spike the shit with whiskey. Let's get her some space to deal," he said softly and received a grunt in response. "This is fucked so hard," he muttered to himself, shaking his head.

"Yeah, but you salvaged it so far," Ripper said as he walked past. "Just keep going, Mason. You'll figure out the win. You always do."

Hearing the confidence in his friend's voice, Mason lowered his head and gripped his hands tightly in front of him, squeezing hard until he could spot veins popping on his forearms. Unclenching his hands, he noted the trembling had subsided, as was his intent. Taking a single deep breath, he blew it out slowly and then turned to walk back to where Merry still knelt next to her husband. The gasping, agonal breaths had ceased, so Mason wasn't surprised Tilly was no longer bleeding. Merry had moved, shifting back slightly, hands now folded in her lap. He grimaced when he saw her knees resting in the dark crimson puddle spreading out in an uneven arc from the body. *Fuck.*

Reaching down a hand, he slipped it underneath her arm, lifting and levering her to her feet. Unresisting, she rose, and once he got her moving, he led her through the backdoor. He knew there were rooms behind the bar and hoped she had extra clothing stored there in case of emergency. *If this don't classify as a fucking emergency, I don't know what the fuck would*, he thought. Leaving her standing in the middle of the hallway, he found and locked the outside backdoor then returned to her side, quietly asking, "You got some clean pants here, Merry?"

She nodded and pointed towards a door on the left, so he carefully urged her that way, opening the door to find what looked like a bedroom. Relieved, he found a dresser as well as another door leading outside, this one already barred and locked. She stood passively while he sorted through the clothes in the dresser, pulling out a shirt, underwear, and pants. Spying a half-opened door in the opposite wall, he walked over, pleased to find a bathroom with a shower. Turning the water on, he twisted it over to hot, standing for a moment until the steam billowed out of the shower, and let it follow him back into the bedroom. "Let's get you a shower, Merry. Here're some clean clothes for you. I'll be waiting here until you're done, but you take your time, sweetheart."

She looked up at him then, reaching out to take the bundle of fabric, her face still registering shock, but also the beginning of a crushing pain. "I'm not," she sucked in a gasping breath, "your sweetheart, Mason. I hate," she drew in another unsteady breath, "you."

His eyes closed, and he pressed his lips together before looking at her again, an answering pain settling in his chest. "I know, hon. I hate me right now, too." He handed her the clothes and took her shoulders in his palms as he gently turned and pointed her towards the bathroom. "I hate me, too."

***

The next day, he was behind the bar at the Monaco, seated on the back of a stool propped against the wall, his feet resting on the cushion. He had intentionally placed the seat directly over the spot Tilly fell, not wanting to think about the events of yesterday every time he saw someone step over the stained flooring. From this vantage point, he could view the entirety of the bar, keep a watch over all the customers, both seated and wandering around. Alert and prepared for danger, he felt the rumble of bikes through the wood at his back before the noise registered to anyone else in the room. He was already off the stool and moving towards the door before anyone else even knew trouble was about to come knocking.

Cutting a glance over towards the pool tables, he saw Ripper reacting, quickly disassembling the stick in his hand, effectively leaving him with a three-foot bludgeon. Looking in the other direction, he paused for a second, shaking his head, because Shooter was still leaning indolently against a wall. His brother appeared markedly drunk, and there was a woman on her knees in front of him. "Fucktard," he muttered, pulling to a stop three feet inside the door and planting his feet, folding his arms across his chest and lifting his head. Listening carefully, he heard the scuff of leather soles on the sidewalk outside, so he didn't flinch when the door abruptly flung open. Holding his place, he stared into the eyes of the man standing in the doorway. Roadkill, president of the Dominos MC.

Upon seeing Mason standing there, blocking the way, the man's mouth pulled into a tight line, lips pressed thin and bloodless. Gaze moving across the men scattered throughout the room, he evidently did not find the face he was looking for and lowered his chin when he looked back at Mason. "Where the fuck is your president?"

"He ain't here. Want me to take a message?" Mason asked this in a flat tone, trying to neither placate nor provoke. He carefully eyed the man, but it was Hawk, the man standing directly behind Roadkill, who demanded the bulk of Mason's attention.

Hawk was a dozen times more dangerous than Roadkill, and the Domino lieutenant didn't have any love for Mason, having been on the losing end of a fighting match more than once. Fortunately for the man, his president had finally decided he didn't need to master that particular challenge after all, and had stopped paying Deacon for a chance at Mason's ass about two months ago. Unfortunately for all involved today, Mason knew eight weeks wasn't nearly long enough for the sting to have faded.

"Hawk, you hear what they're sayin', man? Motherfucker took my fucking bar and he ain't even fucking here," Roadkill spoke loudly without turning his head, still staring at Mason, who stood silently.

"Can't hardly believe it, but I heard it. Given the state of the man's club, are you surprised at him leaving them twisting in the wind like this?" Hawk sneered. Mason could scarcely make out his features in the shadows cast by the door. They still hadn't moved into the room, and most of their men were outside on the sidewalk, not even benefiting from the posturing their leaders were doing.

There were footsteps behind him; coming to a stumbling halt a little behind his left shoulder, with a wince, he recognized them as belonging to Shooter. *Goddammit*, he thought, *why couldn't he have taken his bitch in the back like he normally did? He's going to jack this up, sure as shit.*

Mason knew without looking around that the crowd in the room had separated into three groups. One would be his brothers, the men in the Rebel Fiends. They would have banded together somewhere between his back and the bar. Another would be the Skeptics; he had noted the presence of Bones earlier and knew the man seldom traveled without a half-dozen of his brothers. The Disciples, a club based out of Milwaukee, would be the last group, and they would be over near the pool tables, where they had been seated before Roadkill and his crew appeared.

Four clubs: his Fiends, two friendlies, and one enemy in the Dominos. Though, he knew from painful experience that in a fight against another club like this, the only men he could count on were the Fiends. He would love to believe Bones would have his back, but Deacon didn't like making agreements with other clubs, the one from Milwaukee being the exception. Even that had been done mostly because it would chap the ass of the Detroit Highwaymen's president, and their fragile agreement with the Disciples would never hold during a war.

Roadkill took a quick step forward, lifting a hand to swing, and it was all the movement Mason allowed. Countering swiftly and efficiently, he reached out and grabbed a wrist, turning and twisting it and the man, so Roadkill was suddenly facing the doorway, his arm jacked high behind his back, wrist bent at a breaking angle. "Motherfuck!" Roadkill yelled, struggling to get out of the grip Mason had on his arm. Yanking harder, he forced the older man to his knees, never taking his eyes off Hawk, trying to anticipate his reactions.

Still staring at Hawk, Mason used the edge of his foot to kick the man's legs apart and then stood on Roadkill's boot, twisting the heel to the outside with his weight, drawing another yell from the man. Held immobile with his arm, the threat of a broken leg was real, and Roadkill froze as he realized he could do nothing about it. "Get your fucking hands off me!" he shouted, but Mason ignored him. The entire encounter had taken all of five seconds, and Mason drew in a steady breath through his nose then made a face and blew it back out. "Hawk, if I let him up, can you keep his ass contained?"

Hawk shook his head, taking another step forward to give more of the members crowding behind him a look at their president kneeling on the floor, submitting to a not-yet-eighteen-year-old man. *Fucking shit.* This move spoke to a schism in club politics, exposing the weaknesses of their existing leadership.

"Okay then," Mason said, rubbing his temples with his other hand, affecting a nonchalance he didn't feel. "Roadkill," he said and then paused, waiting. When the man didn't acknowledge it, he said his name again, tugging painfully on the man's arm. "Roadkill?" Receiving an affirmative grunt this time, he continued, "If I let you up, you're going to walk back outside, get on your fucking scoot, and ride home, right?"

"Fuck you. You are fucking *dead*, motherfucker. Dead man walking," came the expected response, and he shook his head.

"Wrong answer," he said, and swept the gun from his waistband, striking the butt of it hard against Roadkill's head, releasing him to slump to the floor. "Get your man and get out," he ordered, giving Hawk a chin lift as he stepped backwards a single pace, keeping his pistol loose and ready in his hand. He heard an intake of breath behind him and stopped Shooter's words with a flick of his hand and an angrily hissed, "Shooter, shut the fuck up."

Hawk shook his head, glancing over Mason's shoulder towards Shooter and then sweeping the room with his gaze. "This place was Dominos'. You took our fucking bar. We need something in return."

"You're getting something," Mason snarled, reclaiming the step he had taken, pointing the gun at Roadkill's head. "You're getting to leave here with all your men breathing."

Hawk stared at him for a long minute and then nodded once. "Point taken, Mason." He motioned to two men behind him, saying only, "Pick him up." He stepped to one side, allowing the men to maneuver the unconscious man out of the bar then nodding at Mason again, he asked, "Where is Deacon?"

"Fuck if I know," Mason responded, the tension in the room releasing somewhat. "He doesn't check in with me every time he takes a shit." There was a ripple of light laughter from both sides of the circle of men, and then Mason asked, "How's Houlihan?"

"Fucking woman caught pregnant again. Third kid, man. I'm so fucking done with diapers and baby shit. This one better be a damn boy, because it's the last time I'm going down this road." Hawk shook his head, shoving his hands into the front pockets of his jeans, telegraphing the altercation was over.

"You know what causes that shit, right? Jesus fuck, man. Wrap up your dick once in a while." Mason flashed a quick grin, and then, just as quickly, sobered. "I don't know where Deacon is, but you can be sure I'll pass along Roadkill's message."

"Fuck," Hawk grunted. "Won't do any good at this point to say he was nearly alone in his decision to come here tonight, would it?"

"Probably not," Mason said.

Hawk nodded. "Watch your back, Mason. Roadkill isn't an easy man. This shit tonight will rankle as much as losing the bar in the first place. He'll be gunnin' for you." He swept his gaze around at the men in the bar and then looked back at the members of his own club clustered in the doorway. "I'll tell you right now, he'll be alone in his vengeance. You got me?"

Laughing harshly, Mason nodded. "Situation normal for a Tuesday, but yeah, I got you."

***

"Aww, fuck naw. No. No. *No*. Don't fucking do this, man." Mason quietly ground out the whispered plea as he watched the tall shadow separate itself from the surrounding darkness in the alleyway beside his house. Shaking his head, he stayed where he was, bent over the side of the truck bed as if he was reaching in for the lone bag of groceries there, waiting for the figure to approach closer. Shifting his stance, he moved his body to cover the gun held in his left hand. Regular practice kept him deadly accurate with both hands, which he found gave an advantage in situations like this, where people might only expect the weapon to be in the dominant hand.

Tracking the figure as it moved towards him, when he gauged there was no way to mistake this as anything but intentional, he lifted his hand and swung around, not surprised to discover Roadkill's features. This was expected. The man confidently aimed a gun at him, and Mason had a split-second to register the muscles in the hand gripping the gun were tightening, to identify the movement as Roadkill working to draw the finger tucked into the trigger back towards his palm. The frozen moment passed and it felt like a mule had kicked his shoulder, throwing him backwards. His grip on his own weapon tightened in automatic response to the noise and impact. He watched as his bullet hit Roadkill in the throat just below his jaw, tearing a wide, gaping wound that fountained with blood. The familiar copper taste of the liquid covered Mason's face and chest before the man fell back onto the driveway, his legs collapsing like a marionette with cut strings.

Yelling, "Fuck, fuck, *fuck*!" Mason turned in a tight circle, searching the area for additional attackers. After a moment, he was shocked to realize Hawk had been serious, and Roadkill was alone in his quest for retaliation. Facing the prone man again, staring down at the lax body in front of him, he drew in a shaky breath; he hadn't meant to shoot Roadkill. Sucking in another breath, he looked down at himself, noticing a small hole in his vest, several inches above his name patch. Then, twisting his neck, he tried to look at his back, but couldn't detect what kind of damage was there. Thank God, his shoulder was numb and didn't hurt...yet, but he was damned sure the pain would be coming soon.

There was a sudden bloom of illumination across the yard, coming from the house beside him as an interior light turned on, and he grimaced in response. *Fucking bitch teacher*, he thought, *she never fucking sleeps*. He hated his neighbor. "Fucking goddamn shit."

He knew the gunshots must have woken her, and also knew she would be the first to call the cops. Was probably already on the phone, screeching about her dangerous neighbor who ran a gang of thugs and thieves. *Gotta clear my shit*, he thought. Without thinking, he leaned over to pick up Roadkill, staggering as dizziness struck him. *Fuck*. The man was not small. Lifting the heavy body was awkward with one working arm, but he managed, tipping the man's torso over the side of the truck bed. Once up on the edge, gravity took over, pulling the body down in a sliding rush. He watched as it landed in a loose pile of limbs, ruined face buried in a drift of leaves against the tailgate.

He shook his head hard, clearing it of the fuzziness threatening to creep in around the edges of his thoughts. "Fuck. Can't do anything about the driveway," he muttered, and then his eye caught on a can in the open toolbox in the truck bed and he laughed at himself. "Sure you can." Even given the late hour, he judged he had less than ten minutes before the cops showed. Knowing how oddly time flowed in moments such as these, he quickly moved the truck, thinking to make sure blood wasn't yet dripping from the drain holes. He grabbed the can of starter fluid and doused the blood on the drive with about half the contents of the can. Pulling a cigarette lighter from an inside pocket of his vest, he used it to light the spray from the can's nozzle aflame, creating a mini blowtorch. He set the blood covering the driveway on fire and then used the rest of the fuel to burn away stray drips, leaving a bubbling mess of asphalt and pea gravel behind.

Tossing the empty can into the back of the truck, he settled into the driver's seat. He carefully backed into the street and then drove away, not knowing for sure where he was going. Pain was setting in, the wound in his shoulder throbbing hard with each racing heartbeat. Gritting his teeth, he managed the shift into second gear then stiffened his injured arm, trying to hold the wheel steady with a suddenly shaking hand while he explored his wound. Blindly reaching under his shirt, his fingertips found a small hole on the front of his shoulder, where the bullet had entered, and a slightly larger one on the backside, where it exited. There was a small amount of blood trickling out of both wounds, and he found himself bizarrely calm, thinking wonderingly it wasn't bad for a gunshot. "He fucking shot me," he muttered in disbelief. Tightly clamping his hand down on the wound, he winced and hissed, "Fuck."

Mason drove aimlessly, no clear destination, making random turns up streets he didn't recognize. He couldn't go to the clubhouse. The club and clubhouse were not options, Deacon having made it clear to all members that any shit they reaped was their own goddamned problem, and nothing—not a single piece of trouble—was to be brought to the club's doorstep. It meant calling Ripper was out, as well as the rest of the club members. He didn't trust Shooter, either, much as he wanted to, so it meant his own blood was out, too. *What the fuck am I going to do?* he thought. *DeeDee...Winger?* He rejected the idea of bringing his cousin and friend into this, and they were hours away at best. He needed help now. He couldn't drive around all night with a fucking body in the back of his truck, and he sure as fuck couldn't go home to where it had happened.

When next he identified his surroundings, he found he was a little way up the street from a bar called Tupelo's. Driving past, he saw bikes in the parking lot and vaguely remembered it was a semi-neutral bar controlled by the Skeptics. Tromping on the clutch, with a jerk of the wheel, he bumped over the curb and pulled into the lot, groaning at the pain as he glanced around. Mason grimaced when he recognized one of the bikes, the truck rolling to a stop even as he wondered if he truly trusted Bones this much.

Any decisions were out of his hands as soon as the door to the bar opened and Bones strolled out, followed by a dozen men. Apparently, they heard him arrive, and came out to discover who had driven a cage onto the lot. The moment when Bones recognized his vehicle was clear, and after stiffening, the man gave what appeared to be a 'wait' hand signal to his men. *That'd be useful in a fight*, Mason thought, *like quiet hunting with the boys back home.*

Rolling down the window was so far beyond him right now he couldn't even laugh about it. As Bones approached the truck alone, Mason reached over with his right hand to try and open the door. The latch gave way abruptly and he nearly fell out of the vehicle, catching himself on the doorframe with a pained grunt. The movement caused Bones to stop suddenly, and his face tightened as he took in the blood covering virtually every inch of Mason's body.

In another bizarre moment in what had become a surreal night—*he fucking shot me*—Mason watched as Bones first nodded wordlessly, and then held up both hands, wagging them back and forth in the air, following his actions up with a casual shrug.

The pain became impossible to ignore, now blooming hot enough to bring an oily sheen of sweat to his face. Distractedly, Mason shook his head, thinking he had spaced out, trying to decide what he missed. He finally gave up the attempt to understand on his own and asked, "What the fuck was that?"

Bones held a palm out towards him, a smirk on his face as he said, "I was debating with myself whether to ask you who you killed or if you are dying. Given the fact you can still speak, I must now surmise you killed someone. However, the conjecture does not negate the fact you look like you are wearing enough blood so you also might be dying. Therefore, I find myself with a conundrum, a riddle to solve. Because while I might like you, Mason, you are a Fiend, and I fucking *despise* Deacon. So now, the question becomes"—he wagged one hand again—"do I let you die, because you are Deacon's, or should I help you live, because you could be a friend?"

"You're asking me?" Mason asked in disbelief.

"Sure, why should I not? Shouldn't every man have a say in when and how he dies?" Bones rested his hand on his belt, tucking his thumb inside the heavy chain.

"If you're giving me a choice, a voice in this, then I say help me out, motherfucker. You actually think I'm going to tell you to let me bleed the fuck to death? You're a crazy motherfucker, but damned if I'm not glad to find you here tonight." Mason tried to stand up out of the truck and dizziness struck again, so he had to grip the edges of the door hard to force himself upright.

Bones took another step towards him and his gaze went to the back of the truck. "Ah, I see the first death of the night is following you around. This will not do, my friend." He turned and whistled, calling two of his men to his side. Instructing them, he said, "Take the keys, oh look...my friend has left them in the ignition like a kind man. Take the truck and dispose of the trash in the back. Make sure there will be no blowback to the Skeptics or this man. I care fuck all about shit leading back to the Fiends, but we will watch Mason's back." He turned to look at Mason, who was shaking his head in confusion. "Where did this unhappy event happen, my friend?"

"My house—" Mason began, but he stopped talking, because Bones had already turned away.

"Go to his home. The address should be in the truck somewhere. Make certain things are as tidy as you can make them." He made a shooing motion with his hands and the men stepped towards the truck.

Mason cleared his throat. Trying to move, he staggered sideways and grunted when the effort jarred his shoulder. "Cops could be there. I got a bitch of a nosey neighbor. I torched the blood; at least, I think I did. The moment was kind of...chaotic."

"Police, we can deal with. Torching the blood, that is good. Fast thinking when presented with a quickly unfolding problem. All which will make our job much easier." He reached out, gripping Mason's belt with one hand, easing his shoulder under Mason's good arm. "Chaos is hard to manage, but as it appears to follow you around, I suspect you will become accustomed to it eventually. Let's get you inside now and take care of your scratch. We have a good stock of liquor, which should make what comes next easier to bear."

3. Growing up

1998

"Fuck, man," the man said with a grin. "This is the best ride I've ever had. Smooth, easy to balance, easy on the ass...she is a fucking dream to ride."

Mason nodded at him. "She's a good bike, man, been good to me. I've had her for several years. Brought her back as close to original as I could, but I'm ready to move on from the Indian. I find myself wanting to sink my ass onto a pretty bike, black with lots of chrome." The Indian was the second bike he ever owned. The first one had been a beater piece of shit he had to work on more than he had ridden for the first years he was in the club.

Heeling the kickstand down, the man who had introduced himself as Harddrive balanced the pretty red and white bike, swinging his leg up and over the black leather-fringed seat. "I have a couple of beauties in my shop"–he hooked his thumb over his shoulder at the building behind him–"so why don't we go take a look, see what speaks to you. We'll determine if we can strike a deal, yeah?"

Four hours later, Mason had his chin lifted in the wind, feeling the low rumble of the Fatboy transferring through the leather seat into his legs and ass. He laughed aloud when his balls started tingling, signaling his cock to fatten and stand at half-mast. He had been in Cheyenne for a week, meeting and speaking with the head guys for a couple of Wyoming and Utah clubs, and now was on his way to southern California. Shooter had finally left the Fiends a year ago, headed home to his daddy's club, and Mason was on his way to visit for a couple weeks. It felt good to be back in the wind.

This trip had afforded him a lot of time to think. Maybe too much, because he had wound up at the painful conclusion he simply couldn't stay patched into the Fiends. He had decided when he got back to Chicago that he was going to petition to go gypsy. He wasn't expecting Deacon to let him leave the club easily, or on good terms, but he would fucking try his damnedest. He wouldn't be able to tolerate the things going on in the club any longer, not after discovering so many examples of well-run clubs. It would hurt like fuck to leave his brothers, but be an anguish of a different type to watch the club continue to circle the drain as it was right now.

Using his reputation to smooth the way, he had received invitations into a dozen different clubhouses under the guise of establishing good relations between the clubs. After the first one, what he was honestly doing was cataloging the differences between an affluent and respected club and the one in which he was a member and officer, and he found the differences to be vast and troubling.

In the years since joining the Fiends, as Bones predicted, he had become accustomed to chaos and unrest, at first thinking it was a result of the lifestyle. The Fiends were never peaceful, always at war with one club or another, and consequently, there were raids and ambushes happening all the fucking time. He had lost a dozen brothers to the fighting...and killed nearly twenty men himself.

Every moment of their lives was tension-filled, and just as he had when he was homeless and staying in shelters, he always slept with one eye open. Waiting. Watching. Mason knew it was only a matter of time before he was caught off guard or came up with his weapon a little too slowly. At that point, he would become nothing more than another name on a scrawled list of dead tacked to a corkboard in the clubhouse kitchen. Disposable. Forgettable.

Deacon likened the club to a lion pride, repeatedly stating things about shifting leadership without actually saying anything. Things like, "When the young lion killed the old, dominant one, he also killed all the cubs belonging to the old male." Mason didn't entirely understand what the fuck he meant, but Deacon would stare at him and say the words as he wiped his blade clean, or holstered his gun before turning to walk out of whatever clusterfuck he had initiated, always leaving the mess for Mason to clean up.

The past couple of years had been the worst. Some days, Deacon appeared to be fucking crazy, and other days, just the right amount of paranoid. Nothing the man did made sense anymore, and Mason had begun to wonder if it ever had, or if he had simply been so young and stupid he couldn't see it before. Every member, each one of them, had to always be watching their own back, and often against their brothers.

He had called and spoken to Winger a few days ago, wanting to talk through some of his thoughts after his meetings with the clubs in Wyoming. The man had fucking apologized to him. Asked for forgiveness and told him he should have caught on to how fucked-up Deacon was before he ever introduced them. Mason took his hand off the bike's grip for a moment, wiping his palm on his jeans before replacing it. *Fucking hands always feel sticky now*, he thought briefly before viciously shoving *that* memory away.

Midway through Nevada, he finally pulled over at a motel, paying for a single night. He had pushed hard the entire trip, making most of it during the dark nighttime hours, spending his days talking to club members. Parking his new bike on the walkway in front of the windows of his room, he stood and admired it for a minute and then, a smile still on his face, carried his small bag inside, locking the door behind him. As he did most things, when he showered, he did so quickly, efficiently, and then stretched out on the hard mattress of the bed, arms folded behind his head. Staring up at the ceiling, he began to run the events of the past two years back through his mind, trying and failing to find where things could have shifted to a different path.

Eventually, he sighed, turning in the bed to roll onto his hip, extending one leg and groaning as he eased a tense and strained muscle in his thigh. Rubbing at the knots with his hand, his fingertips ultimately sought out a dimpled scar there, running over it several times before he pressed hard, gritting his teeth against the sudden pain. Sighing again, he moved, settling into a different position, his hand flat on the surface of the bed. After a few minutes, his eyelids fluttered, closing, and he fell asleep, his breathing slowing and evening out as he relaxed in the time before the nightmares began.

What the hell is that noise? he wondered, lifting his head and looking around the main clubhouse room, discovering the usual collection of drunk or stoned men littering the stained and tattered furniture. The sound built and swelled again, finally becoming recognizable as a man's angry scream.

Mason jerked upright, looking down the hallway towards the source of the noise, knowing even before he moved the location would be Shooter's room. His brother's wife and daughter had gone missing about six months ago, and he appeared to have gone crazy with worry. Shooter had visited Chicago several times since they had been gone and, even though the unspoken consensus was they were most likely dead, his desperation to find them grew with every turning page of the calendar. He had become convinced there was a traitor in the Outriders club, and had petitioned Deacon for help to smoke out whoever was responsible into the open.

Striding quickly down the hallway, Mason reached Shooter's room and flung the door open. It swung wildly, ricocheting off the inside wall and nearly crashing closed again before he caught it with an outstretched arm. Shooter was on his back on the bed, blood covering his chest and belly as he strained upwards against the man he was fighting. Ripper knelt above him, straddling Shooter with a knife in his hands, his face shocked when he twisted to look at Mason. Shooter took advantage of his distraction and shoved hard, Ripper heavily falling off the bed on one side while Shooter rolled nimbly off the other. Mason suddenly realized his pistol was in his hands and he had reflexively pointed it at his best friend...was still pointing it at Ripper.

"What the fuck is going on?" He shouted his question at the two men, the vibrating thunder of his voice shockingly loud and surprising in the small room.

"He fucking tried to kill me," Ripper said, sitting up and laying the knife on the bed. "I came in here because he was yelling, and the crazy man fucking came at me with a knife."

Shooter stood, looking down at Ripper with a sneer. "More like you tried to kill me, traitor. I wondered who was responsible, and now I know it's you, motherfucker."

"What the fuck are you talking about, man? Responsible for what?" Ripper stood, and Mason saw the weeping cuts on his forearms, where the knife had gashed and slashed his skin. Those definitely looked like defensive wounds, but why would Shooter lie? "You aren't even in this club anymore, man. You pussied out and ran home to your daddy. So go ahead, tell me, pussy. What the fuck are you talking about?"

"I'm talking about you killing my wife and kid, taking my old lady and family from me, motherfucker. My daughter." Shooter was shouting, his face red and strained, spittle spraying from his mouth with every word. He looked deranged, and Mason worried about his sanity, not for the first time. Shooter continued yelling, "I'm talking about you trying to kill

me just now, trying to complete the job. Wiping the Morgan name off the face of the earth." Without another word, he launched himself at Ripper, his hands stretched into claws, fingers straining to tear at flesh and clothing. Rip stumbled backwards under the assault, his back thudding into the wall with such force something fell to the floor in the hallway, crashing and breaking.

There was a hard thud against Mason's leg and he glanced down to see the handle of the knife protruding from his thigh muscle, blood already beginning to trail down the material of his jeans. Ignoring the knife for now, he lifted his head and shouted at them, inarticulate with his need to stop them from killing each other.

The two men twisted and grappled, each trying to get the upper hand, Ripper attempting to protect himself and Shooter only caring about dealing damage. They fought back and forth across the room, upending the mattress, breaking the overhead light, and he saw glittering glass pieces scatter down onto the fighters. For an instant, Mason caught a flash of dirt floor and hand-quilted bedcovers, and then shook the memory of Kentucky away.

Shooter clearly wasn't stable, and Ripper had shifted into automatic fighter mode. He sparred with Mason all the time, and had been fighting alongside him for many years now, all of which had molded him into a deadly machine. The two men came together in silence except for grunts punctuating the blows reaching through guards and hissing gasps at the effort of thrown punches. Mason watched as Ripper captured one of Shooter's hands in his own, lifting the arm above the man's head. Their chests nearly touched as they strained against the other then Shooter's boots slipped and slid, and they crashed to the floor, Ripper landing on top of Mason's brother.

With a knee on each side of Shooter's chest, Ripper landed blow after blow on his head and upper body. Mason shouted at him to stop, to get off, but there was no response. The big man leaned over Shooter, his hands settling onto the neck of his opponent, and Mason shouted at him *again, even knowing it would do no good. Ripper had retreated into the quiet space they found when fighting, where pain couldn't reach you and the only thing that could bring things to a close was the end of the fight, in one way or another.*

The sound of a gunshot split the air and he saw Ripper's head lift, a puzzled look on his face as he turned towards the door, hands falling away from Shooter's neck. Horrified, Mason saw his arm had lifted, pointing his gun at the men on the floor. He realized this precisely as he registered the stinging burn of an ejected, spent cartridge on his wrist, and knew he had been the one to pull the trigger.

Shooter shoved at the man now draped slackly over the top of him. Coughing and choking, he was gasping for breath as he wiggled free, his face purpled from lack of oxygen and the blows he took during the fight.

Mason was aware of a growing uproar coming up the hallway. He glanced down in confusion at the growing patch of redness on the front of Ripper's shirt then locked eyes with his friend, watching as he slowly slumped to the side. "What the hell?" Ripper asked breathlessly, lifting a hand to press against the bullet wound in his chest. Repeatedly making a gasping 'huh' sound, he sank back farther and then fell flat on the floor, his boots touching the wall. Distantly, Mason noticed one ankle had twisted inward; his friend was too big for the area he was lying in.

Someone gently took the gun from his hand as, from behind him, Deacon asked in disbelief, "He fucking shot Ripper?"

As if the removal of the weapon's weight had released him, Mason took three steps, falling to the floor at Ripper's side, reaching out to clasp the man's hand. His arm snagged on the knife still embedded in his leg. With a grunt, he pulled it out, throwing it across the room where, with a dull clang, it hit the wall, sliding to land on the floor near his brother. Shooter still hadn't said anything, hadn't moved from where he leaned against the wall by an overturned table.

Mason looked down in time to spot a frown move across Ripper's face, followed by a peaceful expression. He whispered to Mason, "It doesn't hurt, man. Huh. I figured it would hurt, but it doesn't fucking hurt at all."

Hands ripping open the wrecked shirt, the sight of Ripper's ravaged chest struck him like a blow. The gaping injury from the gunshot welled with hot blood spilling over the lip of the wound, flowing around the wall of muscle to soak the floor where Mason knelt.

"Shut up, motherfucker. It's going to hurt, and you're going to be fine. Shut the fuck up; you're going to be fine," Mason growled.

Attempting to press his hands against the wound, they slid ineffectually across the shattered flesh. Coated with crimson, they slickly slipped when he needed them to stay firm. He twisted to discover the doorway filled with Fiends, questioning and shocked expressions on every face as their gazes swept from him and Ripper over to Shooter. "Call a bus," he directed and waited a beat, but no one moved. "Call a fucking bus!" This came out as a shout, and he sat there until he saw the slow shake of Deacon's head.

"No ambulance, brother," Deacon said, leaning in to lay Mason's gun on the dresser by the doorway. "No bus, man."

"Call a goddamned fucking bus," he roared, moving to stand until he felt a tugging on his arm.

Looking down, he saw Ripper's face shift and twist through a grimace of pain and then back to calm. Blank. Peaceful. Tugging at Mason's arm again, he closed his eyes and then opened them again. "I'd have killed him," he whispered on a long sigh, the outrush of air ripe with the stench of death and decay. He sucked in another breath, eyes fixed on Mason's face.

He watched as acceptance of his death settled on Ripper's features, sticking there as surely as his brother's blood was drying thickly on his hands. *"You know that. You done good, Mason. Saved your blood. You'll figure out the win, brother."*

Jerking himself awake, Mason rubbed a hand across his face, leaning up on one elbow in the bed. He reached down, fingertips firmly rubbing the scar on his thigh. Moving stiffly, he shifted until he sat on the side of the mattress and pulled his smokes from the nightstand, lighting one and letting the first drag out on a deep sigh. Cigarette wedged in one corner of his mouth, he restlessly rubbed his hands together, trying to get rid of the lingering phantom stickiness caused by the dream.

The nightmare was never entirely the same. It never followed the exact track the night had taken six months ago, but the end was always unchanged: his best friend Ripper dying in his arms from a gunshot, lying on the dirty floor of Shooter's room.

***

After two more stops in the southwest, he made it to southern California. He found even the air here felt different, unlike anything he had ever experienced. It seemed richer in some way, more essential than everything he had encountered before. It was as if it could change him, alter him forever, and set things apart, transforming even his understanding of everything experienced in his life up to this point.

His plan included an hour-long stop at the Joshua Tree National Park, just outside Palm Springs.

Mason wound up spending two days there. Mesmerized, he sat on a picnic table near his campsite, fascinated by views of the bizarrely twisted trees, which somehow managed to invoke a feeling of poignant loss in him.

The colors in the morning light were brilliant, and he stood in open-mouthed awe as they crawled across the landscape. He drank in the sight of white sand stark against red rocks, gazing in wonder at the beauty of Mastodon Peak in the near distance.

At night, he tracked the purples and pinks creeping across the sky, clouds reflecting the colors of a deepening indigo overhead. The raw beauty of the landscape broke open a walled place inside him, making him long for...an undefined something.

He made friends with an older couple his first night in the campgrounds, invited to share the warmth of their nearby campfire as the evening's chill crept in. Mason was delighted when the woman brought out a harmonica, captivated as she reverently held the tiny instrument. Flipping her long, white braid over one shoulder, she lifted her hands to her face and blew confident, bluesy tunes that reached deep, resonating inside him like the music of Appalachia once had, dragging memories to the forefront of his mind.

He sat, listening to her music, and remembered standing on the edge of the front porch of his family's shanty, surrounded by cousins and church members. He was swept back in time to those moments where, with feet stomping and hands beating out time, everyone sang, faces lifted in joy.

I'm just a poor wayfaring stranger
Traveling through this world of woe
There's no sickness, toil nor danger
In that fair land to which I go

The sounds of guitar, banjo, and mouth harp hanging clear on the mountain air introduced unblemished beauty into a life harsh with unmet need.

I know dark clouds will hover o'er me
I know my pathway is rough and steep
But golden fields lie out before me
Where weary eyes no more will weep

Tonight, thousands of miles and well more than a decade away from that setting, in his mind his mother's delicate, gorgeous voice was raised alongside the pure, childish tones of Bethany, his little sister, singing the old tent revival gospel song.

I'm going home to see my mother
She said she'd meet me when I come
I'm just a-going over Jordan
I'm just a-going over home

Delores and Harold, the couple camping near him, talked long into the night about their children, smiling as they spoke of their son who, like him, was a club member. Dennis, it seemed, had made a home for himself with the Freed Riders in East Texas, but trekked back to Wyoming often to meet up with his parents. Mason found it refreshing and relaxing that these people had no fear of him. As a biker, more especially as Mason of the Chicago Fiends, he was far more familiar with the looks of panic and dread he inspired. *This response*, he thought, *is something I'd like a chance to get used to.*

Bedding down in his tent on top of his sleeping bag, he left the flap open, staring out at the sky for a long time. His brain worked overtime, thinking, considering and rejecting options, while his gaze tracked the movement of the stars slowly whirling in the sky overhead. The song Delores had played at his request ran through his head, stuck on repeat, one exquisite memory of his childhood worth keeping.

I'll soon be free, from every trial
This form shall rest beneath the sod
I'll drop the cross of self-denial
And enter in my home with God

After sharing coffee and breakfast for a second morning, he promised the talkative couple he would stop in and meet their son if he got a chance. Unable to manufacture a reason to delay further, Mason finally packed up his bags and left, turning south and west towards San Diego and his self-appointed meeting with the Outriders. Riding the sweeping curves that wound along the edges of the Otay County Open

Space Reserve, he felt renewed in a way he hadn't for a long time. He was calm and centered after his time in the desert. It was in this mindful state he first saw the Pacific Ocean, the initial glimpse of the vast expanse of water with shifting blue-green colors stealing his breath.

He found an elevated parking area where he could stop, and sat there for a long time, watching the sailboats dancing on the waves, their canvas a mix of unadorned white and splashes of vivid colors. The deep blue water extended out as far as the eye could see, and he sat, staring in awe, convinced he could glimpse the curvature of the earth along the horizon. Everything about the ocean made him feel small, but somehow more entirely connected than he had ever felt in his life.

Mason had never seen anything as beautiful, and before he knew it, he had spent a half day simply staring at the unceasing motion of the water, utterly spellbound. Waves hypnotically advanced up the beach and retreated, shorebirds running along and in the white foam left in the water's wake, beaks working through the sand and liquid.

The ocean called to him more than any woman ever had, and Mason rode to a lot nearer the shore to park the bike. He took off his boots and walked into the ocean, not caring what kind of incongruous appearance he provided. He was in his black leather vest with his blue jeans rolled up around his white calves, standing and walking through the shallow water, playfully kicking at the waves as he sang.

I'm just a-going over Jordan
I'm just a-going over home

He observed the many couples and families, children playing with dogs and the water, or running and playing with each other...or moving through the water and playing with nothing at all. They were carefree and happy in a way he couldn't ever recall allowing himself freedom to be.

I'm just a poor wayfaring stranger

He remembered his sense of amazement at glimpsing Lake Michigan for the first time, taking in the expanse of water along the shores of Chicago, so totally outside his, admittedly limited, range of experience. In his mind, he thought that water differed greatly from this. It was darker and cold to the touch, even in the height of summer. This water felt somehow softer, lighter...like it was more liquid than the Great Lake, more alive. He decided in part it was the color, a shifting and ever-changing blue so crisp and sharp he knew he would see it in his memories for a long time, pulling it up in order to remember the swirling, warm water curling softly around his ankles.

Unhurriedly walking along the beach, he looked down at shells and seaweed mixed with driftwood and other flotsam at the edge of the water. One piece caught his eye and, stooping, he picked up something that looked like a rock the color of translucent spring grass. He turned it over and over in his fingers, fascinated, because it was see-through, but cloudy, nearly like a piece of smoothed, opaque glass. A voice came from beside him and he turned to discover a boy of about twelve, looking at the rock in his hand. "That's a pretty piece. It's big, too." Glancing up at his face, the boy blanched and reflexively took a step back.

Mason squatted down, making himself small so as not to alarm the boy any more than he already had. Holding the rock out towards him, he asked, "What is it? Do you know?"

"It's sea glass." The boy nodded, eyes back staring covetously at the rock.

"Huh. Sea glass," he mused. Turning it over again in his fingers, Mason let his gaze linger on the glass. "It's pretty."

"Yeah," the boy agreed. "You've found a very nice piece. I haven't seen that color before."

Impulsively holding it out to the boy, he asked, "Here, you want it?" Even as the words fell from his mouth, he wanted to yank them back, greedily wanting to keep the glass for himself.

I'm just a-going over home

"No, thank you." He held out a small bucket, showing Mason the pieces he had collected. There were white and blue, brown and dark greens, but none of them as brilliant a color as the one held in the flat of his palm. "I have plenty of my own." Cocking his head, he looked Mason in the face, fearless now that they had exchanged a half-dozen sentences of conversation. "I'm Garrett. You're from away, aren't you? Are you a tourist?"

"I'm Mason, from Chicago." Mason nodded. "Guess you could say I'm a tourist, sure. I'm out here to visit family; thought I'd give myself a chance to take in the sights." He twisted, putting a knee to the damp sand, looking out over the ocean, gaze again tracing along the horizon. "I've never seen the ocean before."

"Oh, wow. I've always lived here. I can't imagine not having the Pacific right here." The boy turned to face the same direction as Mason. "What do you think?"

"I've never seen anything like it. It's amazing." A breeze stirred the air and Mason watched as the boy lifted his chin, sniffing.

"Storms tonight," he said briefly, taking a step backward, preparing to move along on his way up the beach.

I know dark clouds will hover o'er me

"Thanks for the warning." Mason laughed dryly, standing to watch the boy walk away. A short distance up the beach, he saw Garrett approach a blanket on the sand and exchange greetings with the man and woman waiting there. At something the boy said, the man looked up at Mason and raised one hand. Waving in response, Mason suddenly felt awkward.

The sight of the small family was as foreign to him as the ocean had been, and for another little while, he watched from the corner of his eye, covertly studying them. He observed fleeting but affectionate touches passing between the three. The dark-haired woman leaned her head on her husband's shoulder for a moment, face raised in laughter, hand cupping around his bicep as her other hand reached out to tousle Garrett's hair. After a time, he saw them packing up, and smiled as they strolled off the beach hand-in-hand, their boy sandwiched safely between them.

He shook his head, shoved the beautiful, bright green piece of sea glass deep into his pocket, and turned to walk back towards his bike. As he sat, waiting for his feet to dry so he could brush the sand off before putting his socks and boots back on, he thought again about the club. He had already made his decision, and he would be leaving. He would quit, cut his losses, and move on, but now it felt like forsaking the club would be something from which he might not recover.

I know my pathway is rough and steep

When he patched in, he had vowed faithfulness to the club. His mouth twisted in anger, hating the way Deacon's actions had forced him into this corner. He would be damned if he would dump them because things had gotten complicated. Instead, resolving to stay, he needed to figure out a way to fix things. He just had to find the win. *Love ya, Rip*, he thought, fingers absently working across the bottoms of his feet to dislodge the last clinging grains of sand, eyes again on the horizon where the ocean met the sky.

But golden fields lie out before me

***

He hadn't yet had a chance to talk to Shooter, or meet his old man, when a call woke him early the next morning. He had spent the night at a motel, and now reached out to pick up the phone from where it was ringing on the table between the beds.

The question of how Shooter had known he was in town never crossed his mind. He simply got up, rolled his bike out the door, and headed off to meet his brother as requested. Shooter had said they needed to talk; there were things at play Mason needed to know about.

Walking up to the front door of the bar Shooter had named, he found it a little odd the neon lights were dark, but didn't give it much thought beyond that. It wasn't until after he stepped inside the obviously still-closed bar he realized he had been betrayed.

A hard shove combined with a leg tangling with his own brought him down. He twisted as he fell, pulling his pistol out only to have it kicked from his hand, hearing it skitter away, sliding across the hard floor. Looking up, he was stunned to recognize his brother standing over him, arms swinging down, a length of something metal in his hands, and then nothing...darkness.

I'm going home, no more to roam

4. Implications

"You think you're so high and fucking mighty." Mason blinked up, squinting against the harsh light of the overhead bare bulb. Shooter sneered down at him, pulling his foot back and kicking Mason in the back, drawing a low groan from him. "Always so damn self-righteous. Your name always on her fucking lips. 'Don't forget his name, Jonny, Davis Mason.' Even after Pops went to Kentucky and got her back from your crazy-ass old man, she wouldn't fucking stop talking about you."

There was a screech of chair legs on the floor, and Mason opened his eyes again to note Shooter had pulled a metal chair up close. The legs looking as large as columns beside Mason's face. Something landed on his shoulder, shoving at him, and he fell over backwards, bound hands beneath him. Unable to control the movement, he flopped down, the back of his head smacking painfully against the concrete floor. Squinting up through the swollen flesh around his eyes, he saw his brother sitting on the chair, his foot still resting on Mason's body.

"Not so high and mighty now, are you?" The words echoed a little in the enclosed space, but he couldn't summon the energy to respond, eyes drooping closed as he tried to remember how he had gotten here...on this floor.

There was a sudden, loud noise nearby, and it brought his focus back to the man in the room with him. Watching, he saw Shooter's face swing towards what must be a door behind Mason, his look of annoyance quickly changing to one of fear at whatever it was he saw approaching. There was a boom and then the shuffle of footsteps followed by a heavy sigh. "Boy, what the fuck you think you're doing?" Mason didn't recognize the gravel-filled voice, but the disgusted and disappointed tone gave him sudden hope rescue might be within reach.

"Teaching this piss-ant a lesson, Pops." Shooter slid the chair back and shifted his heavy foot to the floor, eyes intently fixed towards the other side of the room.

"This your brother, boy?" Mason tried to turn so he could see behind him, wanting to lay eyes on the man to whom the voice belonged, the man who had stolen his mother, and fathered this crazy bastard on her. Justice Morgan.

"He fucked me over in Chicago. Turned everyone against me. Been against me my whole life, and you know that's true." There was a distinct whine to Shooter's voice now, and if his face didn't hurt so fucking bad, Mason would have smiled. If Shooter was feeling threatened, then this was definitely a rescue.

"That ain't how I know it. Ain't how I heard it either, boy. I understood from Deacon he killed a brother to save your sorry ass. What call do you got to truss him up and beat the shit outta him now?" Hard hands slid under Mason's shoulder, and he saw the outline of a shaggy head against the light before being flipped over onto his front. Face pressed to the chilled cement floor, the split skin over his cheek stung as he focused, feeling fingers tugging at the ropes binding his wrists behind his back, plucking at the loops and loosening the knots until he could twist his numb hands free. He put his palms on the floor, pushing up to his hands and knees then to his feet, moving to put a wall at his back as quickly as he could on shaking legs.

"You okay, boy?" Assuming this question was directed at him, he nodded, even as he kept his eyes on Shooter. His brother's features had hardened into irritated lines, and he stood, hands fisted impotently at the ends of his arms. "Asked you a question, boy. I put a question out there. I expect a fucking response."

Shades of fucking Deacon, he thought. "Yeah, I'm okay." Mason gritted the words between clenched teeth because while it wasn't exactly true, he would never give Shooter the satisfaction of knowing precisely how badly he was hurting. "Motherfucker in front of me won't be for long, though. He's got a world of pain coming his way for this shit." He swung his gaze to the man standing near the door. "You gonna have a problem with that?"

"Goddammit." Morgan ran a hand over his chin. "Yeah, I'll have a problem with that. You need to just fucking suck it up, Mason. I'll deal with John about all of this when it's time." He spoke as if he and Mason were alone in the room, chatting about the weather or something else equally innocuous. "Your mama wouldn't have wanted you boys to fight like this. I'll deal with John," he repeated. "My word on it."

"What'd Deacon say about you stealing all his money, brother?" Shooter asked the question in a jeering tone and Mason whipped back to him, his head lifting as he realized what the statement had to mean.

"You fucking prick," he growled. A tone of angry incredulity in his voice, he ground out his words. "You set...you fucking set me up when you left, didn't you? You goddamn motherfucking little prick." He took a step towards Shooter. "Did you know they nearly killed me before I could make Deacon believe it wasn't me? I was kneeling on the basement floor, wet with my own blood, a fucking knife to my neck. They were going to fucking kill me, you cocksucking prick. They practically did."

The memory of that moment was all but overwhelming. He could once again taste the intense fear of death in the back of his throat, smell the stench of his own brutal panic as the sharp blade slid and tugged at the soft skin of his throat. In agony from torn muscles of elbows and wrists tightly shackled behind his back, he could feel the ripping tug at his scalp where a hand gripped his hair, violently wrenching his head backwards while shouted questions came at him for which he had no answers.

Shaking off the remembered fear, he took another long stride forward, experiencing a thrill of pleasure when he saw Shooter take two fast steps backwards, shoulders hitting the wall hard as his instinctive attempt at escape failed.

Seeing the fear in his eyes, Mason pulled his lips back in a parody of a smile, taking aim with his next words. "You find your wife and daughter's bodies yet, bastard? Oh, wait…it's because of your bastard they're dead, right? Pathetic excuse for a motherfucking father you turned out to be—"

Whatever he was going to say next was lost in the roar coming from Shooter's throat as he launched himself at Mason. Catching him by the wrist, Mason let the man's own momentum spin them, pinning him to the wall and grinding his face against the rough cement. He pushed his elbow against Shooter's spine, holding him in place easily, putting him off balance by kicking his feet wide apart. With his other hand, he pulled the gun from the waistband of Shooter's pants. Flipping the safety off, he placed the barrel tip against Shooter's neck immediately below his ear, pressing hard, making the metal bite painfully into the tender flesh.

"They were going to fucking kill me." His voice was nearly inaudible, remembered pain making it hard to pull in enough air. He tasted the reek of panic rolling off his brother, his face near Shooter's shoulder. "You stole more than fifty large from the Fiends—from Deacon—and made it look like it was me. What the fuck did you need fifty thousand dollars for, huh?"

He shifted his hold, pulling on the wrist he held in his hand, drawing a grunt from Shooter as he leaned into him harder, shoving his face against the wall again. "Did you think there would be no retribution? Did you? You knew they would be on me. Had to know. Were you trying to kill me? They were going to fucking cut me into pieces, make me watch as they carved me up bit by fucking bit. You've seen it happen; you knew."

"But they didn't. From what I hear, as is usual for you, you came out on top. Always on top, you always manage to turn things in your favor in the end. Deacon now trusts you like a son, because of the way everything went down." This came from behind him and his muscles jolted, jerking his head up. He had focused on Shooter to the exclusion of everything else, carelessly forgetting Morgan was even in the room. "I am not gonna let you shoot my boy, Mason. Back it down, suck it up...and walk the fuck away while you still can."

"He set me up." Without shifting his eyes from the back of Shooter's head, fairly quivering with rage, Mason spoke to the man behind him.

"Yeah. And, just like with what he did today, he'll answer to me for everything. He wants my club, but I will not have a traitor over it if I have to beat it out of him. Either he learns his lesson from this, or he leaves the Outriders. There ain't no middle ground here, boy. Either way, he'll answer for both in full."

"I killed a man to save his life." Mason's throat had nearly closed, his voice sounding raw and agonized, even to his own ears. *Ripper.* "A good brother. An honorable man."

"And John will one day understand what it means, son. What kind of cost something of that sort brings to a man. I promise you. But Mason, I already told you once. I am not going to stand here and watch you shoot him." The distinctive noise of a pistol cocking came from behind him and Mason closed his eyes, muscles all over his body tensing, waiting for the fiery cold impact of the bullet. His heart beat once, and then again, and when nothing happened by the third heavy thud inside his chest, he chanced a glance behind him, seeing the gun angled down to Morgan's side. *Fuck.* He could push it, but chances were good Morgan would shoot him. *I'll get my pound of flesh another way*, he thought, a snarl lifting his lip.

Jerking brutally on the wrist in his grip, he lifted the limb until there was a satisfying snap and he felt the sharp crack as the joint gave, Shooter's shoulder popping out of place accompanied by a weak scream of pain as muscles ripped. Releasing his hold on Shooter's wrist, he reached up and wound his fingers into the man's hair, pulled his head back from the wall, and shoved forward hard. Smashing his brother's cheek and nose against the unyielding surface, Mason felt another crunch as Shooter's cheekbone gave way.

Releasing Shooter with a final hard push, he stepped backwards, raising his arms and holding his hands out to the side, gun dangling loosely from the fingers of one hand. Turning to face Morgan, their gazes caught and held, the stare lasting for several seconds as he lowered his arms. "My bike?" he finally asked between pants. Now that the altercation appeared to be over, his hands had begun to shake, pain from the beating bubbling to the surface in rolling waves, breaking over the wall of his self-control.

"Outside. I set a guard on it. You tell Tugboat that Morgan said you were golden. He'll let you leave." Morgan stood there, shoulders drooping as he watched his son sag to the floor, tears streaming down Shooter's face in pain and humiliation. He sighed heavily, speaking deliberately. "You won't be welcome here for a while, Mason. Best get in the wind, son."

"Yeah, I'm getting that feeling," Mason scoffed, walking the perimeter of the room towards the door. He slipped the gun into the back of his pants, tugging his shirt down over the butt.

"Your mother did talk about you to him. All the time, wanted him to know you as best he could from here. It mattered to her, boy." The sudden, surprising offering stopped his forward movement mid-step, and he looked over his shoulder at Morgan, puzzled at the conversational segue. The man continued, "She loved you and your sister. I wish there were a way to make things right, Mason. I only wanted to bring her home. I didn't know what we left behind when I took her back."

"A fuckton of hurt," Mason said. "You left behind a fuckton of hurt." He shook his head, in his mind hearing again a distant, high scream cutting through a Kentucky night, and then he turned and walked out the door.

5. Betrayal

"Shit," he ground out, hips pistoning against her ass. "Fuck." Eyes closed, he tipped his head back, and his hands shifted restlessly across the skin of her back, coming to rest wrapped around her waist. He had the woman bent over the foot of the bed, fucking her from behind, her feet spread wide to allow him between her legs. He suspected her pussy hadn't been tight for a long time and couldn't find an angle that was working for him. Pausing for a moment, he moved her, shoving her feet back together, placing his legs on the outside of her knees. In this position, he finally found enough friction and rub to make the fuck worth the effort. Grunting with every stroke, he set a hard, fast pace, wanting this to be over with so he could go the fuck to sleep.

Tucking his chin to his chest, he opened his eyes to watch as his cock slid in and out of her pussy, wet and glistening in the bright, overhead light. Her asshole gaped a little as she clenched and pushed back against him, and he idly wondered if that hole would be better than her pussy. *Let's see if a little incentive will get her more engaged*, he thought. Lifting one hand, he pinched her ass cheek for a moment then brought his palm down in a hard slap against her flesh. Her pussy tightened down on him when he spanked her and smiled grimly then slapped her ass again, listening to her squeal. Rubbing the mark roughly, he watched as the skin reddened.

"There we go. Tighten down on me, pussy. Clamp that thing like you want it. You like pain, yeah?" He hadn't been aware he was about to speak, and his voice startled him. It sounded thick and rough, intense and entirely unlike his usual tone. "You like that, bitch?"

Her voice high and thready, she responded, "Yes. Like that."

He bent over her back, pushing his hand underneath to find her breasts, plucking at her nipples, twisting and pinching them hard, drawing a shrill scream from her lips, the pain seeming to push her to a quick climax.

"Shut up, you fucking bitch." He grunted. Fingers digging into her hips, he pulled her back onto his cock hard, grinding deep into her as he came, finally flooding the rubber with his semen. He hadn't given a fuck if she had come or not, but at least her pussy got tight for a minute when she did. *Fucking club whore*, he thought. *Useless piece-of-shit pussy.*

He stayed still for a minute, feeling her pussy clench and flutter around him, his breathing and heart rate quickly returning to normal. Pulling out, he removed the rubber and tied it into a knot, tossing it into the toilet when he walked into the bathroom. He washed his cock and balls in the sink, not wanting the stink of sex on his skin all night. Wiping his hands on the towel first, he dried himself and tucked his dick back into his pants, buttoning them closed.

Walking out of the bathroom, he was surprised to find her still in the room, sprawled across the bed and already asleep. He thought about waking and kicking her out, but finally shifted her so she lay on one side of the mattress. Lying on his back, arm tucked behind his head, he stared at the ceiling, thinking.

After his encounter with Shooter, he had holed up in a hotel along Coronado Beach for a week, letting the worst of the bruising and swelling recede. His ribs had been so sore he didn't think he could have ridden for any distance, and the man Morgan had set to guard his bike had told him about the reasonably priced hotel near the Navy base there. From his hotel window, he watched the ocean's waves for hours, thinking.

Finding out how Shooter had betrayed him hurt—he wouldn't lie. Now, in retrospect, looking at Deacon's actions at the time and knowing the facts, he found it even more telling his brothers had been willing to kill him without even establishing he was the one who stole from the club. They were all looking after their own asses so hard they couldn't detect when one of them was working for the club rather than himself.

He had been in Kentucky for two days, first meeting with different club leaders in Louisville and Lexington, which had gone well. Then he had dropped back near home to visit Morgan's local Outriders chapter, receiving a surprise request to stay at the clubhouse before he headed back to Chicago. Glancing over at the woman, he snorted. She was part of his invitation, told in no uncertain terms to make him happy. He sighed, because he had known better than to turn down club hospitality—hence the unwanted fuck.

Shifting on the bed, he angled one knee, tucking his foot behind his other leg, reaching down to touch the lump of sea glass in his pocket like a lucky talisman. Overall, this had been a good trip, perhaps not as profitable money-wise as Deacon wanted, but he knew the exposure to what other clubs did—how they ran things and how they handled situations—would prove invaluable. Every club visited had only highlighted even more exactly how fucked up things were in Chicago under Deacon. He sighed again and settled into sleep, his last thoughts of ideas on how he might get changes into place bloodlessly.

Mason woke and groaned, gripping the sides of his head, trying to lessen the pounding behind his temples. There was a noise in the room and he moved, cracking one eye open to find the woman from last night standing beside the bed. She was dressed in jeans and, he saw with some annoyance, his shirt, and looking past her, he skimmed a glance around the room in surprise. It wasn't the same one he had fallen asleep in last night. "What the hell?" he asked, voice raspy from his dry throat. Levering himself up on one elbow, he winced as the change in position caused the throbbing in his head to turn into jackhammering again.

"Time to rise and shine, sleepyhead." She wore a sly grin, which made him immediately distrust her. *Fucking club pussy*, he thought, frowning at her.

"Where the fuck are we?" Anger swirled in his gut, mixing with fear, because he seriously didn't know where the fuck he was. He swung his legs off the bed on the side opposite where she stood. A flash of irritation crossed her features as he turned, giving her his back as bent over, grabbing his pants where they were thrown in a pile on the floor. Tugging them up his legs, he reached down to tuck his cock inside and froze for a second, recognizing the feel of dried pussy juice and semen on his dick and crotch. Spinning around, he eyed her watchfully as he finished dressing, pulling on his boots before asking again, "Where the fuck are we?" Puzzled by the satisfied expression on her face, he immediately discarded his momentary confusion as unimportant when she answered him.

"Drive On Inn," she said.

"Goddamn answer me, bitch," he snarled. "Don't make me beat it out of you." Somewhat gratified by the look of fear on her face, he growled, "What the fuck are we doing in a motel when we were at the clubhouse last night?" He felt a pulling in the bend of his elbow and saw a bandage, using his fingernails to rip it off and toss it to the floor.

"Night before last," she said, cocking her head over. "Oh, baby, you must have been drunker than I thought."

Did she just say I lost a whole day? He couldn't wrap his mind around the concept. He had drunk enough to black out before, but he sure as fuck hadn't been drunk when he went to sleep. Before taking this club whore up to the bedroom, he was careful to have only a single beer the whole night. She had been the one to bring him his food and that one beer. He looked around the room, the décor supporting her claim they were in a motel. No bags, which meant—

"Where the fuck's my bike?"

"Your Harley is back at the clubhouse. We took my car to Lexington to the JP's, but then you couldn't wait until we got to the clubhouse, so we stopped and rented a room on the way back." She smirked when she said this, rubbing a hand down across her breasts suggestively.

He focused on a single piece of her statement, and his balls drew up as an icy cold settled into his belly. "JP?"

"Yeah, you wanted it fast, and when your daddy wouldn't take your calls, you had Watcher pull a string or two." She smiled, looking somehow predatory as she sauntered around the end of the bed towards him. "You are younger than you look, you know? I didn't realize you were only twenty-six until you filled out the papers. But that's all right; I don't mind being a little older than you."

I'm just a poor wayfaring stranger

Boy, you'll remember your lessons this time, won't cha? he heard his daddy say, feeling the lash come down across his back. With a jerk, he pulled himself back to the moment and repeated the question, his hands beginning to shake in earnest. "JP?" Watcher was the president of the Outriders chapter in his hometown, where he was supposed to stay for a single night. He had known the man his whole life, trusted him like a brother. He snorted, remembering Shooter's face as he last saw him, tears and snot covering his cheeks, blood streaking his chin. He knew all too well not all brothers were trustworthy.

"Baby, are you okay?" She reached out a hand and he twisted away before she could touch him. She had a hurt look on her face as she froze in place. The whore's voice was tender when she called, "Baby?"

"Are you trying to make me believe I fucking married you, bitch?" He ground out the question, because even if it didn't make sense, it was the only thing that came to mind with everything she said and how she was acting. It had to be a joke, but it wasn't funny, and he was going to fucking kill Watcher for this gag when he saw him. Didn't matter if they were friends; he would fucking kill him. Mason rubbed his forehead with the heels of both hands hard, scrubbing back and forth across the skin, because his goddamned head hurt so bad it was hard to think.

"Yes, baby. Don't you remember?" Her voice was quavering now, and if he hadn't been watching her face closely, he might have believed his reaction hurt her. But, he *was* watching, and he saw the gleeful look in her eyes, quickly masked as she clenched them closed, forcing out a tear barely large enough to trickle from her eye.

"No, I don't fucking remember. I don't even fucking know your name, bitch. What kind of game are you playing?" He reached out, gripping her arms right above her elbows, shaking her back and forth. "What do you get out of it? What did Watcher tell you to do, bitch? What kind of fucking game is this?"

"No game, baby," she stuttered the words out, gasping a little at the rough way he was handling her, his grip bruising-tight on her arms.

"You wanna keep this charade up? Okay, keep your fucking game going, but I'm taking your ass back to the goddamn clubhouse. Stupid fucking bitch. I'll let Watcher deal with your shit." Glancing around the room, he saw what had to be her purse on the dresser and stalked over to it, his hand locked around her wrist dragging her behind him. "Fucking bitch." He picked it up and shook it, hearing keys jingle inside. Dropping her arm, he reached inside the purse and dug out the keys, holding them tightly in one fist as he threw the bag to the floor and walked to the door. "If you're coming, then you need to get a fucking move on it."

Back at the clubhouse, he stalked in, followed closely by...fuck, he didn't know her goddamned, fucking name. The entire ride had been silent, except for her occasional forced sob, each one met by his disbelieving snort. Watcher was standing at the bar, and as they walked into the main room, he looked up, the smile dropping from his face as he took in the anger radiating off Mason. Jerking his head to a door across the room, he snapped out one word. "Office."

With a nod, Mason reached back and grabbed her arm, his hand a hard bracelet around her wrist, again dragging her along behind him as he strode into the room, kicking the door closed so hard it rattled the doorframe. "Fucking bitch says I married her." Mason didn't pose this as a question, but he waited for Watcher to either confirm or deny before he said anything else.

Nodding slowly, Watcher's eyes never left Mason's as he said, "You told me it had to be yesterday, brother. I called in a small marker for you. Carrie"—here, his gaze cut to the woman and then back again—"was agreeable."

"Carrie?" Mason hated his voice sounded desperate and afraid. *Weak.* He sounded fucking weak, and it was not a position from which he was accustomed to dealing. He dropped his hand from her wrist and took a step to the side, physically separating himself from the bitch. Leaning his shoulders against the wall behind him, he folded his arms across his chest, trying to find some sense of control in this situation.

"Carrie Sosa," Watcher said, tipping his head towards the woman. "Carrie Mason now, I reckon."

"Oh, fuck no!" His arms flew up as he roared the words, rejecting the idea with every fiber of his being. "This club pussy ain't my goddamned wife. I don't remember a fucking thing after going to sleep here in the clubhouse last night...I guess the night before last, if she's to be believed. Not a thing, Watch."

Tucking his tongue into his cheek, Watcher slowly shook his head in disbelief. "Are you fucking kidding me?"

"Why the hell would I joke about something like this, brother?" Mason asked, running a shaking hand across his jaw before folding his arms across his chest again. "I'm telling you...I don't remember anything past fucking her in the room upstairs, tucking my dick in, and falling asleep with my pants on. Nothing.

"Then, today, I woke up in Lexington, evidence of bare-assed fucking on my cock, and a woman in the room claiming we were married. I have no recollection of talking to you, driving to town, vows, blood tests...fucking. Nothing, brother, there's nothing I remember. Help me understand." Mason's insides were beginning to quake; this had to be a dream...it was like something from a bad dream. A nightmare. He reached up, slapping his face hard once, and then a second time before he barked out a harsh laugh. "This ain't no fucking dream, is it?"

Watcher swung back to Carrie, and with one look at his face, she backed up a step. He snapped at her, "Where's the fucking shit, Carrie?"

"What do you mean?" she asked, taking another step back. Mason moved so he stood between her and the door, pressing his back against the wood. She glanced his direction and then focused back on Watcher, mistakenly thinking he was the biggest threat in the room. "What do you mean, Watch?"

"Where. Is. The. Shit?" he asked again, and Mason watched as a shiver wormed its way up her back. Suddenly, the import of what Watcher was asking hit him, and he jerked as if slapped.

"You fucking drugged me, didn't you?" His teeth ground together as a wave of anger washed over him. The emotion was so fierce he could feel the muscles of his arms coiling and tensing. "You goddamned bitch.

You drugged me...for what? What did you want?" He was beginning to piece things together in his mind, the numbing layer of confusion he felt all day finally melting away. He got to the clubhouse and talked to Watcher then she brought him dinner and a drink, telling him they...what. "'Watcher told me to make you happy,'" he said, quoting her, because it was what she said before sitting on his lap and putting his hand between her legs. Before he took her upstairs and fucked her.

Carrie swung to look at him, an expression of fear chasing anger across her face. He remembered the sly grin and look of satisfaction she wore this morning, and then thought about his condition when he woke up and, suddenly, he thought he knew. His voice was perilously soft, contemplative when he said, "You fucked me bare." Now it was her turn to jerk at his quiet words, and he watched her try to control her response. "You fucked me bare, because...why? Why would you drug me and then fuck me bare? Are you pregnant? You lookin' for a baby daddy, bitch?"

"No," she shot back, and he believed her. The response was instinctive...without pretense. Hiding a pregnancy was not part of her ploy. "I didn't drug you." Ah, but from her body's reactions, this statement was a bald-faced lie, and he called her on it.

"Yes, you did. You fucking drugged me." He reached out a hand and grabbed a handful of her dark hair, twisting his fist in it to pull her close to him, forcing her to her knees even as she screamed out at the pain. Rage washed through him. "I was fucking drugged and you goddamn well did it," he said, still speaking quietly and staring down at her. "Why?"

"Because Shooter told me to," she shouted, refusing to surrender, her hands tugging futilely at his wrist. She didn't have a chance of escaping him; his fingers had an iron clasp on her hair. "Shooter told me to. He made me, Mason."

The desire to hurt someone was nearly overwhelming, and he was shaking with a depth of anger he had never felt before. The strength of the loathing and disgust he had for the woman on her knees before him was frightening in its intensity.

He could kill her with a flick of his wrist, and he knew Watcher would cover his play. He wanted to, had never wanted anything as badly as he did this.

He was furious with her.

Hated her.

She had drugged him. She had lied to him...stolen a day from him, stolen...something else.

Control. She had manipulated him, stripped him of control.

"You goddamn bitch, you better be clean." *Fucking Shooter*. What in the hell was he doing? What was his play with this? Mason had to get himself back in check, focus on Shooter.

"I am," she said breathlessly, her head bobbing rapidly up and down as he stared at her.

"Goddamn well better be, or I'll fucking find you and kill you." Even though he said this in a flat, even tone, he had never before meant any statement as he did this one right now. *Fucking club pussy.* He felt the entire thing spiraling out of control, his ability to handle himself diminishing. Head throbbing, his vision crowding down into a tight tunnel, he could distinguish only her face, and it was shaded with dark, tell-tale crimson. *Fucking bitch.*

Control.

I am a poor wayfaring stranger

"I'm sorry, Mason. I'm sorry. Sorry." The words fell from her lips in a fast torrent. He slowly forced his hand to relax and let her go, and then shoved her away her from him in revulsion, watching dispassionately as her hands went to the sides of her head, shuddering as she rubbed her scalp. He took a deep breath in and blew it out slowly, turning towards Watcher with a heartfelt plea. "Help me fix this, brother."

Nodding, Watcher picked up the phone, dialing a number from memory. After a few short words, he hung up. Looking up at Mason, he shook his head. "So fucking sorry, brother. I'll deal with Carrie and any legal shit. Goddamn, this is screwed up." Looking at Carrie, he snapped, "Once this shit is handled, Carrie, you're out, bitch. I don't want to glimpse your fucking ass around the clubhouse, or my fucking club again. Not a single, goddamned, fucking member. You are out. But, until this shit is contained, you don't fucking leave." Jerking his head at the door, he waited until Mason opened it, and then yelled, "Patches, get your ass in here."

An Outriders member stepped through the door a few moments later, looking from Mason to Watcher, ignoring the girl at first, only looking at her after Watcher finished speaking. "Lock her in one of the rooms upstairs. She eats and drinks, but that's the sum of it. No phone, no wandering our house, no fucking." Pinning the man with his gaze, he pointed a finger and emphasized again. "No fucking." When Patches nodded, he continued, "She's got shit either on her, in her, or in her goddamned car. Find it and bring it to me, brother."

Carrie cowered when Patches reached for her arm, but at his urging, she rose to her feet and went quietly enough. Once the door closed, Watcher dropped his head into his hands, leaning his elbows on the table. "Goddammit, Mason. I swear to God I didn't know you were fucked up, man. You sounded like yourself...normal. I'd have never gone along otherwise. Hell, I questioned you hard, but you seemed solid on what you wanted. Fucking Shooter, man. That dickhead's got a hard-on for you that absolutely won't quit."

"Just help me fix it, brother." Mason settled slowly into a chair across the table from Watcher, the adrenaline-fueled quiver of his muscles the only reminder of the rage he had felt only minutes ago.

"You got it, man. We'll get this shit sorted." He nodded, and then looked up at Mason. "Are you happy in Chicago, brother?"

Mason looked at him warily, glancing over at the door Watcher had pointedly closed behind Patches as the man left the room. "What's up?"

"I'm leaving the Outriders." Watcher dropped this bomb without preamble.

Even though he had been considering the same thing himself, he was shocked, because once a man patched into a club, it was a rare occurrence they would leave voluntarily. "What the hell? What do you mean you're leaving? What the fuck are you going to tell Morgan?"

"I'm gonna tell him my brother started a club in New Mexico and asked me to come out. Unlike his son, Morgan's an honorable man; he'll let me patch out and gypsy. My brother's club is virtually all veterans, and it sounds like they're a good group of men. I wanted to extend an invitation to you, too. We could use good brothers there, and even without the military background, you are one of the best I know.

"I'm aware of rumblings surrounding rumors Deacon is losing control in Chicago, and brother, you do not want to be in the middle of that Charlie Foxtrot when things implode." Watcher leaned forward, spreading his palms on the scarred wood of the tabletop. "Southern Soldiers would welcome you with open arms, Mason. I know the kind of shit Deacon has been into…had you do in the past. I can fucking guarantee you the Soldiers aren't anything like what you've experienced." His voice dropped, and in a near-plea he said, "Come with me."

Frowning, Mason slowly shook his head. "Chicago is where I'm supposed to be, man. I'm not sure why, but I know that fact just like

I know my own name. Yeah, things are fucked up in the Fiends, but I have ideas how to change things, how I can work to fix those broken things and piece us back together. I've gone back and forth in my head these past weeks, trying to decide what to do. It comes down to saving my brothers.

He sucked in a breath and blew it out as he admitted, "I've learned a fuckton from every club I visited on this run, and I can visualize a hundred ways to make the Fiends better." He stood and extended his hand, gripping Watcher's when he stood and reached out. "I'm fucking honored you'd ask me, brother. Fucking honored. It means more than you'll ever know. But I can't, Chicago is my home for now."

6. Take a stand

1999

"Goddammit, Mason. You cannot simply let this shit lie, man. It's shit and you know it, son." Jackson worked himself into an angry lather as he and Mason watched a half-dozen Fiends get ready to leave the clubhouse. Each man had been handpicked by Deacon to ride with him to this meet with a small club from the upper peninsula of Michigan. They were his inner circle, his most trusted brothers. Or, at least the ones least likely to buck anything he proposed. The groups were supposed to hook up at a greasy spoon bar somewhere upstate in Wisconsin, near the UP, but to what end, Mason wasn't sure.

"Hush, old man." He looked over at Jackson warmly, liking his use of the word son. "I'm still trying to sort out what the shine is on this particular deal for Deacon. You of all people know I can't overplay my hand." Mason had been comfortable around the man since the beginning. Early in their conversations, he found out Jackson was from the backwoods of Mississippi. His father had been a Pentecostal preacher, a culture not too far removed from how Mason had been raised, and Jackson grew up sitting in the first pew of small churches across northern Georgia. Now, even after spending decades in Chicago, the older man was still as country as Mason had at one time been, and the two had developed an easy friendship.

Training his eyes on Mason, Jackson said gravely, his voice low and serious, "Girls and brown. That's what they're going up after. Deacon's tired of the shit in the current stable, so he's out to buy some fresh pussy. The Devil's Sins have a connection in Canada, and he's heading up to meet with their second in command, Demon. Each brother you spot leaving today will be coming back with fresh, young pussy on the back of his scoot, and you know not all that pussy is gonna be willing. Motherfucker ain't even taking a cage; he's putting them on the bikes, man. Fucking lack of respect for anything." He spat in the dirt at their feet. "And this is if he stays straight enough to make it back. You seen his arms lately?"

Mason nodded. He had watched as the muscles withered away from Deacon's biceps, seen the festering sores in the bend of his elbows. Deacon always liked blow, but this was harder than anyone had ever seen him party. The man would shoot instead of eat, most days. "Where's Prez getting the money to pay for all this shit?" He pitched his voice low, tipping his head close to Jackson to ask the question, and he flinched at the answer.

"Same place he gets the money for every fucking thing he does, man. Off our brothers' backs, from their sweat and blood. I was in the office earlier when he was pitching his fit about how low things were inside the safe. Chanced a glance, man. There ain't a dollar left in the fucking hunk of iron. He's bled us dry, Mason. You can't let this shit go on." Jackson lifted a hand, sweeping his long hair back from his face over the top of his head. "This ain't the way the club was ever intended to be. Ain't what any of us signed on for. We need you to step right the fuck up, brother. We need you to save us."

He knew this was the kind of action he would never be able to take back. A fork in the road that couldn't be U-turned. Was he ready to commit to the path he had chosen, staying and fighting for the club instead of patching out? Rubbing his fingers back and forth across his lips and chin, he watched the bikes rumble out of the parking lot, keeping his gaze on them for a long time. He saw them grow small in the distance and sighed, turning to the man next to him to ask the question that would kick everything off, knowing his utterance of the words would mark the beginning of the end. "You'd back me?"

"Fuck yeah, I'll back you. Nearly every brother here would back your play, Mason." He nodded defiantly, confident in his answer. "You give a shit and we all know it. With you, with us behind you, we'll thrive instead of die a slow death." Mason nodded and turned back to the street. The bikes were long out of view now, but he stared into the distance, mentally weighing the options he felt were open to him. Jackson gave him a minute then asked, "What you gonna do, brother?"

"Burn this motherfucker to the ground," he snarled, his voice flat and angry. "He wants to kill the club? Then we'll roast him in the goddamned ashes. It's past time for war."

7. Rising from ashes

2000

Mason stood inside one of the connecting doors and looked around the room, breath whooshing in and out, his lungs' quest for air sucking it in hard and fast. It was done. His and Jackson's plans, put into motion, executed today. Now. Done. It was at moments like this when he missed Ripper the most. The tipping points, those damned forks in the road, rare moments of change when he needed someone to tell him he was doing the right thing—he had headed down the right path.

There were six bodies on the floor, stacked along the edge of the walls like rolled up carpets, set out of the way for cleaning. Six bodies. Six deaths had painted the walls red, blood drying in enormous swaths of maroon. Gory streaks along the plaster and woodwork of the bar, splatter on the ceiling and table legs. Six bodies of brothers, men he had known for a dozen years in some cases. Fathers. Sons. Husbands. Six brothers, put to ground, because it was needful for the club.

Hands on his hips, he didn't bother to turn when there were sounds of another scuffle behind him, trusting the men he brought with him to have his back. Hopefully, this would be the last resistance encountered, and *please, God*, let it be ended without more bloodshed. This coup was the final step in what had been a long journey, months in the making since he returned from his cross-country run with knowledge Deacon never intended him to have. Awareness and understanding of what a club should be, how it could support the members fairly, and most of all...how a real club president gave all to the club, unlike Deacon, who took everything.

He first tried to do things the right way, at least what he imagined the right way would be in a better club. Attempted to promote change from the inside out, working his way into a position of trust and influence. Every change he suggested had either been killed outright by Deacon or died a slow death of non-adoption, because there were no incentives for his brothers to want change. Their club was weakened beyond belief, nearly on the verge of closing, because of one man: Deacon.

"Mason." Pirate called his name, and then the man paused to clear his throat and deliberately changed the form of address, jolting Mason with the title used. "Prez."

"Yeah?" he responded without turning around, counting the bodies again, coming up with the same figure. Six brothers.

"Jackson didn't make it, man." There was genuine sorrow in his voice, and Mason turned. Disbelief ran through him, followed swiftly by sadness and the memory of his mother's voice.

I'll soon be free from every trial
This form shall rest beneath the sod

"Are you fucking kidding me? Where is he?" Mason's forehead wrinkled, pulling his eyebrows together. Jackson had become his touchstone since Ripper's death. Hell, the man wasn't even supposed to be here tonight. By all their planning, he should have been at one of the brothers' houses, the intent to keep their old ladies and kids safe.

Pirate led him through the Monaco to one of the back rooms. Turning through a doorway, he saw Jackson's body awkwardly slumped across the threshold of the next room. Stopping next to him, he squatted and first put his hand on the old man's neck to confirm what he already knew from his visual assessment, and then gently shifted him until he lay flat inside the room. There were three bullet holes in his leather vest, the spacing and location giving him hope his friend's death had been near instant, at least. "Get me a tablecloth or something," he spoke quietly, without turning, listening as Pirate moved away.

Reaching out, he tenderly swept Jackson's hair back from his face, plucking the strands loose that had become stuck to his bottom lip. Jackson had a knife in his hand, and Mason retrieved it. Inspecting it, he saw the blade was clean, so he folded the knife closed and tucked it into his own front pocket. "Stupid fucking old man. What the hell were you doing here?" He straightened Jackson's arms, folding his worn and work-stained hands across his stomach. "Just like a preacher's son to bring a knife to a gunfight. Stupid pacifist."

Several other members walked from room to room throughout the building with a predictable pattern of step, step, pause, a grunt or whispered conversation, and then movement again. He had set them to gathering the drugs and firearms from all the hidey-holes and caches Deacon had around. The only people still in the building were his backers, his brothers. In the hour since the shooting ended, Deacon and the twenty-two men who had resisted, the members who fought back, had been moved two at a time back to the clubhouse, and would be held until Mason could turn his attention that direction.

"Prez." Pirate was back, and Mason felt fabric brush across his shoulder. Reaching up, he took the proffered cloth and spread it respectfully over Jackson's body, hiding the destruction of his friend from casual view.

"Thanks, brother," he ground out, standing and turning around. "This was well done. A hard fucking thing, but well done. Wish like hell

Jackson had listened to me, but we'll honor the man...our brother." He took a breath, gripping Pirate's shoulder, thinking fast. So many moving parts to keep track of, but he needed to know what the lure had been. "Send RG to check on the families. Find out why Jackson left. Then, we vacate this place for the day. We have business at the clubhouse."

At the man's nod, Mason raised his voice to be heard throughout the building. "Bring what you've found to the clubhouse. Bring our dead. Church in an hour. We'll torch or clean later, make sure we lock the fucking place up tight for now, brothers." He listened, hearing several noises and words of acknowledgment as he turned towards the backdoor, striding out of the bar and into the night.

***

"You stupid, backwoods motherfucker, you," Deacon said, calmly straining against and testing the bonds that held him in place on a straight-back chair. "You think you can take my club? Think you have the men? The votes?"

"I know I can, Deacon. Hell, I already did." Mason sat behind the desk, turning a gavel over and over in his hands as he looked at the man who, until a couple of hours ago, had been the highest authority in the club. "I have the votes. I have the men." He paused, and then said, "I have the club. My fucking club."

His voice so smooth you would never know he was helpless, tied to a chair, Deacon said, "You don't know what you're getting into, stupid fucktard. Running a club is a complex thing. It's expensive to keep the clubhouse and the bar going. Businesses ain't for the uneducated." He twisted his shoulders, obviously trying to pull his hands loose.

"Don't you mean it's expensive to keep you in blow and brown? Just as it's costly to keep you in the classy hookers you take to the Admiral? Fuck, Deacon, I've been watching the books for a while now. The brothers and I all know where most of the club money goes." Mason laid the gavel flat on the desktop, placing his hands palm-down on either side of it. "We know you fuck us over to keep your own shit flowing. We all got tired of it. I've provided the fulcrum the club needed to shift the balance and get you out of the way of our success."

Deacon's head came up, and Mason could see the muscles in his jaw clench and release. When he spoke this time, it was with a quiet venom, which should have been terrifying, and would have been even four years ago. Now, coming from this tired, old man, it rang hollow, having less effect than Mason would have ever credited.

"You thankless backwoods fucktard. I took you in, showed you how life could be after you left behind the hellhole your daddy raised you in. Let you live here, in my house, called you my brother. Thankless piece of pussy boy white trash. Fucking snake handler piece of shit. I shoulda let Shooter take care of you when he wanted. Should have capped you when you killed Ripper. I could have; not a man would have spoken against it."

He closed his mouth with a snap, cutting off the bitter words. Squeezing his eyes shut, he sat there for a moment, dragging in harsh breaths through his nose, obviously struggling for control. Finally, he shrugged both shoulders and settled into the seat, seemingly giving up on his efforts to talk Mason down. "Twelve years, motherfucker. Nearly half your life spent in my club, my good little pussy boy, always doing what you were told. What are you going to do with me now? Obviously you have a need for me, or you'd have already put me to ground."

Mason was grudgingly impressed; Deacon was discussing his own death as if it were a foregone conclusion, and not something about which he was overly worried. "Yeah, Deacon. You're right. I am what you made me. In the twelve years you've known me, you created this man in front of you. With every fight you forced me into, every ambush you allowed for entertainment's sake, every single thing you've done has brought us to today. It is all on you, man. All on your fucking head.

He stopped and took a deep breath then shook his head. "Yeah, I have a need for you. We're going to make this as bloodless as possible. Finalize things without the club losing power in town. I won't let you strip my brothers of anything else. Goddamn, man. You've already taken enough from us all. I want you to ride with me and talk to the presidents of the Dominos and Skeptics. We're going to let them know you've agreed to step down. I don't want those clubs thinking we're a house divided, today's deaths aside."

Deacon looked down, flinching at the open acknowledgment of the cost from today's fighting, and Mason was glad to get a glimpse of that at least. Motherfucking human, at the end. He spoke over any response Deacon might have had, telling him, "You'll spin them a pretty story about being tired, what a toll the presidency has placed on you. Greybeard status creeping up on you. You figure out some shit they'll believe, since I do not want to be responsible for my brothers fighting a war with the other clubs in Chicago. I won't. It's not going to happen, because we'll nip this shit in the bud. And, we'll take care of this part yet tonight. This, and our final business." He took a deep breath. "And then tomorrow I'll escort Jackson home."

At the name, Deacon's head came up, and he questioned, "Fuck. You sayin' Jackson bought it today?"

Mason nodded. "We're not sure who did for him. He wasn't armed but with his knife. Someone called him away from the families, and he left prospects there who kept control, but he came to the Monaco and found a tight, little grouping of bullets with his name on them."

"Motherfuck," Deacon whispered. "He was the last original Fiends."

"I know," Mason said, "and he was the one pushing me the hardest to do what we did today. He couldn't stand to witness the club going down like it was. Members leaving every month and you not giving a shit, as long as you could powder your nose or belt your fucking arm. Brothers riding broke down, piece-of-shit bikes, because you raised dues time and again until it's all they could afford. It tore him up there was no sense of permanence or strength in the club. He said you'd stolen enough from all of us...from him."

Deacon closed his eyes tightly and took a deep breath, followed by another. He raised his head and looked at Mason, hatred evident in his expression, but there was also an aggrieved respect. "Time I moved on, Mason." He nodded slowly, warming to the part. "It wasn't clear until we had this discussion, but it's time...past time I handed over the reins."

Breaking character for a moment, he glared hard at Mason. "Don't cut my patches until after we talk to the other clubs. They'll believe it better if this is done without visible outward pressure." He held the stare for a second then slipped quickly back into the tired president role, and said, "I think Florida sounds pretty good. On the other hand, Texas, I could do Texas. Somewhere warm, where it doesn't snow for six months out of the fucking year. Somewhere I can get in the wind anytime I please."

Mason stood and opened the door, glancing at Pirate and RG. They nodded wordlessly back at him and turned, moving so he could catch sight of the collection of men on the floor, trussed-up like deer on a truck hood. He counted the twenty-two men he expected and stepped back, taking his knife and slicing through the bonds holding Deacon to the chair. "First audience is the hardest, motherfucker," he muttered, gripping the man's shoulder and pulling him up, shoving him into the room.

Rubbing his wrists and elbows, Deacon looked at the men tied wrist-to-ankle and twisted to glance at Mason. "You don't fuck around, do you?" At Mason's silent stare, he hooted a brief, despondent laugh. "Listen up," he said loudly and launched into a version of what he and Mason had discussed a moment ago. In the end, ten of the men agreed to follow Mason, but a full dozen refused, calling him a traitor, and worse.

Instructing they remain restrained until he returned, Mason escorted Deacon outside, followed by the bulk of his men. *My men*, he realized with a start. *This is my club now. Their faith, my promise. These men, my brothers*. Seating himself on his bike, he looked around, for the first time in a long time seeing a spark of excitement in the faces surrounding him. Everyone here was ready for this change to happen, ready to move forward. Nodding to himself, he twirled a finger in the air and led the pack of bikes off the lot and onto the surface streets, heading toward the meets with the other clubs.

***

Six hours, he thought. Six hours to advertise the change and stabilize the club's position in Chicago. Fourteen since the shit storm began, and now well past midnight. The dawning of a new day only hours away.

"You're with me, because you wanted change." He looked around the room, seeing heads nod in response. "Well, that change starts here. Pirate is Lieutenant, RG is our Enforcer, and Sonic is the club's Sargent at Arms." He looked over at Deacon, sitting quietly on a nearby barstool, and saw his head jerk up at Mason's next words. "First order of business, we got some patches we need to cut."

Standing, he moved beside Deacon, who stood slowly, unfolding himself until he was upright. Mason met his gaze without flinching, proud his hand only shook the barest amount when he reached out to grab the edge of the man's vest. Voluntarily handling the man's cut for the first time in his life, those sacred colors meaningless on the leather now. "Deacon, you've proven yourself false to the brotherhood." In some part of his mind, he knew this had to be a spectacle; it needed to feel final to everyone witnessing this transfer of power, demonstrating the seriousness of the moment.

"No longer a Rebel Fiend." Reaching into his jeans pocket, he pulled out Jackson's knife and flicked it open, holding it with his thumbnail near the sharp tip. This felt right, too.

Shifting his gaze to where his hands needed to work, he commenced snipping the threads that held the president patch to the vest while he continued to speak. "Your role was to lead, but you failed us all." *Snip.* "Failed in the charge to the charter." *Snip.* "Failed in the expectations your brothers left in your hands." *Snip.* "Failed their trust in you." *Snip.* "No longer their president." *Snip.* "No longer our leader." Taking the small patch in hand, he laid it on the bar behind them, and then put his hands on Deacon's shoulders, holding his eyes as he turned the man away.

Snip. He set about working on the patches on the back of the vest, the bottom rocker with the word 'Chicago' first. *Snip.* "The club no longer needs you." Removal of this patch went faster, the threads easier to pluck out without damaging the material of the piece. "This town no longer needs you." *Snip.* "Our expectation is you'll leave, not keep your embarrassment in view." *Snip.*

He laid the patch on the bar next to the first one and saw Deacon's head angling down, looking at the evidence that change was happening at this moment: he no longer was what he had been for so long. Starting to work on the middle patch, Mason looked carefully at the emblem of the club before moving Jackson's knife along the edges. *Snip.* "Rebel Fiends existed before you came along." *Snip.* "You're not critical to the life of the club." *Snip.* "But you nearly killed it, killed our brotherhood." *Snip.* "No longer will you damage the club you vowed to protect with your life." *Snip.* He laid the black and white image of a widely grinning devil's head on the bar, touching the edge of the fabric with one fingertip. "No longer your colors."

There was stark silence in the room as he returned to the back of Deacon's vest, hands steady as he cut the threads on the final patch, the top rocker, which spelled out the club's name. "No longer Rebel Fiends." *Snip.* "No longer a brother." This went much faster than any of the rest of the patches had. *Snip.* Renaming the man felt right, and he didn't allow himself to think beyond the next movement of the knife. *Snip.* "No longer Deacon, but *Cut*." *Snip.* "No longer anything to us, Cut."

Stepping away, he laid the final patch on the bar, the small pile of dirty fabric a poor conclusion to years of association. "Pirate, escort Cut off Fiends' property, would ya?" Turning his back on his former president, with his body language, he told everyone in the room how unimportant the man now was to him, to their club, their brotherhood.

His heart swelled when the clear sound of Pirate's smooth response rang through the room. "Sure thing, Prez." Deacon—no, *Cut*—Cut sucked in a harsh pant at the hard-earned designation being given so freely to another, and then Mason held his breath as he listened to their footsteps moving away.

He stood there, taking in the first shallow breath when the swelling tones of bike exhaust pipes sounded in the parking lot. The second breath came as he listened to the diminishing noise as it moved off the lot and away. A third breath, deeper, freer as he realized it was happening. Deacon, gone. Out of their club—out of their lives. The cost of change was seven deaths: six men loyally defending a club riddled with parasitic leadership, and one brother. A brother he knew would count the cost worthy.

When Pirate returned to the room and nodded at him, he drew a deep breath, swelling his chest, stretching muscles so long tensed that their release felt like freedom. Mason shifted to look out at the men still lying tied on the floor.

"Any man who wants to change their decision can speak up now. We'll have a chat." He waited a beat, and when no one spoke to fill the silence, he nodded decisively. "Alrighty then, you've all made your choice. RG, bring me a Cut."

Once all the ex-members had been escorted out of the clubhouse, Mason looked around at the exhausted men standing in scattered clumps around the room. *Time for the next change*, he thought. He took a deep breath, releasing it slowly before saying loudly, "Church, motherfuckers. Not like before, with only officers. This is an all-member church, so pull up a fucking chair." He walked behind the bar where all the removed patches had been laid, gently resting his hand on them.

"First order of business, you've all been calling me by a title today I've not been granted. I won't take it by force; it's a trust that must be freely given, has to be earned. And freely accepted, which I would do." He paused, and RG jumped into the moment of silence.

"Mason, you're the motherfucking president." Shaking his head in forced amusement, he leaned back into the cushions of the couch where he was sitting. "You want it all official like? Okay, man. I nominate Mason president." Before Mason could even respond, a chorus of "Seconded," rang out. This single word came from several throats around the room, and the men laughed tightly.

RG grinned and looked around the room. "No opposition? Good. Motion fucking carried. Next order of business, Prez?"

Mason laughed. "Alrighty then, motherfuckers. You all heard me name our officers earlier. Any discussion surrounding those decisions?" Headshakes met his question, but there was no conversation or chatter, so he nodded. "Okay." He looked around carefully, meeting each man's gaze unflinchingly. "What we had wasn't working, brothers. We all knew it, saw the evidence every day when we eyeballed ourselves in the mirror. So we took a chance, took a chance on each other. This is our chance to remake ourselves. An opportunity to draw a line in the sand and separate our new, sane club from the insanity of what went before. I think we can all agree we lived up to the name 'Fiends,' whether we wanted to or not." His mind went back to the hundreds of fights he had been forced into, all for the sake of the club, the rich purses lining undeserving wallets. Limp bodies slung into the trunks of cars or the back of trucks, dull-eyed dead rolled into ditches and shallow graves. "It all changes today."

He continued, "This is not something I do lightly. I want every man Jack of you to know and understand that truth. As much thought as I've given to the takeover today, and I won't mince words with you, of all people. This was a planned coup, bloodier than I wanted, but brothers, control over the club had to be stripped from the man who was our president. I read once that history is written by the victors, so I know...I fucking know our history will show this was a needful thing." He took a calming breath, resting his hands on the bar. "As much planning as went into today, more has gone into this next thing."

I'm just a poor wayfaring stranger

Bethany's voice rang in his ears and he shook his head to dislodge the memories. "No longer Rebel Fiends, we will be known as the Rebel Wayfarers from here forward. Got a guy working up a patch for us right now, because I fucking had confidence in all of you. Confidence we would emerge the victors today. Confidence we'd come out on top, because it was the only way this would shake out. Confidence. A Wayfarer is someone who travels. A wanderer. The definition will tell you a wayfarer goes typically on foot. But we're fucking Rebels, man, so we can make it what we want. Rebel Wayfarers, with Chicago as the mother chapter." That more than anything else he said drew a hiss of whispers from around the room and he nodded.

"Fuck yeah, you heard me right. Mother chapter. I have ambitions. I have confidence in you, remember?" He raised one clenched fist. "We're going to make this motherfucking club something to be proud of, something others will admire and aspire to become. Every man in the room is a founder of the mother chapter, as of today. Fucking originals, one and all. Every man who will fly the new colors with me will also bear the weight of a new charter. We want the same things, brothers. We want safety for ourselves and our families, security in our club and how it's ran, stability and room to grow our brotherhood. We all want the same things." He thumped his closed fist against his chest and then rested it on the bar top, tension running through him, because these changes were crucial for what he wanted in the long term.

"The patch supports our intent, and will serve as a reminder to every member who wears it that we have strong leadership not afraid to enforce the laws. Law number one is no hard drugs." He glared at a man near the door who had openly laughed. "Pervert Dan? You got something to say, motherfucker? Spit it out."

"Yeah, Mason. How the fuck do you think we're going to make money if we can't sell shit?" Leaning back against the wall, his hands tucked into the small of his back, the man seemed relaxed as he asked his question.

"Did you fucking listen to me? No. I said one thing and you caught sight of another, so let me be perfectly fucking clear. No brown. No. Hard. Drugs. We drop all trade in heroin. That's it; it's the only change there." Glaring again, he asked, "Any more fucking questions?"

Dan shook his head and Mason continued, "Law number two is no working girls. Flesh trade stops as of right fucking now." Looking around the room, he saw no argument on any faces. "We take the few girls left and sort their shit out to a good daddy, someone who'll take care of them. Or, we set them up with a little dough and pat them on the ass as they walk away. Their choice to stay in the business or go, but our choice to stop the trade." There was no discussion, so he dipped his head and moved on.

"Law number three is no heavy weapons. We got enough shit with the gangs and all the iron they bring to the streets. We do not need to add to the imbalance by selling fully-A shit to babies. There's shit going on in the world that don't feel right, brothers, and I won't be a party to making this country a less safe place to fucking live. I don't care what kind of green they throw at us. Our fucking country, our fucking charter...our fucking club." He looked around the room again, his gaze moving from man to man, seeing no disagreement or disputes. "And that's it, those three laws are plenty, and they're what we'll use to guide the club going forward. Easy enough to remember, and the patch will back it up."

From an inside pocket of his vest, he pulled a piece of paper, smoothing it on the wood of the bar. "A skull, to remind us of the cost from today, when we had to put brothers to ground. When a man who stood with us went home in a fucking box. The skeleton key shows our fucking backbone, brothers. And, the three prongs are the three laws. This is our warded lock, the sacred trust from the officers," he gestured to the men around the room, "to you. We are the Rebel Wayfarers."

He repeated the phrase, growing in volume with every repetition, the men around the room, his brothers, joining in. "We are the Rebel Wayfarers. We are *Rebel Wayfarers*."

***

He stood still, looking around the shop at the illustrations and drawings on the walls and ceiling, cartoons and line drawings fighting for space alongside intricate artwork in stark, black lines. There was a scuffling noise behind him, and he turned to find a woman walking towards him. Greeting her with a smile, he said, "Dagger, hon. Good to see you again."

"Mason." She held out her hand and he gripped it, palm-to-palm, then used it to pull her into him, folding his arms around her for a moment. With a grin, Dagger stepped back, tucking her thumbs into her front pockets. "I have the drawing finished. Ready to look it over?" Nodding, Mason followed her back to a small room off a narrow hallway. "Were you planning on left or right? I drew it so we can go either way; it's easy to flip if needed," Dagger called over her shoulder and Mason responded.

"Left, I think. There's nothing already there for you to work around, and it's closer to my heart, so the symbolism isn't lost on me. Did you like the idea I described?" He was a little nervous, never having done anything this meaningful before. He had some big ink, as well as several small pieces. There was one swirling tribal covering a shoulder and part of his chest, and then continued down his side and ran low across his hip. Only one of his current tattoos had meant anything to him. Deacon didn't like him having naked skin; he thought ink was more intimidating, so had mandated many of Mason's tattoos.

"Yeah. Fuck, yeah. It's fucking amazing, man. Wait until you see it. I'm super excited about this one." She pulled a rolled-up piece of paper from a cubby in the bookshelf lining one wall of the room and motioned for Mason to sit in the chair taking up most of the space. Untying the satin ribbon holding it closed, she held the edges of the paper so Mason could make out what was on the surface of the page.

Sketched in broad, aggressive strokes was a phoenix, the design intended to go from the back of the hand, up the arm, and over the curve of the shoulder. Flickering fire, feathers in motion, the strength of the wing captured in mid-downstroke, even the fierce look on the bird's face...everything about the artwork looked perfect to him. He loved the colors used in the sketch—everything drawn in blacks and grays, reds and yellows—making the proposed tattoo look scorching and formidable. "Did you get the saying worked in?"

He followed the tip of Dagger's finger where it pointed to the drawing, and saw the quote. Worked seamlessly into the rising feathers of the phoenix's wing, he read, *I choose to become*. "Nice. It looks incredible. I don't want to change anything. Fucking perfect, Dagger. When can we start?"

"Now, motherfucker. I blocked off the rest of the day for you. This kind of detailed full-sleeve is gonna take a few sessions, but we can get a lot of the outlining done today." She cocked her head, looking at Mason. "What does the phrase mean, man? The phoenix I get, because your club is rising from the ashes of the past. The metaphor is clear, but Carl Jung? Shit's pretty deep."

Mason nodded, looking at the drawing again. "There's a quote from Jung that goes, 'I am not what happened to me...I am what I choose to become.' It seemed appropriate to the situation. You know, it's not only me, but also the entire club moving forward. We're not the sum of what happened to us in our past; we're moving ahead, forging our own fucking path. God help the fool who gets in our way."

As she prepared her tools, he shrugged out of his leather cut, folding it over the small chair in the room. He patted the patch on the back, still crisp and clean with newness, the skull in front of mustache handlebars sporting a paisley patterned bandanna and a fierce scowl on its bony face. It held an ornate skeleton key gripped tightly between its jaws, three teeth on the bar of the key. Reaching behind his head, he grasped the collar of his long-sleeved Henley and pulled it over his head.

Dagger looked at him and reached out a finger, touching a small, detailed tattoo on his collarbone, smoothing over the colors embedded within his skin. "Dude, I like that one. What does it stand for?"

Mason looked down at his shoulder, remembering the kick of the shot hitting him, the struggle to decide who he could count on. He thought about the flash of despair felt when he realized he didn't trust his own president, his own club. The stylized bear claw covering the scar from the bullet hole had been Bones' idea. He had sketched out the design quickly, and then accompanied Mason to the tat shop to direct the laying on of ink to his satisfaction, talking the whole time of the bear representing truth and luck, being the symbol of a warrior. Mason smiled, looking up at the tattoo artist, deciding to hold this story close to his chest, because it was too big to explain. "Not much. Bears are tough motherfuckers. I decided I needed to be tougher."

8. Building a family

2002

"You sure about this, Prez?" Red, one of their newest members, asked the question.

Mason nodded. "Yeah, abso-fucking-lutely sure, brother. It's the right thing to do."

He heard sounds of assent around the table in the office of the clubhouse, where they were in the middle of an officers-only church meeting. Looking over, he nodded at the thin young man seated near him. "Myron says the bar could turn a profit now that we've got shit under control. I vote we let those profits go to Merry for two years. As long as the bar can make enough money to support itself, anything over expenses goes to her."

Myron nodded, clearing his throat. He seemed nervous, and Mason knew it was because of the present audience, since one-on-one, the man was talkative and funny. *He's going to have to get over it at some point*, he thought with a silent snort. *I got plans for the man.* "Myron, go over the numbers, would ya?"

He tuned out as the ideas were laid out; he didn't have to pay attention, because he had listened to it a dozen times already and had full confidence it would succeed. He had worked on the plans hard enough, and long enough, getting expert advice as needed.

When he first decided to go to college and began taking courses, he sought out a couple of the professors who were willing to mentor the lone adult in their classrooms. Earlier this week, he ran the idea past his economics guy a final time.

After looking through the documentation and information, as well as checking some figures on the projections, Professor Grinnell sat back in his leather chair and looked at Mason over steepled fingers.

"Mason, it looks like you have planned for everything. If I didn't know better," he said, "I would never believe you didn't already have your MBA. This is a sound plan, and I'd invest in it if you were entertaining offers. The only change I will recommend is for you to go ahead and incorporate now, because, knowing you as I do, I don't believe you'll be happy with merely the one business."

Mason pulled his focus back to the present, looking around the room and seeing the mostly bewildered nods from the men. Half the brothers who had come through the changeover had left in the first year. He expected most of the rest of them would leave in the next few months, as it became apparent he wouldn't budge on the three laws. His eyes drifted from man to man, and he lifted his chin in pride, because the holes left by long-time Fiends members had all been filled with *Rebels*. Good men, good members. Good fucking club.

I'm just a-going over home

Much later that night, he sat in his accustomed spot behind the bar, ass on the back of the stool and boots on the seat. He was looking out over the quiet crowd of citizens mixed with bikers from various clubs. Everybody was minding their own shit tonight, and he was relaxed, felt like things were falling into place. Today, the club's officers had voted, and over the next few months, reparations would be made, debts settled. The biggest one—the one with really no way of making things right—the one they held with Merry being the first. She stood beside him, leaning her shoulders against the wall. He had explained the plan to her, and was now waiting for her response.

"Did you know I cleaned up while you rode to Mississippi?" The question seemed to come out of left field, and he looked over at her, startled into shaking his head. He knew the mess and disaster inside the bar had been all sorted out by the time they got back. While he remembered being surprised, because it hadn't been something he ordered, he had taken it as a gift and put the thought away.

"Yeah. It was a…it was so bad. The boys had cleaned out…well, you know. But, there was blood everywhere. I spent three days washing, cleaning, and then cleaning again. Scrubbing. Bleaching. Trying to set things to rights. I knew you had your hands full, first with Deacon, and then getting Jackson home." She sighed. "I didn't think it would ever all be done with. Didn't think *I* would ever get done cleaning. It seemed an insurmountable task." She looked at Mason and then turned her gaze back to the room.

"Then, I got the ball rolling, breaking it down into bite-sized chunks. I took it one table at a time, one three-foot section of wall at a time. As long as I could make the job into something I could understand step-by-step, I could do it. I had confidence I'd come to the end eventually. And I did." She swallowed noisily, forcing down her reaction as her voice softened, filling with regret when she said, "I hated you for a long time after what happened with Tilly." He made as if to speak, and she quieted him with a look. "Hush. Just listen. Hated you for his stupidity and Shooter's actions. Simply because you were there…because you were present, even though I could tell from the beating you wore on your face that you had fought against it, fought for us. I hated you, because I couldn't hate Tilly. Mason," she turned to face him, "I need you to know I don't hate you anymore.

"I don't hate you, or the club you're building. I can see the differences you're putting into place, and I can see the differences in you. You've managed to take a project so massive it could crush you, and you've made it work, piece-by-piece. In the process," she tilted her head, looking up at him, "I think you're remaking yourself, too. A better Mason than we had before. I can't hate this Mason." A smile slipped on and off her face as she said, "It's been a lot of years, sweetheart. I hope you don't hate this Mason, either."

He stared at her, not speaking, holding her gaze until she nodded, accepting what he could offer her for now.

They sat for a while longer, silence setting easy between them. Finally, Merry stirred herself, offering him a small smile. He stretched out his hand and she took it, clasping it between both of hers. "Tomorrow is the anniversary," she said quietly, and he nodded. "I'll need a ride, son."

"Anytime, Merry. Whatever you need. Anything you need." His response was immediate, and she smiled again. "I'll pick you up in the morning, and we'll head out to pay our respects."

"Tilly was a good man," she said softly, and he nodded. "You are too, Davy. Don't lose sight of it. You matter, son." He dropped his gaze to the floor, not having a response.

She took a breath. "Go ahead and rename the bar, hon. It's an extremely sweet idea, because, as I remember him, Jackson was a decent man, and using it to honor him is a good thing. It will provide a feeling of continuity to the club, show them all his loss is remembered and balanced as cost against the triumph you're building now. We loved the bar, not the name. The name Monaco was something that came with it when Tilly and I bought the place. I'll officially sign it over to you...hell, it's been yours for years now anyway. But don't pay me the profits." He quirked an eyebrow up at her, asking a wordless question. "You said Myron is a genius, right?" He nodded. "Tell him to invest it for me."

9. Slate

2004

Standing at the end of the bar, he scanned the room and immediately saw the new customer sitting on a stool, looking wide-eyed around the place. Mason scoffed under his breath. The kid had probably accepted a dare to come into the biker's bar, and now didn't quite know what to do. He walked over, leaning on the bar directly opposite the kid, and pinned him with a stare. "You in the right place, man?"

Outwardly, he was impassive, but he flinched mentally in surprise when the kid mentioned Watcher's name right off the bat. Seems his old hometown friend had sent him a package; now he would simply have to figure out what the deal was. He knew Watcher's brother had been killed on a run to Cali a couple years ago, and Watch had taken over the Southern Soldiers club as president. He and Mason kept in touch regularly; they enjoyed hearing about each other's life in and outside of the club. Stories about Watch's wife and daughter gave him hope that one day he would find the same. Love and loyalty wrapped up in a woman he would want to spend his life with, not merely a nameless, faceless, voiceless fuck to ease the tension of the day.

Right now, his first order of business was to respond to the kid's question, and he laughed, pulling a mug and filling it with draft beer while they chatted. Taking his money, Mason rang up the sale then turned back towards the bar, seeing the watchful angel tattooed on his shoulder for the first time. It was different from others he had seen. This one held a gun and a sword, looking down at the words 'My Brother's Keeper.' *Interesting ink for someone not in the life,* Mason mused, thinking if Watcher had sent him, then maybe the kid had a taste, after all.

Glancing around, he saw trouble in the making, with a bunch of Dominos members seated near a tableful of Disciples. Those two clubs had a long history of rubbing each other the wrong way, and he knew he would have to keep his eyes on them to avoid issues today. *This shit's a full-time job*, he thought, rolling his shoulders tiredly.

Walking down the bar, he had a quiet word with two Rebel members, seasoned brothers he trusted. Tug had come to him by way of Morgan soon after the reformation of the club, and had fit in as if there were a Tug-sized hole waiting for him. Bingo was a greybeard Mason had known for a while, and the man was solid. Had a shit sister in Fort Wayne, but the man himself was reliable. At his signal, they rose and walked towards the kid, and Mason gave the two members seated on either side of him a chin lift, silently directing them to sit elsewhere.

He gave the kid a few minutes to settle in with his new drinking companions, the Rebels bracketing him like bookends, then turned and walked to the end of the bar. Bingo and Tug restarted a conversation begun a couple days ago in church, jumping back into the middle of the argument, and Mason was amused to watch the kid try to politely ignore them. Then, when that didn't work, he turned his head side-to-side, looking at them in turn as they spoke.

Bingo drew Mason into the conversation, and shit got a little heated, but then everything settled out as he expected it would. In the end, he gave Bingo permission to head down to Fort Wayne and start a Rebel chapter, if he was so inclined. This was club business of a kind that generally went on behind closed doors, but he was exploring a feeling he had about this kid and wanted to figure out how he would react.

He took things in stride pretty well, and Mason was surprised at his own pleasure in the interaction. Introducing himself and the two Rebels who had been torturing the boy, they received his name in return, Andrew Jones. *Time to get down to brass tacks*, he thought, asking, "What did Watcher send you here for, kid?" He had a sudden thought. "You aren't wearing any colors, so you better not be affiliated. Jackson's is neutral, but we don't fucking tolerate anon shit."

Andy paled and shook his head, and Mason nodded, listening as he spoke eloquently about being on the road for a while, looking for a place to land, but not finding it yet. Everything he said made sense, and he resolved to call Watcher at the first opportunity to find out what he had to say about the kid, what the story was.

Busy mixing drinks, he partially tuned out the next part of the conversation until Bingo stood abruptly, gripping Andy by the arm and yelling excitedly. This in turn caused the kid to jerk to his feet, turning the barstool over. The entire place went silent as everyone tried to determine what the problem was. Mason stilled for a moment, watching the altercation. *Fucking shit*. He hadn't pegged the kid for a fighter, but his response was interesting. Andy had settled into an alert defensive stance, loose and ready to react, and certainly looked like he could take care of himself.

Mason reached out and smacked the side of Bingo's head. "You don't go grabbing strangers, Bingo. What a fucking moron. Sit back down, kid, or take him outside so he can stroke off to the Indian. It's a secret fantasy of his." *All this shit over a fucking bike*, he thought, shaking his head.

Some of the tension left Andy's body as Bingo rushed to apologize, and at his words, the kid eased off. Seeming unsure of himself for the first time since walking in the door, but obviously not wanting to offend, he reluctantly invited Bingo out to look at his bike. Mason looked across at Merry, and then over at Red, signaling he was going outside, even as he noticed the kid using the mirrors around the room to track everyone's movements behind him. *Observant fucker*, he thought with a snort.

When they rounded the edge of the building, Mason stopped in surprise. *No fucking way*, he thought, tuning Bingo out as he looked at the '47 red and white Indian Chief the kid was riding. There was no way this was the same bike he sold a few years ago out west, but as he looked closely, he thought he even saw familiar dings from stones on the front of the tank. *No fucking way.*

Pulling his attention away from the bike when the kid asked about their rides, Mason was proud to point them out to him. Things had changed a lot in the years since he had taken over the club, and his brothers all had rides that were better than decent, and most of them were newer models. Recently, he had acted on an idea of buying a bike garage for the club, which would allow everyone to work on their bikes where all the tools needed were available. No more blocks in a driveway and making do with what was on hand.

He heard shouting and groaned; something was going on out in front of the bar. *Something was always going on*, he thought. *No fucking rest for the wicked.* Taking long strides, he turned the corner as the door of the bar opened again, spilling fighting men onto the sidewalk and street. Turning, he saw Andy had followed him and appeared to be evaluating the action. Interestingly, it looked like he quickly picked out the real trouble from the opportunistic shitheads looking to bust skulls for fun.

Mason watched as the kid edged around the group, apparently putting himself into position to help if needed. Yelling and shouting, striding through the men, Mason stopped most of the shit, but left the two major ones alone, and turning to Andy, he said, "Come break these fuckers up, man."

Without hesitation, Andy stepped forward during a momentary lull in their movements and grabbed the two men by the back of their heads. He smashed their foreheads together before pushing them away from each other, then asked quietly, "How's that, boss?"

Shocked at the efficiency of the move, as well as the composure the kid had shown after getting shoved into a situation as potentially dangerous as this had been, Mason laughed hard for a minute, and then watched as Andy placed the wall strategically at his back. It looked as if he had only now recognized the danger he put himself in by stepping into the fight, even if it were on request.

This reaction reminded him briefly of his own uncertainty at that first fight, his initiation into the Fiends, when his only security was knowledge he had Winger at his back. Shaking off the memory, Mason called over to him, raising his voice so he shouted over the murmuring men, "No motherfucker here will put a hand on you for this." Twisting, he swung his gaze to the now-silent men assembled in a rude ring. "You fuckers hear me?"

He assumed after the altercation and his statement that Andy would stick close, but Mason had already turned to walk into the bar by the time he realized the kid wasn't following. Looking over, he saw Andy was walking quickly away, already nearly to the corner of the sidewalk where it turned into the lot. *What the hell?*

"Where the fuck are you going?" he called, receiving a casual flip of a hand in response.

"Headed out, thanks," the kid said, turning the corner and moving out of sight. Mason sighed and followed. He had an idea for how this kid could help out around Jackson's, and the barest glimmer of a thought about the club. But first, he had to get him to fucking agree to hang around. Rounding the corner directly behind Andy, he found him staring at Bingo, who was still standing in place, eyes fixed on the classic bike.

Mason laughed and called out, referring to the man's temperamental bike when he asked, "Bingo, what the fuck are you doing, brother? Your girl is going to see you cheating on her, and she'll take her revenge...you know she will." He laughed again.

Bingo looked over at Andy with a longing expression on his face. "She's beautiful, man. I'd give a fuckuva lot for one just like her; cherry red, virgin white, fringe on the seat, chrome so bright—that poetry nearly fucking writes itself."

Mason slung an arm around Andy's shoulders, feeling him tense under the firm hold. He was thin, but wiry and muscled. He would be quick and sharp, and Mason had already seen him in action. As he turned them to walk back to the door, in a wheedling tone, Mason said, "Come back inside and have a beer; I'd like to offer you a job. Bingo will be out here for another hour, but he won't fuck with your ride. He'll simply lust from a distance."

Andy came along willingly enough, and Mason parked him on a stool behind the bar. Shit like today's fight had been happening too frequently for his peace of mind, and he knew the place needed an enforcer fulltime. The problem was he didn't want to use a Rebel, because there could be all kinds of blowback if it appeared the member was misusing his colors in any way. If Watcher vouched for the kid, he might be a perfect fit as an unaffiliated bouncer. *Unaffiliated for a time, anyway*, he thought with a snort, surprised at his own admission of how right this kid felt.

Stepping into the backroom, he pulled his phone from the pocket of his jeans and made a call. "Watcher," he said warmly at the answering response on the other end of the line. "You sent me a present, didn't you?"

"How do you like Andy, man? He's something else, isn't he?" Watcher explained, "He hung around my Soldiers for a few months. We weren't a good fit for him, but he's fucking solid, Mason. Took him on a run into Old Mexico with us when a fucking shipment went missing. He stood in the doorway of the house we were doing business in and faced down a dozen Machos on his own.

"Pops called him a fucking Ice Man. Motherfucker took a bullet in the leg for my club, and then before the lead had even stopped flying, he was taking care of brothers who were wounded. Tied his shit off with a rag and jumped in to help my men.

"Man has a sense of right about him. It's hard to explain. Like...kids and dogs trust him. Hell, Mason...I trust him. I told him to hunt you down, because I know you need good brothers, man. This one has a feel about him; I truly think he's going to fit in there. He's green in the life, had a hard fucking start with me, but I don't think it's turned him off.

"He's been wandering for a couple years, slipped through East Texas and Memphis on his way to you. He simply has to find his home. He takes care of his baby brother and his grandparents up in Wyoming. I got the sense his pa was dead, but couldn't really find out anything about his ma." He laughed, and the ease of the humor flowed up the line, making Mason smile. "I like the man. He could do worse than hang around with you."

"Thanks for that, motherfucker." Mason laughed again. "Wyoming, huh?" *What were the chances*? "Anything else I need to know about the kid?"

"He isn't a kid, Mason," Watcher spoke earnestly. "No kid could have faced down my crew the first day we walked into the bar where he worked. He fucking took Spider down, Mason, and you know how crazy that man is. Andy can handle himself in all kinds of fights, too. The man should have calm and composed tattooed on him somewhere."

"Alrighty, he's not a kid," Mason agreed readily. "Thanks for sending him my way." He was about to hang up, when he heard Watcher say something else that surprised him into a grunting response. "Huh?"

"I said he already met Bones. Bones gave him a verbal marker, man." The tone of Watcher's voice expressed volumes. A marker meant Andy could call on Bones for nearly anything and receive help. Both Watcher and Mason knew the president of the Skeptics didn't take to many people. If he liked the kid—Andy—well enough to give him a verbal marker, it meant a lot. Just as it had meant a lot for Watcher to tell Andy to use his name as an introduction.

Mason shook his head. "Well, hell. Appears I gotta keep my eye on him now, Watch. He cracked the skulls of the Dominos' Veep and the Disciples' Sargent at Arms not an hour ago. They won't stop fighting about fucking territory, stupid shitheads. Seems he's gained the attention of four out of five major Chicago clubs in a single day. The man might not thank you for sending him here once he understands how this could go sideways for him." Mason laughed. "Bones? Really?"

"Yeah, I know. But, Andy's a good man. Watch his back. Peace, brother," Watcher told him, and Mason responded, "Shiny side up, man."

Disconnecting the call, he picked up a case of beer, carrying it out to the bar and looking towards Andy. He was still sitting on the stool behind the bar, but he was visually tracking trouble over by the pool tables. Glancing at Mason for permission, he waited for the nod and then stood, strolling over to the men who were arguing. Within a minute, he had shit sorted and was back on the stool, drawing a snort from Merry as she walked past. "Keeper, Mason," was her only comment.

***

"You are lucky he came to you first," Bones said, tipping his beer up to take a slow, deep drink.

"Not sure luck had anything to do with it," Mason said, rolling his bottle between his palms, wetting his hands with the condensation gathered on the surface. It had been a roller coaster day, starting with officially patching Andy in as a prospect after months of testing and recruiting him, followed by a bloodbath at the strip joint the club owned. Mason had also found out Monster, a holdover from the Fiends who had made officer a couple years ago, had instigated some near-traitorous troubles. He spread rumors that caused the death of another prospect today in the midst of that bloodbath. Not what he would have wanted for Andy's initiation into the club, but the man had stood firm with his brothers today, regardless of the odds against them.

"I saw the man that day, as I did today, bold and courageous. Also undoubtedly curious, nearly dangerously so. He would have done well as a Skeptic, Mason...as you would have." Bones tipped his head back, looking over at him with a grin.

"Why'd you give him a marker, man? You didn't even know his fucking name—"

Interrupting him, Bones said, "And now he has a different one. Offered by his president, which means a great deal. I should know. *Slate*, I like it. As I said, I saw something in the man. His is a will that can change the direction of fate, I believe. When I look at how he was today, standing firm...calm and cool in the middle of a fierce firefight. Hell, Mason, I am not sure he even broke a sweat until you walked in and he feared your wrath...feared your disappointment in his actions. I must say, he reminds me much of you." Leaning forward, he laid his palms on the tabletop, staring across the room to where Slate stood, back against the wall as he watched the crowd in Jackson's. "He is following an agenda, even if he does not yet recognize it." Sitting back, he stretched his legs underneath the table, nodding slowly. He pulled a laugh from Mason when he finished with, "Much like you."

10. Wreckage

2009

"No, you shut the fuck up and stop arguing, Myron. Just buy the fucking thing." He punched angrily at the disconnect button on the phone, even as his shouts still echoed in the room. "*Fuck!*" he yelled, giving in to frustration and throwing the phone across the room, barking out a laugh when a hard hand caught it before it shattered against the wall. "Thanks, Tug, you saved me a few hundred dollars."

"What are you buying now, Prez?" He tossed the phone onto the paper-covered desktop in front of Mason, eying the chaos where there normally was strict order.

"Baugh's bike shop in Norfolk, if I can swing it." He scrubbed his hands across his jaw, feeling the bristle of his growing beard. Every time he quit smoking, he grew out his beard. He snorted, wondering how long it would last this time. "Did you look at the last load of bikes we got from Bear and the Baugh brothers? Bear's a motherfucking genius. I know Robinson can wrench with the best of them, but even he admitted he'd have never thought about some of the modifications. With the waxers and weekend warriors wanting bikes, we have to find a way to keep our line speedy. I'm not going to have money going to other shops when it could be hitting our cash registers and benefiting our brothers."

Bear was Rob Crew, a retired Navy man working in a custom bike shop owned by his friends Donny and Dennis Baugh. Mason had found out about the garage when Red bought one of their bikes, and he hadn't wasted any time partnering with them. The other man they were talking about was Lane Robinson, a Fort Wayne member.

"Why are they selling?" Tug asked. He had been one of the men who went out to test the waters, and quickly reported back he liked the quiet bike mechanic. Slate had traveled out with him, too, and in the intervening months, he and Bear had become good friends, making more than one road trip together.

"Donny's closing the shop. After Dennis' carjacking and shooting, he doesn't want to keep the place open. Says he needs to focus on getting his brother well. I'm going to try and buy it instead, keep Bear on to run the place." He ran a hand across his jaw again, wishing the hundredth time that day for a smoke.

"Why not let Donny close it and move Bear up here to work in our shops?" Tug sat casually in the chair across the desk from Mason, one ankle crossed over his knee. "He got along with everyone well enough. Hell, he's already got a club name; I'd say he's past the hangaround status. Double hell, Mason, I've heard you say more than once that one of your few regrets was ignoring my good advice about hiring the man years ago. You gonna blow me off again?"

Mason slowly shook his head. "You know what, old man? That actually makes a lot of sense."

Tug laughed. "Gee, thanks, brother. You make it sound like I don't usually have good ideas."

He picked up the phone and made a call, talking to Baugh about Bear's situation, and Donny agreed to have a chat with him, extending an offer on Mason's behalf.

"Told you I have good ideas," Tug said once he had hung up the phone.

"Fuck you, Tugboat," he responded smoothly, without rancor. Grinning, he said, "You have the best worst ideas of anyone I know." Texting the change in plans to Myron, he didn't wait for the sarcastic response he was certain would come before tossing the phone down.

"Fuck you, too," Tug said with a laugh. "You headed down to Springfield this weekend with Duck and the boys? It's graduation day, finally."

Mason shook his head. Ever since Reuben Nelms, Duck, patched in, he had talked several members into helping him keep track of a woman. Attached to, or interested in, Mason hadn't bothered to figure it out, only caring as it affected the club. Attending the U of I college there in Springfield, she was finally done with school and he was glad, because this meant his members would be able to stay the fuck in town and closer to home.

Even though Duck had frequently asked him to go, Mason had always managed to be busy whenever this kind of event came along. "Nah, I got shit to do, man." He sighed. "Think Duck will ever get over whatever it is drawing him to this woman?"

"No idea, man. I haven't set eyes on her yet. He said she's moving to Chicago, though; I suspect with easy access it's unlikely his obsession will fade." He shifted in his chair, setting one ankle atop a knee, his movements telegraphing how uncomfortable he was with the next question. "How are things with Bingo?"

"Shit. Things are shit. Thanks for fucking bringing it up, bastard. I know I'm gonna have to make a change there, but I can't find my way clear yet. Maybe he'll slide back okay. I got no fucking idea right now." He loved the greybeard and respected him immensely, but the man's nieces and nephews were eating up his life, making the club take second seat in a way that didn't sit right. Chapter presidents needed to be able to dedicate themselves to their club and brothers, and Bingo couldn't do it right now. Mason scrubbed along his jaw again, and Tug laughed.

"You quitting again?"

"Fuck you," he said, his voice carrying a little heat this time, because this was a topic that stung, too. He seldom failed at anything, but he had returned to this spot again and again, trying to quit. Swiveling his chair to prop his feet on the corner of the desk, his hand rested on the lump in his front pocket and his fingertips unconsciously traced the outline of the glass. "Every time I think I've got the things licked, some kind of shit happens to suck me back in." He cut a look towards his friend, lips curled as he said, "Shooter called."

"What the fuck does the little bastard want?" Tug was the only one in the Rebel club who knew the full story of what Shooter had done to Mason. He had known Morgan for decades, had known their mother, and been around to watch Shooter grow up. Tug had seen the evidence with his own eyes, but even with that, initially he found it hard to reconcile the boy he knew with the stories he had been told. Over time, he trusted Mason enough to know they had to be true, and he now harbored a disappointment in Shooter.

"He's coming to Fort Wayne to visit Judge." Mason scowled down at the desk. Judge was Shooter's son, a nephew Mason had never met. Morgan had never wanted Shooter's kids to know about their connection with Mason, and he honored the request through the years, even after Morgan was gone. He found it amusing Shooter's boy was called Judge in the club, given his grandfather's name had been Justice. He scoffed softly, thinking, *Family.*

I'm just a poor wayfaring stranger

His thoughts turned to Kentucky, and then to Nashville, and he thought about the last time he had seen Bethany. Shaking himself out of the memories, bringing his attention back to the conversation, he looked up at Tug. "If he does, I'll want you to go down and meet with him."

The phone lying on the desk rang and he looked down, expecting to see Myron's info. He frowned, because instead, it was Bingo, and he picked up the phone and answered, "Yeah?"

As he listened to the man on the other end of the phone, he slowly dropped his feet to the floor, sitting up in the chair. It was as if he couldn't drag in enough air to keep going, as if he had been gut-punched by Ripper. He shook his head, trying to focus on what Bingo was saying, "...the hospital with her now."

"Say again, Bingo? Hold on. Let me put you on speaker. I got Tug here." He laid the phone on the desk, looking up at Tug with what felt like desolation settling into his chest. "Say again, brother."

His voice was raw, filled with heart-wrenching pain, and the sound of it hit both of the men in the room, tightening their muscles against an unexpected blow. "Both Winger and Lockee, man. The ER doc said they were DOA, didn't survive extraction from the truck. A bunch of us are here at the hospital with DeeDee, Mason. She's tore up, man. Hoss has her right now, helping her keep it together, but we need you down here." Bingo sucked in a deep, shuddering breath and he knew the man was hurting just as bad as he was. Bingo and Winger had been friends for as long as Mason had known the men.

It was impossible to focus on the words. It was like his brain was stuttering, his thoughts skipping from memories of watching his sixteen-year-old cousin climb on the much older man's bike and leave the holler forever, to remembering the warm feeling of security standing in the middle of a parking garage fight ring, because he knew Winger stood behind him. Dead? How could Winger be dead? Beyond being brothers in the club, he had always felt the man was truly family in a way that transcended the in-law thing.

"Is the gal with her? The redheaded one Lockee is...was good friends with?" Mason asked, dropping his head into his hands.

"Yeah, Melanie is with us. She lives with them now...with DeeDee, so we called her as soon as we got word. I had a brother pick her up and bring her to the hospital. Dee had already left the house when we got there, so she rode over here on her own, brother. I've never seen her like this. Doc gave her some pills." There was a noise away from the phone and they overheard Bingo tell someone to hold on. "We're pulling out in five, Mason. See you when you get here, brother."

"Yeah, catch you in a few hours, man." Mason closed his eyes, letting the soothing darkness wrap around him, thankful Tug was silent, isolated by his own world of pain.

***

"You listening, Prez?" Mason lifted his head, raising his gaze from the toes of his boots to Slate's face. His friend. His brother. He hummed a question, shaking his head, because he had been a thousand miles away, lost in memories of Winger. "I talked to Bear. I'll head down to Virginia in a couple weeks and bring him back to Chicago with me. Mason, he seems a good fit, man. We gonna patch him in if he's interested?"

"Yeah. Convince him, brother. Sometimes we have to recruit the worthy ones. I walked into Baugh's garage the first time, and the rightness of the man hit me square in the face. I saw the tribute he made for his wife and daughter, and I knew. I totally knew he needs what we have. I'm with you. I think he's a good fit. Bring him home. Let's help the man heal." He rolled his shoulders and stretched his neck, watching Slate wince a little at the cracking noises his neck made. "You don't smoke, do you?"

"Boss, you know I don't. You need a cig? I'm sure there's a dozen—"

"No, I'm tryin' to quit again," he interrupted as he scrubbed at his chin with his fingers. "Thought it would be obvious." He snorted a laugh. "You ever been addicted to anything, man?"

Slate was silent a minute then shook his head. "Not me. My mom, though. Well, you know all about her story, how fucked up she still is. Where the hell you going with these questions, Mason?"

"No fucking idea. I can't wrap my head around Winger and Lockee being gone. I want a smoke so bad I can fucking taste it, bitter and delicious on my tongue." He sighed and then looked at Slate again. "We had an impressive number of members show for the funeral. Was good to see, man. I won't lie; I was surprised to pick out so many different clubs represented in the escort. This was a hell of a sendoff for a good man."

He sighed again. "The Fort members voted; they want to move DeeDee and Melanie into the clubhouse. I'm not sure at all how I feel about it, but it's their house. If it helps them heal to hold Winger's family close, then who the fuck am I to tell them no?"

Slate nodded, making a noncommittal noise. He was a mother chapter member, but Mason used him as a fixer where things had gotten bumpy. It helped, because he wasn't personally invested in any of them, but he was often deeply involved in many of the chapters they had chartered.

"You know Robinson well?" Mason asked about one of the Fort Wayne members, and Slate shook his head. Not surprised, Mason snorted and continued, "Bingo and Deke think he's solid for officer here. Bingo wants to promote him today." He shifted, crossing ankle over knee. "There's shit here in the Fort. I can't even get a handle on some of the members, man. He's one of them. I absolutely do not fucking know him. Not the first thing."

"DeeDee likes him," Slate said with a shrug. "She's a pretty good judge of character."

"Truth," Mason said shortly. "I talked to Winger last week about him. Told me he trusted him with his girls. That says...said a lot, too."

They sat in silence for a few minutes, and then Mason stirred himself, unfolding and standing. He looked down at Slate, a frown on his face. "When you headed down to Norfolk?"

"Couple weeks, why?" Slate cocked his head, his forehead wrinkling.

"No reason." He stood there, trailing a fingertip across the edge of the table, back and forth. "You ever wonder why things work out the way they do, man?"

"Every single fucking day." Slate laughed, the sound brittle and humorless in the room, drawing the attention of several members near the bar.

"Me too," Mason said heavily. He paused, looking over at the nameless party dolls standing patiently near the pool table and gestured to one of them, waiting until she made her way to him and slipped her arm around his waist before he walked away. "Me too."

***

"You don't fucking speak," he whispered in her ear, pressing his chest against her back. "It gets to be more than you can take, you have your signal. Do you remember your signal, bitch?" She nodded, moving her hand to snap her fingers.

The woman he selected from the group downstairs would remain faceless and voiceless for him, exactly the way he needed her to be. This wasn't about connecting with someone; it was, as always, club politics. Those women had been offered up as entertainment, selected because they didn't have a connection to any members. They were only at the clubhouse to party and hook up with a member if they could...even at a fucking funeral.

While she would be able to crow and lord it over the other club whores that the national president had picked her, the next time he was in town, he would again look right through her. By the time he went to sleep, he wouldn't even remember her hair color, bottle blonde though she was. He couldn't snub the chapter, so he would fuck her, but Mason never planned to put tail on his bike. It was best he didn't let the woman get any ideas. Stomp the shit into the ground before it had a chance to set roots.

"Okay, I'm gonna fuck you now. Be silent, and when I want you to move, I'll fucking move you." She nodded again, and he pressed a hard hand between her shoulder blades, bending her at the waist.

"Hands beside your head," he said softly, watching as she moved, precisely as he had known she would. In a scolding tone of voice, he said, "Oh, honey, did I say you could move? I thought I told you I'd fucking move you." Eyes focused on what he could glimpse of her face, he smiled grimly as fear swept across her features. "You don't fucking speak," he repeated himself and waited for her nod.

Drawing back, he let his open hand fall on her ass three times, two on the left and one on the right. Rubbing the palm-shaped red marks until she winced, he reached up and shifted her hands nearer her head then looked down at her. "Your pussy tight?" he asked, and she nodded. Chuckling darkly, he murmured, "We'll see." Using his knee and thigh to push her feet wider, he stepped up behind the woman, unbuckling his belt and laughing humorlessly at her cringing wince when she heard the leather sliding through the loops of his jeans.

"Not into that, honey," he said, dropping the coiled leather on the mattress near her face, his lip curling when she flinched backwards. Conversationally, he said, "I like my hands on you, no doubt about it, but mostly I'm not into hearing a bitch while I'm getting off. As long as you're fucking silent, we'll get along perfectly fine." She nodded again, and he laughed aloud when she quivered underneath him.

"Don't be scared, honey," he said, unbuttoning his jeans and shoving them wide while he pulled out his cock. This would be all the undressing he did tonight. Taking a rubber from where he had laid it on the bed, he rolled it down his length then slid two fingers inside her, gathering her slick juices and spreading it over the head of his sheathed dick.

"Shhhh," he said softly, thrusting his hips forward, sinking his cock halfway with one slide. "Not too tight, bitch,"—he muttered, humor in his tone—"but not too bad, either." Setting a fast pace, he thrust and plunged in and out of her pussy, rough hands on her hips pulling her back into him. "You into a little pain?" He asked the question already knowing the answer, and he laughed once again when she shook her head, eyes widening but lips still intelligently sealed. "Too fucking bad," he grunted, lifting his hand and slapping her ass, feeling her pussy clench around him. "There we go," he muttered, spanking her again.

11. Bridging the gap

2010

Mason leaned his hip against the back of a chair, looking out the window across the distinctive city skyline. He stood without moving, eyes tracking an airplane as it rapidly gained altitude, making a wide, sweeping turn out over the lake. Across the room, the man seated behind the desk cleared his throat nervously, and Mason felt a wave of pleasure. This was a noise made by someone who was afraid, and having this man frightened of him was an excellent thing. Tucking his hands into the front pockets of the suit pants, he lowered his gaze from the window and turned his shoulder slightly, angling the slightest amount towards the man, granting him an opening to speak.

"I don't know if I can give you what you've asked for, Mr. Mason."

He snorted silently, impressed. The man's voice had hardly quavered when he spoke.

"I know you can, Williamson." He turned, fully knowing the imposing figure he made silhouetted against the expanse of sunset-colored glass. "I want two things from you, and both are easily obtained. I want the police report on the attack on Mr. Ramos. The *real* report, not the canned information your department feeds the feds. And, I want the paternity test results. I will walk out of here today with both of those in my hands, because, Williamson, you do not want me to leave without them."

Bones, Salvador Ramos, had been caught in an ambush a month ago and hadn't been able to find anything to indicate who was behind it. Badly beaten, he was still recovering from the broken ribs he claimed had been gained by arguing entirely unsuccessfully with an aluminum baseball bat. Mason had a glimmer of an idea of who could be behind it, but wanted to see what the gang task force had to say before he would raise the curtain on that accusation.

The other matter was something he still couldn't completely believe. Watcher had called him nearly four weeks ago, told him to come home. Wanted to meet him down in Kentucky, said there was something he would need to see with his own eyes. Knowing the man wouldn't ask without reason, he rode down, hitting the road within thirty minutes of taking the call.

Already seated in the diner Watcher had specified, he looked up when the man walked in without a word of greeting. He sat across from Mason and stared at him for a moment, tongue pressing against the inside his cheek, and then shook his head and silently pointed across the street.

Scanning the area, Mason knew he was missing something, but he couldn't figure out what was so concerning. The only thing he could see was a kid squatting down next to a little 50cc dirt bike; it looked like he might be tweaking the chain. The kid's movements were relaxed and comfortable, but there were moments when he moved that telegraphed pain, and Mason knew the boy must have gotten a caning recently.

The kid stood, gracefully unfolding from his crouch. He flipped the hair back off his forehead in an astonishingly familiar movement and Mason's breath wedged tightly in his throat. Caught in these fleeting moments between childhood and the teen years, the boy was beautiful. He had a strong jaw, which looked too wide for his face now, but Mason knew too well the boy would grow into it eventually.

Hair as dark as a raven's wing, it was barely long enough to brush the top of his shoulders, which were wide for such a young boy. Mason knew without a doubt, if he could see them, those eyes hiding behind the drift of hair across the young face would be grey as steel. Without shifting his gaze, he reached across, gripping Watcher's wrist tightly, grinding the bones together and drawing a pained sound from his friend. His tone was low and dangerous as he asked, "Watch? You wanna explain to me what the fuck is going on?"

"Two words, brother." Watcher took a deep breath, twisting his arm out of Mason's grasp. "Carrie Sosa."

Pulling himself back to the present, Mason smirked a little when he saw the sweat covering the commissioner's upper lip. Seems his long pause might have had a beneficial effect. "Do we have an understanding?" He stepped towards the desk, reaching out to drag the plush armchair back a few feet before sitting down. "I'll just wait here, shall I?"

He hadn't always been this comfortable dealing with the kind of people who gravitated towards official positions in normal societal authority, but over the years, out of necessity, he had developed a shit-meter that gave him insight into which of these men could be pushed and which could not. He was unable to ultimately influence only a meager few, and his success was part of the reason the Rebels had thrived in Chicago in the ten years since being formed. He had been branching out for years, building small pockets of support in communities and cities across the Midwest, and there were official chapters in four cities, making good on his founding day boast that the Chicago chapter would be the first of many.

Thanks to brothers he had found and patched into the club, like Slate and Bear, they had been able to keep a handle on most of the shit that came with growing pains for a club. Robinson, renamed Gunny on the day they laid Winger to rest, had played an important part, too.

Mason suspected this hit against Bones and the Skeptics was from a Michigan club he had been considering absorbing. They were probably trying to set their spike in the rail and make any move on his part more difficult. If he could place the act at the feet of the Devil's Sins, he knew he would feel somewhat responsible for the injury done to his friend. However, he would be far more pissed they would take such a cowardly, sideways swipe at him.

Resting an ankle across one knee, he propped his elbow on the arm of the chair, reaching into his jacket and pulling out a package of cigarettes. "You don't mind, do you?" At the man's quick headshake, he nodded, and then frowned, tilting his head marginally as he voiced a gentle reminder. "Shouldn't you be making a phone call about now?"

Watching Williamson begin to make the calls necessary to set the wheels in motion, Mason drew on the cig, letting the smoke drift slowly past his lips, watching it wreath the overhead lights in a haze. His mind turned back to a month ago when his world turned upside down for a different reason than finding out he had a son. The fucking teacher who had been his pain in the ass neighbor since he bought his house had finally sold hers and moved out. But, who she sold it to, dear God...he remembered trying to explain to Slate about the woman he had seen moving in. His words had stumbled over themselves in their hurry to leave his mouth, because he couldn't say enough to explain her and his instant attraction to her.

Mica Scott. Even when he didn't say her name aloud, the words in his mind had the ability to calm him, bringing his attention back to what was important. As he had often done in the past four weeks, he picked and plucked at the edges of his attraction to the woman, trying to find the pattern and texture of the emotional fabric. Abso-fucking-lutely unlike anything in his experience, his obsessive desire for her was overwhelming at times, causing him to do or say things he would have never believed he was capable of.

To protect her, because he had an irresistible need to keep her safe, he had named her Princess, giving her a title but no rags to wear, because she didn't know...could not know the significance of the phrase. There was something about her that drew him, and since his first sight of her, he had been circling doggedly. While she seemed fragile on the surface, he knew down in her bones she was tough, strong, and courageous—and she was so fucking beautiful she stole his breath. Her eyes were the exact shade of the sea glass he plucked from the sand on the California beach so many years ago. It felt as if he had been preparing for her the whole time, while in the same instant, he knew he could never be ready for her.

A movement drew his attention, and he saw Williamson had lifted his gaze and was looking over Mason's shoulder towards the door. He held his position with some effort, because it went against everything within him to keep his unprotected back towards the door, but he had to continue to deal from a position of strength in this room. A pretty woman strode past him, her hips giving a subtle shimmy, which told him she had seen him and liked what she saw. He watched her walk, and the slide of fabric over her muscled ass should have been mesmerizing, but all he could see were sea-green eyes and dark hair. Nothing compared to Mica.

Shifting his gaze back to the man, he ignored the woman, hearing a little huff of disappointment as she left the room. Holding out one hand, he waited, silently demanding the policeman give up the information. When Williamson half rose from his seat, leaning across to place the file in his hand, Mason accepted it, tapping long fingers against the folder, eyeing the man with distrust. "Everything I want is here?"

"Yes, Mas—" With a scowl, Mason shook his head, and the man flinched, backpedaling. "Yes, sir, Mr. Mason. Everything should be there."

He stood, tucking the folder under his arm. "I'll let you know if it's not." Turning, he strode from the room, letting the door slowly swing shut behind him.

***

"Are we one-hundred percent sure it's the right info?" He thumped his fingers rapidly against the top of the scarred desk, anxiety making him restless.

Myron looked up at him somberly, nodding. "Yeah, it's clear, Mason. You read everything right. Chase Sosa is your son, no doubt about it."

Leaning back, Mason took a deep breath. The fucking bitch had his son. She had his boy for twelve fucking years, and he hadn't known. *My boy*, he thought, *she fucking kept my boy from me. Control. She fucking did it again, stripping control from my hands.* He cut his eyes over to Myron. "He healthy? Home life okay?"

"Pending, Mason. Intel is pending. I'm still waiting for the report, but we should have it from our guy by morning at the latest. If you'd told me about this when you first got word, I'd have it all in hand." With a shrug, Myron slid the folder onto the desk, giving it a little push to the center of the surface. "But you didn't, so we wait. But, boss, from what you know about her, do you genuinely think things have been good?"

"Fuck, no," Mason gritted out the words. "Bitch kept my fucking boy from me for twelve years. That is not a recipe for anything good. If it hadn't been for Watcher, I still wouldn't know about him. I want him here tomorrow." His voice lowered an octave, rage giving it a gritty edge. "Get him up here, Myron. I gotta meet my boy." His breathing became erratic and shallow, and he felt shockingly near tears. Twelve years lost with this boy...his son. Chase. "Get him for me."

"Mason, no. Boss, I need you to think, man. You're feeling but not thinking, and that isn't like you." Myron settled back into the chair, focusing his gaze on Mason's face. "He's twelve, and she's had his ear his whole, entire life. You've got no idea what she told him about you. For all you know, he thinks some other man is his father."

At those words, Mason stood with a wordless roar; reaching down, he flipped the desk over with a crash, scattering papers across the room. The edge of the desktop scraped down his shin, forcing Myron to stand and jump back with a yelp. Standing in the sudden chaos, Mason shouted, clenched fist thumping savagely against his chest, "He's *my* fucking boy."

"Yeah, you know that. *Now*," Myron shouted back at him, face red with the effort of trying to break through the shroud of pain and anger Mason was feeling. "You didn't even know about him a month ago. Do you think he knows?" His voice softened as he said, "Mason, I can't...I won't be the one ordering this boy kidnapped and brought to you. There's a right way to do this, Prez. Think for a minute. *Think*. What's the shine for her if she keeps the boy a secret? Why would she do this?" Myron was scowling at him as he reached down to rub his leg, but Mason had frozen in place, considering his words.

What was the benefit for her? This whole thing was a calculated move. *Twelve years. A fucking long-term play.* With distaste, he remembered the feel of her pussy the one time he recalled fucking her. This had been planned right from the beginning, when Shooter had paid her, threatened her. The man's wife and daughter missing at the time, everyone thought they were dead, but then he had found them in a little town in the desert, brought them home.

Tug had been there on that day, patched into the Rebels, but visiting old friends out west. He claimed Shooter's reactions were touching, human; said he had been destroyed at the two years lost with his family. Believed he had been further ruined by the knowledge they left him by choice. All of this wasn't until a full year after Kentucky, so what had his plan been?

Shooter kept in touch over the years, calling occasionally, always the first to initiate contact. More than once, Mason thought he registered jealousy in the man's tone when talking about where he grew up in Kentucky, the family's holler. Was it a thread that could lead to the plot?

"Find out who my daddy has in his will." Spell broken, Mason stood upright, looking away from Myron, uncomfortable with his response to the whole situation with the boy. "Tell me as soon as you get the report from our guy. Thanks."

Dismissed, Myron left the room as Mason looked around at the mess and snorted, bending over to begin gathering the papers. As much as it chapped his ass to think it, his old man owned the better part of two counties down in Kentucky. Valuable land, with assets not listed on any official inventory. If someone wanted the holler, there were few routes open to them, unless his father was changing tradition and would will the properties to someone other than his first-born son. Setting the desk upright, he laid the folders back in place on the surface, aligning the edges in tidy piles, working with his hands while his mind steadily turned over all the possibilities.

Softly, he said, "Chase Sosa." He snorted and then shook his head, revising his statement in a firm tone as he yanked the door open and stalked from the room. "Chase Mason."

***

"Wasn't anything I wanted to happen," he whispered, curling his hand around her ankle.

"I know, son," she responded quietly, her voice as soft as her fingers ruffling through his hair.

"I shoulda talked to them before we climbed on the bikes. Or, maybe I coulda said something after we got there. Shouldn't have rushed in like I did." He shook his head, his cheek rubbing against the fabric of her dress where it lay across her legs.

"Can't change the past." She said this matter-of-factly and he sighed in frustration. "It says a lot about you that you want to, son, but what's done is done."

He closed his eyes then groaned, and opened them again when the world swung in tight circles around him. "I ain't gonna be sick."

He could hear the smile in her voice as she responded, "Of course not. You're the biggest, baddest biker in town. Can't have you getting sick from a little vodka, now can we?"

"If I could change any one thing, Merry…" he started, his voice trailing off. Head still cradled in her lap, he stared at the granite stone in front of them, gaze tracing the edges of the letters spelling out his failure. "I still hate me." Sighing, he wasn't aware of closing his eyes again, never knew when the darkness of unconsciousness closed over him like dark water in a deep, flooded mine. Her answer to his statement fell on suddenly deaf ears, but he had long since given up seeking absolution for his sins anyway.

***

"You're really my dad?" The boy's face twisted in disbelief. He drummed his thumbs nervously against the edge of the table in a fast-paced beat. They were seated in the diner in Straight Creek, about fifteen miles from where Mason had grown up. Carrie was from Straight Creek, and this was where Chase had been living all his life. Movement caught his eye and he looked up, sighing as he recognized the waitress walking their way. They had met in a long-ago summer camp. Every time he came back to Kentucky, he found reminders of his father and the shit he saw and lived through before running away.

"God, our Lord, please lead this sinner through," his father shouted, hands on Davy's head as he prayed over him. "Make him accept the error of his ways." Face crusted with vomit and blood, he tipped his head down, passively allowing the touch, even though it turned his stomach. Church camp in the summer was a time to bring together the youth of their community, teaching them about God in ways the government would certainly frown on, teaching them things that couldn't be covered in church on Sunday morning.

Last night had been one of the worst, fourteen-year-old Davy fighting back against the man who came to his bunk. The girls would be arriving today, which would mean things would go back to normal for him. Normal, meaning the only thing he would have to worry about would be the matches organized by age group. Unlike the rest of them, Davy was most often pitched against older, more seasoned boys, his father always trying to teach him the humility that should come from a beating.

A beating like the one last night, one that would scar the soul as much as the body, because while he had punched and kicked, he had not been successful in anything except deflecting attention to the boy in the bed next to him. Held in place by hard hands, he had been forced to watch as his father bent over the bunk, grunting as the boy's head moved back and forth rhythmically.

He shook his head. This woman seemed to have recovered from those traumatic days, and nodded without recrimination as she approached. He watched as Chase leaned into her hip when she rested a protective hand on his shoulder, giving Mason a hard look. He liked that his boy had people like her around him, people who wanted to protect him from hurt.

"Nancy," he said, inclining his head.

"Davy Mason," she responded, her gaze bouncing between him and the boy, and he saw realization dawning on her face. She mouthed the words 'no way' at him, and he nodded somberly. "Okay. Y'all let me know if you need anything at all. But, knowing him like I do, I already know Chase wants this." She brought a small plate with a single piece of apple pie from behind her back, waving it teasingly in front of the boy. "He never says no to my pie."

"No, ma'am, I sure won't say no." Chase grinned up at her, but the smile didn't reach his eyes. "I like pie." She set the plate and a fork on the table, and then turned to walk away. Chase's attention immediately transferred back to Mason, the smile falling from his face. "Are you?" The kid's chameleon ability said volumes about what his life had been, and seeing it, even if he hadn't already read the report, Mason would have known what kind of shit Carrie had rained down on his boy. *My boy.*

"Yeah, boy. I am." Mason struggled to keep the tone of pride from his voice, but he couldn't stop the quirk of his lips when Chase picked up the fork and shoveled a big bite of pie into his mouth. His smile died when he saw the tears welling in the boy's eyes and heard the catch in his breath. "Chase," he said, and then paused. "Son," he tried the fit of the word in his mouth and liked it there, "you're wondering where I've been. Why you had to grow up without a daddy." Eyes down to the table, Chase nodded, chewing long past when there should have been fruit or crust left in his mouth.

"I found out I was your daddy about twelve hours ago." This statement brought the boy's gaze up to meet his. "I first saw you not quite a month ago. Before that day, no one ever told me I had a son. It's been the longest fucking"—the boy's eyes widened at the word—"month of my God damned"—his eyes widened farther—"life."

"If you saw me, why didn't you say anything?" Chase scooped another bite of pie and shoved it into his mouth, but he looked stricken.

"Chase, you're twelve. From what I hear, you're a smart boy. Why don't you tell me why I waited until I was sure?" Mason didn't know why he wasn't simply answering the boy's question, but now that he had said it, he knew he wanted to hear what Chase would say.

Chewing slowly, he traced circles on the tabletop near the plate with the tines of his fork. Mason raised his head, calling over his shoulder, "Nancy, can we get a glass of milk and some more coffee, please?"

"Sure thing, sugar," he heard, and shared a grin with Chase when the boy's eyes flicked up at him.

"Some things never change," Mason muttered, and then said, "Thanks," as she set the milk and a pot of coffee on the table. She smiled and walked away, retreating once more behind the counter. He returned his focus to Chase to see he was ready to answer and nodded encouragingly, waiting.

"Because you wanted to be sure. You didn't need to put yourself out there unless you had to. No one wants a burden." Chase nodded, so absolutely certain of his answer that this, too, spoke volumes about the garbage he must have had to listen to all his life. Sudden pain made Mason's heart stutter in his chest, and he wasn't even sure for a moment if he could speak.

"Eeehhh. Wrong." Pushing past the pain, Mason made a loud buzzer noise and forced a grin at the boy. "Yeah, I wanted to be sure. Only because I wasn't willing to come in and turn your life upside down if it wasn't true." He pointed a finger out the window, ignoring the half-dozen Rebels waiting there in the shade, indicating where Chase had been when he first saw him. "As much as I wanted to run across this road and grab you when I saw you working on that old dirt bike...boy, you deserved the time for me to be sure, so I wouldn't fuck things up for you."

He laid his palms on the table, leaning over and bringing his face down to the same level as Chase. "If I'd known about you, there's no way I'd have stayed away. No fucking way. You mark that, boy. You're my blood, my son"—a warmth spread through his chest at the word—"and you would never...*will* never be a burden to me. You tracking what I'm sayin'?" Chase swallowed and nodded, eyes wide as he listened.

Mason blew out a hard breath. "I hate like *fuck* I've missed twelve years of your growing up, but I can tell you now I won't miss anything else. You can mark that, too." He sat back in the seat, forcing a relaxed posture, resting both elbows along the back of the booth. "I'm sure you have questions, Chase. I can't promise I'll answer everything, but no question is off limits. Ask away. Whatever you've got, ask."

The boy reached out his hand for the glass of milk, and Mason saw he was trembling. Shoving down his anger at everything about this situation, he tried his damnedest to project calm and easy, exactly like he did during a rival club sitdown. Inwardly, he snorted, thinking, *I can do calm. Fuck yeah, I'm so fucking zen I could put myself to sleep.* Chase's chin tucked far down into his chest and he could barely make out the muttered word. "Anything?"

"Yep," he answered easily, "anything."

"She...Carrie said—"

Mason interrupted, "You call your mom by her first name?"

Chase ducked his head again, nodding. "She said she's too young to have a son my age, so I can't call her Mom anymore."

"You're shitting me?" The question burst out of Mason before he could put a clamp on it, and he saw the first glimmer of humor cross the boy's face as he shook his head. "She's...*Jesus*...never mind. What did Carrie tell you?"

"She said you never wanted to be a dad, and that was why you didn't come around or help with bills when things were bad." He spit out the words quickly, and cut his gaze up to Mason's face then back down to where he was still fiddling with the fork. "So it's not true?"

"Not a word one," he affirmed, his voice ringing with confidence. "Twelve hours, Chase. That's how long I've known I had a son."

"So it wasn't anything I did?" The vulnerability in the whispered question cut him to the heart, and impulsively he reached across, folding both of Chase's thumping, jittering hands in his own.

"Boy, look at me." He waited until the grey eyes, so like his, lifted to look at him. "I am some kinda glad to see your face. There isn't anything you could ever do...not one single thing would cause me to turn away from you. You're my blood,"—his voice deepened, growing rough—"my son. Love for you is already bone-deep in me."

***

"What do you mean I have to wait?" He was yelling into the phone at Myron, who was patiently trying to explain the ins-and-outs of Kentucky custody laws.

"Judge said the boy has to stay in counseling, and you have to keep a visitation schedule for a full year before she'll consider the transfer of custody. He barely turned thirteen, Mason. While his age means he could legally pick his residence, you said not to push him, so that route is closed to us." Myron sighed, and Mason could imagine the man rummaging through the files on his computer. The skinny geek liked his toys, and his office at the clubhouse reflected his electronic passions.

"Then get me something we can use on Sosa. There've got to be fuckups in her past we can leverage—" He stopped talking at a negative noise from Myron.

"You're president of a 'biker gang'...those are the judge's words, not mine. As much as I know you've cleaned things up since starting the Rebels, we're both aware we're not squeaky. We go digging on her, there's a whole lot more she could dig on you." Mason recognized the bite of frustration in his voice as he continued, "I wanted to bring you better news, Prez. I think you'll have to ride this one out, man."

It had already been six months since he learned about Chase. He made it down for every visitation, not losing his cool even when Carrie jacked him around about getting his boy. On the lawyer's advice, he had rented a small apartment in town, giving them a semi-permanent place to stay when Chase came over.

"Myron, it chaps my ass she's not being called out on the fact she stole my son. Stole my boy for twelve goddamned years." He gritted the words out, realizing his hand had tightened on the phone, his knuckles standing out in stark whiteness around the device.

"Boss, you already know how it looks, same as I do. You were married to her for a day and then filed for an annulment. She claims by the time she knew she was pregnant there was no way to get ahold of you. If we go there, then the fight becomes an ugly he said/she said argument, and no one wins. Certainly not Chase."

Myron made a little noise and Mason knew he was moving restlessly. "Give me a bit, Prez. I'll try to discover if there was any way she could have known where you were, how to contact you. Six more months, and I know you can do this, Mason. Just six months. Get together with your boy today, spend some quality time with Chase, and then come home to Chicago. Slate said for me to tell you Mica's been coming to Jackson's regular-like. Almost like she's looking for you."

He sighed. "All right. I'll be in the wind on my way back in the morning. Tell Slate to call if he needs me."

"Will do."

Disconnecting the call, Mason scrubbed his palm across his jaw, feeling the whiskery bristle on his skin. Mica had been getting more comfortable with him for a while now, and if she was coming around looking for him...he smiled, the corners of his mouth curling up softly. He had introduced her to his Rebels, following a slow and steady pace, making certain they all knew her status first. Princess of the Rebel Wayfarers motorcycle club was as official as his own title of president, and every man knew she owned them. The other clubs had gradually become accustomed to the protective nature the Rebels had towards her, and understood the protection extended to cover the people she loved, such as her best friend, Jess Nalan.

He sat on the overstuffed armchair in front of the apartment's big windows, thinking about his next-door neighbor in Chicago with the sea-green eyes and soft lips, which so often stretched into a generous smile.

12. Kentucky hollers

2011

"Ma?" His question wavered into the darkness, his fears nearly overwhelming him and stealing his voice. The shadows pressed in against him from all sides, covering his senses like a blanket. It was as black as if he had taken the cage down a hundred feet into the mine with his pa.

Standing still and silent, Davy turned to put his back against a huge oak tree, feeling the lingering warmth of the Kentucky summer day radiating from the rough bark pressing through his thin, canvas shirt. Sounds still came from the darkness surrounding him, and his breathing sped up, terror taking residence in his mind.

"Ma, where are ya?" Noises near and far came from all around him, directionless and frightening, the effects of nightfall amplifying the simplest and most innocent of rustling leaves and cracking branches. Slowly and methodically, he quietly shuffled his bare feet until they were underneath the covering of crunchy leaves, and he could dig his toes into the coolness and solidity of the ground beneath his feet, grounding himself, and creating a sanctuary in his mind. Hiding like a toad underneath a log.

"Ma," he whisper-shouted, trying to hold back the terror causing his limbs to shake. It was dark and he was alone. He had set out all his new snares like she told him, resetting the others as he picked up the three rabbits caught since this morning. Now, the coppery smell of blood coming from the carcasses tied to his shoulder strap seemed to float all around him, in his imagination the scent drawing predators closer with every moment he spent in the woods.

Why would she bring him out here and leave him? She wouldn't, he knew it, so something must have happened to her. Not long after she had separated from him, telling him they would have a better chance of finding game for supper if they walked different paths, he heard a loud roaring and a scream. That had been in the gloaming of twilight, and she should have met him by now. They had done this many times, and she never failed to collect him before going back to their shack.

What had the roar been? It had sounded mechanical, echoes multiplying the sound until it seemed to surround him. Muffled by the trees and hills, even the scream had seemed foreign and strange, and he couldn't be sure it'd been Ma at all. There had been talk of panthers in town a couple of weeks ago. He had been sitting on a bag of corn in the back of their farm truck parked in front of the feed store and heard old man Hearny say them panthers could sound just like a woman screaming. Maybe he'd discovered one of them stalking in the darkness, looking to panic its next meal into a hopeless retreat.

Ma'd never leave me, he thought again, then shook his head in dismissal, feeling the ends of his too-long hair trailing across his bare neck as he absently slapped at a skeeter on his arm. She had left when he was little and been gone a long time. Pa said she was gone for half his life, which meant she had been away for four years. Come back just this spring, she had dragged into the house in the middle of the night, face thin and pinched, clothes threadbare and dirty.

She and Pa had scrapped like hounds over a coon, shouting and skittering back and forth across the shack. Davy and Bethy had crawled underneath the kitchen table, cowering there and watching their parents fight until Pa pinned her against the wall, his hand on her neck holding tightly as her face turned a dark purple, mouth gaping open in a breathless scream. Pa finally turned her loose, letting her slide down, collapsed like a rag doll on the floor, legs splayed wide, ankles turning in weakly as she coughed and choked.

Later, Pa'd bred her like one of the mares, bending her over the edge of the bed set against the wall in the main room. Shouting scriptures and repeating words from past sermons, he had her dress hiked to her hips and pressed himself against her shanks and back. Davy pulled Bethy over to his pallet then and covered her ears, holding her face against his neck so she couldn't see.

He watched his ma's face and knew Pa was hurting her. She wasn't acting like the mares who squealed and kicked but then huffed in excitement, pushing back when the stud finally hit their hole with his big thing. Ma wasn't huffing or squealing; she was standing still. Not fighting, the look on her face desperate and long-suffering. She was taking the pain for some reason Davy couldn't figure out.

The force of Pa's body hitting hers was driving her up onto her toes. He could hear the thud of her heels hitting the floor, watched as they made deep impressions in the swept dirt. He stared at her feet as she was rhythmically rocked up and down, toes…heels…toes…heels, gaze darting up to see the dark necklace of bruises around her throat. She was crying soundlessly as she forced her fist into her mouth and bit down hard enough to have bright red blood painting her lips like one of the harlots Pa preached about. But this was his ma. She couldn't be no harlot. The red mixed with her spit where it bubbled around her fingers, and he saw her silent tears leaving thin wet tracks across her soot-covered face.

That was four months ago, and since coming home, Ma'd settled back into life in the compound. She cleaned and mended, cooked and canned, gathered and hunted, as was expected from the women. Pa had bred her a lot, but he'd been calmer as the days passed, and Davy didn't have to protect Bethy anymore. This was more like the Pa he vaguely remembered from before Ma had been gone, the one who laughed and ruffled their hair. Not the Pa left alone with a weeks-old girl child who cried like a stuck pig every night. This Pa was more interested in putting a baby in Ma's belly than punishing her or the other members of the church.

He'd been sitting on the front stoop, shelling peas last week, and overheard Ma crying to her sister about someone named Jonny who she missed. It made Pa real mad when he asked who Jonny was, and Pa had gone to the barn to have a talk with Ma. She found him later as he was gathering eggs with Bethy, telling him to remember a name: John Morgan. Dark bruising already spreading across her cheek, she reached out and cupped his chin in her hand, holding his gaze with her own as she said, "Don't forget, Davy. John Morgan, I want you to always remember that name, baby. John Morgan."

Bethy had asked who John was, and Ma told her, "He's only a little older than your brother is, sweet girl. My strong sons, John Morgan and Davis Mason, and my beautiful, sweet baby girl, Bethany Mason. Remember those names, all my babies."

Davy had leaned against his mother's side, resting his head on her rib bones as he said, "Love you, Ma."

As she always did, she responded back with, "And I love you more, baby boy."

I'll stay here another pass of the clock, *he decided, looking up at the waning moon and taking note of its position in relation to the tree he leaned on. He wasn't lost, could never be lost here in his family's holler, on land that had belonged to the Mason family for more than four generations. I'll wait for her. I'll always wait for her.*

Disturbed by the dream, Mason roused himself from the half-sleep he had been drifting in and out of for the past several hours. He propped himself up on one elbow, his gaze sweeping across the pictures on the wall above his bed. He settled on a black and white image of a young girl leaning against the fender of a truck. Unsmiling, hugely pregnant, with bare feet and legs, her broad jaw partially hidden by the sweep of her long hair, she stared into the camera. The truck was parked in front of a wooden shack, and indistinct figures were barely visible seated on the stoop in the background. The emotions evoked by the photograph were loss and despair, which exactly fit his frame of mood tonight after the party he had thrown.

He sighed, falling heavily back into the bed on his back, one hand scrubbing across his scalp, feeling the bristle of his short hair against his palm.

His cell rang on the nightstand, and he rolled over, picking up the phone to catch sight of Mica's name on the screen. "Babe?" he spoke softly into the phone and listened, her audible breathing the only response for a moment.

Finally, she said, "Hey, are you awake yet? Can I come over? I had a bad dream and don't want to be alone right now."

Surprised, he frowned. She left the party at his house earlier with Rupert in tow, as Mason had intended. His obsession for her needed to be put aside, because he knew he would ruin her, wasn't the right man for her life. He believed Daniel Rupert was a good man, something he felt she deserved. He asked her, "Isn't Daniel with you?"

Even through the phone, the tears in her voice were clear as she hiccupped, "No, Daniel isn't here."

What the fuck? He had watched them kissing on her back porch steps. Held his breath when she leaned into the man and then kissed him, their intimate moment tearing Mason's heart in two before he could force himself to turn away from his kitchen window. What the hell did Rupert do that he wasn't with her right now? Why wasn't he there to soothe her, to take away the dream and fill her night with sweet? Shaking his head, Mason told her, "Oh, babe, I'll be right there."

13. **More**

"Why are you here?" The words hung in the still air of her backyard, trees casting dark shadows around the edges of the space, bright moonlight reflecting off the windows and onto her face. "Mason, we...I can't—"

"Shhhh. Babe, I know." He spoke quietly, but still glimpsed a flinch from her at his tone. God, he wanted to hold her, stroke her body, hands running over her bare skin as he had done only once before, touch her...love her. Now everything had changed, the balance of their relationship shifted, and he knew it. *This is your own fucking fault*, he thought grimly. He had practically thrown her at Rupert more than once, and would have to fucking live with it—live without her love—because he had seen how they connected on a level that was deep, and real. He had too much shit rolling thickly through his life to fuck this up for her, because if anyone had earned the sweet, it was Mica, and there was zero sweet to be found within the borders of his existence.

Her hand lifted, bringing her fingers up to touch his face, and he stood quietly, letting the feel of her skin against his sink into him. He groaned silently, clamping his teeth together as unwanted heat built low in his belly, his cock fattening, growing thick with desire. "You've told me more than once I can't be in your life." Her voice was so soft he had to focus to hear her clearly. "What changed two weeks ago to make it suddenly okay for us to be together like...that?"

He could tell she needed honesty, so he cracked open the door normally kept tightly closed on his heart, telling her, "I needed you, babe. You...you were looking for a way to forget, to move past your nightmares. A way to build memories not filled with pain and betrayal. You've lived with all the shit in your head for so long, and Daniel wasn't...ready yet. I was and you let me in. You called me, and I answered your need the only way I knew how. You let me take care of you, let me love you." He reached up, cupping her hand, holding it in place on his face with his hard palm, branding his skin with the heat.

"Babe, I needed to know what love felt like. After everything over the past few years, I couldn't even glimpse it anymore. Mica, babe." He sucked a breath in through his nose, his lips parting as he slowly breathed it out, staring down into her eyes. "You are so strong, my treasure...you showed me love. Not fleeting attraction or even lust coming together in a meager moment, but a full measure of love, something to take with me all my life."

She hiccupped a sob and his throat tightened in response, absorbing her pain. The last fucking thing he ever wanted was to hurt her. *Fuck.* The thing he most feared was losing her from his life, and he knew because of his actions their hard-won friendship was at risk. He gripped her hand tight, pulling her towards him, wrapping his arms around her and holding her tenderly against his body, cradling her as gently, as if she might break.

"There are different kinds of love, you know?" He spoke with his cheek pressed against the side of her head, whispering near her ear, "We each had something the other needed, the kind of thing that only comes along sometimes. But now, babe? You and Daniel have a thing that's always going to be there for you. He's it for you." He wished he could laugh, but the sound stuck in his throat, refusing release. He swallowed hard and, with a voice thick with emotion, said, "He's...hell, a blind man could see how much he feels for you. And, I've seen how totally you care for him. That's true, babe. That's always."

There was a low rumble in the distance and he straightened, squeezing her tightly for a moment before taking a step back. They were standing on her back porch and were far too exposed, but she had come home early and his Rebels weren't here yet. He knew he had to cover her until they arrived, but damned if he could find it in him to go inside her fucking house. The house that, for him, was now filled with memories of her naked, moving beneath him. She had welcomed him into her bed for one night, urging him with words and touches. That house was where she had kissed his hands, and then his lips, and then been spread before him, his to do with as he pleased. For one night.

And, he had pleased. With his hands, lips, tongue, and cock, he made love to her, watching her face as she shattered around him. She had been so real and genuine, drawing him in and giving him room to open himself to her as he had never done with a woman before. Denying his own pleasure to find hers, it was the first time he had ever wanted to be selfless in bed. His name on her lips, cried out in passion, was all the repayment he wanted...needed.

There had been no pain, nothing forced...no thoughts about club business or advantage; he had simply loved her, face-to-face and heart-to-heart. He memorized every touch, every sound, knowing this single chance would be all he ever got of her. The woman he had wanted for more than four years had given herself wholly to him, and he had greedily taken every part, holding it all close, because it was good, and true, and right in the moment. Their sometimes.

He took another step back, dropping her hand, missing the connection and heat immediately. They couldn't come together again like that, and he knew it. Hell, they both knew it. She needed Rupert, and he had the club. He would always put his brothers first; it had been part of his makeup for too long to change now. He could hold onto the memory though, hold it fucking tight and close, because she had shown him the possibility of love, and now that he had a taste of it, he found he wanted it again. Was desperate for it.

Deliberately, he slipped his club mask into place, watching the corners of her mouth turn down at the change in his expression. Three bikes turned into the alley between their houses, parking near his garage. Without turning to look, he knew it would be Tug, Slate, and one of their new prospects, Tucker. "The boys will keep you safe, babe," he said softly, and she nodded.

"You can't stay?" The question hung in the air between them like her statement had earlier, and he stared at her, turning over the idea before finally shaking his head. Rejecting her broke him in a way he didn't expect. He always said he would give Mica anything, but it seemed he found the exception to the rule, finally.

Turning from the fresh hurt blooming in her expression, he watched his men tromp up the steps to the porch, Tucker bypassing them to move inside with only a chin lift. Slate frowned at their closeness and shook his head at Mason. "Prez." He greeted Mica with only a quick nod, and then walked on into her house. Tug stepped near, wrapping his arms around her from behind, tickling her neck with his mustache, and drawing a real smile to her face. Seeing it, knowing she was safe and comfortable with his men, Mason moved to go, pulling himself up to stand straighter. Tonight's business wasn't going to be pretty, and he needed to prepare himself mentally for what was to come.

He heard a softly called, "Mason?" and turned around just as she flung herself into his arms. Instinctively, he cradled her to him, their bodies aligning in a way that made him groan silently. He held her, the softness of her curves imprinting themselves on his memory, the ache in his chest making it so fucking hard to breathe, because he knew this was right...felt so fucking right. He let his hand slip down her back, hovering for a second above her ass, pulling her tight against him before he stroked upwards, gripping the back of her neck with one hard hand. The air was so still around them he could make out the sound of his palm moving over the fabric of her clothes, the rasp of her breath in her throat...the sound of her heartbeat speeding as he caressed her.

"I'll be back tomorrow, babe," he whispered, feeling her nod against his shoulder. Deliberately slowing his breathing, he felt hers begin to match it, felt her edging away from whatever precipice she had seen in her future. Calming himself to calm her, he stood motionless and held her until she shifted, indicating she was ready to pull away...ready to leave him. As they separated, the sounds of the night gradually became audible again, the whir of locusts filling the trees.

Without another word, he crossed to his truck and backed out into the alley, his mind replaying the past few minutes as he dissected her behavior, trying to understand. Absently, he watched bugs flickering through the lights of his truck as he drove away.

About three hours later, he was finishing the meet with Bones, when his phone vibrated. Pulling it from his pocket, he frowned to glimpse Tucker's name on the screen. *What the fuck is the prospect doing calling me?* he wondered, immediately getting pissed off at the conceit of the man. "Yeah?" He barked the word into the phone, and then froze, his muscles locking in place as the man's words sank in.

There had been an attack on Mica in her home, his three men sitting idle in the next room. One fucking room away, and she had still been targeted. Tug came on the line and, with a few tersely worded phrases, indicated how serious this was, his last words before disconnecting a plea for Mason to hurry.

He sat, struggling to control his breathing, shaking fingers pressed to his forehead and cheek, mouth twisted in anguish as he thought, *I promised her safety.* He remembered his last glimpse of her as she went into her kitchen, glancing over her shoulder with a soft smile as she waved goodbye.

"Mason, what is wrong?" Bones asked him, holding out one hand, palm up. "You are white as a ghost, man."

"Motherfuckers touched Mica," he whispered, his voice raspy with rage, and he watched as Bones' head snapped back.

"Who would care to anger the Rebels so?" He drew a breath before asking, "Was it Shooter?" His questions made Mason pause for a moment, considering. It was interesting how quickly his friend's thoughts went to his brother, interesting and damning, because now it was all Mason could think about, too.

"It's probably her ex," he said, shaking his head to reject the idea his brother could be involved. Jerking abruptly to his feet, he took long, hurried strides towards the outside door of the Skeptics' clubhouse. The Skeptics members had only just finished loading the back of his truck, and he gave them a quick wave of thanks. He nodded at Red, who had settled into the back of the vehicle to watch over the squirming cargo. "Pop one if you need to make a point, brother," he said, his voice low but audible to the unwilling passengers. Red opened his mouth to laugh soundlessly, watching as the eyes of the bound and gagged men in the back of the truck widened with fear. They didn't know they were already dead men, only kept breathing as long as they had information he needed.

"Mason," Bones called from behind him, and he paused only long enough to look over his shoulder. "Skeptics stand with Rebels, if you have need of us. Call me; let me know if this is a first strike. Let me know how things go." He nodded solemnly, and Mason nodded back, moving to climb into the truck and leave.

14. Whatever it is we do

The entire drive home, he turned over Bones' words in his head. Pausing at a red light, he texted Slate a question, wondering at the lack of response. Slamming his hand hard against the steering wheel in frustration, he barked out a harsh laugh when he caught sight of himself in the mirror. *Hell, you look like a crazy man*, he thought, taking in his wild eyes and curled lip.

Caught by the next light, he fired off a text to Tug, who immediately answered. The man had already rousted a response from the Rebels; a group of their members were even now on their way to his house. Tug texted one more word with a question mark, and Mason responded back with **No**. They would not be letting Rupert know until he had a better idea what was going down.

Parking his truck haphazardly in the alley, he jumped out while it still rocked on its springs. He quickly told Red he would send a couple brothers as soon as possible to help keep the prisoners contained, receiving a grunt in response. Trotting across her yard, he took the back porch steps two at a time. Pulling open the door, he stopped for a moment, shocked and immediately enraged at what he saw.

Mica stood in her kitchen, Slate casually reclining in one of her chairs while she cleaned blood off his face.

That shouldn't be too bad. But, it *was*.

Shocked. Yeah, he was that. Shocked, because he could see she was beaten all to hell, her ribs already purpling along one side. There was a large necklace of bruises covering her throat...*oh, God, her throat*. Suddenly, he smelled deep earth, bitter and dark, the scent belching from the open mouths of the mines, followed by sweeter dirt, rich with promise, the aroma of spring's first turning of the sod. Shaking his head, he continued his visual sweep, taking in the darkening bruises on her arms and legs. There was blood on the inside of one thigh, and he felt sick at what it had to mean.

Enraged.

He was enraged, because the reason he could see the damage dealt to *his woman*—alarm skittered across his brain when he registered those words—was because she was nearly fucking naked. Mica, who didn't do casual, didn't do naked. Mica, who was fucking chaste as a fucking nun, was virtually naked in her kitchen. Leaning over Slate's face, her breasts barely contained in lace dipping close to his mouth, his hands in his lap down beside her bare pussy. Even when Mason had fucked her—*made love*, his brain supplied—half the time, she had hidden her body underneath the covers.

She looked up at him, and those eyes...her beautiful, sea-green eyes were empty. They stayed empty and emotionless for a single beat of his heart, then another, and finally, he saw the color amplified by the welling tears he would give anything to never fall, never touch her cheeks. He would give anything to deflect her pain and fear, and never see the gut-wrenching knowledge of his failure reflected in those eyes.

Crossing the room in two steps, he swept her into his arms, curling himself around her possessively, trying not to think about the feelings ricocheting through him. He couldn't let himself think that he loved her;

he needed her to be okay. And then, he couldn't think at all, because he felt her body beginning to shake, muscles quivering all over as she instinctively knew she could let go.

He had her, so she was safe.

In his arms, she was safe and could react to what had happened.

She was safe. *Always*. Not sometimes, but always.

Hours later, he had her tucked safely into his bed. She had been in his bedroom. In his home. *His*. Her dark hair spread across his pillows as he had often imagined it, her body curled up on his bed. She was his. Had been his.

Not now, though. She kept asking for Daniel, and he finally relented, calling to tell the man to come, because she needed him. Not Mason, she wanted Daniel.

Then, she left.

Left with Daniel, Mason standing watching from his doorway as they drove away, lights still shining brightly from the windows in Mica's house across the narrow alley.

Mason hadn't been allowed to keep her, not anything of her. The only thing remaining in his house was the scent of her body on his sheets. The arguments Daniel presented were sound, much as Mason hated to admit it. There was nothing to dispute, because he knew the security the man had was far superior to three bikers drinking coffee in the kitchen while she got the shit kicked out of her in her own goddamned bedroom. Her safety was far more important than his...what? Lust? His...*love*? He laughed aloud at his own confusion. *You don't know what love is*, he scoffed, *never had it in your life, but what Bethy showed you. What do you know of love, you sad bastard?*

If he hadn't left her, hadn't rejected Mica's softly voiced request, could he have stopped it? If he had stayed, would she be undamaged right now? Unharmed and safely in her home, next to his, where he could walk over and call on her anytime he wanted. He did leave, and staying had not even been an option, because he had business to deal with. Club business seemed to always be between him and her, but his brothers depended on him. He had worked too hard over the years to build the club, only to let his brothers down now, hadn't he? But...what if he had stayed? If he had only stayed...

He shook his head and stood from the couch in his quiet house, walking through the kitchen to the back patio, where he pulled up a plastic chair, propping his feet in another one. Leaning back, he stared up at the cold, star-filled sky, thinking of times not too far in the past, when he and Mica would do this. Before her ex-boyfriend raised his piss-ant head. Before Daniel helped save her. Before she loved the hockey player.

"Not mine." He spoke the words aloud quietly for the first time, eyes flicking from constellation to constellation in the winter sky.

"She was never going to be yours." The voice came from behind him and he rolled, rising and spinning from his chair to face the intruder whose identity he already knew. Shooter took a step forward out of the shadows. "You need to get the fuck out of her life if you want her happy."

"That a fucking threat, *brother*?" Mason sneered the word, jolting as his hand met an unexpectedly empty holster at his back. *Fuck*, he had taken the gun out when he was helping their EMT tonight with Mica. It was resting on the dresser in his bedroom, placed there out of caution, and now frustratingly out of reach. *Don't let him know. Just play along*, he thought.

"More like a promise. Only because I know you, not because I'm going to do anything. You should leave her alone, brother. Let her live out her life as a citizen." Shooter looked at him, tilting his head to one side. "Is it too big an ask? You backing away to keep her healthy? She didn't look like she was doin' too good tonight when she left in the big car, man. All bruised up and shit." Quizzically, he tilted his head the other way. "You do that shit to her? Fuck, man, I always gathered you liked dark, but didn't know your tastes ran *that* dark."

"What are you doing here, Shooter?" He forced himself to ask this in a bored tone of voice, as if he were already tired of the discussion.

"On my way to the Fort, thought I'd stop in and visit my little brother." He pulled out the chair Mason's feet had been in, gesturing to the other chair as he sat. "How are things going with your son?"

Mason dragged the chair over, placing the heels of his boots on the edge of the railing, staring into the darkness of the backyard. "I know why you did it, bastard. Ain't happening, Shooter. You won't get the land."

"Yeah, I expected you'd figure it out. Can't blame me. Your little mountain is worth a fuckton of cash and promises. I didn't think it would take you so long to be curious about Sosa, but I guess you had your hands full, what with betraying your club and all." This was said in an even tone, because Shooter wasn't trying to pull a rise from him; in fact, he was just calling things as he saw them. "Where'd Gunny take the bangers?"

It didn't surprise him Shooter knew about the men the Skeptics had found and detained for him. The four had been part of a crew hired weeks ago to kidnap Mica by her twin brother, Michael Scott. Their only instructions had been make it hurt and make her absence permanent. The Rebels already dealt with the foot soldiers, but these men were the officers and should know more about the chain of command for the orders. Hopefully, they would know more, because Scott had turned into a dead end for anything to do with her ex, which is who Mason suspected had actually been behind the attack. *Both attacks*, he mentally amended with a curl of his lip.

The first event being her introduction to Rupert, he thought and snorted. He and Daniel had made it so the bangers weren't successful in their efforts. However, it had been just the first in a cascade of shit, with everything seemingly determined to knock down his chance at a relationship with her like a house of fucking cards. It had taken far too long to locate the bangers afterwards, but it was satisfying to know they would be breathing their last soon. *Motherfuckers shouldn't have touched her.* She would never know what happened. Mason would continue to make sure the hard side of things was always kept far away from her.

He ignored Shooter's question, instead asking one of his own, "How are Edith and Luke?" He didn't honestly give a fuck. As far as he was concerned, they were probably tainted with the same brand of crazy as their old man, but he dragged them out, because he knew the girl was one of Shooter's hot buttons.

"One of your boys keeps sniffing after her." The scorn in his voice was surprising, but there was also an underlying flavor of fear Mason found interesting.

"Who?" he asked, but thought he probably already knew.

"Your man Bear keeps showing up where she is. Judge said it's happened too many times for it to be accidental. He asked me if the guy was mental, because he never talks to her. Never talks to her, just watches from a distance." Shooter shook his head.

Mason shifted, crossing one ankle over the other. "Yeah? Good for him." He moved again, reaching behind him to the rock wall and pulling a pack of smokes out of a nook there. Wordlessly, he offered the package to Shooter, who accepted one. Mason shook his own cig out, reaching back to replace the pack, and then he leaned up to take a light from Shooter. Cupping his hands around the one holding the lighter, their gazes locked over the flickering flame. "He's a good man," he said, dragging deeply before leaning back and blowing out the hot smoke.

"Yeah, I caught that. Judge has a hard-on for him though. Not sure what happened there, but they got sideways at some point." Shooter cut a glance over at him. "You going after this woman?"

"You see her walk out of my fucking house?" It was all the answer he would give, the only thing he was prepared to hand to his brother.

"Sorry, man. Gems like her are fucking hard to find." Shooter drew in a shaking breath, surprising Mason with his next words. "Mama was one of those for Pops, like Kimberly was for me. He told me once that he never knew what she'd run home to, when she went back. He didn't know about you and Bethany until they were already miles in the wind.

"Did you know I was nine when Mama left the first time? Something had happened in the club; she saw something Pops didn't intend her to ever catch sight of and she ran away. He said she panicked, kind of how Kimberly did when she found out about the whore and my son, Roxy and Luke. Pops said he never knew how she wound up in Kentucky, or with your daddy." He took a drag off the cigarette, the ember glowing brightly in the darkness.

"Her sister was there. Aunt Barbra," Mason said quietly, and Shooter made an inquisitive noise.

After a few minutes of silence between them, Shooter said, "You wouldn't think it, but I was too young to remember her when he brought her back. By then, she'd been gone so long I don't think I even knew who she was. Empty face trying to fill a hole I didn't even know existed. She'd been gone four years, and then was back for four more. I was seventeen when she disappeared the last time. She wasn't even gone half a year, but you could tell she'd been through a lot in a short period. She never quit talking about you and Bethy. Pissed me off. I was so angry I had to share her with people who didn't even know I existed. She had a life in Kentucky that didn't involve me, my own mother carrying on with people who didn't give a fuck about me. I was mad as hell when I realized she left because she picked you and your sister over me.

He sighed. "I think Pops was sorry how things went down, because she wasn't cut out for club life. He should have left her a citizen. Being his old lady put a big fucking target on her back and was what killed her in the end."

Mason jerked. He never asked how she died. He knew from a cursory discussion with John early on that she was gone by the time they met in Chicago, but he never questioned the how of it. He carried his own anger at her abandonment of him and Bethy, and the things that happened to them without a protector, without a mother to care and give a shit that people were beating your kids. That they were getting fucked over, again and again. He didn't ask, didn't fucking care, because until he was grown, he assumed she had forgotten them. Put them aside as readily as smothering covers thrown from a too-hot bed. The lie put to rest by Morgan's words in a cement block bunker far to the west, news of her recounted love for them forever paired in his mind with the taste of blood in his mouth. He always figured an illness had taken her. "What happened?"

"One of the Mexican clubs torched her." He said this casually, and Mason's breath stilled in his chest at the ease with which he talked about their mother's death. "Caught her out on the freeway and boxed her in. They gassed up and lit the sedan she was driving. Stood around and watched it burn. Pops said he heard one of them popped a cap when she got down to screaming, so at least there's that."

The air chilled around them and the night deepened as they sat in silence for a long time, cigarettes long ago stubbed out against the soles of their boots. Shooter finally stirred, rising slowly to his feet, groaning as he stretched. "I better get in the wind, brother. Think I could bump into you in the Fort sometime?"

Mason lifted a hand. "Yeah, let me know next time you're in town. I'll head down and we'll do...whatever it is we fucking do."

15. Lingering images

2012

He stood in the parking lot for a moment, twisting to look at the dark building behind him. Shadows lay deep around the edges of the River Riders' clubhouse, only the lights from his Rebels' bikes illuminating the lot. Mason was trying to figure out exactly what had just happened inside there. Not the party still going on, it was just biker normal. Nor the drama with the bangers coming in, waving guns around, because while unexpected, even the drama had been handled with relative ease by this club's members.

No, he was contemplating his surprising reaction to the chestnut-haired and hazel-eyed woman still inside those doors. He shook his head, swinging his leg over the bike seat and starting the engine. Tug idled over to him, pulling up alongside and facing him. "What happened, Prez?"

Mason shook his head again. "Fuck if I know, Tug. Shooter's girl had just gotten here—"

Tug interrupted him with a nod. "Yeah, I saw Eddie in the parking lot on her way in. Her and some gal."

Cutting his eyes over, Mason asked, "The gal? Do you know Willa?"

"Willa...What the? No. *Jesus*, Mason. What happened, boss?" Tug looked carefully at him, and Mason shrugged, not sure how to respond. His confusion must have shown, because Tug continued, "I'm asking why we're pulling out of here hours ahead of schedule?"

"Huh. Yeah, just some bullshit." He sucked in a steadying breath. "Bangers came in toting the prospect Bootleg had manning the lot." Bootleg was the president of the Fort Wayne River Riders, the club his nephew, Judge, was currently patched into. "They had a couple of pieces, were waving them around. Riders took care of business; it was no problem, really. They have them downstairs right now, working to figure out what they were thinking." He shrugged. "Shooter's fucking pissed, because Eddie was here when it went down."

He stretched, pulling a small piece of crumpled paper out of his jeans pocket. Smoothing it, he read what was written, and a slow smile spread across his face. Tucking it securely into his wallet, he told Tug, "Let's hit our clubhouse for a quick one before I head back to Chicago."

A few minutes later, seated at the clubhouse bar, he looked at Bingo and Tug. "Bear's on his way west. He won't be back for a bit, so make arrangements as you need to, brothers." He sighed. "I'm flying to Texas tomorrow morning, so I gotta get in the wind here pretty quickly."

Bingo asked in surprise, "Texas?" while Tug simply smiled.

Mason nodded at them. "I'm bringing our Princess home, one way or another." Mica had been holed up at her aunt and uncle's ranch in East Texas for weeks now, and he was fucking tired of her avoiding his calls. He stayed there as long as he could after...everything, but now it was time to bring her home.

"I have a plan." He grinned. "Tugboat, you know how you promised her you'd learn her how to ride?" Tug laughed aloud and nodded, taking a long pull from his beer. "I bought a pretty little Sportster for her.

Gonna be delivered to the ranch tomorrow afternoon, along with my new bike." At Bingo's raised eyebrow, he scoffed, "Shut the fuck up, old man. You know you like chrome as much as I do. Anyway, we'll discover how long she can resist the call of the road." He took a drink of his beer, and then tipped the top of the bottle towards the backroom. "DeeDee and Mel doin' okay? It's been a tough couple of years."

Tug nodded. "She's getting there. You gonna say hello since you're in town?"

Mason shook his head, looking over at Bingo. "Slate's gonna put together a welcome back party for Mica. It'd be nice to have DeeDee there. Why don't you ask her to ride Winger's bike? It'll put Mica at ease to meet another woman rider there, I think."

Bingo nodded and then stood, slapping the bar top with his palms. "I gotta go, Prez. Kids will be getting ready for bed soon. I try to be there for the little ones."

Mason looked at him, taking in the drawn look on his face. "Everything okay, old man? You still doing good with your sister's kids?"

"Yeah," he responded. "It's all good, Prez."

After he left, Mason finished his beer, rolling the bottle between his hands. Tug sat beside him, seemingly patient. Mason said, "Shit's sideways with him. I don't have a handle on it yet, but shit is definitely sideways." He turned to look at a table of men across the room, only half of which would meet his gaze. "Shit's sideways in the chapter, too, Tugboat. We'll have to sort this sooner rather than later."

"Yeah, but not today." Tug leaned back, propping the heel of one boot on the stool rung.

"Nope, not today." He sighed, and then said her name softly, "Willa." He paused, closing his eyes for a moment, then directed, "Tell me what you know, old man."

Tug took a deep breath, blowing it out, ruffling the edges of his mustache. "She's best friends with Eddie, Shooter's gal. I don't know much about her, boss. I saw them out together once, and I thought there was a chance Judge had something going on there. She was awful excited to see him, even though he was pissed as hell they were out drinking." He looked over at Mason. "Honestly, Prez, it's about all I know. You want me to do a sweep?"

"Yeah. Find out what there is to know." He nodded, remembering the way she watched him, thinking again of her body. When he imagined fucking her, it wasn't like he generally took his pleasure. He had thought about taking her as he had Mica, soft and slow, buried balls-deep inside her pussy, watching her break underneath him. Tonight, in the clubhouse, even fully dressed and without employing any touch, she had responded to him in ways he hadn't expected. Her nipples tightening and arching up for his mouth, looking like pencil erasers through the thin dress. "Find out everything."

Mason shook his head, pushing his arousal back with some effort. "Judge was asking about Texas."

At his statement, Tug sighed and reached up to rub across his new scar from the thump on the head he took in Houston from Mica's ex. He had been knocked out for most of the fight with Ray Nelms, had only come to when Mason and Slate were dragging the bound and unconscious man towards their horse trailer. "What was he wanting to know?" Tug chanced a glance, and Mason grinned humorlessly at him.

"He was only digging. There isn't anything to know. Nelms isn't breathing her air anymore. Slate's man, Blackie, came through for us. His boys took care of the trash, both in Houston and Longview." Tug sucked in a breath; this was the first time Mason had implied he was behind Mica's father's disappearance. He nodded in response, acknowledging what Tug had already figured out. "Yeah, Scott's buried somewhere west of Longview. You didn't see the motherfucker standing there, bald-faced and proud of what he'd done to our girl. It wasn't enough what he'd done to Mica, but then he stood there and threatened her baby sister. After everything Nelms had done to her...to both of them, and then he thought he could threaten her, too."

Tug shook his head, the look on his face somber. "You'll get no judgment from me, man." He pounded his chest three times. "She's a fucking treasure."

Mason shook himself, standing and stretching. "I gotta get in the wind so I can bring her home, brother. See you in Chicago."

"Yeah, Prez. Safe travels, man." Tug clasped his shoulder, and Mason walked away.

On his ride back to Chicago, he had ample topics to keep his mind occupied, mostly surrounding Mica and their busy past few months. She had settled into a steady relationship with Rupert; it had been hard to watch, but pleasant to see her get the sweet after everything they had been through. Then her ex raised his piss-ant head again, stripping everything from her.

After Nelms had threatened her friends, she broke things off with Daniel, tried to cut everyone out of her life, attempted to go it alone. Mason hadn't put up with her shit, forcing himself and the club back into her circle. He went along with her when she didn't want to tell Daniel what was going on. If he was honest with himself—here, he snorted, because he was arguing with himself in his own fucking head. *Who else would I be honest with?* If he were honest with himself, he would admit he went along, because he hoped it meant she didn't think Daniel was strong enough to be with her during hard fucking times.

In response, he kept her safe and kept her secrets. For weeks, he danced around what she wanted, pushed up against what he knew needed to be done. Then, her cousin came to town, bearing news her ex, Nelms, had reached out and snared a member of her family, dragging them into her nightmare. His Rebels made a move to track him, but the man slipped their net in Texarkana. Finally, they caught a break, because his own trap set in Houston backfired, and then they had him.

Mason shuddered, thinking of how Mica looked, small form huddled on the ground with her worst nightmare rearing over her, the vicious expression on his face telegraphing his intent to kill her. He was fully certain if they hadn't stopped him, Nelms would have murdered her. He had already drugged and raped her baby sister, leaving the girl pregnant in an effort to get Mica home. With the level of planning required for his plays, and in the wake of his twisted evil, killing the woman who dared to escape him years ago had to be on his agenda.

But, they saved her. In the end, they pulled it off, getting there in time. Saved her and handed Nelms off to a Texas club Slate held markers with, and those men had taken care of the cowboy in a permanent way. Mason had pictures to prove it, showing Nelms lying twisted in a ditch, sand shoveled over his face. He kept that picture for a while, long after her bruises faded. He kept looking at it because of the hurt the man had caused the woman he loved. He looked until his rage finally subsided, when he knew she realized it was over.

He saw a flash of Willa's face and shook his head.

But then Mica got stuck. She wouldn't come home, so he stayed in Texas with her for weeks. She had a thousand excuses not to go back to Chicago, excuses about her family, her sister. It wasn't until he got her drunk that he found out the real reason she refused to leave—because she feared what her daddy would do to her sister in her absence.

Mica had been a magnet for heartbreak since she was in her early teens, with her mother dying too soon. Her father, sick bastard that he was, had turned to Mica for his physical release, molesting her for the first time only days after they laid her mother in the ground. When she was a senior in high school, she was finally beginning to plan ahead, readying herself for adult life, when her father had brutally raped her best friend.

In an effort to save her friend from small town humiliation, heavily influenced by the guilt Mica felt because she hadn't been able to stop the attack, she testified against her father, telling everything he had done to her over the years. The things he did left scars on her, both physical and emotional, and Mason had seen their aftermath come to the surface many times in the years he had known her. Recently released from jail when they arrived in Texas, her father had stood in front of Mica mouthing off about her baby sister, Molly. In that un-fucking-tenable situation, of course, Mica would want to stay where she could protect Molly. He shook his head. *Of course, she would.*

Once he caught sight of the truth and recognized the shape of her fear, Mason arranged for the same bike club to pick up Trenton Scott. When they understood the need, when he explained the source of her pain, the club had dealt with Scott with no expectations of debt or repayment. No marker needed. They simply took care of the entire business, and he was grateful. That was another picture Mason held on to for a long time: the sick fuck's weeping face turned upwards from the deep hole he was in, sunshine barely reaching him as the dump truck's bed began to tilt, sliding its payload into the hole, burying the man like the filth he was.

Everything had come to a head about a month ago, and recently he got the feeling Mica understood her father wasn't off on a post-prison bender, but actually wouldn't be coming back to their family ranch. Ever. The last time he called and spoke to her, there was a definite sense of homesickness in her questioning about their friends. He was willing to make a bet their girl was finally ready to come home, even if she hadn't yet admitted it to herself.

She needed to be home, and he needed her there, even if Daniel was the right man for her. Even if he could only watch from the sidelines. She made him better, made him want...more. At the thought of more, an image of Willa flashed in his head again, and this time he allowed it to linger, thinking again of the only touch that passed between them tonight. The brush of her hand light on his as she took the initiative and tucked her phone number into his palm. Even the memory of that slim contact was enough to make his cock begin to stiffen, and he laughed at the absurdity of flying up the Dan Ryan with a boner.

16. Heartbreak

"Goddammit," he muttered, angrily rolling and stuffing a few pieces of clothing into a bag. Last night should not have fucking happened. *My head is so fucking messed up right now. I want a goddamned, fucking cig*, he thought then snorted. Even his thoughts sounded angry in his own head. A soft noise sounded, the rustle of bedsheets against bare skin, and he glanced up, eyes catching on the small figure stirring in the bed. He studied her reflection in the mirror fastened to the hotel wall, futilely trying to maintain a mental distance from her.

Last night, she caught him off guard, using his own words against him as she lowered to her knees, his cock in her hands...her mouth. His attempts to run her off backfiring as she leaned in and kissed his tattoo, the one she never knew was because of her, the phrase reminding him every day he could never be worthy of her, that his love for her had no place. *We accept the love we believe we deserve.* Looking up at him, with one breath, she told him they were all wrong for each other, told him he would never be able to let her in all the way, never be able to let her love him because of who he was. Then, with her next, she said what he most wanted to hear, giving him something he never dreamed he would be lucky enough to have again. She gave him her. "But we can have sometimes, when there is need. Let me be your sometimes...until you find your always. We can have this."

And, he let her. Never taking his eyes off her, he watched as her lips enveloped him, feeling the heat and softness of her mouth surrounding his hard, throbbing cock. Watching as her hand tried and failed to encircle the girth of his dick, small fingers jacking him in counterpoint to the movements of her head. He placed his hands on either side of her head, not directing her, simply wanting...needing to touch her. Under his palms, he felt her cheeks hollow as she sucked hard on the crown of his cock, felt her jaw open as she worked her tongue across the slit at the top, absorbed the vibrations of her moan when she tasted the pre-come she found there. "God, babe," he groaned. "You feel fucking perfect, mouth on me. Fucking perfect mouth."

Her sea-green eyes had fluttered and closed as she worked his cock, but every time they opened, he locked his gaze on hers, wanting to hold onto the intimacy of the moment. Leaning against the wall, he widened his stance, silently inviting her hands to wander, to explore, and she did exactly what he wanted. Keeping her mouth moving on his cock, she used her fingers to thread and pull her way through the dark hair surrounding the base of his shaft and balls, caressing and weighing his sac in her palm, framing the root with her fingers and shifting back to stroke his length again.

Encouraging her, he said, "Just like...mmmm, babe. So fucking good. Everything you do feels so fucking good." Her mouth on him had been utter fucking perfection, hot and tight, tongue dancing along the ridge of the head, mixed in with just an edge of teeth. Sucking him into her mouth and to the back of her throat again and again, for long minutes she teased and pleased him. Bringing him to the brink, tonguing along the veins standing out on the surface of his cock and then backing off with soft kisses and gently blown air across the head.

He reached down, pulling her off him and to her feet, drawing her up the length of him, feeling his slick cock pressing into her still-clothed belly as he kissed her. Under his questing lips, he felt hers, swollen from sucking him, responding, kissing him back. Beginning slowly, he licked along the seam of her lips with his tongue, silently demanding entrance, and she gave way, opening to him. Softly, he stroked his tongue into her mouth, twining with hers and tasting the bitterness of his own fluids. Her eager reaction had him groaning into her. He held her delicately, his hands cupping her face, holding her to him while he caressed the skin over her cheekbones with his thumbs. Murmuring against her lips, he asked her, "My sometimes?"

At her nod, the acknowledgement of what they were doing, his hands tightened and he leaned in, trapping her lips beneath his, devouring her. Twisting, he put her back to the wall and pressed against her, feeling his cock throb between them, hearing her gasp softly at the single-minded way he pursued her. Pulling back when he felt her tremble, he wrapped his arms around her, lifting and carrying her to the bed. Give her sweet, *he thought desperately.* Let *her see the sweet.*

Still holding her, he reached down and swept the comforter and blankets to the floor, settling her into the middle of the bed, her tanned skin in dark contrast to the white sheet. He wouldn't let her hide from him this time, obscuring her curves and body with concealing covers. "So fucking beautiful, babe," he said. Breathing hard as he looked down at her where she waited for him, he palmed his cock and muttered, "Not sure I can put you aside again. My sometimes."

"Then don't, Mason," she whispered, raising her arms to welcome him. Stooping over her, he lifted one hand to her face again, his palm caressing up her throat until he cupped her cheek as he bent to cover her lips with his, kissing her with tightly reined hunger.

His other hand worked at the snap of her jeans, and he tugged them down her legs, staring up at her in frustration when they caught on her boots. Find the sweet. *Squatting beside the bed, he watched her face as he unlaced the boots, slipping them from her feet and, one at a time, tossing them carelessly over his shoulder, drawing a quick laugh from her as they thudded into the wall.* There it is.

Pulling her jeans off, he tucked a long finger into each sock, sliding them down and off her feet, drawing her toes to his mouth and pretending to bite them, wanting...needing to hear her free-sounding laugh again. Finally, he smiled up at her when it echoed through the room, light and bright and so fucking her. *"Don't eat me," she said, and then blushed when the double meaning of the words caught up to her.*

He gazed up her body, taking in the perfection laid out before him, his mouth opening in a hungry gasp when he saw the wetness saturating her panties. Those pretty satin panties, very nearly the color of her eyes, now dark with promise between her legs, because she wanted him. Him. *She wanted him...in her mouth, in her body. "Babe." There was a tone to his voice he only remembered one other time, when he had her in her bed. "Sucking me make you hot?" She made a noise he took to be agreement as, naked, he prowled up her body, trailing kisses and touches with his tongue as he moved, his fingers tracing invisible designs on her skin. Slipping his shoulders between her legs, he used his fingers to stretch the fabric over her mound, licking his lips as it outlined every line and fold of her pussy.*

Moving his mouth closer, he nuzzled against her, smelling the deliciously musky scent he remembered from before. "Fucking loved eating you, babe," he muttered, opening his mouth and sucking her panties between his lips. "Couldn't get your taste out of my head for weeks. Can't wait to get my mouth on you again." Stiffening his tongue, he traced the center of her core, pressing the fabric between her pussy lips until he came to the hardened nub at the top, dragging a sigh from her as he pressed and flicked hard against it.

He sat up and reached out to strip her panties from her body. Muscles tense with need, his cock was throbbing in demand, and he told her brusquely, "Take off your shirt, babe." She sat up, pulling the shirt over her head, disheveling her braid further, and he watched as she unfastened her bra and discarded it, unbidden. He drew a hard breath at the sight of her breasts tumbling free, trembling and shaking with each gasp she dragged in through parted lips. "Mica, I want my hands on you."

He knew she wouldn't understand the importance of his next words, but said them for himself, to cement the difference between her and the women he had fucked over the years. "Want your hands on me. Babe, I want to hear you. Want my name on your lips. No holding back. If this is my last chance with you, then I fucking. Want. Everything." She nodded and leaned forward, kissing him hard, licking his lips, stripping the faint flavor of her pussy from his mouth.

He moved back between her legs, using his thumbs to open her, putting her delicate folds and nerve-laden flesh at his mercy and on display. Remembering what she liked, he licked her hard, asshole to clit, not rimming her but coming close before moving up. Trapping her swollen clit between his lips, fluttering the tip of his tongue across it a dozen times, he worked to bring cry after hard cry to her lips. He felt her hands on his head, pushing the short hair back, her fingertips tracing across his brow and down his temple. Her hand moved down to find his, where he held her open, and she curled her fingers around him, seemingly needing the touch.

Mason shifted and fucked her with his tongue, lapping up her wetness, eating at her as if he were starving for her, which he had been. For months, he had been a starving man. Every time she rode on the back of his bike, he imagined her like this, her pretty pussy spread out for him to feast on. Each glancing touch, each moment spent in her company since then, he had wanted her under him.

Grinding his erection into the mattress, ignoring his own desire, he pushed a finger inside her, listening to the keening sound she made, her hand tightening on his. His gaze flicked up her body, watching as her mouth opened and closed, lips tucked between her teeth with a sigh of his name. "Want to hear you," he reminded her, and ate at her when her *eyes fluttered open, that beautiful sea-green drinking him in for a moment before her lids sank closed again.*

Slipping his hand free of hers, he pushed it underneath her ass, lifting her hips to his mouth. He nearly faltered when his fingertips felt the scars covering her cheeks, remembering the first time he saw them, knowing what they meant even before she shared her secrets with him.

She was so broken when he first met her, so determined to make her own way and afraid to ask for help with anything. It had taken her thirty minutes one day to ask him to look at her car, because she didn't want to give anything of herself away, and asking for help meant accepting people would know bits of you. With pride now, he watched as her eyes opened, her gaze finding his as she called his name again, "Mason." Not broken any longer, this woman wasn't afraid to ask for what she wanted, and he felt her hands on his head, pulling his mouth tightly against her, demanding what would take her over the top, the movements and touches that would bring her the most pleasure. "Please," she pleaded hoarsely, and he smiled, his mouth still on her. It was with satisfaction he brought her to the brink, wanting to see her slide over the edge of the wave, knowing he would be at the bottom to catch her and lift her high again. Knowing he had all night to make her come, make her cry his name, to fuck her like he dreamed of every night. To love her.

Now, he stood there, watching as she woke, knowing nothing would be the same. There was no way he could go back again, wouldn't allow them to make the transition back to merely friends after being inside her. Feeling her clench around his cock as she came a second time from his deep, rhythmic thrusts, then feeling her come again, when he pressed hard on her clit with his rough thumb, drawing his name in a deep groan from her lips. He reached down now, adjusting himself in his jeans, and looked back up to find her smiling at him.

"Mornin', Mason," she said softly, her voice rough with sleep. She sat up and yawned, stretching with the sheet in her hands, the silhouette of her body showing through the cotton.

"Babe." That one word was all he could choke out, because for a moment, he thought he had seen love on her face. He hoped.

***

He knew he told Slate to accept no arguments from Daniel about attending the party, but their conversation had been two days ago, and now he prayed, for once, that his second was unsuccessful at something. Turning onto their street, he motioned for Mica to take the lead, watching with pride as she swayed the bike around him, taking point in their procession of two. He saw her falter as she looked ahead, seeing for the first time the large number of bikes lining the street near their houses. But then he saw that damn chin come up and could nearly feel the determination radiating off of her.

Pulling in beside her, he looked around and, with a grateful sigh, realized Daniel wasn't there. His brothers, Dickie and J.J., were, but no Daniel. *Goddamn, the stupid motherfucker isn't going to show*. Finally, something was going to go his way without it being hard. Motioning for Mica to park her bike, he rode to his own garage, backing his pipes to the building before he put down his kickstand. Eyes never leaving her, he watched as she confidently backed onto the pad his boys had poured for her a while back. Saw her take off the helmet and reflexively reach up to smooth her hair down as she looked around, a slow grin on her lips. Every gesture was graceful, and brought him back to last night, her body moving underneath his.

Mine. The thought prowled through his mind, and he watched her affectionately greet his brothers, not even realizing he was moving until he came up behind her, gripping her around the waist possessively. For the next hour, he walked the party with her, his hands always on her, claiming and marking her as his own. He was always protective of her, but this was different. This was stingy, selfish behavior, because he believed she had given herself to him entirely. Her words named it 'sometimes,' while her body said 'always.'

Standing beside her, he felt a persistent buzzing in his pocket and pulled out his phone, surprised to read Shooter's information on the screen. "Babe," he said, leaning down to brush her lips with his as he had done a dozen times since they arrived home. "I need to take this." She nodded and smiled up at him from her position on a blanket then turned to continue her conversation with Road Runner and Jess.

"Yeah?" He put the phone to his ear, walking away towards the back of Mica's house, where Slate stood on the porch with Tug and Myron.

"I need your help." The request was spoken plainly, no opening greeting to soften him up. He grunted but stayed silent, listening. "I'm having problems with a club here in Cali. Motherfuckers think they can jack my shipments whenever they are running low on cash."

"Why would that be my problem?" He was genuinely curious, because this wasn't something he and Shooter did. They didn't ask each other for favors; it wasn't in their nature. Didn't fit their uneasy relationship.

"I'd like to think because it's my problem," Shooter laughed. "Mostly it's because Deacon is part of their crew. You released him, man. Doesn't it make you responsible for his actions?"

"Fuck you," Mason said. "Man runs his own life, so it sure as shit isn't my problem if he's fucking up yet again. Old man screwed himself in Florida and Texas, outwore his welcome there in a hard way; it sounds as if he's traveling the same road now in Cali. Hell, you've met with him and encouraged him through the years to pull all kinds of shit. Enjoy, man. He was your president before he was mine." Mason laughed at the groan he caught over the phone. "Seriously, how the hell are you getting jacked? They got someone inside the Outriders?"

"Fuck if I know." The frustration Shooter was feeling was right there in his voice, riding the waves of anger and betrayal. If the other club had someone inside, then it meant a brother, someone Shooter trusted, had turned traitor. For that man, whomever it was, it wouldn't be something survived if true.

Mason made out a shouted name and his head whipped up, his heart sinking and pain blooming in his chest when he recognized the man in a suit headed his way. "Lemme think on it, figure out if there's anything I can find out. I gotta go, brother," he said and disconnected the call.

Daniel had showed after all, looking every inch the successful businessman he was, walking across the yard in a tailored suit and silk tie. *Mica never got to see me like that*, he thought, and realized he was already thinking about her in past tense. Mason had always kept a distance between them, and now he frowned at the realization of just how separate he held her from everything else. He had only ever given her the biker part of him, but not even all of that, only the parts he thought she would be able to stomach. Not the father and family man he was...wanted to be. Not the harder parts of himself. He never showed her the man he could be when protecting his own. Even having her last night, he only gave her sweet, telling himself it was what she needed, not the sharper edge of his desires.

Oh, she saw pieces of his hard side once, the first time she met Daniel. He had been amused when she felt remorse over his minor injuries from the fight. So fucking minor, but he had goddamn well taken care of business when he had to, and she never asked about what she had seen during the fight. *Maybe she was still wearing the blinders you gave her*, he thought, snorting a laugh as he watched Daniel walk up the steps onto the back porch.

"Hey, man, glad you could make it." Mason held out his hand, struggling to keep from clamping down tightly during the shake, quickly shifting to a forearm grip to remove the temptation to hurt the motherfucker, a hard ache taking up residence in his chest.

Stepping back and tucking his hands into his pockets, Daniel looked at him and nodded, probably going over the last conversation they had. The one where Mason had told him he was going to Texas to bring Mica home, and called him a stupid motherfucker. He told him he would be making a play for her love. After a minute, Daniel asked softly, "You got her to come home?"

Mason nodded. "Yeah. It was time; she was finally ready." He held a hand out, pointing towards the grill where Mica lay on the blanket, hidden by the crowds between the porch and her. "She's over there." He saw with surprise his hand was steady, even as he felt a liquid tearing in his chest, breaking the pain apart and giving him room to speak. "She's good, man. You should go talk to her." He paused, taking in a breath. "She'll want to see you."

"Yeah, all right." Daniel ducked his head and then cut his gaze back to Mason's face. "We okay?"

"Yeah. It's all good, Daniel," Mason lied, turning his back and dismissing the man to go and...claim Mica. That's what he had just granted permission for Rupert to do. For the last time, he had given her away.

Clenching his jaw hard, he looked at the men left standing on the porch with him and saw understanding on their faces, which somehow made everything worse. Looking at Tug, he opted for club business over personal, saying brusquely, "Shooter's having problems with a club in Cali."

Tug nodded. "Judge said as much the last time I talked to him. Some club from the south of Diego is dogging Shooter's ass every time he turns around."

Mason scrubbed across his jaw. "Shooter said Deacon rides with this club." From Tug's plain look of surprise, he didn't know this tidbit, and Mason felt better for providing information, being the first to know.

He turned, protectively putting the wall of the house at his back and casually seating himself in one of the patio chairs, knowing he wasn't fooling his brothers. He watched as Daniel made his way across the width of the yard, noting as he stopped occasionally to speak to people. He recognized the exact moment when the man saw Mica, identified it by the stillness that swept across his frame, knew it from how the muscles of his shoulders and back tensed. Mica might have run from their relationship first, but he had been the one to reject her a few weeks ago, and this meeting could go either way.

Mason closed his eyes briefly when Mica stood, meeting Daniel halfway, and when he opened them again, he saw her reaching out to twine her fingers with his. He turned away, and for a moment thought he heard Shooter's voice again, telling him as he had weeks ago, *She was never going to be yours*.

A minute later, and her soft voice stole gently across his skin as she asked Mason to walk with them, with her and Daniel, and he couldn't find it in himself to tell her no. He had to see with his own eyes this was what she wanted, what she needed. Standing close as she told Daniel about the ride up, and how much fun she had learning to handle the motorcycle, Mason was swept with a wave of both pride and longing...and loss, because her love for Daniel shone so brightly. If the man couldn't glimpse it, he had to be blind. What he had seen on her face this morning wasn't love, at least not love like this. His sense of loss was so strong Mason had to step back, folding his arms across his chest to try and give himself some separation from them, and damned if she didn't reach up, untucking one of his hands and clasping it in hers.

She pulled his hand to her chest and he felt the softness of her breasts on his fingers for a moment before he felt the hardness of the back of Daniel's hand pressed against his. She wasn't looking at either of them, simply staring across the crowd and holding their hands against her in an unconscious representation of their triangle relationship, him on one side of her, and Daniel on the other. Pinned between the two men, Mica was joyous and giggling, unaware of the rage and desire sweeping through him feeling her touching him while seeing Daniel's hand in hers. Rising to her toes to kiss each man on the cheek, she settled back onto her heels, still holding their hands, happiness radiating from her.

He met Daniel's eyes over the top of her head, and Mason felt that liquid shattering in his chest again. The moment where they stood as equals in her affection passed, and Mason watched jealously as Daniel gathered her to his chest with his free hand, nuzzling into the side of her face, dropping kisses along the edge of her jaw. Each movement, every breath, seemed to sink punishing knives into him, the vicious pain swelling and growing inside him as he could see the undisputed ownership in the other man's actions.

This morning, she was mine, he thought bitterly, interrupted when Slate called his name from across the crowd. One word was enough: Tucker. The prospect who disrespected the club's princess, the prospect they drubbed out of the club months ago. Seems the man had finally surfaced, and now, here Mason was—he looked back at Mica, watching as she smiled sweetly at something Daniel whispered in her ear—putting the club first. As he always knew he would have to, he had to walk away. She had never been his. Would never be his. He reached down and touched the lump he carried in his pocket, the state of mind usually evoked by the brilliant green sea glass now entirely too far out of reach.

He took in a breath and uncurled his hand from around Mica's, softly telling her, "Back in a bit, got club business to deal with, babe. Stay here." He looked Daniel in the face, their gazes locking as Mason challenged him, hoping the man would recognize the charge as what it was, his relinquishment of the woman. "Keep her safe, brother."

Not waiting for a response, he turned and moved across the yard, hearing first Slate, then his other men, fall into formation behind as they swept through the crowd. He felt the soles of his boots thudding heavily onto the ground, striding steadily towards the business that made him finally sift through his dreams of a relationship with Mica like dust.

17. Find love again

"What the hell do I know about being a full-time father?" He asked the question without expecting a response, somewhat surprised when one came.

"Seems like you're doing a pretty good job so far, Prez." Tug looked over at him, lifting his liquor-filled glass in a mocking salute. "You just love 'em. Love on 'em, correct 'em when they're wrong, whup their ass when they need it. Just do what you're doin', Mason."

He nodded, looking around his living room. "Nearly a fucking man, my boy. He tries to fight with me all the time. I'm not sure what the motivation is anymore. I wondered at first if he was feelin' guilty about missing Carrie when she dropped him off like she did. Lately, it simply seems he hates me instead of her. She hadn't even told him she was gonna dump him. It's how he feels, you know? Like she dumped him. There isn't any joy in this for him, not that I can catch hold of anyway. I'm so fucking glad he's finally here with me. It's what I wanted every moment since I found out about him, but he can't see past whatever's in his mind." Mason sighed, letting his head lean back against the couch.

A couple months ago, Chase's mom had brought him to Jackson's and dropped him off with no warning, accompanied only by a small bag of dirty clothes. In the years since Mason learned about him, Chase had resisted even coming to visit his dad in Chicago; forget anything about moving there.

Because of it, Mason faithfully made his trips to Kentucky twice a month. Chase had been happy enough to stay at the small apartment, seeming to enjoy the days spent there with Mason and whichever of his most trusted brothers could make the run. He had kept the knowledge of his boy tight during that time, since Chase was not in a position where access could be controlled, and it made it hard to protect him. He didn't want to give any enemies thoughts of leverage, but more, he wanted…needed to keep his boy safe.

Then the decision was taken entirely out of his hands by the same bitch who kept them apart for twelve years. She threw them together, mixing oil and gasoline with a careless stir, and they hadn't heard from her since she drove off the lot in a spin of smoke and rubber. Since then, Chase had been bouncing between Mason's house and the clubhouse, pretty much staying wherever Mason wasn't at the time.

"How's the recruiting coming, boss man?" Tug laughed. "You sure about this one? I'm still not seeing it, Mason. He's a nice guy, but patching in the hockey player? You sure?"

"Yeah, Jase will be a good fit. Man fucking loves my cousin, but how in the hell he believes he's going to be able to do anything from here is beyond me. Hell, why she's running is beyond me too. She should know the hunt only makes things even more interesting for a man like Jase Spencer." He laughed; Jase was another fucking hockey player, best friends with Daniel. He had hooked up with DeeDee after Mica's party a few months ago, had bravely wooed her in full sight of all the club members. Mason thought things were going somewhere, but then she bolted, heading back to Fort Wayne early, and then holing up in her suite at the clubhouse.

"Did you set that up?" Tug asked, and Mason grinned.

"Nope, that one wasn't me. Hell, you were the one who pushed her, from what I understood. Brothers were talking about the dance between you boys and her for weeks, man. In any case, in every way, she needs him. And, we need him. I can spy where he fits, long term. There's a certain satisfaction in pressing a puzzle piece into place, feeling how it locks there where it fits so well." *Fuck, I need to stop drinking*, he thought. *My mouth is running too much tonight.*

"Bear settling into place, too?" Tug leaned his head back, mimicking Mason's posture.

"Jesus fuck, man, I can't figure him out. Just when I think he's back in a decent place, I find him back on the fucking brink again. I simply want him healthy, ya know? Nothing more or less than healthy and sane." Mason sighed. "Pike, Slate, Bear, Tater, K.C., hell...every-fucking-body has baggage, man. You're the only one I know without a history fucking with your head. Fucking baggage."

Tug laughed loudly. "You never got to meet my old lady, did you?"

Mason shook his head twice, rolling it so he could look at his friend. "Nope. I think the night I met you, the night you were on bike gardia...guardnian...fuck." He took a breath, blew it out noisily, and then continued, speaking deliberately, "...guard duty, *fuck*, she was already gone, wasn't she? The night Shooter tried to fucking kill me. *Again*. How many fucking times was *that*...fuck. Bastard. But you'd already lost her by then, right?"

"Yeah, she was gone." He recognized the deep sadness in Tug's voice and found himself longing for even the bone-grinding anguish of that emotion. Sorrow so rich and intense could only mean their love had been strong, a passion matching or even greater than the grief that still abided years later. He wanted to know how his friend had managed to have such an intense love with a woman, and still have the club, too.

"Was she a good one?" Mason asked. "Good with the life? Did you ever think she might have been better out of it?"

"Fuck no, she was terrible before the club. I never doubted she was the one for me; she was fucking born for the life. Except for our families, she turned her back on everything to do with her government name as soon as someone gave her a moniker. Nytro." He smiled, looking up, but evidently seeing something other than the ceiling. "She was hot, wild, a little out of control all the time, and un-fucking-stable the rest of it. The best old lady I could have ever wished for."

"Does it ever get better? When you lose someone...someone you love like that? I look at Bear, man, and he's hurting all the fucking time. Is love worth it?" Mason dragged a hand roughly across his face. "Fuck, I'm too drunk to talk shit like this. Ignore me, brother."

"It gets easier, but it's never better. From what I've seen, I think you have to find love again for it to get better. I know I ain't there yet, but I think Bear will get there eventually. I hope you do, too, Prez. Love, yeah. Love is always worth the struggle." Tug lifted his glass, seemingly surprised when it was empty.

Mason held out his glass, and Tug let him pour a splash inside before they clinked the glasses together, grinning. "Here's to both of us finding love again."

18. Guilt and pain

Mason leaned back in his chair, looking out at the crowd gathered in the sunshine streaming down into the backyard of the St. Louis clubhouse. Months ago, he had nearly closed the chapter here after finding out some of the members were not following the main club laws. Bear and Tug had talked him into keeping the chapter open, but he made certain their president, Pike, knew his own continued good health depended on following the straight and narrow where the three tenets were concerned.

It had proven to be the right decision, and tonight was his validation, seeing the members and their families enjoying the party and each other. He brought in a dozen non-officer members each from Chicago, Fort Wayne, Kansas City, Memphis, and Little Rock, because as Gunny had pointed out to him once, it was important the different chapters have familiarity with each other. Building a sense of family—brotherhood—was important to him. To them all.

Members and officers circled around where Mason had seated himself, moving in patterns all night long that were both interesting and telling to watch. He could tell the chapter officers who had problems with other chapters by their avoidance or aggressive approach. He made mental notes about needed conversations either with him, or with Bear and Slate, the two men he seemed to lean on more and more. He kept both men busy, sending them out to the remote chapters for weeks at a time, gathering intel not only on the chapter members, but also local LEO, and town or city politicians.

Expanding their base of operations meant more relationships to manage, and not only within the club, but also with the citizens who infringed on their businesses. So far, he had been able to manipulate most events to their advantage, but much of it was putting the right peg into place at the right time. He had been fortunate so far in finding the right people or opportunities. He would have to find another piece to his puzzle soon; he had given Fort Wayne to Slate not long ago when Bingo stepped down as president. This would be one of his last runs with the man for a while, because Slate now had shit of his own to deal with in the Fort.

Mason grinned, watching as an entire herd of kids played on the playground, sliding and swinging on equipment bought from a school that was upgrading theirs. The money went to a good cause on both sides of the equation, because it helped the school out at the same time it delivered the unspoken message to members that family was not only welcome, but expected. This kind of subtle reinforcement helped retain the good men they needed, letting them know having families wasn't an automatic reason to patch out, as some clubs did.

His eyes flicked up and over, catching a glimpse of a body moving purposefully through the crowd straight at him. The look on Slate's face drew him to his feet and his chin lowered slightly as he read the desperation and fear there. Before the man could even open his mouth, Mason was saying, "Tell me."

"Bear hasn't checked in for too long, Prez. He's in Des Moines, and I have a feeling something's gone sideways." Slate pulled at the back of his neck nervously. "His last message said he found shit and he gave me four names. When I call up to Des Moines, no one's seen any of them for a day or more. Mason, something's gone sideways. I know it."

Mason pulled out his phone and tapped a speed dial number. He put the call on speaker and stepped towards the clubhouse wall, gesturing for Slate to follow him. "Myron," he spoke over the other man's greeting. "Track Bear's phone."

"On it," they heard, followed by rapid tapping of computer keys. "Just outside Des Moines in a rural area. It looks like it hasn't moved for about ten hours, boss. You want a location?"

"Yeah, text it to me, Slate, Goose…and Pike." Goose was the club's EMT, a good man, trustworthy and dependable, and might be necessary if things had gone bad for Bear. As for Pike, well, he might as well get this lesson out there, if things turned out the way he suspected. "We're heading out now, and I think we're—"

He looked his question at Slate, who supplied, "About six hours out."

Mason continued speaking, shortening the time frame, knowing how they were going to ride. "—four hours. Stay on his phone. Slate's going to send you some additional numbers to track. If anything changes between now and then, you buzz the four of us again, okay?"

"You got it, boss. Need anything else waiting for you?" Myron was a list-making planner, and it usually made Mason grin, but today he was grimly glad of the trait.

"Yeah, make sure someone in Des Moines can get a good kit for Goose. I'm sure he's got stuff with him, he usually does, but if Slate's right, he's gonna need more. I'll talk to the men there in town. Don't show my hand, brother." As he waited for Myron's acknowledgement, Mason looked at Slate, who nodded. "We're in the wind, Myron."

"Okay. Ride safe, boss." Mason disconnected the call, looking over at Goose and Pike, who were staring at him, phones in hand. With a nod, he sent them to the parking lot while he went over to talk to Tug, whom he would leave in charge here in his absence.

***

Riding up to the edge of the clearing where the abandoned warehouse sat, Mason lifted a fisted hand, pulling the column of motorcycles to a quiet halt. He killed his engine, heeling down the stand and lifting off the bike in a single, smooth movement. Pulling his earpiece off, he tucked it into the pocket of his jeans, turning his head and freezing into place for a moment as a gasping scream came from inside the building. He swept his gaze in a circle, marking each man's face, cataloging the fear and anger on their features. He said, "Myron was able to remotely activate Bear's phone. Our brother is in there hurting, and there are four traitors to our club doing their best to break him. Trust me when I say you do not want to listen to what I've heard for the last half-hour."

He looked around at the men he had picked for this run. The group was not only the three he left St. Louis with, having been filled out as they passed through both Kansas City and Des Moines by officers, as well as officers and visitors from other chapters they had picked up along the way. Five chapter presidents and twelve other officers stood here to take in today's business, and, *please, God*, let it force them to study their own members with a more jaundiced eye to keep this shit from happening a-fucking-gain.

"We go in hard and hot. I don't give a fuck if any of those four survive, but for the information they might still hold." Pulling his gun from the holster in his waistband, he locked his gaze with the Des Moines president. "Tater, these men are your responsibility. You tell me right the fuck now if you won't be able to deal with whatever shit we find."

The big, red-haired biker ducked his chin but kept his eyes on Mason. Unblinking, he said, "I got this, Prez. My chapter, my charter...my fucking mess. It's on me."

Mason reached out, clasping the man's shoulder. "It's on all of us. Rebels forever—" His mouth stretched into a grim line as the men around him echoed the rest of the statement. "Forever Rebels."

An hour later, he leaned on his bike's seat, watching as club members trailed in and out of the warehouse, carrying bags and crates of weapons. He reached into his shirt pocket, pulling out a crumpled pack of smokes, looking at the package in his hand for a minute. With a sigh, he shook one out, replacing the cigs in his pocket, flicking open his lighter with one hand. He took a deep draw off the cigarette as he lit it, the scent of burning tobacco replacing the stench of fear and blood in his nostrils.

"Gonna have to shave again, man," he heard and half turned, watching Slate walk up beside him.

"Yeah," he grunted, seeing a dozen members coming out in pairs, carrying heavy bags between them. These bags had handles on either end, and they swayed and bent in the middle as the burdens inside shifted with the movements of their attendants. Tater stood in the doorway, holding it open for the laden men with the heel of his boot. He looked over, catching Mason's eye, and nodded. Mason told Slate, "Alrighty, everything's out of the building. Let's torch this mother."

Slate yelled across the weed-covered lot, calling in several members waiting there with gas cans, sending them in so they could prepare the building for the purge needed to cover evidence of the deaths that happened here today. Mason watched them moving in, and then asked, "You hear back from Goose yet?"

"Yeah, he said it's mostly what he expected to find. They're already on their way back to Chicago. He said he's going to lock Bear in a room at the clubhouse for a couple days until he's breathing okay." He cut a glance over at Mason, and the weight of that look settled on his shoulders. "This isn't your fault, Prez. He knew better than to go it alone like he did. He's worked this shit long enough. I've worked with him enough to know he was aware of the danger."

Shaking his head, Mason grimaced and said, "That's the whole fucking point, man. He knew it. Had full knowledge of the danger, but did it anyway. Fucked his own track, knew it, and did it anyhow. He's been going at this for a while now; I don't know how we can keep him from hurting himself. I've never met anyone with as deep a self-destructive streak as he has, and it fucking breaks my heart. It's been a decade since he lost his family. Hell, he's been a Rebel for years, part of our inner circle nearly since he patched in, and I can't seem to find a way to help him. I can't find the shine, man."

Slate nodded, his mouth drawn down in regret. "I've seen the same, but he's better now. Seems like as long as we get him back to Fort Wayne every few weeks, he's better. I wish he'd take the jump where Eddie's concerned. Motherfucker wants her; this much is clear. I'm not sure why he's balking at the connection."

"Probably because both Tug and I waved him off his approach, man." Mason laughed harshly, the sound entirely without humor. "You sure you wanna wish Shooter or Judge on him? Seriously? We both know Eddie comes with the potential for a fuckton of blowback."

Slate made a face and nodded slowly. "Yeah. I know she does, but there's something there, Mason. Something real…and right. You haven't seen him after he's caught sight of her, whether he talks to her or not. He's…lighter. More like when he's fresh off a run, not as deep into himself and his pain."

He responded immediately, ready to grasp any hope of saving his brother…his friend. He would do anything to keep from glimpsing again what he had seen in the man's eyes today. "Then we push him that way. You invited him to relocate to the Fort, and I'll make certain he takes you up on it." Mason's eyes tracked the last bag while it was loaded into a van, watching as the doors slammed, followed by the echoing thumps of a flat palm signaling readiness. The vehicle took off, leaving a plume of dust in its wake.

"Naw, man, I don't want to take him from you. I know you need him in the shops there in Chicago." Slate looked around. "Looks like we're about ready to go, Prez."

Mason nodded and took a last drag off the cigarette then straddled his bike, backing it towards the door where the members were exiting the building. He motioned one of them to lay a trail of gasoline down before he tossed the can back inside, and then gave them all a 'move along' chin lift. Waiting for his members to head out, he shook his head as he felt a mix of pride and pain at the quality of each man's ride. Pride, because this was what he always wanted for his brothers, giving them the ability to own the bikes they desired, and live the life they craved, regardless of the cost. And pain, because a trailer headed out thirty minutes ago had six scoots on it, the riderless bikes symbolic of the real cost of their business today.

Looking over his shoulder, he flicked the spent cigarette into the doorway, watching for a moment as blue flames licked inside and outside the threshold, curling up into the chill night air. Setting his face forward, he gunned his bike hard, working up through the gears as the fire took hold within the building, the slow-growing roar and whoosh lost in the sound of motorcycle engines as he gained on his Rebels. They split to either side of the narrow road, leaving him to ride the line between the columns until he was in point position, the men behind him collapsing back into a staggered riding formation, following his lead.

***

Sitting at the head of the table, Mason looked around at the men he had gathered into the crowded room. They were in the office of the Des Moines clubhouse, and he had Tater pull in the remaining local officers, as well as the men he brought from St. Louis and Kansas City. "Bear told me today this shit went deep," he began, taking his time and meeting every man's eyes. "We saw just how deep when we dealt with business."

He paused, seeing the pained look on Tater's face. "We can't always know how brothers will respond to...temptation."

He stopped speaking for a moment, hearing an eerie echo of his father's voice in the room. *And, as righteous followers of the faith, we have to rise above those base responses to temptation. Rise above, and stay the course.*

"We simply have to stay the course." He winced at his word choice, and then continued, "Tater, I'm going to let you weigh in on the chapter. You say your piece, and then we'll go around the table, thumbs up or thumbs down, brothers. Sometimes you just have to know when to step back."

You can't always predict the path, but you can always stay the course.

"And sometimes you can see clearly when it's time to chart a different path."

Get the fuck out of my head, old man, he thought grimly.

Nodding at the chapter president, he settled back into his chair, ready to listen. Tater responded with a chin lift, and then looked around the table before focusing back on him. "Prez. This is on me, not my brothers at this table or in the other room. I shoulda seen what was going down; it shouldn't have taken someone from outside to figure there was a division in the chapter." He swallowed, glancing over at his remaining officers. "None of us did, though. And to find out it went beyond the four members, and up into the officer ranks..." Tater shook his head, and in his mind's eye, Mason saw the last two body bags carried out of the warehouse today.

Taking a deep breath, Tater lowered his head, staring at the table for a minute, then lifted his eyes to meet Mason's gaze with quiet strength. Tater was a commendable man, a trustworthy brother. He hated like fuck this happened, and hoped it wouldn't break him. "I can keep a lid on things. I know how important it is to the club that all chapters be treated equally, and I don't expect any special handling, Prez. But I'm telling you I can keep a lid on things. I've got some damn good members, brothers I trust with my life—"

Mason interrupted, asking, "Would you have trusted Danz and Shifter with your life? I know Bear did." Those were the names of the Des Moines officers outed as traitors today, their bodies in the last two bags placed in the van.

Tater stared at him wordlessly for a moment then clenched his jaw and nodded, telling Mason honestly that he had misjudged them. People Tater had trusted, people who betrayed him and the club, had called for the beating Bear had endured on all their behalf.

Their gazes locked solidly and Mason waited. Waited while keeping his posture loose and relaxed, giving Tater time to work through things in his head. Waited, because he was halfway glad it had come to this during the plea, so the other men didn't have to vote, since it could leave bad blood behind. He had seen it go down that way more often than not, rifts torn between brothers and chapters. At least this way, the decision was all on him, and every man seated at the table knew it. He waited, and finally, Tater sighed, his face settling into implacable lines, jaw clenched tight as he spoke his acceptance through gritted teeth. "How long?"

"Now." Mason pushed back from the table and stood, turning to his Kansas City president. "K.C., how many can you take? We've got about 80 members to find homes and jobs for, less ten percent or so to cover the ones who won't want to make a shift. Think on those numbers for a minute." He nodded towards another man at the table. "Stan, you ponder it too. Little Rock isn't far. Could be a solution for some of the men."

Pike cleared his throat, but Mason stopped his words with a shake of his head, pulling out his phone. "Nope, you got shit you're still clearing, Pike. You sit and settle your own shit before you take on anyone else's."

"Myron," he said into the phone. "We're closing Des Moines. Do what you need to do immediately then text me the details on properties and businesses." Without waiting for a response, he disconnected and turned to Tater. He needed to shore up the man's confidence, make sure he knew Mason's approval and trust still rested on his shoulders. This was a big sidestep, but not a failure, because they had good members they could shuffle and keep.

"I could use some good men in Chicago and Fort Wayne, and you are my first fucking choice. Tell me who you recommend and who you think will need cut, because they won't pull up stakes. We won't leave any nomads from this. What we will do is cut their patches respectfully and let them go gypsy, so they can get into another local club if it's what they need. No one's forced into moving; no families get split up, man. Let's work our way through this, brother."

He reached out a hand, gripping Tater by the forearm. "You're a good man, and I'm proud to call you a brother. Sometimes you simply have to cut deep the first time to avoid a second round."

19. Moving forward

Her voice echoed the one leading her, repeating the words that would bind her to her husband. He had eyes only for her, but she had half turned away to face the groom, and all he could see were small portions of her face. He recognized her look of concentration, knew her little frown was because she was trying to ensure she got everything exactly right. He could see the love written there as Mica looked up into Daniel's eyes.

Mason sat near the front of the church on the bride's side next to Molly, her baby sister, and silently snorted a laugh. Mica had been fucking adamant he come to the wedding. Then she focused on convincing him he was her family, and the damn woman wouldn't be silent until he agreed to sit here, where she could catch sight of him. She wanted more from him, but he hadn't been able to see his way clear to granting her other request.

For her, the night of the party had been a turning point. Not only because Daniel had stayed with her, rekindling their relationship, but Mason had opened up for the first time, giving her a glimpse of the club life she had been insulated from for so long. He had admitted to protecting her, even at the cost of others' lives, and she hadn't flinched at his words. The longer he talked, the angrier he had been at himself, because just as he always knew—as he always *fucking* knew—she had a strength in her that was bone-deep. Now he held the bitter knowledge that if he only trusted her more, then things might have been different between them.

But he hadn't, and they couldn't go back from that. Couldn't go back before the hotel, couldn't go back before her bed. Even as he had seen Daniel's shadow waiting in her living room that night, he knew there was no win there for either of them. With his words, he first claimed her, caressing her softly as he promised she would always be his, and then he told her she owned him, and finally, he released her and walked away.

A month later, Daniel had come to him with the ring he had shown Mason once before, and Mason freely gave his blessing. He guessed in a way she was right, because he was her family, always would be. He brought his focus back up to the couple, seeing them standing close together on the riser in the front of the church. Daniel was holding her delicately, kissing her tenderly with his eyes wide open, as if he couldn't believe how lucky he was.

Sighing, Mason was about to get up, when Molly reached over and patted his leg. He smiled at her and she leaned sweetly into his shoulder, telling him, "You done good, big man." That was all she said before she stood and applauded the bride and groom as they began walking back up the aisle towards the rear of the church.

Mason was surprised when Mica pulled Daniel to a halt next to him and reached out her hand. Twining Mason's fingers with her demanding ones, he felt the unfamiliar, warm metal of her rings, the odd intrusiveness of the symbol of her marriage to Daniel grating on his nerves until she reached up with her other hand and cupped his chin. "Love you, Mason," she whispered, leaning in to kiss his cheek.

"Love you more, babe," he returned, pressing his lips to the curve of her cheek near her ear. "Do right by the man."

Nodding, she turned back to Daniel and they continued up the aisle. He dropped his gaze to the floor for a moment, and then a flash of chrome came into view. He grinned at Daniel's older brother, J.J., watching as he angled his chair over to where Mason stood next to the hugely pregnant Molly. He had been sniffing after Molly since she came to town, and recently, she seemed to return his interest. J.J. wasn't grinning now, though; he was looking past Mason worriedly.

Turning, he was surprised to find Molly sitting back down on the pew with a perplexed look on her face. He moved past and sat beside her, so he and J.J. bracketed her on either side. Reaching out for her hand, he was surprised at the strength with which she gripped him.

"Molls, baby. I was watching. Are you—" J.J. didn't finish his sentence before Molly was nodding, and Mason nearly laughed aloud at the frightened expression that flashed across the man's face. He raised his head, looking at the groups of people scattered around the room, seeing the one man he hoped to find. He whistled softly and then called emphatically, "Goose."

Making his way across the space, Goose took in Molly's posture and the pasty color of J.J.'s face and a broad grin stretched his lips. Looking over at Mason, he asked, "We got a little Scott on the way?"

"Yeah, I think he's decided to make this day even more memorable." Mason grinned up at him as he maneuvered between J.J. and the end of the pew.

Crouching next to Molly's knees, he put his hands on her thighs and looked into her face. "Tell me what you're feeling, doll. Everything, from emotions to physical. Tell me what you're feeling."

She leaned forward a little, and Mason slid his hand down her back, softly rubbing and stroking along her spine. "Tightness around my middle. Some hard pain in between my legs. It's like period cramping on steroids." Mason felt her muscles tighten beneath his fingers and watched her face crumple a little. "It's coming in short waves." She looked up at Goose then over at J.J., holding out her hand to him, tears not far away. "I'm scared."

"It's gonna be okay, Molls." Mason was impressed with Daniel's brother. The color had returned to his face and his hands were steady when he reached out to take hers. "We're all right here with you, and you can do this, baby. I know you can."

Goose had been doing his EMT thing, unobtrusively touching Molly's belly with a flattened palm, taking her pulse, counting her respirations, and Mason noted the change in his expression when his gaze dropped to the wooden pew. Glancing down, he slid sideways to avoid the growing puddle, and grinned up at his Rebel, a man who had been present for far too many end trips on the path of life. He was pleased Goose would be there for this one just starting out.

"Molly, sweetheart," Mason said softly, cupping her elbow in his hand. "Let's get you out this side door next to us, yeah? Goose can pull up the van; we'll get you comfortable." He looked over at J.J. and said, "Assuming you're driving yourself?" He was surprised at the headshake he got in return.

"I'm staying with Molly." J.J. rolled his chair backwards, and then called over to where his other brother, Dickie, was talking to their mother. Pulling him over with a head tip, Mason listened as he quietly told Dickie what was happening and asked him to bring his truck to the hospital after the reception. "Don't tell Mom yet; let her bask in Danny's happy for a little while before she worries." Mason knew she would worry; Darlene Rupert had fully embraced not only Mica as a daughter, but also pulled Molly into their family, making several trips to Chicago to meet with and pamper the girls as they organized plans for the wedding.

By now, Goose was waving from the side entrance to the church and he levered Molly to her feet, watching her eyes widen as she realized her dress was wet. "It's gonna be okay, Molly. Like J.J. said, we're with you. We got you, darlin'." He realized as he said the words they were true, and had been since she arrived in Chicago on the bar's doorstep. She had been scared half to death, pregnant, and only twenty years old. Immediately, she had become part of the club, as surely as her sister was, and now every brother would protect her at the cost of their own life. Including him.

"You got a name picked out?" He asked the question casually, trying to distract her. He let her lean on him as they moved slowly towards the van parked just outside. "It's a little boy, right?"

She nodded, taking in a shallow breath and pausing for a moment as another pain overtook her. He grunted as her hand tightened hard on his arm, and he saw J.J.'s hand slip around her other one, giving her something else to bear down on. "Tomas Andrew Scott," she said finally, taking another step forward.

He grinned. "Daniel's middle and Slate's first? Good on the kiddo, those are some big boots to fill."

She smiled up at him, and he was surprised at the love in her face as she said, "Yeah. But, if it wasn't for Slate, I don't think I would ever have had the courage to tell Mica what had happened. Because Essa trusted him, I did, too. He's a good man. A truly good man, exactly like you." Her hand tightened on his arm again, and they paused until she could resume their slow pace to the door.

Goose reached out, taking her from Mason and backing into the van, holding both her hands as he led her up the steps.

She looked back and said, "So is Daniel. He's a good man and he loves my sister." Still looking over her shoulder at him, she didn't say the words aloud, but was clearly thinking that was like him, too. Instead, what she said shocked him, and he stared at her wordlessly. "You know you're my choice for my son's godfather, Mason. He needs everyone in his corner I can wrangle there, and you are my only pick for that position. We all need you. More than you would ever believe, we need you."

Mason stepped back, breaking the lock her gaze had on him. He watched as J.J. lifted himself into the front seat, and Mason waited for the door to close before taking the chair over to where Dickie was waiting beside a truck with a winch on the back, ready to handle the wheelchair. He stayed there outside the church's side entrance, watching as the small convoy of vehicles pulled out, taking Molly away to the hospital. Mason found himself torn. On one hand, he wanted to be there when little Tomas took his first breath, but even more, he felt he needed to witness the beginning of Mica's journey with Daniel. Full fucking circle.

His indecision was broken when he felt a small, warm hand cup his, where it hung by his thigh. "You wouldn't give me away," she said, leaning into him. "Will you give me a dance?" His throat too tight for words, he nodded, following her into the rowdy party that was a hockey team and biker club's version of a wedding reception.

***

Shouting a joking, "Fuck you," down the stairs in response to a salacious comment, Mason moved down the hallway to his room in the clubhouse. Kicking the door closed behind him, he didn't bother locking it, knowing none of the club whores would dare disturb him without an explicit invitation. One he hadn't issued in long months now, preferring his own hand to the feel of pussy around him that might require a fucking conversation or any kind of give and take to get.

He staggered a little as he toed off his boots, watching as they fell in a tangle with his socks next to the wall. One of the boots had angled oddly, and for a moment, he felt the weight of a gun in his hand, seeing a foot-filled boot twisted awkwardly against the molding along the bottom of the wall. Shaking his head, he pushed those memories of Ripper away, unbuckling his belt.

Letting his pants sag to the floor, he stepped out of them and shrugged his cut off, hands automatically working to respectfully fold the vest and place it across the back of the chair near the bed. He paused, hands still on the garment, and lifted it, tilting his head as he looked at the patches sewn with care onto the black leather.

On the back, the name of the club rose over everything, Rebel Wayfarers. The small MC was near the emblem for the club, the scowling skull. Across the bottom of the vest's center section was Mother Chapter – Chicago. He grinned, remembering how he had named it and worn the patch for years before it became truth, a promise to himself he looked at every day when he donned the president's persona for the club.

On the left front, below the bullet hole he refused to have repaired, was a smallish patch that said President, followed by one bearing his name, Mason, and then another lined up below with the word Founder.

On the right, in a curving arc around the side, he saw the dark orange words National President.

Scattered across the remaining real estate were a variety of patches. 1%; God Forgives, Rebels Don't; GDMFSOB—that one made him laugh, because he had a citizen woman ask him once what it meant. He had enjoyed watching her face flush red when he told her, "God Damn Mother Fucking Son of a Bitch." He had helpfully volunteered the meaning behind the DILLIGAF patch, enjoying watching her squirm just a little. "Does it look like I give a fuck?" She had turned away then, walking back to her friends in the bar as fast as her too-tall-for-comfort heels would allow.

Some of his patches were more light-hearted, his favorites being Fuck This, Let's Ride; If it has tits or wheels sooner or later you've got problems; and Don't ask to ride my bike and I won't ask to fuck your wife.

With pride, his fingers traced the logo for the club's bike shops, FWO, Fucking Wide Open, and then moved to the two that stood for the motto symbolic of the relationship between all the brothers in the club, RFFR, Rebels Forever, Forever Rebels. He folded the vest again, draping it across the chair, and reached behind his head to tug his shirt off before he remembered he had worn a button down today, out of respect for Mica. Sitting on the edge of the bed, he fumbled with the buttons, finally succeeding in removing the shirt.

Mica, he thought as with eyes closed. He watched again as Daniel danced song after song with his new wife, her face lifted in love and laughter to his. Mason had stood along the edge of the room, arms empty, heart full for her. He could be glad for her, because, as he had often told himself, she deserved the sweet, and it was exactly what she had gotten today. Merry had sidled over to him at one point, leaning close and laying her head against his arm. With a sideways grin, he remembered her words. "Mark my words, son. You'll have this for yourself."

He had tipped backwards on the bed at some point in his reverie, and now sat back up with some effort. Leaning over, he reached down to tug his wallet free of his pants and opened it, pulling out a small piece of paper. He stared at it for several minutes, and then tossed his phone and the paper onto the nightstand, twisting away on the bed to remove temptation from sight.

20. Chase needs more

He stood in the lot, watching as Tug's bike turned a corner, disappearing from view. Sighing, he turned to walk back into the clubhouse, stopping when he saw Myron standing there. "Not right now, Myron. I ain't in the mood." He stomped over to the door of the clubhouse, pulling it open and walking into the main room, the thin biker turned implausible accountant at his heels. He snorted, thinking, *Suspect I have that bass-ackwards. I think he's always been a bean counter, and I just found the biker in him.*

He stalked into the office behind the bar, and once inside realized the door had failed to close behind him, which meant Myron had followed him, regardless of his wishes. *Goddammit, I only want a fucking minute*, he thought. Without turning, he said, "I'm pretty sure I mentioned I wasn't in the mood, man."

"Slate's in Fort Wayne, Bear's flat on his back, you sent Tug off with your boy, and now you're looking like someone stole your lollipop, Mason. I think you need to talk whether you are in the mood or not." Myron pulled up a chair, reaching back to slap the door closed now that he was safely on this side of it. "I'm all you've got, man."

"Fuck you," Mason said good-naturedly, a smile quickly sliding on and off his face as he turned to face Myron. "I don't need to talk about anything other than the reports you still haven't gotten me on the businesses in Fort Wayne I want to buy. Jase is nearly tee'd up, man. Give me shit to feed him when he's ready."

"Do you enjoy this kind of thing? Pushing and pulling people around until they are sitting where you need them to be?" Myron idly picked at a thread on the seam of his jeans, cutting his gaze up at Mason when he remained quiet for too long.

"Yeah." He admitted softly, "I kinda do. It's what I'm good at, bringing the right people to the table to solve a problem. Slate's good at it, too, but he tends to stick to a smaller scale. It's why we work so well together, because I'm all about the big win, man. Find the win."

"What did Chase do that was so bad?" Myron tried for casual and failed.

"It's not what he did. Fucking and drinking...hell, when I was his age, I was prospect patched into the Fiends, getting my ass beat on by grown-ass men all the time, fucking when and where I felt like it. It's where his mind's at, more than what he did." Mason glanced out the window again, seeing the office building a few blocks away. That was where he needed to be right now and he sighed heavily, knowing he wasn't getting away from this conversation anytime soon.

He reached out, pulled the chair from underneath the desk, and slowly took a seat. "His head's pissed at me, but I can't get a twist on it, can't figure it out. Him being pissed at his mom—now *that* I can track. What I can't track is why he's avoiding me and treats me like I'm going to beat the shit out of him anytime he's around me. But then he feels ballsy enough to do shit like this. I guess I should be grateful he's not talking trash behind my back."

Myron's mouth moved, his lips pursing, and Mason looked carefully at him, seeing the man...actually seeing him for the first time in a while.

He was such a young kid when they initially hooked up, not long after he established the Rebels. He had forced all the members into community work, looking to build trust with the business owners and people in the neighborhoods surrounding the clubhouse and club activities. One of the things they frequently did was volunteer at a homeless shelter, the best of the various places Mason had frequented when he first moved to Chicago.

He had first seen an eighteen-year-old Myron sitting at a long table, surrounded by dirty, disheveled men in mismatched clothes, their shoes most often held together with twine or tape. Myron had stood out, because his clothes were reasonably clean and his shirt tucked in, but what caught Mason's attention was the jar of buttons he was holding. Tilting his head back and forth, his hands had turned the jar upside down and then right side up, then upside down again, the buttons cascading to and fro along the inside of the jar, contained yet fluidly in motion.

Moving close, Mason had asked, "What the hell are you doing with a big ole jar of buttons, boy?"

Jerked from his daydream when he heard Myron's voice in the office, he realized he had spoken aloud when Myron gave the same response he had that night in the shelter. "Counting them."

Laughing, Mason said, "Born bean counter if I ever met one."

A wry smile on his face, Myron nodded. "You pegged me from the get-go. So what's up with Chase?"

Mason stilled, turning the puzzle that was his son over in his head again, and he grunted in recognition, because he thought he might have finally found a seam in the picture. "He wants to be me. Not the me I showed him when I visited twice a month in Kentucky, but the me he found in the bar when Sosa dropped him off. The me who has a thousand brothers and isn't afraid of anything because I have them all at my back." Lifting a hand, he rubbed hard across the back of his neck.

"Like with Mica, I only let him discover the parts I thought he could take, but he's tougher than I thought. It was probably a surprise when he got up here, because he'd only met a couple of our guys up to then. I made sure they were the men I was most comfortable with, the ones I trusted the most, so I could let my guard down around them. So in the first setting down home, he got to glimpse the brotherhood we had, the respect they held, but wasn't awed by it. Now," he laughed harshly, "he's fucking overwhelmed his old man has all of" —he swept his arms out to the sides, in a parody of a show's host— "*this* at his disposal."

Myron made a stifled noise, and Mason looked at him, making a motion for him to talk. "Probably more like he's impressed his old man is a powerful leader who's earned the respect of so many other powerful men. He's in awe. I think he wants some of it, sure. But, I think what he wants most is for you to see him like that…like how you see the members. Like his opinion counts for something. How you look at the men who surround you, badasses all, present company excluded." Myron laughed. "Prez, I think you sometimes forget how much your attention and respect matters to the men around you."

"No. I never allow myself to forget. I never forget the significance. That's why I hold it so fucking tight, because it means more when I let it go." He paused, remembering, then looked down. "Aww, fuck." Mason cleared his throat, shaking his head. "A few weeks ago, in the middle of another conversation halfway turning to a fight, Chase asked when he could patch in, become a Rebel." He felt a hard twist of anger at himself in his chest. "Fucking shit, Myron. I laughed and told him to come back and talk to me when he was eighteen."

"Ouch, boss," Myron said, shaking his head. "You knocked his legs out from under him. It told him he wasn't worth the attention. Hell yeah, I'd have gotten out of your line of sight, too."

"*Fuck.* How'd I fuck this up? I knew I wasn't…fuck." He scrubbed his hand over his face. "Goddammit. First Sosa drops him off like she's putting a bag of trash at the curb. He's any old errand that needed doing before she could move along, and then today I send him on his merry way with hardly a word. I fucked up hard."

Myron laughed. "Nah, you didn't fuck up. You hurt his pride, sure, but now you've given him space, which he seems to need. You've also handed him mentors, people he can build a rapport with, people you've already shown that you trust. He'll do okay. He knows you love him, boss. It's on your face every time you look at him."

Mason sat for a minute, soaking in Myron's words, and then stood, stretching. "I gotta get to work. Meet you early tomorrow morning before the board meeting?"

"Yeah, boss." He felt Myron's eyes on him, watching him walk out of the room, and then heard him speak, obviously thinking Mason wouldn't hear him. "Mica knows you love her, too." The statement caused a hitch in his step, and then he continued pacing steadily up the hallway towards his room.

***

Mason was going over the plans for a charity run in Little Rock, reading the notes from the chapter president, when his phone rang. He looked over, seeing Slate's info on the screen, and picked up immediately. Before he could say anything, Slate's voice rolled from the speakers, torn and raw with emotion, "Mason, *Brother*. I don't know what to do, man. This is so fucked up."

Mason spoke quietly, trying to infuse his few words with the wealth of confidence he had in his friend. "Slate, talk to me." He didn't know what the problem was, but as wretched as Slate sounded, he thought it was likely about a woman. He knew Slate and Melanie had gotten together in a way that seemed solid. In his mind, it had been a foregone conclusion and a good fit, since she was already in the life as much as an old lady would normally be, and Slate loved her to distraction. He had named her Princess, same as—

Goddamnit. He threw up a wall, because he needed to put those thoughts aside.

"I don't fucking know where to start." Slate's voice broke, and he cleared his throat. "DeeDee came in to talk. *Motherfuck.* Mason." His breathing was fast and raspy with distress. "She said after Winger and Lockee died, Ruby slid off the path a little. Started looking for an exit strategy, sounds like."

Mason interrupted with a question. "Ruby?"

"Melanie," Slate explained. "It's the hair some." There was the bare edge of humor in his voice for a second, but then it was gone. "But mostly it's because she's fucking precious to me. Ruby." Mason made an agreeable noise, and Slate continued, "The UP Michigan club that's caused all the shit over the years, part of what they did was take Ruby."

Mason interrupted again, "I remember it, man. It was right after I suspected they'd had at Bones, but from what I understood, she went willing on Demon's bike. Rode up with him like a pro. A few months later, Bingo went and brought her home, but I'm sure she went willing. I assume she came back willing, too, so things must have gone sideways for her."

"Sideways," Slate scoffed softly. "That's a fucking gentle way of putting it." His tone made Mason's blood run chill and he suspected he wasn't going to like what he was about to hear. "She went willing, but it ended when he walked her into a storage closet and locked her in right after they arrived at the clubhouse in Iron Mountain. Motherfucker kept her for his; at least he didn't pass her around. But, he beat her and fucked her, and then beat on her some more. Bingo never told you about this?"

Her face flashed in front of him: brilliant smile on a fragile face surrounded by falls of curly red hair. Sunny, beautiful, happy. That was the Melanie...*Ruby* he carried in his mind. Mason shook his head and then choked out, "Nope. First I'm hearing of the shit."

"From what DeeDee said, I dunno. Maybe he doesn't know what went down. Ruby plays her cards fucking close to the vest. She's quiet and deep, but Prez, she has so much fucking fear. You haven't seen her; it's like coaxing a beaten dog out from underneath a porch. You know you gotta move slow and easy, careful not to spook her, because you also know if you try and grab hold, try to drag her out, she'll fight you with everything in her." His voice tight with anger now, Slate growled, "He fucking did that to her. He took a woman, who from all accounts was bright and quick to laugh, sassy and fearless...and he turned her into a mouse who freezes at the barest scent of cat, eyes big and round, shaking. I may never get to discover what she was before Demon; that's how fucked in the head she is by his shit. He fucking did that to her...my woman."

"Yours?" Mason let the question slip before he could stop it then waited for an answer.

"My. Fucking. Woman." He could hear the panting breaths between each word, recognized there was hurt still unspoken by his friend.

"Brother," he said. "There's more, isn't there?" He knew from Slate's pain there had to be, but Mason honestly didn't know if he could stand much more.

It had been two years since he got the call from Bingo asking for approval to make a run to the UP to retrieve an errant child. That's how he had taken the message when he got it, indulgently giving the go-ahead for the run, believing she had fled from the pain of losing her family and was only now being gathered home. The call came nearly two years after he saw the report about the ambush Bones had lived through, when he suspected the Devil's Sins of treachery to avoid being taken over. With everything happening with Chase, he hadn't followed up on it soon enough, and by the time he looked again, the trail had gone cold.

"Yeah. Fuck yeah, there's more." Slate pulled in a breath, raw agony washing through his voice when he continued, "When he figured there wasn't anything for him, when she didn't know anything about the Rebel operations, he turned her out. Into the snow, he turned her out. He let her make one call before he locked the gates behind her, but...Prez."

There was silence on the phone for a long minute, and he let Slate take his time, waiting until he was ready to continue.

"She was pregnant. Before he took her out of that closet...that fucking cell, he gave her something to purge the baby. Then he kicked her out, left the clubhouse and locked her out. She waited for three days in the snow, alone. She miscarried alone. She's only ever told DeeDee anything about it, and I suspect even there...she...not everything was spoken. Mason...brother, she's carried the load of this alone this entire fucking time."

The door to the office opened abruptly and Red stuck his head in, and then, with a wide-eyed headshake, pulled it back closed. Mason became aware he was standing, his fist pulling back from a bloody hole in the wall, muscles trembling with the strain of holding still. "Goddamn, man." He spoke to Slate in a low voice, "We find him—he's yours."

Tears evident in his voice, Slate asked, "What do I do, Mason? How do I...help her? She trusts me a little, but how can I help her trust me with this? Why the fuck would she ever trust a swinging dick again, man? How do I bring her into me? So much. God, I love her...so fucking much. If you love Mica half this much, I don't know how you fucking breathe, knowing she's outside of your control. I know I give you shit about the princess, but I get it now, I do. How do I do this, man?"

Mason took a deep breath, pushing down the pain and guilt. Slate didn't need to know he could probably have prevented this, if he had focused more on the club, instead of his own shit. Standing here right now, he could visualize what would have been a clear window of opportunity, but after being distracted by the knowledge he had a son, he had sorted through that, instead of following up on the club information he had been handed.

He swallowed hard and said, "You love her. That's what you do. She's responded to you; something in you speaks to her. Find a place of stillness and let her keep listening. You need to know it all, man, but you'll have to torque it in so she feels safe telling you. You can't react in the ways you're going to want to, so find a place of stillness where you can listen to her, too." He sagged, leaning against the wall, eyes on the damage he had dealt, mind on the damage he hadn't prevented. "You keep her first, and you love her. You've fucked her, right?"

Slate made a harsh noise, and then corrected him, and Mason jerked as an echo of his own words to Daniel about Mica slipped through his head. "Made love, not fucked."

"Yeah. So, you just love her. Give her reassurance, so when she opens to you, she knows it won't make any difference. Tell her. Show her. Love her." Mason sighed. "I'm here, brother. You need me, I'm here. You need me there, I'm there, man. Anything."

"Thanks, Mason." Slate was quiet for a minute, and then said, "DeeDee's moving to an apartment."

"Hmmm. Why now, after living in the clubhouse this long?" *That's curious*, he thought.

"I caught Jason Spencer sneaking out of the clubhouse a couple mornings ago." Slate snorted. "Knew he was in town, because he called Tug, but it surprised me to stumble across him here."

"I could have told DeeDee the pursuit makes things more interesting." Mason barked a brittle laugh. "She seems okay with him being there?"

"Yeah." It was Slate's turn to laugh. "Actually, I should thank him. It was them being in the suite together that sent Ruby to my bed the first time. Nothing happened, because club business cropped up, but she met me in the lot and wrapped herself around me, wouldn't let go. Gave me the balls to take the next step when it was opportune. Don't tell Jase, though. His head's big enough as it is."

"Yeah. Glad they hooked up. Dee's been alone for too fucking long." Mason sat in the chair, leaning his elbows on the desktop. "I'm here if you need me. Love you, brother."

"In the wind, man." Slate disconnected the call and Mason put his head in his hands, trying to push the images from his mind of a tiny redhead standing alone in a snowbank in the cold, bent double with cramps as her child pushed from her body too soon. Imposed on those pictures were thoughts and memories of Molly, supported on all sides by people who loved her, people who waited eagerly for her to bring a new little life to them.

Another fucking mark against all that is Davis Mason, he thought, sneering at his own false sense of importance. Standing, he walked over and opened the door, calling into the main room of the clubhouse, "Tell Woody he's got a repair job in the office."

He was leaning back in the chair when his phone rang again, and he saw it was a forwarded call from one of the bike garages, FWO2. With a bitter grin at the tongue-in-cheek name for the shop, he answered the phone, expecting to find a delivery delayed or something along those lines. "Yeah?"

"Hi. Is Rob Crew available? I asked the guy who answered the phone, and he told me to wait, so I thought he was finding Robby." The woman's voice was smooth and low, but poised and confident. Mason grinned.

"Who should I say is calling?" he asked, using his best monkey suit voice.

"This is Maggie Crew, his mom. I know it's passé to have your mom call your workplace after you're about twelve years old, but I needed to talk to Robby and he's not answering his phone." She seemed verging on embarrassed, and Mason was intrigued even more.

"He works at the shop, yes. Is everything okay, Missus Crew?" *Confident concern, this will likely draw her out*, he thought.

"Well. Um. I'm sort of in-between things." She said this with a little laugh, which flowed over him like the taste of chocolate on his tongue, causing his dick to pay attention.

"Missus Crew." Intentionally lowering his voice, he addressed her with an intimate tone, wanting to know if he could provoke a reaction out of her. "I asked if everything was okay."

"Well, yes." She laughed again, but it wasn't the same. Now it sounded brittle and tight, and he felt like an ass for making her uncomfortable. "And no. See, I was going to come visit Robby. It's been two years since he's been home, and I thought a trip to Chicago might be in order."

Two years? Bear was more fucked up than he had known, or he kept the man too busy to make time for his only surviving family member. Now Mason felt even more like an ass, because his mom was sweet and sounded cute. *MILF*, he thought with an inward chortle, and then he told her, "He's not in Chicago anymore, ma'am."

"Call me Maggie, mister..." She paused, giving him an opportunity to introduce himself.

With a grin at her blatant manipulation, he complied. "Davis Mason. I'm a friend of his. Maggie, when you said you are in between things, what did you mean exactly?"

"Well, I kind of sold my house." She paused after saying this, and then laughed nervously, the smooth tone back in her voice and he grinned, reaching down to tug at the head of his semi-hard cock. "I'll need to be out in a couple weeks, and I thought perhaps I could stay with Robby for a little while. I miss my boy." She paused again, and then asked, "Do you know where he is?"

He thought about the sterile set of rooms Bear had kept above the garage here in Chicago, and was glad he had moved the man to Fort Wayne. Slate had gotten him an apartment in the building he was moving into, and even if it was a club-owned building, it was still a damn sight better than living inside a club business.

"Yes, I do, Maggie. Is this your cellphone number?" He glanced at the number on the screen, recognizing the New Jersey area code.

"Yes, Davis." He nearly laughed aloud at her use of his first name. Only people who didn't know him called him that, so he corrected her, not wanting there to be any missteps the first time he saw her in person.

"Call me Mason; everybody does," he instructed, gratified to hear her repeat his name. His cock was standing at more than half-mast now. Her voice was simply...mmmm. *Kind of like Willa's voice*, he thought, and just that fast, he was fully hard and having to work to control his breathing, rubbing a hand roughly across his crotch, picturing Willa's face in his mind. With some effort, he pulled his thoughts together, saying, "He moved to Fort Wayne, about five hours east of Chicago, over in Indiana. I'll text you his new address. I have it in his personnel file."

"Mason, do you think he'd be okay with me visiting?"

He hated how unsure she sounded, hated the part he had played in giving Bear any excuse to stay away from family, from his mother, who so obviously loved him. "I think he'll be delighted to see you, Maggie. Would you like me to call and let him know you're coming?" She had said a couple weeks, so it might not be right away. This would be good, because while Bear was pretty much healed up from Des Moines, he wasn't entirely bruise-free, and he would hate for her first sight of her boy to be harsh.

"No, I'll finish up here and then make my plans. Who knows? There's a chance he'll call his old mother back before I get on the plane." She laughed again, but he could hear the underlying current of hurt. He knew the two of them were close during Bear's school years, and even after he married, when he was in the Navy.

From what Bear had told him, it sounded like he was her rock after her husband died, and in return, she had been his when his wife and daughter were killed.

Family.

Was it right to worry about Bear's family, if he had just been kicking his own ass for worrying about his son? Shit got all kinds of confusing when you got away from the club, and family was the most bewildering of all.

"Maybe he will. You let me know if there's anything you need, Maggie. Save my number when I text you the information. If you need anything, you call me. You can call me any time, okay?" He liked her easy manner, and had a sudden thought, wanting to reassure her. "Rob's got a lot of friends in Fort Wayne already. We'll make sure everything's okay with him, all right?"

She made an agreeable noise and thanked him, disconnecting the call. He texted her the information and waited for her confirmation before flipping back to the phone application, making a call of his own. "Tugboat, I'm going to need you to watch out for someone in a couple of weeks…"

21. War

"Mason, phone!" Merry shouted, and he walked to the front room of the bar from the stockroom. He frowned at the phone she handed him, surprised to find it was his. He thought it lost, because the last time he remembered seeing it was in Jess' hands earlier tonight, and she was like a crow, always taking shiny things.

They had been celebrating a strategic win for the Mallets, Daniel and Jase's hockey team. The whole team had come to the bar following the game, and it had been crowded and loud. Not too loud for him to hear Jase's statement about moving to Fort Wayne, though. While he had been expecting something along these lines, he hadn't thought it would happen mid-season.

Every time he fucking turned around, Daniel did something, highlighting what a great guy he was. For him to be willing to negotiate a trade for his friend so he could chase a woman, taking a hit to his team's championship chances, made him either the stupidest motherfucker around, or a genuinely good guy.

From the look on Mica's face tonight, it was clear she thought Daniel was a genuinely good guy too. He snorted, putting the phone to his ear and saying, "Yeah?" as he thought, *Damn good thing too, since she fucking married the guy*. He froze mid-step, hearing chaos over the phone line, voices raised in the distance, the sound of someone retching closer by. He pulled the phone back and looked at the screen; it was Hoss, Slate's second in Fort Wayne.

"I'm waiting here, Hoss." He clipped the words, hearing an inrush of breath, and then made out what Slate was saying in the background, "She was standing with me, here. Ruby was right here." At those words, Mason roared, fisting the phone in his hand, "I'm fucking waiting here, brother."

Silence descended on the bar, all faces swinging to look at him, Rebels' hands finding holsters and weapons, boots moving to positions by the exits. There was noise on the line and then he recognized Goose's voice. "Prez. Ruby's been taken. Slate got knocked out, and he was the only one with her. They were in the apartment garage, had just gotten home. She was out shopping then—"

Mason interrupted him, speaking over his rushing words, "Goose. How long?"

"We aren't sure. Maybe an hour?" There was noise in the background, and he heard an affirmative grunt.

Mason's mind was racing. There had been so much happening in the Fort, so many chances for things to go sideways, for people to look for vengeance. Slate finding an ongoing skim at the gun range, cutting two brothers in the process of investigating, but the third was still in the wind, Rabid. Bangers were a constant threat, but they would have killed Slate outright. Which left a couple of other options, none of which was good. "Manzino?" He said the name of the drug dealer they had displaced, and heard another noise in the background of the call. He shouted, "What the *fuck* is happening there, Goose?"

Hoss' voice came over the phone. He muttered, "Sec, Prez. Sorry, man, let me get—" Then, away from the phone, his voice continued, somewhat muffled, "There are cameras in the garage. Find the footage and get it to Myron." Back to the phone, he said, "Prez. Ruby looks to be the only thing they were after. They didn't get to Slate's apartment, and they didn't take the bike or car. He's all jacked up, but it might just be from hitting his head. Goose said he smells like he was dosed with ether. I dunno."

Mason said, "Manzino or Rabid?"

"No idea, boss. It's a cluster, man." Hoss was reliable, dependable, and he had his place in the club. As second in the chapter there, the man had to be good with prospects, and it seemed like he could get past the guard on most folks to find out what they were thinking. For this, they would simply have to get him something, or someone, to work with. If things were clawing through the air like this, and Slate was incapacitated, it was a goddamned good thing Bear was already there. And Gunny, too. Mason knew he would be on this hard, with focus. They would handle shit until he could get there, and then Hoss would be there to help him figure out the rest.

His mind was still racing a hundred miles an hour, going a dozen different directions at once. Speaking aloud, he talked through his thoughts, bringing things into focus. "Bring DeeDee in. Hoss, think, man. Who else? If this is a hit against families—" He stopped when he heard Hoss suck in air, this being something he clearly hadn't considered. "You call DeeDee right now. Call Bingo. I'm gonna send Jase your way. Keep me the fuck updated, because I'm going to sit tight right here until we know which direction the wind is blowing. Don't leave anyone vulnerable, brother. Call them all in. I got the bit about the security videos; I'll prep Myron so he knows it's coming his way. I want him to determine if he can track Ruby's phone."

"It's turned off; he already tried. The brothers have been pulling all the markers they could think of, making all the calls to try and find out anything." Hoss sounded out of breath, and Mason recognized Slate in the background again right before the sound of bikes roared through the speaker. "I'll call, boss. We're in the wind."

He sent a quick text to Jase, telling him what was going on, and then another asking him to call as soon as he got it. Within a minute, his phone rang and he answered, finding a nervous hockey player on the other end of the line asking, "What can I do?" He liked the attitude, and it went a long way towards supporting what he was about to ask.

Filled with wrath that someone had the balls to touch a claimed member of his extended family, Mason ground his teeth together tightly before he spoke. Not only was Ruby Slate's old lady, but she was his cousin's daughter in every way that mattered. The overwhelming anger came through his voice loud and clear as he told Jase, "Get your ass down there. DeeDee's gonna need you, even if nothing else happens tonight and especially even if she doesn't think so right now. I'm hanging tight here until things are resolved, then I'll be in the wind myself. Mother*fuckers* don't know what they stirred up with this shit. They do not fucking understand how it is. We will coat the motherfucking streets with red. Get to the Fort, someone will text you with DeeDee's location. She's being moved right now, to make sure she's safe."

Just as any of his Rebels would, Jase's only response was confirmation and a plea. "I'm on my way, Mason. Keep her safe for me."

***

He closed the bar, sending Merry home and running everyone out, allowing only Rebel members to remain.

War.

Slate had called, told him it wasn't Manzino, or Rabid. The threat had come from an old failure of Mason's that no one but he knew about. Demon of the Devil's Sins had taken Ruby. They would be going to war with the Devil's Sins. Slate was currently putting plans in motion for a raid on the Sins' Fort Wayne clubhouse, where they felt it was most likely the club had stashed Ruby.

There was a ragged touch of insanity in Slate's voice, and Mason offered to leave now to come down, offered to be there for the outcome, but even before the answer was voiced, he knew Slate wouldn't be able to wait. He needed to know for himself if the most likely scenario had played out. Most likely, because both Mason and Slate knew there was no reason for the Sins to keep the woman alive. Ruby.

Offering the only comfort he could, Mason told his brother, "I know this is shit, Slate, but you didn't find her only to lose her. She's your fucking always, man...not happening." He waited a beat to be sure Slate had heard him, and then disconnected the call. Now it was a waiting game, and Mason was fucking terrible at that.

He tried Demon's phone, laughing harshly when it went to voicemail, then made a couple calls to more stable members of the Devil's Sins. He made certain they were aware of what was going down in Fort Wayne on the Sins' side of the table, carefully not passing along anything about the clubhouse or the raid currently underway.

Hoss called at regular intervals, telling him one word nearly every time, "Nothing." Mason sat in his usual spot, but didn't interact with his members. He felt he needed to keep himself tightly in check, keep things under wraps, because if he didn't—if he let the monster loose that had been roaring in his chest for the past four hours—he would kill anyone who even fucking looked at him wrong. His muscles were tense, screaming for something to do, something to rend into pieces. Someone to make pay for everything his brother was going through.

Vengeance.

The one word had been rumbling in his head since he got the call. Someone would pay for tonight's work, and pay in red, not green. There would be a reckoning for this hit, and it would cut fucking deep. He jerked as the jukebox kicked on, doing its random thing, and then he froze at the song that began playing. Hellyeah's *Sangre por Sangre* flowed out of the speakers and across his skin. They had the fucking right of it, man. *Blood for Blood*. Vengeance.

His phone rang and his mouth twisted as he answered with a flick of his thumb, unmoving when he spoke into the earpiece he wore. "Yeah?"

"Got her, and it's bad. All I know, Prez."

He grunted in response to Hoss and disconnected the call, sitting with his elbows still propped on his knees, patiently counting his breaths. It rang again and he answered, again only saying, "Yeah?"

Harsh breathing, then Tug's voice jarred Mason off the chair, had him slamming a fist against a mirror on the back wall, watching as the slivers of glass fell amongst the bottles of liquor there. "Rabid." The Rebels in the room came closer, moving against raw instinct to get away from the danger radiating off him, looking for ways to support their brothers, their president.

"Are you fucking kidding me?" Mason didn't even recognize his own voice. "Not Demon? But he was on the security—"

"Both, Prez. We found a bunch of Sins' members in the house, caught up to Demon on the main floor. But Rabid—" He sucked in a breath. "Rabid had her in the basement, Mason. He'd put his talents to use on her."

"*No!*" He shouted the denial, the images now rolling through his head, causing his stomach to lurch inside his belly. Rabid's talents had always been more savage than the club needed now, in these days of prosperity, peace, and calm. His military background was specializing in making people talk, and occasionally he played a part in club interrogations, but most often, Mason found his methods too brutal to stomach. He breathed the word out again in desperate rejection. "*No.*"

His mind was racing at full speed. Rabid had cheated the club and been caught. Then the coward ran, leaving his partners twisting in the wind. He knew being captured would mean death now, because not only had he stolen from his brothers, but had proven himself a traitor, too. What was the shine for Rabid doing this? Something in this whole mix wasn't lining up. Maybe it was vengeance against Slate, since he was the one to uncover the skim and cut the rockers? Not enough. Shit still didn't line up.

"They're taking her to the downtown hospital, Mason. It's bad. Goose worked on her for a long time. He stayed on her until the bus got here. He brought her back twice, man. We're cleaning up after the party, but we'll need to have a bonfire soon. Got some trash bags to carry out, and some swinging meat to take home. Leftovers will be at the house. You gonna come down to see to things?" Tug spoke cautiously, carefully wording the information as if their calls were being monitored, and with everything going on, Mason knew it was a good tactic to take. He felt his lips pull back in a humorless grin. Swinging meat, indeed.

"Yeah, I'll find my way down in a bit. Got a couple calls to make here. Keep me posted, brother." Without waiting on a response, he disconnected the call. Reaching into a drawer under the back bar, he pulled out pieces to a small pre-paid phone. Assembling it and dialing a number from memory, he waited until it was answered, and then said, "Tell Watcher that Mason said he's going to war." Hanging up, he dialed again, delivering a similar message, "Bones needs to know Mason's going to war." *Twice, Goose brought her back twice.* He would wipe the goddamned club off the face of the earth.

Thinking for a moment, he pulled out his wallet and took out a card. Referring to it, he dialed another number then said, "Andrew Jones needs Estavez. We're going to war." There was a burst of Spanish on the line, and he responded with, *"Entrar en guerra,* yes, *war."* Disconnecting the call, he took the back off the phone, pulling the battery before throwing it back into the drawer, looking around the bar as he wordlessly whirled a finger in the air.

***

He wheeled his bike into the hospital parking lot, backing into a space. Idly wondering how long it had been since he had been inside one of these places, he thought, *Molly*. Then he reached back further and remembered Mica's stay in a hospital in Chicago after the botched kidnapping.

He and Daniel sat side-by-side in the uncomfortable waiting room chairs for hours. Daniel carefully picking at the edges of Mica's relationship with Mason, trying to figure out what there was between them, clearly distrusting the 'just friends' vibe he knew Mica was putting out there.

Mason stayed seated on the bike, remembering the feel of Mica in his arms at the wedding reception, the satin of her white dress under his palms, her body moving to the music with his. Fucking Daniel fucking watching from the fucking sidelines with a smile on his fucking face, because he had won the woman and could be generous. He could be generous, because he knew this would be all Mason ever got from her again. Innocent as the white fabric implied, his interactions with her would never again be sensuous, and wild, and so fucking good it stole his breath...he shook his head at his thoughts.

Standing up off the bike, he walked in, following the arrows on the wall to the wing where Ruby's room was. He stood in the doorway of her hospital room for a long time, observing the occupants. Slate sat unmoving and silent, watching her sleep, the look on his face at once fierce and vulnerable, the deep love he held in his heart for the woman there on his features for anyone to see. Mason watched as Slate's eyes tracked from her slightly parted lips, down to her chest, where he appeared to be counting her breaths, back up to her eyes, covered by closed and still eyelids. Over and over, reassuring himself she lived, she breathed; she still existed in a way that meant they could be together. His woman.

I'm just a poor wayfaring stranger

Even though he was glad Slate finally had found this for himself, he still couldn't silence the tiny jealous voice inside gloatingly reminding he would never have the same. *Give the woman who holds your heart away to another man like you did, no way around it, you're gonna end up alone.* Ruthlessly pushing the thought down, he spoke to his friend, working hard to have confidence ring true in his words. "She's going to be okay, Slate. You got her, man. You got her back." They talked for a few minutes, and then Slate put words to the guilt eating away at his insides, the thing that would likely haunt him for a long time.

"This shit is so fucked up. I feel useless, Mason. I can't do anything to help her. They stole her from my side, man. She was by my fucking side, and I couldn't keep her safe. It was touch and go too. She nearly died in that basement, because I couldn't keep her safe. She wasn't fucking breathing for the longest time; Goose saved her life." *Brought her back twice.* Anguish twisting his features, Slate swept his arm towards where she lay in the bed. "Look at her, Mason; look where she is...what she's gone through. This shit is because of me, because of us. It hurts so fucking bad, man. How can I do this?"

Mason watched him, considering and rejecting words of comfort and reassurance. He remembered his shock at Shooter's nonchalance regarding their mother's murder—dead because of the club. Maybe death shouldn't be a surprise when you dealt in pain all the fucking time—and Ruby knew the play, she had been part of the club all her life. Hell, she had been a pawn before, too.

That was probably the hardest piece to swallow, but he thought at the end of everything that happened today, Slate didn't need those reminders. He simply needed permission to keep her. He didn't need to be told the pain could easily circle back around again, coming at you from a different angle every time, so you never knew where to guard. He needed to be told it was okay to still want what he had, even knowing it could be taken away at any time. Mason reached out and clasped his friend's arm, speaking from the heart, saying, "How can you not, brother?"

Slate had no response, and Mason stood with him for a few minutes, and then said, "I'm not staying, just needed to stop in on my way to the clubhouse to verify for myself how she's doing. I'm taking care of these fuckers tonight, Slate. You stay here and be with your lady. Our brothers and I have this under control, and we will handle things as needed. The hard shit's *here*, man; I don't envy your path."

He could still see the uncertainty in Slate, and knew the man was considering putting Ruby away from him for her own safety. *It would fucking break him*, he thought. Pulling Slate in for a one-armed, back-thumping hug, he said softly, "But she is fucking *worth it*. Like Mica would say—she's your always, man. You are one lucky motherfucker; not all of us find ours."

Back outside on his bike, he sat for a minute, and then pulled out, turning the opposite direction from the clubhouse. Winding his way back out to the center of town, he set course for an apartment building in New Haven, trying not to think too much about what he was doing. He parked in a corner of the lot, killing the bike and sitting there, waiting for what, he wasn't entirely sure.

After about twenty minutes, a small car pulled onto the lot, turning into a resident's parking spot. With hungry eyes, he watched as Willa climbed out of the car, phone wedged between her shoulder and ear as she leaned into the backseat to gather her shopping bags. Scanning up and down, he thought she looked good, her long hair loose and swinging down between her shoulder blades, a happy smile on her face.

He found himself smiling back, returning the expression, even though she couldn't see him. She bumped the car door with her hip, casually closing it, and he frowned when she didn't lock the vehicle, but instead moved towards her apartment. The small alcove that held her front door had odd acoustics and reflected her voice towards him. "No, he hasn't called, Eddie. I'd have told you." Arms full of bags, she was fumbling with her keys, and he frowned again, because she wasn't paying any attention to her surroundings. Anyone could come up on her, and she would never notice them in time. *Who the fuck is she talking about?* he wondered. "I know what Shooter said, but he's so dreamy, though," he heard before she opened the door and disappeared inside.

Mason realized he wasn't the only observer in the lot when a bike started nearby. Looking over, he froze when he saw Judge pulling out. The man didn't look at Mason as he left, but there was no way he could have missed seeing him pull in if Judge had been sitting there before Mason arrived. He realized his muscles were clenched, tight and tense, and he carefully shook his hands out before starting the bike.

Until he had seen Judge, he had felt soothed, comfortable. Just watching Willa's graceful movements seemed to calm him, something he had never experienced. Even with his frustration at her lack of self-preservation, he had been better simply being near her. He remembered the draw that had pulled him across the River Riders' clubhouse to her side, the challenge he had been willing to issue Judge for her without even knowing her name. She gave him her number that night, and he had used it several times. Never speaking, he called only for a chance to hear her voice utter a few short syllables. *Enthralled and fucking mesmerized by another citizen*, he thought. *Fuck me.*

***

"Fucking Rabid was an asshole." Tug thumped a fist on the desk.

There was a pause, and then when he didn't receive a response, Tug said, "Motherfucker." Mason nodded in tired agreement.

"This was goddamned shit business." Tug leaned back in his chair, tilting his chin up towards the ceiling.

"What an evil fucking night." Tug rubbed his hand down his face, smoothing his mustache.

Mason snorted. "You gonna keep stating the obvious, old man?" He had come back into the office after talking to Bear, and that shit had nearly torn him up. Seeing the man taking giant backward strides, losing all the ground he made in past months, was fucking hard. He had tried for a compliment, and Bear had swole up, gotten pissed off, which was at least emotion, something the man attempted to keep a lid on all the time.

"I'm taking Bear to Chicago with me. I think he needs Rabid's kids. Bingo told me he has a good bond with the boys. He's already got durable power of attorney, so custody is next, and then adoption if it works out." Mason ran his fingernails through the beard on his jaw, scowling. "He'll fight me on this. I know it."

"He's had a busy couple of days," Tug said with amusement in his voice, and Mason raised an eyebrow at him. "His mother showed up like you said she would. First time I saw her was in the apartment garage right before we came back here; she tiptoed through the blood and puke on the floor as if it was just another puddle. Never flinched at the black leather or bikes, only smiled at me when I called her Missus Crew." He paused, and Mason saw the look on his face change, softening even more as he said, "Beautiful smile."

Mason snorted again, this time with more humor. "On the phone, she's something else. I can't wait to meet her in person."

Tug dropped his gaze, hiding his expression. "She's...interesting. Glad she's here for him."

Mason looked at him with a half-grin, and then it faded. "This was shit work tonight; you're right." He sighed. "Slate's destroyed, man. I'm fucking glad she's going to be okay. He'd have been ruined if she bought it. How'd he go from zero to a hundred with Ruby so fast?"

"Wasn't fast, brother. He's been after her since he took over the club. He simply gave her the room she needed to come to the same conclusion." Tug lifted his coffee to his lips, blowing across the hot surface. "Did you hear Eddie showed up in the clubhouse for Bear the night before last?"

"Fucking shit. Are you serious?" Mason would never have pegged her for a first-move kind of woman. "Shit, I need him in Chicago for a couple. You think it's going to monkey wrench his play?"

"Doubtful, after seeing the two of them finally admitting what they've been dancing around for so long." Tug cut a glance over at him. "It was a powerful thing to witness, Mason. He basically claimed her for everyone to see right there in the clubhouse. I've never seen as possessive a move as him walking towards her. Hell, it made me half-hard and I ain't into men." They both laughed, and then Mason sighed.

"Judge is in town." He offered this with no context, wondering where Tug would take it.

"I understood Shooter recalled him." Tug shook his head. "Dammit, that boy never did like to be told what to do. Still, if Eddie's here in the Fort, is there a chance he's back on babysitting duty?"

Mason shrugged, draining his coffee cup. "Dunno. Saw him on the lot outside Willa's apartment."

At his admission, Tug slowly shook his head back and forth. He knew about Mason's quiet obsession with the woman, having handed over a folder full of information months ago. He softly asked, "Is it like that, then?"

Knowing what he meant, Mason sighed. "No fucking idea, old man. I want..." He trailed off as he looked up, their gazes catching and holding for a moment as he admitted, "Fuck yeah, I want. But, I got shit to clean up before I can think of anything like her. We're going to have to rub the Sins out after this. You know it. I know it." Mason stood, shifting his shoulders until his cut sat comfortably again. "Gonna gather Bear then get in the fucking wind."

"Ride safe, brother," Tug called after him, and Mason flipped two fingers in a mock salute as he walked out the door.

22. Sweet love and joy

2013

"It's been a long fucking couple of months, man." Ankles crossed on one corner of his desk, Mason lounged comfortably in his office chair, looking out over the city as he listened to Slate on the phone. "She's back to a good place. We're in a good place. Don't fuck this up for me, Prez."

"I need you, brother." And, he did. There were problems in a few of the chapters, and he needed someone he trusted to pay them a visit, straighten shit out. Report on what couldn't be dealt with immediately and quietly.

"She's pregnant," Slate said, and Mason dropped his feet to the floor, sitting up straight in the chair.

"Congratulations, man." He knew he wore a goofy grin, but he wouldn't trade this moment for anything. To know Slate and Ruby had come back from where they were only three months ago, finding their way to this instead, it was worth every effort he had expended to scrub the earth of those motherfuckers who had hurt her, hurt his family.

"Yeah. DeeDee's over the moon." Slate's voice held pride, and Mason laughed.

"And you aren't, motherfucker?" He had a sudden, terrifying thought, and asked, "How long...when's she due?"

"She didn't catch until after, Mason. It's all good." Slate spoke quietly, clearly knowing what his fear had been, and was able to immediately put it to rest. Mason blew out a silent, relieved breath. That would have been heartbreaking, especially since he knew the history between her and the fucker they had rolled off the back of a boat only a few weeks ago.

"Good fucking deal, man. Being a to-be daddy won't get you out of club duties though, and I need you like I said." He ran a hand across his chin, feeling the short bristles of his five o'clock shadow. He flipped through other members in his mind, but no one other than Bear and Slate would do for this. "I can't send Bear; he's barely beginning to make his way with Rabid's kids, man." He paused, thinking, "I've got Tater, but he's tracking Rabid's damned brother. That little motherfucker is going to try to cause shit. I know it."

"I get it, boss. I'm on it. What do you need me to do?" This was Slate's go-to phrase, the words that had driven every selfless sacrifice the man had made throughout his entire life. Mason fucking hated hearing them come out of his mouth again, because of him, because of the club and the harsh demands it placed on all of them.

"Lima, Indianapolis, Bloomington, Memphis, Little Rock, Texarkana...half-dozen others. The rest are all smaller chapters than those first six. And, brother, I'm most worried about Memphis, because shit smells every time the wind blows from their direction. Then hell, man, it'll extend the trip, but Watcher'd like to get together with you in New Mexico. He wants to talk about what we're going to do with the new Diamante chapter near him. I suspect Estavez will be in attendance.

He's got a toe in the water there, too." Mason scrubbed along his jawline again.

"Four weeks, then. Maybe longer." Slate sighed. "I'm feeling like taking folks with me would be bad, Mason. Make a hard job harder. From what you've already sent over, I don't think I want to roll in looking like the club is descending in force. I think I'll do a solo run, out and back. No more than six weeks." He laughed. "When Ruby gets pissed about this, I'm having my old lady call you."

"You do that, man. I'm happy to take it from her any day," Mason said with a grin, disconnecting the call. No lie, he was pleased to take it from her, because if Ruby could bitch at him, it meant she was on the breathing side of the sod.

Bethany's voice was high and sweet as she sang, "I'll soon be free from every trial. This form shall rest beneath the sod. I'll drop the cross of self-denial. And enter in the home of God." Mason jerked and looked around then shook his head at how memories had a way of sneaking up on us.

***

An hour later, he stepped out of the office building's lobby and came to a sudden halt, staring in disbelief at the woman distractedly making her way up the sidewalk. "No fucking way," he muttered, moving to follow her, getting close enough to get a real look at her face, and then going back on a foot with shock. *Goddamn*, he thought, *it is her.*

Willa walked up the sidewalk, a tiny backpack riding on her shoulders, and he watched as she consulted her phone then stopped to look up at his building with a frown on her face. She keyed something in on her phone then shook her head, looking up at the building again. Moving slowly, she swung in a small circle, taking in her surroundings, looking puzzled by something. Her gaze skittered across him and he quickly turned his head, hiding his face by bringing up his right hand as if he held a phone in it.

She walked past him and he couldn't help himself; he sniffed the air, catching a hint of the scent that had made him crazy the one time he had gotten close enough to smell her. Squaring her shoulders, she marched up to the revolving door. He grinned broadly when her determined strut changed to a ridiculously slow pace as she passed through the sedately circling entrance. Looking at the resident map on the wall near the elevators, he watched her eyes catch on the listing there and was suddenly and absolutely certain she was there for *him*. He watched her read *Mason Corporation,* and then was surprised when her shoulders slumped.

The traffic on the sidewalk flowed around him as he stood, watching her through the glass, business people and office workers hurrying home to their lives and families. He saw as she took one step back then bumped into a man, and Mason registered the man's fingers moving on the backpack, tugging something out, even as he bent close and mouthed an apology for running into her.

She turned and came outside, followed closely by the thieving asshole, who didn't realize he had sticky-fingered his way into a nightmare. Mason watched for a moment as she looked at her phone, punching in something else and frowning at the results. He tracked the asshole's movements, even as he eyed Willa, noting when he strolled into a parking garage while Willa turned and walked in the other direction.

Shaking his head, he gripped the handle of his briefcase tightly in his fist and turned his back on the woman, following the dead man instead.

Seated in his car twenty minutes later, he looked down at the journal in his hand. He had found it tucked inside the case of the tablet the man had stolen, which now sat in the passenger seat next to Mason. What engrossed him and held his rapt attention was the information scribbled on the papers in front of him. Loads of information, all handwritten, with notes and cryptic acronyms and underlines...about him. His name, his age, several addresses here in Chicago, including the one where he had nearly run into her just now. One in Kentucky, from decades ago.

She appeared to be investigating him. What he couldn't figure out was why? After everything that had happened, and all the things that had gone wrong recently, he didn't believe he could trust his own instincts anymore. What if he had it wrong and she was a danger he hadn't yet recognized? He shook his head, not buying what his thoughts were trying to sell. He shook his head again and drove home, making a call to Fort Wayne on the way. Tug reinforced his belief she was not a threat, which hopefully meant she was interested in him instead. He pulled up into his driveway, looking across at the house that was once Mica's home, seeing Molly standing in the window, waving.

He waved back as he walked inside, fingers working on the tie he had already loosened in the car. In fifteen minutes, he was back outside, pulling on his riding gloves and settling his ass on the bike. Taking the long way to Jackson's, he let his mind empty of the day, focusing on the ride instead. Trying to push away the guilt of sending Slate on a run when his woman was hardly even back to normal yet. Dropping thoughts of Tug's praise for Maggie's lasagna into background noise mode. Letting the knowledge Eddie was spending lots of nights with Bear settle into a box of goodness he could pull out later.

He sought the still center riding often brought him, but today he found the stillness disturbed by thoughts of Willa. Why was she in Chicago? Why did she appear to be cataloging details about his life? Was she an uncharted danger? Was she an opportunity? Which were the right answers?

Backing into his parking space at Jackson's, he still hadn't found his center, and then was immediately thrown even further off kilter when he walked in the backdoor. Looking into the bar through the one-way mirror Slate had installed long ago, he saw her. She was in his bar. His fucking bar. The last place he expected to find her, but given the amount of intelligence she had gathered, maybe something he should have anticipated.

Seated at one end of the counter, she sat swiveled around on her stool so she could view the entire room. The more he noticed about this scene, the less he liked it, and he found the ramp to rage was fucking slippery today.

There was a glass on the bar in front of her and he frowned. It was half-empty. Already. She couldn't have gotten here much before he did, and her drink was half gone. Surely, she wouldn't be stupid enough to get drunk in an unfamiliar bar in an unfamiliar city? Even if she couldn't tell this was a fucking biker bar off the bat, any woman set down outside of her usual surroundings shouldn't be fucking drinking alone. She didn't have a single care for her own safety, it seemed.

Merry opened the door leading into the bar and he quickly shifted to one side so Willa wouldn't be able to see him, making a face as Merry grinned at his obvious evasive maneuver. "Shut the fuck up," he growled, and she openly laughed, shaking her head.

"Who we hiding from today, old man?" She pushed the door closed and moved to stand next to him, making a noise when she realized what he was looking at—who he was looking at. Anticipating his questions, she put him off by saying, "She hasn't been here long and she's not drinking...well, not actually. She asked for a near-virgin margarita, so it's what she got. It looks real, but there's hardly anything in it, boss. She said it's window dressing."

Tilting her head to look up at him, he knew she scanned him head-to-toe and he felt exposed, knowing she would recognize the tension in his bunched muscles, in the tightness in his jaw, as out of character. Other than DeeDee, he had known Merry longer than anyone else in his life and knew she could read him in ways others would miss. Quietly, she said, "She's important to you." Eyes on Willa, he silently nodded and

Merry reached out, clasping his forearm in her firm grip, surprising him with a softly spoken, "Good, I like her."

She turned and looked through the glass at the room beyond with a sigh. "You staying back here?" Still silent, he nodded again, knowing she'd see the movement of his reflection. "Okay, Mason. I'll get Red to help me on the floor. You do what you need to do, son." She patted his shoulder, walking back through the door and into the bar.

He stayed in the backroom until Willa left at nearly midnight, frustration evident on her face.

Throughout the night, she consulted her phone several times, and he laughed when the tablet pinged more than once. He knew the tracking would show it close enough to her location she would think it a program glitch. The next time he glanced over, the factory reset screen was showing, and he knew she realized it had been stolen and had taken steps to brick the motherfucker. *Smart woman*, he thought proudly, leaning forward on his arms, palms propped on the wood holding the glass in place, face close enough his breath fogged a small circle with every breath.

For hours, he watched, so completely focused on her he simply couldn't see anything else. He drank in everything she did, every emotion crossing her features. Every single thing about her. Filing it all away, storing it up so he could pull it out later to examine it. The way she moved when she didn't think anyone was watching, the differences and how things changed when she knew eyes were on her. The focus given to each person who walked in, her unmistakable disappointment at each new face. She was clearly looking for a singular someone, and he suspected it was him, but told himself he didn't know why.

Then he realized he was trying to fool himself, remembering how she responded to him that night, his voice, his verbal demands.

From her reactions, he suspected she had never experienced this kind of instant attraction before. Knowing the type of methodical and analytical person she was, he wondered if she was trying to catalog it, decipher it. She put herself out there, gave him her number, but then he didn't use it. At least, he hadn't that she knew of for certain. He hadn't called and chatted. Hadn't asked her out. Hadn't hit her up for a hookup. Didn't give her any indication this thing went both ways, so now, she was working to figure it out, which meant figuring him out. She wasn't stalking him. From her perspective, she was probably purely researching her reactions, trying to define the attraction...maybe even what felt like a need for him. Mason smiled when her shoulders slumped at another customer's entry to the bar, and then he shifted to full alert as a man approached her.

"Bones." He shook his head as he whispered it, even though there was no one to hear. "Don't fucking do it, brother. She's *mine*." Cutting his gaze towards the glass, Bones grinned widely as if he knew Mason was there, and his entire body tightened and tensed at the blatant challenge. A moment later, he realized the man was smiling at Willa in the mirror, having caught her gaze because she had been using it to watch his approach. A growl filled the air of the backroom, and he didn't recognize his own voice. "*Mine.*"

Mason read his lips as Bones spoke to Willa. *What is a lovely lady such as yourself doing seated alone in this bar? Beauty should always have an appreciative audience.*

Motherfucker, he thought then watched her duck her head, shaking it slightly. She had moved, no longer positioned where he could view her face, but he watched as Bones reacted to her obvious rejection with a predatory grin. *The motherfucker thinks the hunt is on*, Mason thought as he pulled out his phone with sharp movements, tension apparent in every rigid muscle. Anger evident in his tone, he held down a button and barked the words, "Dial Ramos' cell."

Bones reached into his pocket, an irritated look on his face until he saw Mason's name, then a genuine smile crossed his features as he answered, "My friend, I hope you have no problems for which you need assistance." He looked up at Willa and said smoothly, in a voice pitched for her ears, "I find myself trying very hard to convince a beautiful lady to allow me to buy her a drink."

"Back. Off. You leave her the fuck alone," Mason snarled. "She's *mine*." He had the satisfaction of seeing Bones' eyes glance at the mirror then back to Willa in shock, the look on his face smoothing from charming to expressionless.

"Truth, my friend?" He spoke the question quietly, and Mason could hear the hard crack of pool balls in the background.

"Truth, brother." He didn't say anything else, knew he didn't have to, because Bones nodded then disconnected the call and put the phone back in his pocket. Without another word to Willa, he took up station behind and beside her stool, impassively standing guard over her without Mason even having to ask.

She twisted on the stool to look up at him, startled by his abrupt change in demeanor, and Mason watched as she recognized the change in mood in the entire bar as those present reacted to Bones' unspoken challenge. After a moment, her shoulders slumped with disappointment she had been made, was no longer anonymous.

She stayed much longer than Mason expected, not giving up her quest until nearly closing time. When she finally left in defeat, it was with a silent escort of a dozen bikers, a mix of Rebels and Skeptics. Forty minutes later, Bones returned to Jackson's and nodded once, knowing Mason still stood there watching.

***

Seated on the customer side of the bar, Mason found himself surrounded by friends, watching and listening as Slate and Daniel joked back and forth. It had been a couple months since he sent Slate on his run, and a few weeks ago had happily given permission for him to fly Ruby out to New Mexico. They had been too long apart as it was, and

Mason knew it from the way Slate sounded when he checked in on the road.

Motherfucker had surprised him, though, asking Ruby to marry him. Most brothers didn't take that step, treating the 'Property of' patch as a wedding ring, but damned if Slate didn't want the whole thing. He said he didn't want to leave her any loopholes, but from what Mason could determine, he didn't think she would be taking any outs left to her anyway.

Molly had lined up a sitter for the evening and was seated with Jess and Jess' girlfriend, Brandy, in a booth opposite Ruby and Mica. He allowed himself to peek at the two pregnant women sitting side-by-side and smiled. Those were happy faces, and he loved seeing the expression on Mica's features.

Bones leaned close and said in a low voice, "She is no longer your compulsion, I think." He sat back on the stool, glancing over at Daniel and Slate, who stood nearby talking to Road Runner. "I never knew how you found friendship with the man you handed her to, but I'm glad you did. Your friends bring a welcome layer of normal into our lives."

"Not an easy road, man," Mason admitted then trailed fingers across his bare chin. Bones saw and laughed.

"Smoking again? Those sticks will kill you one day, my friend." He glanced behind them at the women and frowned. "You should take Willa to the wedding. It would do Mica good to watch and see you with someone."

Mason frowned, glancing back to see Mica's eyes on him. She waved, and then turned back to Jess with a smile. "What do you mean, brother?"

"I mean she pays attention. She notices. She has guilt. Let her observe you with someone you could find happiness with, and I believe she will move on completely." Bones picked up his mug, draining it as the group crowded around the bar. "Slate," he called as he stood from the stool, smacking the mug to the bar top and pulling attention their way. "Remember, I'm bringing hundreds of Skeptics to the wedding. We expect food in grand quantities." He stepped back, seeing the array of dishes Road Runner had placed on the bar, and made a face. "And none of this frou-frou food, either. Meat. We'll want copious amounts of meat. Skeptics require manly food." He waved. "I'll see you in a couple weeks."

Mason sat, listening to the chatter of voices around him, secure in the knowledge every man here was one he trusted with his life. He let himself think about what Bones said, suggesting Mica was still invested in their relationship somewhat, and he was surprised the information didn't stir anything in him. There was no thrill of excitement that he could still be fighting for her affections, no pleasure in knowing he might cause a wedge between her and Daniel.

Instead, he found his thoughts returning to Willa. Her study of him, coming out of her way to Chicago to try to find him. Her frustration when she was entirely unsuccessful. Her outright rejection of Bones' advances, showing both men he was not what she was looking for. Mason knew the man was handsome in his own way, the tattoos on his friend's skin a bad-boy draw for many women, but she hadn't been interested in a walk on the wild side, her presence in the biker bar aside. He should use the number she gave him for more than a titillating window into her world, an opening granting him the sound of her voice for two or three words before she disconnected.

"What are you grinning at?" Mica asked, easing herself onto the stool next to him. She turned to look at him with a smile, her green eyes sparkling. Reflexively, he touched the glass in his pocket, tracing the edges of it through the fabric of his jeans as he remembered that day on the beach beside the Pacific, the peace he felt simply sitting and watching the waves.

He started to respond and then was struck dumb with a different memory, knowing between one breath and the next why Willa drew him so deep. Every time he was near her, whether in the same room, across a parking lot, or separated by a thin pane of glass, she gave him the same sense of calmness he had found beside the wide expanse and ceaseless movement of the ocean. She drew him in deep, and simply being near her was enough to let him breathe easier.

Bones' voice rang in his head, *'She sees. She has guilt.'* Nervously licking his lips, he reached out to cover Mica's hand with his palm and told her, "I met someone."

Her answering smile was blinding.

***

Smiling, Mason stood in the hospital hallway, looking through the glass at the tiny bodies filling the nursery beyond. He knew the nurses were nervous, but he would be damned before he told a single one of his brothers to vacate in order to mollify some citizen's sensibilities. Mica was theirs, and it meant her son was, too.

He focused on a bassinette near the window. There was a blue-edged card in the front pocket listing the vital statistics of the occupant. Small fists punching the air, the baby's face had crumpled into angry folds, his mouth opening and closing with shuddering jerks of his tiny chin. Feeling a presence at his side, he cut his gaze over to see Daniel. Still dressed in scrubs from the delivery room, the man looked exhausted, hair sticking up on top of his head as if he had been running his hands through it repeatedly. Mason knew it actually had been Mica's fingers pulling and tugging at the man, and smiled to himself at the memories they had built today.

"He's a strong boy," Mason said and saw Daniel's face soften, a smile of wonder settling into place. "Dark hair like his momma."

Daniel nodded and sighed. "She's finally sleeping. I can't imagine how she stayed awake as long as she did. Had to be exhausted long ago, but she wouldn't go down until you told her yes." He scrubbed at his face tiredly, saying, "Jase is driving up this weekend. He'll stay at our place for a couple of nights. Molly should be here soon. She needed to pick Tomas up at the babysitter." He looked up with a sly grin. "J.J. is coming with her. Apparently they were at her place last night when I called, but both their phones were turned off."

Mason glanced behind them, seeing the mass of black leather, jeans, and pegged boots filling the hallway for as far as the corridor stretched, the vast number of bikers the reason for the nurses' disquiet. "It'll be good to talk to Jase. We all miss seeing his ugly mug around the bar." He snorted a laugh. "I wondered how long it was gonna take your brother to break down Molly's walls. Mica's baby sister has more strength of will than he counted on, I think. She's protective of her boy, too, along with her heart." Folding his arms across his chest, he returned his gaze to the baby in the nursery, noting the child had begun to quiet himself, finding the side of his fist with his mouth. "She is something else, Daniel."

He felt a hand on his arm and turned, seeing Daniel staring at him. Fatigue etched on his face, it looked as if the man needed to find somewhere to get horizontal or he would be falling down on his own soon. Lifting a questioning eyebrow, Mason waited for him to speak.

"Mason," he started and halted, swallowing, the uncharacteristic reticence giving Mason pause. He watched as Daniel tried again. "I just...wanted to thank you."

With a nod, he reassured him, saying, "There's isn't anywhere else I'd be, man. She's a fucking treasure." Out of the corner of his eye, he saw several of his Rebels lightly tap their chest with a closed fist, signifying they had heard him and echoed the sentiment. "She's strong. She did really well, and so did you, Daniel. Congratulations again, you have a good-looking son."

"No. Not thank you for being here, but…thank you for her." Daniel's eyes crinkled at the corners and Mason stilled. "You think I don't know what you did for me? She was yours, heart and soul, there for you to keep, but you let me steal her away." His voice trembled and he paused, clearing his throat. "I love her, Mason. She's my life, and I'll be forever thankful you saw your way clear to doing what you did. I have you to thank for today, for my son." Mason felt the Rebels around them freeze in place, silence radiating out in concentric rings, his men poised and waiting for his answer, as was Daniel.

He stared for a moment, watching the gratefulness fade and fear begin to take its place on Daniel's features until Mason sighed, saying, "Shut the fuck up. Mica's always made her own decisions." He would give the man this today. Could offer this, because last night, after she had gone into labor, Daniel called him in a panic when she wouldn't leave for the hospital until she talked to Mason. Daniel knew the connection between the two of them was as strong as it had ever been, maybe stronger now she was safely out of reach, married to Daniel. With everything happening tonight as it did, he could be generous and give the man this truth. "She chose you, man. She loves you."

After Mason talked to her, reassured her, and promised to meet them at the hospital, Mica had finally consented for her husband to load her into his car and drive her. Then, she had stubbornly waited in the ER for Mason to arrive, insisting he be in the labor room with them. Nearly twenty hours later, her son was born, Jonathan Mason Rupert, and she had asked him to be godfather to the boy.

23. **Not soft**

As Bones suggested, he had invited Willa to Slate and Ruby's wedding. Now, Mason stood in a hotel hallway, frustrated, his forehead resting against the cool wood of a door, eyes closed. That thin barrier was all that stood between Willa and him. A now naked Willa, if the rustling sounds coming through the door were her taking off her clothes, as he suspected. Groaning silently, he couldn't make himself move away. His room was just up the hallway, right next to hers, and he knew from his glance inside yesterday that their beds shared a wall. They would sleep head-to-head again tonight, a mere four inches of wood and plaster separating them, much like the fragile door did now.

God, he wanted to fuck her; he found it necessary to know what she tasted like, to study how she moved underneath him. Needed to watch as she broke and came hard around him, his name on her lips. He had wanted her for weeks...months, was obsessed with her. Found himself dreaming of her voice, her laughter. He had been hard all fucking day, wanting her...but his invitation had offered her something else instead. A promise to leave her unclaimed, never counting on how badly he would need her.

"What the fuck are you doing, old man?" His softly uttered words echoed from the door, and he pushed off the surface, hearing the wood creak underneath his palms. His eyes opened when he heard the latch move, felt the draft of air on his face as the door opened, and then he swallowed hard at the vision presenting itself to him. Willa stood there barely a foot away, wearing what looked like a t-shirt and nothing else. He could follow the swell of her naked, full breasts against the fabric of the garment with his eyes, mark the shadow cast between her thighs where it covered only enough to be tantalizing.

"Mason," she breathed, and goddamned if he didn't like hearing his name roll from her lips. The tip of her tongue flicked out while he watched, wetting her full bottom lip, and he saw the gooseflesh rise on her bared shoulder. Fuck, he liked everything about her, including watching her reactions to him like this. He slowly and deliberately trailed his gaze down her body, watching as her nipples visibly tightened and hardened, rising into peaks he could examine through the shirt. Without saying anything, he lifted his gaze to her face and quirked an eyebrow, waiting for her to continue speaking.

She hadn't appeared nervous all day. Not until now. Throughout the day, surrounded by men he controlled and others he didn't, she hadn't been afraid. Even meeting the significant people in his life like Mica and her little family, baby Jon and Daniel, Molly and Tomas...none of it had thrown her. His thoughts briefly flashed back to the night Mica had Daniel's son, and her need for him to stand alongside her husband as she pushed new life into the world. Without realizing it, he allowed the moment to slide away, focusing instead on the woman standing in front of him, smiling as he did so.

Rivals and enemies had both been present today, standing alongside his friends and brothers. As he did before extending the invitation, he briefly considered what it might mean to have the knowledge out into his world about this woman being important to him. Distracted by the sight and scent of her as he had been all day, in watching her, he lost that thought, too. She took a deep breath, not to lift her titties towards him, although the effect was the same. No scheming played a part in the reason behind the breath, because she wasn't manipulative like club bitches were. She drew that breath, because she needed it, because he affected her the same way she did him, down to his soul.

Like the first night he met her, the first time he saw her...he wanted her. As they had been then, her movements were uncalculated, natural, and because of that, even more alluring. "I heard something in the hallway, but I thought you'd gone to your room."

Fuck, she's a little kooky. He gave her a look, humor lifting one corner of his mouth in a crooked smile. "So you thought you'd open the door dressed...undressed like that?" He raised a hand, trailing the backs of his fingers down her cheek to her throat, loosely cupping his palm around the column briefly, feeling the fast thud of her heart. He watched eagerly as her mouth opened and closed in response to his thumb sweeping back and forth. Curling his fingers around her shoulder to the edge of the shirt, he trailed his fingertips along the fabric for a second, and then dropped his hand back to his side, watching her shudder in response.

"I like you, Willa." He said this plainly, so there would be no mistaking his words. "I like you, so I'll warn you off one time." *What the hell am I doing?* He had a moment to think then his mouth kept moving. "I'm probably not the man you want in your life. I'm hard, and I couldn't give a shit about easy. But goddamn me if I don't like you wrapped around me on the back of my fucking bike. You've been around enough to understand the meaning behind my words, babe." He paused, watching her face as she reacted. "You tell me no, and I'll try to be good with it. I won't like it, but I will not push you into something you aren't ready for. I'll walk away right the fuck now, get you a ride back to your apartment with someone I trust. But, I like you, and I wanna fuck you." Her mouth dropped open as she took in a quick breath at his bluntness. "Not here, not right now, because I can give you this little bit of time to think. But babe, if you don't wave me off...then it'll be soon."

He moved towards her, pressing his chest against her breasts, watching as that damn tongue slipped out to slide across her bottom lip again. "When I fuck, it's hard. I'll consume you, babe, fill you with fire inside and out. Think you want that, sweetheart? Think you want me? You want soft, you need to look elsewhere, because I don't give a shit about easy or soft. But if you want hard, that I've got in spades, and I like liking you…wanting all of this with you." When she would have spoken, he pressed a finger against her lips, stopping her words with a soft, "Shhhhhh. Think on it. Sleep on it. If you want to know what I'm thinking…well, you can listen through the wall to me jacking off thinking about you." Her eyes widened and he smiled.

"Night, babe," he said, stepping back.

Their eyes caught in a stare and she gnawed on her bottom lip for a long minute, but then her chin came up and he smiled again at this evidence of her courage. She could be a good match for him. "G'night, Mason," she said in a singsong voice then stepped back and out of view, pushing the door closed slowly, letting the latch seat softly in the frame. He stood there for a minute, and then smiled widely as an unmistakable giggle sounded from inside her room. *Definitely kooky.*

24. Judge

He pulled back, carefully staying hidden in the shadows of the hallway. Watching and listening to the interplay between Mason and the girl who had piqued his interest, making him wonder exactly what the man wanted. When it kicked off, he immediately thought their conversation could be important, and he wasn't wrong. The words they spoke to each other were interesting, and even more telling were the undeclared places in their chat. He found it fascinating to hear her given a generously defined out option. He knew most men in Mason's position would simply take what they wanted...but not him. Not Davis fucking Mason. "Too fucking noble for his own goddamn good," he muttered, turning to walk back outside to the bonfires where the singing and guitar playing was still going strong.

At one time, he thought Willa might be a match for himself, but it hadn't worked out. He played at it for a while, spent time with her on the grounds of spending time with the bitch. Lies. He had moved on finally, been assigned shit to do by his old man, which took him away from the Fort in any case. Her being with Mason wasn't anything to him except an oddity to consider. A fucking strange twist in his life. Lies. Shrugging, Judge let the door close silently behind him.

25. Strange bedfellows

"Prez," the voice on the phone said, and Mason lifted his head, glancing at the screen to mark the time.

"Yeah?" His voice was hoarse with exhaustion, even though it was barely early afternoon. He hadn't been in bed long and had been looking forward to losing himself in a few hours of sleep.

"They had a problem over at Slinky's," the voice said. He still couldn't place which member this was, but knew it was someone he should recognize. Slinky's meant Fort Wayne, which reduced the possibilities somewhat. *Fuck, I'm tired*, he thought, shaking his head briskly in an effort to drive back the cobwebs. It had been a hard few days since Slate's wedding.

He had come home to Chicago to find two local clubs were back to jacking with each other over territory, so he had stepped in between them once again. If those fuckers didn't start clearing their own shit, he would take them both over, close 'em down, bring the members in, and make 'em all fucking Rebels.

"What's the problem?" he asked, levering himself into a sitting position on the edge of the mattress. He stayed in it so seldom anymore his room at the clubhouse was only sparsely decorated. Tacked up on one wall was a single picture of him with an older biker, arms slung around each other's shoulders, mountains in the distance behind them. One of the first road trips he took with Jackson. Then there was a picture of his boy, seated on a picnic table next to Mason, the two of them smiling at something in the distance, the picture framed and sitting on the dresser where he could see it easily.

"DeeDee called. I'm on my way to her place now. One of the dancers got smacked around; she wants me to check the girl out." Finally recognizing the voice as belonging to Goose, he nodded and then realized the man couldn't see him.

He cleared his throat and said, "Okay. I'll call Hoss. We'll figure out what happened. Did she say if it was a customer who smacked the girl around?" That would be the worst-case scenario, since it would mean the members assigned to security weren't doing their fucking jobs. Which would require he have a conversation with someone about getting their fucking priorities straight.

"Don't think so, but yeah, Hoss will know for certain." Goose sighed. "With Slate still in Georgia, I just wanted to keep you in the loop, Prez."

"Appreciate it, man. Ride safe." He hung up the phone and tapped a number, waiting for the call to connect.

"Hoss, talk to me." His approach was always the same—simple, open, direct, and blunt—because he found the best results most often came when you weren't worried about fluff, and didn't try to steer the conversation.

"I wasn't there, man. I left not ten minutes before she walked in, Prez. But, I know it didn't happen at the club. Evidently, her bastard of an ex-husband found her at the motel where she's been living. Best I can tell from reports is Gunny's already wrapped things up with the dickhead. He and DeeDee are taking the girl to her house to meet up with Goose so he can take care of her, check her over." Hoss knew better than to waste his time with pleasantries, and he appreciated the consideration.

"Okay, keep me updated as needed. I'm gonna try to get another couple hours shuteye. Text Slate and tell him to call me later if he can get a signal beachside, but let him know you talked to me, so he doesn't worry." Mason yawned, the hinges of his jaw cracking and popping. "Thanks, Hoss."

Disconnecting the call, he set the phone on the nightstand, shifting to his belly and wrapping his arms around the pillow, tugging it towards and under his head and upper body. The position put his bare cock in firm contact with the mattress, and as his hips moved, he felt it stirring, responding to the pressure and texture gliding across his skin.

"Fuck," he muttered. Shifting a little farther and arching his back, he remembered how it had felt to have Willa's thighs wrapped around him on the bike, how her jeans-clad calf felt under his palm when he stroked down and back up her leg.

He had taken her to the wedding with the hopes of seeing how she would react when surrounded by hundreds of his brothers and friends. If she appeared the least bit skittish, if she had been hesitant or afraid, his path forward might be less clear.

She hadn't, though. She seemed to be at ease, comfortable and chatty with members of his club family. Certainly aware she was under careful scrutiny, she responded to every question with collected poise, her answers honest and open as she comported herself admirably. *Strong, confident, sexy as hell...she could be a perfect old lady for the national president of a powerful, nationwide MC.* He shook his head, snorting at his thoughts. *Stupid shithead, I just want to fuck her, not keep her.*

Oh, yeah, he had wanted to fuck her bad that weekend. He made a humming sound deep in his throat, nearly a growl, because merely thinking about her made him want to fuck her; that was for sure. He had even half-ass planned to at the hotel, but when he called to tell her she would be riding up with him, something about the nervousness in her voice got to him. So he changed his mind, making reservations for two rooms instead. He thought about their encounter in the hallway, the way her breasts had pushed at the shirt she wore for sleeping, the way the skin of her shoulder felt underneath his hand.

If only she were here right now, he thought, and groaning, reached down and smoothed his palm up the underside of his now engorged cock. Rolling to his back, he slowly began stroking himself, and as he had the night after the wedding, he kept her chestnut hair and hazel eyes in his mind. Seeing her plump lips and imagining them wrapped around...he groaned again, folding his fingers around his cock more firmly, his other hand sliding down to cup his balls, pulling and tugging firmly at his sac.

In his mind, he undressed Willa, had her face-down on the bed, hands caressing the rounded curves of her ass. He imagined his hands on her hips, tugging her backwards and up onto her knees before he slammed deep inside her.

Hips thrusting his cock through his fingers, he bit back another groan. It was nearly torture to have a picture in his head of him taking her hard and fast from behind like he preferred, her breasts swinging pendulously with every thrust, nipples teased erect from friction against the sheets. Especially when he hadn't gotten close to her pussy all weekend, unless one counted her sliding up behind him on the fucking bike, her heat and scent wrapping around him even at speeds of eight-five.

Can she come on my cock alone, or will she need my hands? he wondered, bicep bulging as his arm moved quickly up and down, the length of his stroke becoming erratic. Eyes closed, working the mushroom head of his cock, he watched the scene play out in his head, of his hand reaching out to wrap his fingers in her hair, tangling themselves in her curls. Stroking root to tip now, hard and fast, he visualized tugging firmly to pull her head backwards, exposing the sweep and angle of her neck. Using his grip to steady himself, he powered into her, hearing the slap of flesh on flesh. Dimly, he was aware of the mattress shaking, bedsprings complaining about the ferocity with which he was masturbating.

Please, she said. She was begging to come, whispering the entreaty over and over, and he slipped one hand under her belly, landing two fingers sharply on her clit, the snap of the slap and quick, rubbing pressure on the bundle of nerves pushing her over the edge. She tightened around him as she came.

His fingers tightened around his cock. He shifted back to short strokes, focused on keeping the rim of the head bumping over the calluses of his fingers, rough and wild. He groaned a final time as he came hard, hot streams of semen splashing high on his belly and chest as he drew breath in and out in gasping pants.

He lay there for several minutes, feeling the sweat on his chest and shoulders beginning to dry, his breathing slowly evening out, muscles gradually relaxing. Reaching down, he grabbed a shirt off the floor and used it to scrub the abundant evidence of his activities from his skin. *You are so fucked*, he thought as soon as he realized this climax from his hand was better than the last dozen he had shot off into voiceless, faceless pussy. "Keep trying to tell youself you don't want to keep her," he muttered, punching his pillow.

Rolling to his stomach once again, he sought the solace of sleep in his solitary bed. His dreams that night were filled with Willa, and in these illusionary scenes, he took her slowly, face-to-face, stroking her soft skin, murmuring in her ear of love.

***

Fuck, he thought, leaning his head exhaustedly back against the wall of the bar. He always seemed to come home to Jackson's when things fell to shit. It was unbelievable to him. Everywhere else in his life could fall apart, but simply being present in Jackson's—the scene of his greatest failure—would help to ground him. He heard a noise and cracked open one eye, groaning when he saw Bones seated at the bar in front of him, silent and still.

"We're not open yet, ninja motherfucker," he said, closing his eye again.

"I need you, Mason." Those words struck fear in his chest and he slowly sat up, frowning at his friend.

"No flowery words of wooing? You think simply an 'I need you' is enough to get in my pants these days?" He joked, but was rapidly evaluating the face in front of him, not liking a bit of what he found. Since he had gotten back from the wedding, it had been one fucking crisis after another. Bear left; the man fucking ran off and left a cluster behind. In the aftermath, Mason had worked with Tug and Maggie to make sure the kids he had adopted were going to be okay after yet another fucking abandonment.

Dominos and Disciples were fighting again. Fuck the again part of the thought, because their conflicts seemed to be constant these days, but he couldn't find out the reason why. It wasn't Hawk's girls this time, because Mange had already laid claim to the oldest one, and Houlihan, Hawk's old lady, had forced him to be okay with it, because it was what the girl wanted. No, this current conflict seemed forced from the outside, but he couldn't find the trigger...yet.

In Fort Wayne, the dancer beaten by her ex-husband turned out to be Jase Spencer's kid sister, working for the club in the strip joint DeeDee managed. Talk about a potential for drama. Fucking soap opera. Mason snorted, thinking, *As Slinky's Turns*.

Now he had fielded a call from Willa telling him Eddie was missing. His niece, but no one knew about the relationship except Tug. He had turned out a response, getting his brothers there in the Fort in the wind to check on things. One of the members had been supposed to be watching out for her with Bear gone, but he had been called away to deal with some bullshit with another dancer, leaving her exposed. Mason knew everything had to be connected, but he couldn't figure out which pieces held it all together.

"No. Just bald need," Bones spoke again, and Mason jerked in his seat, having nearly forgotten the man was there. "Diamante took two of my warehouses."

Mason sat up, looking Bones in the face. Anger lodging hot and sharp in his chest, he said, "Las Cruces Diamante? Are you telling me fucking *Lalo* came to Chicago? *My* fucking town?" According to Watcher, Lalo was the brutal president of a club whose entire membership thrived on terror and destruction.

Laughing soundlessly, Bones shook his head. "*Chicago* Diamante. You are behind the times, my brother. Did you not receive my messages about the new club in town? When did you turn into an ostrich, burying your head in the sand?"

With a shake of his head, Mason said, "I've been kinda caught up in my own shit." He looked down at the seat between his boots for a moment, and then looked up at his friend. "Anything, Bones. Whatcha need, man? Rebels stand with Skeptics; you know that's truth. Has been for years now."

"I simply need to trust that Hawk and Mange won't be looking my way during this time of unrest." Pressing his palms flat on the bar top, he said, "I can—how do you like to put it?—clear my own shit. But, Mason, I need you to step up and clear yours, too. You have long left those clubs too much room to wiggle, and now they have tangled themselves all up on their leashes. Time to tighten the hold, my friend. Shorten the leash and bring them into the fold."

Mason laughed bitterly. "Easier said than done—" But he stopped speaking when Bones shook his head.

"You let the Devil's Sins run. You let them run for years, and we all saw the pain your mistake brought to your club...your family, in the end. Bring these two to heel before lightning strikes again." He cocked his head, evidently seeing the shiver running up Mason's spine at those words. He had used them not long ago to refer to his attraction to Willa, likening both Mica and Willa to lightning, and asking Slate if it ever struck twice. *Fuck.*

Not something you haven't already considered, he thought, turning over the list of pros and cons he had written in his mind. If done right, this could strengthen his already powerful club by giving them dedicated members who had an established leadership paradigm. Paired with the businesses they owned, bringing them in made even more fiscal sense. *Time to man up.*

"Okay." He sighed, ran his hand across his jaw, and said, "Okay. I'll handle it. I think you have the right of it, man. I'll clear my shit, brother. My patch on it." He thumped a closed fist to his chest.

With a satisfied nod, the man across the bar stood. "Belief in your words runs deep for me, my friend. There will come a time when I too call you President, I think." He sighed and turned, walking out before Mason could recover enough from his surprise to respond.

***

One day later, the Rebel Wayfarers had grown by two additional chapters. North Chicago and Milwaukee, the former Dominos and Disciples clubs, had patched in without bloodshed or loss of any brothers. It had been unreal how quickly things had moved once he made the first phone calls. Mason laughed when he remembered the face of the man who made their patches when told they needed a hundred and twenty new ones by the weekend.

Tater was proving a valuable asset in Chicago. Mason had set him up with the responsibility for the successful integration of those clubs with the Rebels. With the failure of the Des Moines chapter still haunting his eyes, Mason knew this would be a charge he took seriously. He liked the man and could envision a dozen ways he could use him both in Chicago, and elsewhere.

Now Mason was sitting in the clubhouse office in Fort Wayne, waiting on Bear to arrive from the east coast where he had been holed up for two weeks. After talking to Tug, he found they agreed the best way to handle this was to lay it out for him, to simply tell him what was going on with Eddie as soon as he arrived. If things worked out as he hoped, Mason would be able to spend the evening with Chase while details were organized. Tomorrow, the club would be on the move, heading west to bring one of their own home.

Earlier in the day, he talked to DeeDee about the gal, Sharon. Gunny had moved her to his house as soon as she was well enough, and now he toted her everywhere he went. She said it seemed an obsession at first, but now when Sharon was around him, the man seemed centered, stable for the first time since she first met him. Mason's gaze swept the room and smiled grimly, seeing only male faces. Hauled her everywhere except to the clubhouse tonight, which was a good thing, because business like this was just for the brothers. No old ladies or girlfriends were needed for the hard conversations to come.

He felt his phone vibrate and pulled it out of his jeans, surprised to read Donny Baugh's information on the screen. He stepped back into the office and kicked the door closed as he answered the phone, anticipating some shit about Bear was about to come out. "Yeah?" he answered, propping an ass cheek on the corner of the desk.

"Dennis remembered something, Mason." The somewhat nasally voice brought Donny's face to mind, the twisted, white scar from his facial reconstruction surgery worn proudly, like a badge of honor. Born with a cleft palate deformity left poorly corrected too long, the man was short, years of living with a feeding tube taking their toll on his growth and stature. He was also a man with a prickly sense of honor. Mason generally liked him despite his attitude, but Donny had pissed him off recently with a refusal to pass messages along to Bear until threatened.

"Yeah? So the fuck what?" Mason wasn't the least bit surprised to find he was still angry with the little man.

"The guy who jacked him, Dennis thinks he saw him at Slate's wedding." That statement drew tension into Mason's every muscle. There had been enemies as well as friends at the wedding, but no one who would have any beef with the Baugh brothers. *Unless it was because of the partnership they formed with me*, he thought.

"Who?" Without thinking, he barked out the single-worded question, and then, as he heard Donny's preparatory intake of breath, he found himself suddenly wanting to turn back time. Turn it back to before the call, so he could decline it. There was so much shit in the wind right now, and he knew...even before Donny spoke, he knew what the answer would be.

"It was a guy from California named Judge. He hung on the fringes, but Dennis saw him talking to Bear late on the last night." The sound came down the line of Donny moving restlessly, and he knew it had cost Dennis something to find this memory amongst the other lost ones in his head. "It was something in the way the shadows lay across his face that triggered the memory, and he's been working to piece things together since we got home."

"You think he's got the right of it?" Mason wanted the response to be no, but he already expected Dennis wouldn't have said anything unless he were certain.

"Yeah. He's sure. He believes he has this right, and I'm convinced he's not wrong. The night he was carjacked...the night he got shot, he said he remembers this guy leaning in through the passenger window and telling him, 'Tell them blood is thicker.' Do you know what it means?" Donny's voice deepened as he said, "Why would anyone want to..." He paused, and then asked the painful question, "Mason, was Denny hurt because of the shop? Because of my ambitions?"

"I don't know, Donny," Mason lied. "Let me figure some shit out up here. We're waiting on Bear right now; he should be here within the next couple of hours. And once he gets in, we'll be making fast decisions on what's gonna happen over the next couple of days. Tell Dennis thanks, man. Every bit of info helps."

"Yeah," Donny sounded unlike himself, lost, and Mason wanted to reassure him.

"It's good he found a memory from so close before the shooting, isn't it?" Dennis had been shot point blank in the head by the carjacker, surviving against all odds, but not without a cost.

"Yeah, it's good. Neuroplasticity is always good with TBI. You and I both know I'm lucky to still have him around. It was a near thing for a while." Mason heard a noise in the background and Donny said, "I gotta go. He's yelling for his guitar."

"Music man, always the taskmaster." Mason allowed himself to smile as they disconnected the call, thinking about watching Bear and Dennis play their guitars by firelight at Slate and Ruby's wedding. He scowled to think Judge had been there, floating around, maybe even enjoying that same music...something nearly made impossible by his actions.

26. **The Devil we know**

Forty minutes, he thought, looking at his phone. It was all the time it took him to tear a brother's world apart, and then give him the blocks to begin building it back again. Shooter had called for Eddie's return to the west coast by any means necessary, and they learned Judge had acted on the demand, taking her home by force. Earlier, Tug had recounted for Mason his role in returning Eddie to her father once before, back when she was a teen, both men shaking their heads at how things had rolled around again. "Don't let him fool ya," he told Tug, "bastard has way more than one trick."

So many plates to keep spinning, he thought, seeing Jase walk through the door with his arm around DeeDee's shoulders. Thank fuck she had gotten her head on straight, because she needed the man in a way clear to everyone who had a chance to see the two of them together. Maggie was home with Bear's kids, but she knew her son was back in town, because Tug had called her, promising to keep her updated as he could and signing off the call with a softly spoken, "Love you." *Second plate.* Hoss had pulled Gunny over to chat earlier, and the man had declared his intentions about Jase's little sister. The fucking jarhead had latched onto that little dancer and seemed determined to keep her safe. *Plate number three.*

Slate called his name and he looked up, raising one eyebrow. He heard, "Daniel's friend came through. We've got the jet for a week; Myron and Digger are working to find an airfield to suit our needs." Mason nodded, turning away and going back to scanning the room. Slate had done the hard thing and sent Ruby home earlier today. She was huge with his baby and looked exhausted, needing the rest, even if it had to be with brothers in the apartment protecting her. *Plate number four.* Mica had called him earlier, worried because Jon had a cough. *Like I could fucking do anything about it*, he thought irritably, but he had put Goose on the phone with her and the man had calmed her nerves. *Number five.*

Benny, Slate's baby brother, strolled through the room with Chase in tow, both carrying guitars and disappearing upstairs. *Six and seven, all rolled into one.* His phone rang and he looked down, cursing to recognize Watcher's name showing on the display. *What the fuck now?* he thought, saying, "Yeah?"

"Bones called and mentioned you might have absorbed his pain this week." Watcher was never one to mince words, and Mason appreciated it, especially right now, when things were so chaotic around him. "I'm gonna say good on ya, Mason, but you coulda called me, given me a heads up. Still, good on ya, brother."

He grunted in response and then said, "Yeah, seemed the least I could do for an old friend. He's dealing with the Chicago Diamantes, which is headache enough." He had last spoken to Bones about twenty-four hours ago and could only trust things were still headed the right way there. *Eight.*

"I believe he was able to get the storage situation settled to his satisfaction without difficulty." Watcher sounded smug, and the uncharacteristic reaction made Mason frown.

"How so?"

"Estavez and I cut them off from any assistance from the...home team, shall we say." *Interesting*. It meant the Soldiers and Machos had joined forces to take down the New Mexico chapter of the Diamantes. "Wanted to let you know Deacon's got a paddle, man. He's stirring shit as fast as he can. Understand from folks he's even talking to Shooter these days."

"Yeah? I'm thinking about making a visit out west soon, so there's a good chance you and me will have some notes to compare." *Nine*.

"Sounds good, brother. Let me know if you need me. Soldiers will stand with Rebels any day of the fucking week." The words brought pride to Mason, swelling his chest. This was what he had wanted when he knocked Deacon off his pedestal, a club others wanted to be affiliated with, a club men wanted to join, fought to become part of. *Ten*.

"I know it, Watch. That road travels both ways, brother. I'll be in touch."

***

With shaking hands, Mason slowly typed in a group text and hit send. The missive went out to national and local chapter officers, and a few additional people who mattered, and simply read: ***Got them. Bringing everyone home alive.***

Those few words could never convey the terror felt when he realized once again Bear was set on self-destruction. That he had taken all their careful plans, backed by hard-won intelligence and on-the-ground knowledge, and thrown them out the window, tearing off on his own.

Mason looked down the length of the plane to where a bruised and battered Bear slept. Awkwardly belted into a seat and covered to the neck by a thick blanket, he was slumped over, dried blood crusting his lips. In the seat next to him was Eddie, her dark hair pulled back into a ponytail. Her head was on Bear's shoulder as she slept, too.

Across from them sat the surprise of the night, another strange cog in the wheels that seemed to spin around Mason all the time. Joel Graham, Bear's brother-in-law, had been standing outside the Outrider's clubhouse, firmly planted beside Bear when they rolled up in a hurry, having chased their brother from the airfield when he left without them. Bear had been staggering on his feet, but he was holding tight to an unconscious Eddie, clutching her to his chest as if someone would dare try and take her again.

Joel...Blue Line, was president of the Malcontents, the club who had been stinging Shooter for a couple years, and the man had proven a valuable ally. Once Mason had Bear and Eddie loaded into a van and headed off the compound property back towards the airfield, Blue Line had turned back to the building with them and helped rain destruction on the club. In one night, Mason had effectively dismantled Shooter's club, putting to ground all who tried to fight, torching the colors of every member, dead or alive.

It had been a satisfying moment. Standing and watching as Duck systematically stripped the cuts from each body, every man, and threw them in a disordered pile, soaking them with gasoline they found in the garage. In the chaos surrounding them, he held Shooter in place with a tight fist in his hair. Upright but kneeling at Mason's feet, the man had been forced to watch as the symbol of his club—the club entrusted to him by his father—burned to ashes.

Blue Line then made some calls, and through a process that wasn't yet clear to Mason, traded detailed information on the Outriders' operations for Rebel immunity from the night's business. Mason shifted in the seat, hearing the quiet ping over the plane's sound system indicating they were about to go airborne. He looked around at the men he brought with him, noting the only one who showed any real damage was Bear. *Stupid motherfucker*, he thought then remembered the way the man had held Eddie, as if she were the most precious thing he had ever experienced, and wondered if possibly he had seen the last of the old Bear. Perhaps this time the man would be willing to look forward instead of back.

Judge was the only real sore spot in the night's business, having somehow gotten in the wind and ghosted clean away. In the hours since the fires died down, there were no reports or sightings; no one had heard from or seen him. He was just gone...*poof*. Staring down at his hands, Mason flexed the left one, watching the inked head of the Phoenix slide across the bones and tendons with his skin. Mason hadn't shared Dennis Baugh's reclaimed memories with anyone yet. It hadn't seemed the right time or audience.

Mason leaned his head back as the plane gained speed, bumping over the ground. Shooter was going to jail, hopefully for a long fucking time. Judge had nearly killed Eddie with the dope they used to keep her quiet in the van from Indiana to California, and Shooter had laughed about it. Had laughed about everything, the death of his brothers, the destruction of his club...everything. The only time he stopped was when Mason asked about the club's charter, telling him it was 'safe.' Then he laughed again as Mason tore the safe key from around his neck, knowing that would be where it was kept, because it was Deacon's way, and Shooter had been raised by Deacon as much as he had been by Morgan.

In the safe, Mason had found reams of information on the club's operations and allies, with surprising notes on plans involving him. Already, some of it was on the way to Gunny, in the hopes it would help him find Judge. The ex-Marine was tenacious, and once set on the scent, he wouldn't give up, no matter what he found. They had spoken at length, and he explained about his relationship with the Morgans. Gunny had earned his confidence a dozen times over the years, and now he had trusted in the man's discretion, taking a chance and telling him nothing was sacred. Look everywhere.

With a lurch, the plane left the ground, finding its wings and lifting into the night sky to take them all home. Mason tipped his seat back and closed his eyes, listening with amusement to his brothers arguing over what movie they wanted to watch. He fell asleep with their good-natured complaining in his ears. The dream began with a memory...

He looked down at her, sleeping in the bed beside him, her dark hair spread across the pillows. Smiling, because she looked sated but tired, he reached out a hand, dragging one fingertip down the slope of her nose, pausing on her lips then traveling to her neck, absently tracing back and forth across her skin. He knew he had to go soon, had to catch a plane, bring Eddie back.

She had been surprised that evening when he opened her front door and invited himself inside. She had obviously been expecting someone else, and he felt a rush of resentment at whoever she had left the door unlocked for. Standing in her small kitchen, frozen in place, she held a wooden spoon suspended over a pot of water, drips slowly gathering and dropping from the bowl of the spoon back into the pot. There were a variety of ingredients spread out on the counter near her, packages and notecards lying in piles. Chaos in cooking, *he thought with a snort.* "Whatcha making?" *he asked, padding across the room towards her.*

"Mason," she breathed, and he laughed, feeling how natural the sound felt in this room. Liking the feeling.

"Pretty hard to make me. Not hard to make me hard; you just have to breathe for that to happen, babe." He stopped in front of her, crowding her space, remembering the last time he had seen her, leaning against the outside of her apartment door when he dropped her off after the wedding, eyes drooping sensually, knees weak from his kisses. "Willa, you should lock your door."

"One of the foster kids from upstairs needs some supper. I told him I was making maccy cheese." She gestured at the pot, tipping her chin up to look at his face. "If he has to knock, he won't come in. So I always unlock it and then leave the food on the table."

"You leave food on the table?" He leaned in closer, running his nose along the curve of her cheek, drawing in a lungful of her scent with a silent groan as the muscles in his stomach tensed and clenched in response to her nearness.

"Yeah, he's too nervous to ask, so I leave it in a container. He comes in, I wave, he waves. He picks up the bowl and leaves." Her breath caught for a moment when he nuzzled behind her ear, and he loved hearing her reaction to him. "No nerves needed, nothing much to say. Easy, breezy. But, this way I know he gets fed regularly. They aren't a great foster family, but better than most, so as long as I can make it right all around, he's good there." She lifted one shoulder in an uneasy shrug, the motion jerky, awkward.

He liked how her mouth ran when she was nervous; it underscored the kooky he enjoyed so much. She shrugged as if this was situation normal in Willa World. He suspected it might be, but still... "Babe," he said softly, nibbling along her neck, lips moving across her soft skin. "Doors have locks for a reason."

She nodded and said cryptically, "Danger comes in all sizes."

He pulled back to look at her face, because it wasn't what he expected her to say. He wanted her to tell him he was right, and she would lock her door from now on. That she would take care of her...for him. "What?"

"Look at Eddie." She sounded so sad, and he found he needed to change that, so he leaned in again and softly kissed her lips, placing the barest amount of pressure against her mouth, watching as her eyes fluttered closed.

"Lock your doors, babe," he said against her lips, not wanting to be distracted by tomorrow's business.

"Why would Judge do it? He'd watched and taken care of her for years. Why would he hurt her now? I liked him. He was nice to her...nice to me. Why would he do this to her, his own sister?" Tears trembled at the edges of her lower lids, and mesmerized, he watched as those glistening diamonds clumped in her lashes. "Why now, when Bear's already destroyed her? Lukie Pookie. I liked Judge, dammit."

"Bear's back, babe," he said, lifting one calloused finger to gently clear the tears from her face. "And we're getting Eddie back. That's one of the things I came here to tell you." He leaned in and kissed her again. She responded to his touch with more heat, and he pulled back, smiling to catch her stretching to stay in contact with his mouth. "And to visit you. I'm real glad to see your face, babe." He cupped the back of her head, and then glanced over at the pot. "Water's boiling." Fingers in her hair, he tilted her head, covering her mouth with his own, slanting and moving against her, pressing her back against the countertop. He ground his hips into her belly, working her lips with his, teeth nipping.

He pulled back when they were both panting, her eyes half-lidded, those tear-clumped lashes still evident, but now her face was flushed, swollen lips parted, and there was heated desire in her gaze. "Babe," he said with a slow grin. "Water's boiling."

She squeaked and jumped sideways, brandishing the wooden spoon. "Maccy cheese," she said, her voice breathless, but threaded through with determination. Grabbing absurdly large oven mitts, she picked up the pot of water, dumping it in a gush of steam into the sink. He winced, thinking the macaroni wasted, and then peeked over the edge of the sink to find she already had a colander waiting and smiled at her prep work. Still wearing the mitts, she picked up the metal strainer and shook it, draining water from the noodles. Glancing back over her shoulder at him, she grinned broadly. "Just maccy for now, but soon...soon, there shall be cheese. Or, at least processed cheese substitute." She picked up the spoon and stirred the noodles, draining the last bits of water from the pasta before returning it to the pot.

"Alrighty, babe. We've got mac and cheese for the boy upstairs who doesn't want anyone to notice he's hungry, but you see him anyway.

Your door is unlocked so he doesn't have to knock, and the dish?" He paused until she pointed the spoon at a cabinet, where he found a dozen throwaway containers waiting. "And the bowl of food on the table, so he doesn't have to ask for it." Handing her a bowl and lid, he smiled, leaning in against her back to bite the side of her neck gently. "Mac and cheese it is."

She sighed and rested against him, eyes closed as she stirred the butter, milk, and squeeze cheese mix into the cooked noodles. A sudden noise in the room had Mason reacting quickly, spinning, pushing her behind him and ignoring her squawk of surprise. There was a boy standing not ten feet away, and Mason watched with disbelief as he stalked another step closer, his hands balled into tight fists at the end of thin arms.

"You get away from Miss Willa," the boy said in a low voice, and Mason fought off a grin. The kid was wound tight, nostrils flaring with anger, and he was trembling with the need to keep Willa safe from…him.

"Jimmy John Michael Thomas from Dorkimus Extreme, I'd like you to meet my friend Mister Mason of the Masterful Mystery Movements." She pushed past him, putting herself between him and the boy, and he let her, for now. She squatted down, and a little of the cloud lifted from the boy's face. Mason knew now he must have thought Willa was being hurt.

Gaze locking with the little man over the top of her head, Mason silently snorted at the thought an eight-year-old boy would be competition for Willa's affections. She reached a hand out behind her back, towards him, flipping her fingers insistently, silently asking for his cooperation. He sighed, squatting on the floor behind her, slipping his thick thighs around the outside of hers, taking amusement from her reaction the instant she realized there was a large, erect cock pressed against her ass. She eeped and threw him a startled look over her shoulder then settled her gaze back on the boy.

"I have a problem." Even without being able to catch sight of her face, he knew from her tone she had scrunched up her nose. "I made too much food. There's no way Mister Mason and I can eat it all."

"Miss Willa, I know how you hate things to go to waste." The boy nodded solemnly, reaching up to push his dark hair away from his face, the movement revealing a painful looking bruise on his cheek for a moment before the hair flopped back to cover it. Mason frowned at the sight, remembering Willa saying this foster family wasn't bad, wondering exactly what constituted bad in her book.

"I have this one ginormous bowl." She stood, leaving Mason kneeling on the floor. "And it's full to the brim of cheesy goodness." He heard the snap of the container's lid popping into place, but kept his eyes on the boy, who continued to watch him steadily. She walked past him, past the boy, and put the container on the edge of the table. "I can't find it right now, but if you find it, could you take care of it for me?"

The boy tipped his chin down, looking at Mason with a fixed gaze from his grey eyes. Mason felt uncertain, as if something hung in the balance in this moment, and he swallowed then nodded slowly at the boy. "You got that?" He asked the question without being certain exactly what the answer should be, but then the boy nodded and he took a relieved breath.

"Yeah, I got this." He nodded then jerked his head towards Willa, where she had moved to lean against the counter in front of the sink. "You got that covered?" he asked Mason.

Seemed the boy fancied himself a little bit of a hard ass, and at his reaction, Mason fought to kill a smile. He liked that about the kid, Jimmy. He nodded solemnly and said, "Yeah, Miss Willa's covered." He got a chin lift in response, and the boy left the room silently, thin arm reaching out as he passed the table to snag the bowl off the surface. A moment later, Mason heard the snick of the door clicking into the frame and he pushed off the floor, rising to his feet.

"Thank you," she said earnestly, lips stretching with the full, generous smile he liked so much, and he nodded.

"Masterful Mystery Movements?" He grinned back at her as she laughed and rolled her eyes.

"First thing that came into my head. Sorry." He watched as she looked at him, the hilarity of the moment passing and the smile fading slowly from her face as they stood apart, separated by only a few feet of space, but it suddenly felt like much more. He watched her chew the inside of her lip, gaze dipping to the floor, and she stood a little straighter, no longer comfortably lounging against the cabinet. "Mason," she started to speak, and then her voice trailed off. Licking her lips, she began again, "Mason, why are you here?"

His head recoiled backwards and he froze. Mica had asked him the same question once. Mica, his first real love. A citizen. Just like Willa. Panic settled in his chest as his thoughts tumbled through his head in a rush. What the fuck am I doing here? Am I painting myself into the same fucking corner again? He registered movement and looked over at her. She was waving a hand in his direction. "Hello? Where'd you go? I asked why you are here in Fort Wayne. Is it because Eddie's missing? You said Bear's back?"

With a huff of relief, he moved towards her. Thinking could wait for tomorrow, when there would be club business to handle, but for now, he could deal with her. "Yeah. We have a line on Eddie, but my boys needed a little time to get transport set in place. I wanted to check on you, babe. Like I said, I'm real glad to see your face."

Slipping his hands around her waist, he curved them down and under her ass, lifting and balancing her on the tiny edge of the cabinet. "You do your thinking, babe? You decide what you want?" She nodded and he stilled his hands, which had been restlessly roaming her body, stroking and caressing her. "Gonna tell me?"

Her head dipped again and she leaned forward, pressing her face into his neck while her legs rose on either side of his hips. Her whisper came, soft as the night stealing across a desert sky, and she gave him everything when she said, "I want you, Davis Mason. All of you. Hard...and soft, if you can find any. I want it all."

He pulled back, looking down into her face. She looked so certain, so assured of her decision, that he found himself questioning on her behalf. "You sure, Willa?" She nodded, eyes locked on his, and he smiled, hearing his own satisfaction when he said, "Well, alrighty then." Lifting her in his arms, he carried her up the hall, pausing and retreating to the front door when he remembered. Reaching out, he twisted the deadbolt and put the chain on. With a frown, he asked, "That all the security you got?" She giggled and nodded, pressing her cheek against his chest. He shook his head, and then cupped his hand back underneath her ass to press her tight.

Once in her bedroom, he let her feet slip to the floor and, with a growl, told her, "Clothes off. I want to see you. Want to discover everything I've been thinking about, dreaming of." She stared at him for a moment, and he felt a thrill of fear, but then she stepped back, hands moving to the waistband of her jeans. He watched her undress, seeing her legs revealed as she pushed her jeans to the floor, tilting his head when he became confused at her actions. "Babe?"

"Uh huh?" This had been grunted from underneath the shirt she was removing over her head. It was a feminine grunt, but a grunt nonetheless. By his count, this would be the third shirt she had taken off, and she still wasn't down to skin.

"You got a thing for shirts?" Efficiently removing his own clothes, he unbuckled his belt and pants, letting his jeans sag while he took out his wallet, removing two condoms and placing them on the dresser. Replacing the wallet in his pocket, he let the jeans drop to the floor with a noisy clatter of wallet chain and pocket coins. Folding his cut, he

draped it over the edge of her dresser, and then picked up the condoms, seeing she was now working on a fifth shirt.

"I hate bras." She said this like it made sense and he laughed...hard. Her head peeked out the armhole of the camisole she was currently removing and she scowled at him. "Seriously. I hate bras. But I hate having the girls play peek-a-boo headlights, so when I'm home, I just layer up."

"Got many more layers to go, babe? I got a knife here somewhere." He pretended to search the floor, laughing again when she eeped and scampered away to the other side of the bed.

"Last one," she muttered, her hair wild around her head from the tussle with her clothing. She gripped the tiny shirt and threw it at him, and he laughed aloud when it lightly fluttered to the floor barely halfway across the room.

"Mmmmm." He hummed with pleasure, taking a long look at her bare form. "You naked up real nice, babe." He held out his arms, staring at her face, wanting her to come to him without having to ask. Wanting her to want him, to want to feel them together. To trust him enough to give herself over to him. And, she did.

Delicately sidestepping the clothing strewn across the floor, moving as if to unheard music, she waltzed over to him and folded herself into his arms, sighing as he wrapped himself around her, pulling her close. "Now that's nice," he murmured, lips pressing against the side of her head.

"Mmhmm." She made an agreeable noise and he laughed, which in turn made her laugh and say, "You rumble when you laugh."

"I rumble?" He laughed again just to hear her giggle, and she didn't disappoint. He moved them towards the bed, arranging her beside him as he propped himself over her on one elbow.

"Hmm." He hummed again, threading the fingers of a hand in her hair, using his grip to tilt her head backwards. Moving his lips along the edge of her jaw, he slowly made his way to her mouth, where he nibbled and ate at her. Teasing her, he dipped his tongue slowly into her mouth then retreated when hers moved to tangle with his. He laughed, lips pressed to hers, and then his mouth opened when he felt her fingers wrap around his cock.

"Not laughing now, are you, pretty boy?" Voice light, she teased him, tightening her grip, and he stilled. He had never had anyone play with him in bed like this. "Mason?" She said his name questioningly, and he tilted his head to look at her. "I didn't...I mean, I didn't hurt you, did I?"

"No, babe," he reassured her, shifting and pulling his cock out of her grip, missing the heat of her hand immediately. Kissing along her shoulder, he moved his hand to her breasts, lifting and plumping the one farthest from him while he nuzzled and licked the other. She gasped, and he repeated the movements that had drawn the noise, pulling another short intake of breath from her.

"You could never hurt me," he said, taking her nipple into his mouth and sucking gently. He slipped his thigh between her legs, lifting his knee to push them wide apart, dragging his leg up and against her pussy. He trailed the sole of his foot down her calf then lifted his knee again, pressing hard against her while he sucked harder on her, tweaking and pinching her other nipple.

He pulled back to look at her, loving the glassy-eyed stare she gave him. Softly, she whispered, "It's like you're everywhere. That's amazing." He moved his lips back to her nipple, felt her fingers on his shoulder, and knew she was looking at the tattoo. He waited, but the expected questions never came. Instead, her fingers moved to his neck, and then his face, and she cupped his chin in her hand, lifting his face towards hers for a kiss.

He shifted to lie between her legs, cradled by her hips. Wrapping one arm underneath her, he lifted her shoulders, nipping hard at the muscle on the side of her neck. Still caressing and plumping her breast, he shifted the hand that was underneath her down, sliding it under her ass and pressing her up against him there. "I can't get enough of your skin, babe," he said, smiling against her throat. He shifted his body slightly, loving the feel of her all along his front. "You're soft, and you fit into me exactly right," he tightened the muscles in his ass, pushing his cock against her. "All the right places."

"Gonna fuck you, babe," he warned, pushing up onto both elbows, letting her sink back into the mattress with him on top of her. He reached out, pulling one of the condoms off the nightstand and opening it. Sitting up on his knees, he gripped himself, smirking to catch her avidly watching him apply the condom. "You've seen one of these before, right?" he asked, pressing down on his cock with his thumb, releasing it and letting it slap back up against his belly.

"Asshole," she grumbled, and he laughed.

"No, babe. See, this's why I asked. We don't want any confusion, do we?" He bent over her again and slipped his hand underneath her again, pushing down past the curve of her ass and levering two fingers between her cheeks to stroke the tight hole there. "That's an asshole," he instructed then lifted an eyebrow at her as he slowly caressed her puckered entrance with his fingertips, causing her to shiver. "What you were ogling a minute ago is a cock."

"Dickhead," she blurted then clapped a hand over her mouth with a giggle.

"Mmmm. It's sometimes called a dick," he agreed, pressing the first few inches inside her with a slow glide. "And it's got a head." He tightened his abdominal muscles, twitching his cock hard to pull a laugh from her he could feel down to the root. "What you feel there, that's the dick head, babe."

She gasped when he shifted again, pushing into her farther before he stopped. He had only gone this far with one other woman without setting boundaries, and was torn about what to do next. "Babe," he said softly, "I fuck hard."

She nodded, matching his tone when she spoke, "You told me there wasn't anything soft or easy to be found in bed with you."

"If it's too much, babe. If I get to be too much and you tell me stop, I'll listen, okay? You tell me stop, and I promise you, I'll listen. I'd never hurt you." He was trembling as he spoke, the struggle to hold himself back nearly too much, but wanting her to hear the truth in his voice. "You feel so fucking good wrapped around me, your cunt around me. Wanna fuck you, babe." He was nearly wordless now. "Need you. You."

She moved under him, lifting her hips in invitation, and he accepted, plunging deep inside her and holding there, then pulling back only to thrust back in again and again. Rough and fast, he covered her body with his, sweat coating them both and making their skin slippery, hard to hold. He wrapped his palm around her waist, and then moved it under her ass, pulling her up against him.

She made soft little sounds of encouragement and he fucking loved it, loved hearing her. He loved her hands on him and told her so, feeling the never-ending slip and slide of her palms over his biceps and shoulders, down his pecs and along his sides then back up to his head.

Muttering, face buried in the pillow beside her head, he said, "So fucking good like this, so different, you're so good, babe. Can't wait to bend you over, take you standing, have you everywhere. Fuck you. Touch you." He sucked in a breath then grunted as she tightened around him, and he pounded hard and deep, grinding into her, feeling her hips lifting up against him again and again. "Fucking good." She drew him in, initiating a scorching kiss, their tongues fighting for touch, teeth clashing as they nipped at each other brutally.

"You want me from behind, Mason?"

He heard the question and answered without thinking, the words coming in between pants of air, "No, face-to-face, just like this. I want to see you. Need to. Some kinda glad to see your face, babe. Fuck you. Goddamn, you feel good under me...around me. Right." He reared up in bed, never pulling out of her, but moving to his knees. His hands on her hips as he rocked into her in that position, pushing deeper inside and watching her titties bounce and shift with their quick, hard movements.

Breathlessly, she told him, "More." And he gave her more, using his thumb to press and flick her clit, feeling her tighten around him. Her fingers holding onto his wrists as he shifted back to her hips with his hands, pulling her onto him one last time, grinding into her as she arched backwards, chin lifting towards the ceiling, coming hard around his cock.

Vibrating with the tension of holding back, he waited for her to finish, stroking her belly and sides gently, using the edge of his hand to wipe the sweat from her skin. It had been as fast and hard as he had warned her, and...God...she had given him back everything he needed. He watched carefully in order to identify the moment she began sliding back down the other side, and when her eyes slowly opened, finally focusing on him, he smiled and simply said, "Again."

The second time was slower for her, and as they moved together, he studied the deep, rich pleasure held in her eyes and on her face. Cheeks lifted in a constant half-smile, the crinkles never left the corners of her eyes, and when she looked at him, it was with an expression of bliss. Touching him, rolling her body along his, everything about the act made evident the joy she held inside her at being with him. Giving that delight to him, handing it to him freely, she let him feed off her emotions as he desired, bringing both of them so much farther up the slope. Never greedy, not his woman, always giving him everything.

Raising her smiling lips again and again for soft lip touches, she slid her nose across his cheek to whisper in his ear how good it felt to have him inside her. The intimacy of the moment disarmed him entirely.

Seduced by the connection forged between them, he couldn't catch his breath, couldn't do anything but move with her and listen as she talked to him. Called his name. Told him how glad she was he had found some soft for her, and he realized he had. This wasn't fucking, not even remotely. This was something else entirely, and he soaked up the experience, because making love was novel to him, happening only twice before in his whole life.

This time, when she came, it was with her eyes wide open, staring into his. Her hands cupped the back of his head and neck, forearms straining to hold their foreheads together as he moved inside and above her, keeping that connection throughout her climax. As she peaked, her mouth partly opened, lips curling at the edges as she breathed his name, forcing him to feel everything sweeping through her. Wonder, surprise, amazement...love.

Now he lay next to her as she quietly slept, and he thought about the business of the day. Her eyes had been so bright and unclouded last night as they made love. He didn't want to be the reason she worried. He liked her personality as she was, light and easy, bubbly and full of giggles. The girl who didn't lock her door, because an eight-year-old boy might need refuge. He leaned down and softly kissed her lips, smiling as she made a noise. Even in her sleep, she was searching for his lips again when he pulled away.

Then he forced himself out of her bed, dressed, and left. Carefully locking her door with the key Gunny made for him, and he rode away, back to the clubhouse and club business.

He woke for a moment when the plane bounced in the air, peering down the fuselage to see his brothers were quiet, most of the men peacefully dozing. Everything was good for once, and he closed his eyes again, chasing his memories back down into sleep, searching for a return of the feeling of joy he found in Willa's bed.

27. Legacy in ruins

Getting fucking tired of hiding, he thought. Straddling the seat of the bike he used to escape the compound, Judge watched as the plane taxied and took off, wings wagging for a moment in the wind off the Pacific coast. He had been ready when things went to shit last night, but had still barely gotten out in time when Mason had showed with the cavalry.

Even then, he hadn't traveled far; hunkering down in one of the hillside lookout alcoves he had talked Shooter into constructing last year. Seemed the Rebel intel on the compound didn't include recent changes like those, so he felt safe enough to sit and watch. Safe, at least, until the feds came calling. He took his leave at that point, but by then had heard enough to know the location the Rebels based their raid out of. Over the hours he sat and waited, he made sure to identify and mark every one of Mason's people, memorized every fucking face, especially the big motherfucker who burned the patches.

He had been on his way to check on Eddie when he saw Blue Line and Bear moving through the maze of hallways, and had instinctively paced them, staying hidden. Carefully staying just ahead, he used shadows and turns to conceal his presence before ducking into one of the rooms near hers, assuming she was their destination.

In the van, he hadn't honestly been trying to kill her, but the fucking bitch simply wouldn't shut up. Even when she was knocked the fuck out, she moaned and cried, and was noisy as shit. It had gotten on his fucking nerves until he just wanted some peace and fucking quiet. Babysitting her was shit work to begin with, always had been...and then to have to deal with her fucking mouth? Shit work, always his lot.

With the hallway door open slightly, he had watched through the small gap as the two men paused in front of her door, Bear visibly shaken by the sight meeting his gaze through the small window. Blue Line had spoken quietly to Bear, and then it sounded like he slapped the door in anger. Judge's lip raised in an unconscious sneer now when he thought about the president of the Malcontents, Blue Line. His father had been considering a merger of the two clubs, which was what Eddie was supposed to help move along. She was intended to be a...peace offering.

Bear had reacted strongly to the man's words, but called him 'Joel' in response, using his government instead of his club name, and was apparently surprised to have ran into him. Not only in the compound, but the fact Blue Line was in the life had stymied him. Which was fucking odd, because it would indicate a personal knowledge of the other that predated Bear's association with the Rebels, which tracked back nearly a dozen years, as Judge well knew.

Then shit had gotten decidedly interesting, because his old man had stepped out of the room behind the men. From his vantage point, he could examine Shooter's face, and the anger he saw there was frightening, especially to someone who had been on the receiving end entirely too many times. He remembered the shock that replaced the anger on those well-known features when Bear reached out, bruised and battered as he was, still able to lift the older man in the air with two hands on his neck, choking the life out of him.

Fucking good riddance, he remembered thinking as his old man was tossed like a sack of trash into the room he had come out of only minutes before. He watched as Blue Line and Bear retrieved Eddie and, with clinical remoteness, marked her pallor and stillness as they moved up the hallway past his hiding place. Still alive. Once he was certain they were gone, he stepped out and across the corridor, slowly opening the door to find his father not dead, but coughing and groaning. *Pity*, he thought again now.

Then...they had themselves a little chat, him and his old man. Through a little pugilist persuasion, he found out a wealth of knowledge he had never before caught wind of. He was suddenly able to recognize connections, where before he had only known blank pages. Shooter was still breathing when he walked out, he made sure of that, because he now had a better target for his focused hatred.

"Fucking family," he muttered, watching the plane until he could no longer catch sight of it in the twilight sky. "Goddamn fucking family always screwing up my goddamned *fucking* life." He switched on the motorcycle, deftly turning it on the narrow access road and heading back into San Diego. He had watched his legacy demolished tonight, members killed or arrested, inventory confiscated or burned. Ruined. Everything he had worked for since he was twelve years old swept away in a single motion. "Fucking Davis Mason."

28. Running scared

"She's a sneaky little woman." Mason smirked in admiration. He was standing in the waiting area of the ER, waiting for Bear to be taken up to a room, when he heard the news.

Deke, one of the Fort Wayne officers, grinned back at him, nodding. "Our Ruby can keep a close secret, boss. I guess she'd known she was going to have twins for at least a couple months, since before they got hitched, but she never said word one to Slate."

He glanced back into the treatment room, seeing Eddie still seated on the edge of the bed there, Bear's hand gripped tightly in both of hers, eyes trained on his sleeping face. "Bear's gonna have to stay here a few days. They're worried about his lung staying inflated this time." Over the past couple of years, their brother had been on the losing end of more than one fight, and this time his punished ribs had sliced into one of his lungs. The medic Tug's nephew had arranged in Cali had patched him up for the flight, but it was evident to all of them the man needed a doctor as soon as they had landed.

Mason yawned, his jaw cracking loudly. By the time they got to Chicago then hopped to Fort Wayne, Eddie was awake, the drugs that had still been in her system in San Diego finally working their way through. Mason had to be the one to tell her she had been betrayed by family. Her man had damn near been killed by them, and her own future was on hold until they could find Judge.

He was proud of her then, watching as she gritted her teeth, holding in the flood of questions she naturally wanted to spew, asking only the most important ones. Growing up around a club, she had been in the life nearly all of hers, so she quickly sorted through the extraneous to the critical. She asked about Bear, his head resting in her lap, her fingers nervously running through his hair. Then she asked about his kids, adopted from a member Mason had put to ground, and about her father and brother, not flinching at the answers of jailed and in the wind. Then, she finally asked about Willa, and he had been happy to set her at ease on that topic, at least.

"Where's DeeDee?" He didn't turn but trusted Deke would still be standing there, because he hadn't yet dismissed him.

"Upstairs, standing outside the nursery, watching over the little lumps." There was a smile in Deke's voice that made Mason happy to hear it. Damn but they needed more good like this, things to celebrate.

"And proud pappy?" He turned, grinning to spy the open-mouthed amusement plain on Deke's face.

"Probably still yelling at Ruby." They shared a wry look. Slate wouldn't live this one down for a long time, if ever. Cautiously, Deke told him, "Jase is up there with DeeDee, boss."

He nodded. "Good. We're getting closer with him. Thanks." Deke nodded and moved off as Mason turned to look back into the treatment room, seeing the nurses there with a gurney. Eddie stood, taking a single step back away from the bed, watching like a hawk while they transferred him. Mason froze when he heard a loud beeping coming from one of the machines, and waited to discover if it was a false alarm, rapidly growing concerned when the hustle and bustle of the medical staff didn't slow.

Eddie's voice was raised with questions that were going unanswered, so he added his to them. "What the fuck is going on?"

One of the white-coats raised his head, saying, "He needs surgery, after all. We're prepping him to move now." His eyes swept from Eddie, who wore a bloody men's shirt, to Mason, who had lost his shirt entirely, leaving his cut over bare skin. Raising his eyebrows, he said cautiously, "There's a waiting room for surgery. One of the nurses can show you, brother, but I need to move him now."

Mason nodded, noting the acknowledgment of his club and rank. Hands reaching out for Eddie's shoulders, he pulled her back against him, moving them both out of the way of the staff. He walked up the hallway with her, following the gurney with Bear's body on it until someone stood in front of them, hands out, barring their way. Once pointed to the waiting room, he parked her in a chair and made half a dozen calls before taking up position behind her, one hand on her shoulder.

Deke and Pinto were the first to arrive, followed closely by Gunny. That gave Mason his first glimpse of Sharon, Jase's sister, and he frowned. She was so slight; next to the huge ex-Marine, she seemed waiflike, awfully fragile. Then she smiled up at Gunny, and Mason's heart nearly stopped at the sight of the love shining through. From the look Gunny returned, anyone could recognize the man was so owned. She was just a little thing, but his woman owned him. He would die before he let anything happen to her again. Whether Jase knew it or not, he could sleep easy about his sister now.

Seeing Slate in the hallway, Mason abandoned his post, walking quickly towards him and wrapping both arms around his friend, the strength of the embrace acknowledging everything that had happened in the past seventy-two hours. Without saying a word, they exchanged the understanding that life was fragile and friendships like theirs hard to hold. Pulling back, he wasn't surprised the wetness in his eyes matched what he saw in Slate's. Scowling, he gruffly asked, "Is Ruby okay, man?"

"Yeah, she's better than okay. She's gonna be the best little momma." Slate grinned and Mason realized, for once, there was no strain on the man's face, his brow was unfurrowed, and his smile was unreserved. "My babies are so stinkin' cute, man. You gonna come up and see?"

"Wouldn't miss it for the world, brother. Not for the world." He hit Slate's shoulder lightly with a closed fist. "Twins? Fucking twins, and you couldn't tell she was carrying?"

"Fuck you," Slate said fondly, grinning. "She told me our peanut was okay; that's all I ever wanted to know."

"What'd y'all name 'em?" Mason asked, yawning again.

"Allen Martin, after my dad and Winger, and Danielle Susan, after Lockee and Mom." He offered this with a small smile, and Mason knew before his recent trip Slate would have never named his daughter after her grandmother. He wasn't sure what had happened in Colorado, other than Slate had gone to visit his mother for the first time in years, and he came back lighter and happier than anyone had ever seen him.

"Good names, brother," Mason said, glancing back into the waiting room in time to watch Willa enfold Eddie in her arms. He studied the tearful reunion for several drawn-out minutes, not hearing or paying attention to anything else except Willa, seated not twenty feet from him. Finally, she lifted her head from where she had burrowed into Eddie's neck and unerringly met his eyes, seeming to know by instinct where he was. He looked at her for a long time, her gaze locked on his until she mouthed the words 'Thank you' to him. She waited for his slow nod before tipping her head back down and burying her face into Eddie's shoulder again.

***

Mason's head came up when he heard the sound of the key in the front door lock, and he impatiently ran a palm down his stomach. After everything, she was finally coming home, and he was waiting. Halfway surprised at her silence, he was frowning at the door when she finally appeared, her head peeking around the doorframe. "Mason?" The quiet question caused something to tighten in his chest; he forced the feeling down, putting a smile on his face as he looked at her.

"Yeah, babe?" He had to fight to keep his voice even, but she would never know it. He could do laidback and casual. *Fuck yeah, I can*, he thought.

"Just...making sure it was you," she said quietly, leaning her shoulder against the edge of the doorframe.

"Babe," he stated in a scolding tone. "You notice my bike outside?" He knew she had. He had parked it bold as brass on the sidewalk leading to her apartment, so she would have to step around it to get inside.

"Uh huh," she agreed, still not smiling.

"You recognize that bike?" Maybe she never paid much attention to the differences between his scoot and other rides.

"Yep," she said, popping the 'P' and tilting her head.

"You expecting anyone else here tonight?" This answer might piss him off, but he knew from Tugboat and his other watchers that she didn't have anyone, hadn't had a partner for a couple years.

"Nope," she said, making the same popping noise on the 'P' she had done before, one corner of her lips lifting for a moment.

"Then why you calling my name like a question, babe?" *And, what the hell is she still doing all the way across the fucking room from me?*

"Just making sure it wasn't a dream." Now he got a smile from her, a ghost of one, but still it turned her lips up at the corners, and he liked he brought a little humor to her tonight.

"No dream, I'm right here, Willa. Yours for the taking, if you want." Clamping his lips shut, he ran his words back through his head, confused. *What the fuck did I mean by that?*

Unwinding herself from the doorframe, she took a hesitant step towards him, and then pulled herself to a stop. "I don't want to sleep with you." She blushed, and he enjoyed watching the color move up from the top curves of her breasts, along the column of her throat, and into her cheeks. "Not *sleep* sleep. But I would like to sleep...with you."

"Okay." He huffed out an exasperated breath, and then clenched his teeth for a moment. He never had anyone turn sex down before...no, that wasn't right. He had never put himself in a position to give women the chance to turn him down before. Sex was always about political maneuvering or a pure physical release—*except with Mica*, his internal voice offered, and he scoffed. Looking at Willa, he was not offended, merely surprised. Not that he had offered, but...he snorted at himself. *You're layin' naked in her bed when she gets home from seeing her best friend in the hospital. Of course, she knows you want to fuck her.*

"Can I hold you? Can you give me that?" He asked this, only knowing how important the questions were after they left his mouth, when his chest and belly clenched, waiting, slowly relaxing as he watched a soft smile cross her full lips.

Her head dipped then her eyes lifted back to his as she said, "I'd like that."

Me too, he thought, flipping back the covers for her to crawl into her bed beside him. Softly, he told her, "I'd like that a lot, babe."

He held her through the night, unsleeping, watching as she moved in and out of a doze. Each waking brought more questions, some silly, some serious, but she was never surprised to find him when she woke. She was as relaxed as if she slept with him each night, and he found comfort in the ease with which she accepted him into her bed, her house, and he hoped...her life.

"Did you know he used tequila to drug her?" Her tone was put out, aggrieved. "Tequila? Asshat. She loves tequila." Muttering, Willa turned her face into his neck and went back to sleep as he frowned.

Snuffling and sighing, she grumbled, "There are never enough extension cords." He laughed silently at that one.

"I gave you my number," she whispered, turning her face away from him.

"I know," he said back, kissing her shoulder. "I called you."

"Not for weeks and weeks. Months. I'd given up hope." Still whispering, he watched her stick out her bottom lip in a pout.

"But I called," he repeated, and she nodded as she went back to sleep.

"Not the sprinkle ones. I'd rather have baklava." She sighed, nuzzling into his chest with a shiver. "Turn up the heat, wouldja? Hospitals are cold."

"Mmmm." She hummed, pressing her lips to his shoulder. Nipping his skin, she whispered, "You're so dreamy."

Shifting against him, she drew her leg up across his thighs. "What will you do to Judge when you find him?" He liked knowing she didn't question his ability to locate the man, but wondered at the question and concern for the snake who had hurt her friend.

"Why do you want to know, babe?" He waited, wondering after a minute if she had gone back to sleep, and then she answered.

"Because I'm confused about how I feel right now. I liked Judge; he seemed like one of the decent guys, but wasn't. I can't stand that I misread him so badly. It makes me question everything else in my life." She rolled away from him a little, turning into his arm and resting her head on his bicep. "I liked him." Her hand smoothed up and down his forearm, slowly stroking his skin.

He stilled. She meant she was attracted to him. His Willa had thought about Judge sexually, had maybe wanted to fuck him...and now it made her doubt other things. He knew she was wondering about her attraction to him. That insecurity was probably behind her not wanting to '*sleep* sleep' with him tonight. *God-fucking-dammit.* "Just because we like people who turn out to have asshat tendencies doesn't make us a bad judge of folks, babe. Hell, there's lots of people I've thought I could trust who proved themselves so far on the other side of the asshat line by the time we arrived that I couldn't even eyeball back where we started."

"Yeah, but you're a badass biker dude who deals with lots of other badass biker dudes all the time." Her voice was muffled, and he felt the first hot tear strike his skin, rolling down the curve of his muscle. "It's more likely you'll run into asshats in said badass settings. I'm a public school tech wizard. I don't run in badass circles. My badassery opportunities are remarkably limited, and I still found an asshat."

"Willa," he said softly, shifting to put his chest against her back, tugging her tightly against him. He nuzzled into her hair, finding the skin of her neck and biting it softly then placing an open-mouthed kiss there. "I liked him, too." *He's my blood*, he thought.

"Yeah, but you didn't *like him* like him." He had hoped he was wrong, but she utterly laid that to rest. *Dammit.* She reached down and cupped her hand around the outside of his thigh, tugging. Answering her unspoken plea, he moved to push her top leg forward, resting his knee between her legs, wrapping her up a little tighter.

"Babe," he said with a warning clear in his tone. "I'm a patient man, but you don't want to be talking about other men you find attractive when I have my cock pressed against your nearly bare ass." She eeped and snuffled, and he arched his hips forward, pushing harder against her, drawing another eep out of her. "Especially when I had to leave your bed the last time to go take care of the shit that same man left behind. Hard as fuck to walk away, and that shit is on him. I'm not patient by nature, but I can be, and I'll respect you not wanting to fuck tonight, but I'm not immune to wanting you."

They lay quiet for a while, and he thought maybe she had slipped back off to sleep, when she whispered, "You didn't want to leave my bed?"

"Fuck no, babe. You were naked and beautiful, and I'd just been inside you and found out I liked being there…liked it a lot. In every way, you fit me like a glove, butter soft and delicious. I didn't want to leave, no fucking way." He kissed her neck again, feeling his cock bump against her ass when it jumped and twitched in response to the memories flooding his mind.

"The door was locked," she said.

Pulling a page from her book, he simply said, "Yep," popping the 'P.'

Silence again for a minute, and then she whispered with wonder in her tone, "You liked it?"

"Babe," he said, rising up on one elbow so he could roll her onto her back and examine her face. Eyes closed, she stayed in profile, head turned to the side, refusing to look at him. "Yes, babe. I liked it a lot." He cast his mind back, thinking of the time he had spent in this bed, with her in his arms. He told her he was a hard man, that he fucked. He told her he would stop if she needed him to, but never once had he told her what was really going on. What he was feeling.

"Babe, look at me," he said, and her eyes opened, flicking over his face before closing. "Keep 'em open, smartass." Schooling his face to an impassive expression, he waited until her gaze was firmly settled on him then he smiled at her, lifted cheeks crinkling the corners of his eyes. His smile brought a warmth to her eyes that caught fire inside him until he nearly couldn't stand the heat and tightness in his chest. "I loved being inside you, Willa. That night...to me, what we did in this bed wasn't fucking, babe. It was much more than that, so it's okay if you felt it was more. Because it was, at least for me." Her hands, which had been stroking up and down his sides, paused, stilling in place as the import of his words struck her.

Leaning down, he nuzzled her cheek with his nose. "It was a lot more, babe. Hardest thing I've done was to peel myself off you and crawl out of your bed. No joke." He kissed her softly. "I told you to think and you said you'd done your thinking. You know what being on the back of my bike means, babe. You're mine, you tracking?"

He waited until she nodded, and then continued, "Mine in every way that matters. You don't sleep or *sleep sleep* with other men. I can't be here all the time, but I'll come to you every chance I can, Willa. This means you don't make unscheduled trips, because I need to know where you are. *Need to*." He thought about her trip to Chicago, deciding to keep his knowledge to himself for now. "Mine, you tracking?"

"I'm tracking, Mason," she said softly, eyes open, gaze still fixed on his. There was a soft smile playing at the corners of her lips, and he leaned down to kiss her soundly. Her hand crept around the back of his neck, cradling him close when he would have pulled away.

"Alrighty. We already talk, but we'll do more. Babe, I call, you pick the fuck up, because if you don't pick up, I'll have brothers out looking for your ass." She made a noise and he paused, moving back and waiting, then prompted her with, "Yeah, babe?"

"I work, Mason. I can't always answer my cellphone." She scrunched up her nose, and he remembered the boy from a few nights ago and how she sounded when she was trying to put him at ease. The thought made him smile at her again, and the corners of her eyes crinkled in response.

"I get that, babe. I can be reasonable. But, when you're outside of work, you pick the fuck up. And, you lock your car, starting today. Lock the apartment, too. We can discuss hiding a key and telling the boy where it is, but you're going to take care of *you* first. Before anything else, you take care of you." He leaned in and kissed the tip of her nose. "Because you belong to me, and I make damn sure my property is taken care of. You don't lock up, don't pick up, and we'll have a different discussion."

"Property?" The word came out on a surprised rush of breath, and Mason grinned.

"Property of Mason," he said, nodding. "Yeah, buddy." Then he froze, because it was too much...too big a step, too soon. He thought in confusion, *What the fuck?*

"I'm no one's property, Mason. You can't own people. That's kinda illegal," she contested his words hotly, and he was surprised at himself he didn't argue.

"Okay, but you need to take care of you...for me," he said, leaning in so he could nibble on her earlobe, not wanting to look into her face right now. "So you pick up, you lock up, and you talk to me." He slipped a hand down her belly, sliding his palm against her skin all the way down between her thighs. Curving his fingers, he found her wet and slippery, and he pressed a fingertip gently against her clit. "But right now, babe," he murmured against her neck, "I want to stop talking and get you off."

"Mmm hmmm," she hummed in response, and he grinned.

She slept again, afterwards, and he held her, gaze fixed on her face, tracing the contours of her features with his fingertips. She woke one last time before he had to leave. He knew it, because her hands started moving over his skin again, and without opening her eyes, she told him, "I could love you, Mason."

Once he was certain she was asleep again, he nuzzled into her hair, dropping a kiss on the side of her head. Feeling how she nestled trustingly into his side, he softly said, "I could love you, too."

***

"Yeah, she matters," he confirmed, reaching out to pluck a blade of grass, trapping it between his thumbs and lifting it to his mouth. Producing a loud whistle when he blew across it, he turned to see a smile on Merry's face.

"You gonna bring her back up here, introduce me properly?" She had her hand on his back, rubbing slowly up and down underneath his cut. They were seated on a blanket kept in the trunk of his car for this purpose, the bedding laid to one side of Tilly's grave. "I liked her when I got to meet her that once, but I'd like to see the two of you together." She tilted her head, looking at him from the corner of her eye. "I hear good things about you when you're with her."

"What kind of things, woman?" He was genuinely puzzled, because he didn't act anything but himself, ever.

"I hear you laugh, that you take the time to enjoy things. That you aren't only about the club—" She stopped when he shook his head.

"Club comes first, you know it. It's how it has to be to make things right for my brothers. To keep things profitable." He looked at the words on the headstone; they still had the power to wrap bands of steel around his chest. Tillery Thompson, beloved husband and father.

"You'll always do that, son. It's part of who you are now. I'm talking about you taking time for you, to build something with this woman. The one time you had a chance at love before, you couldn't take it. She wasn't right for you anyway." She said this dismissively, and he laughed.

"Will anyone be good enough, Mom?" He was teasing her, but saw the smile on her face fade. Was something wrong with her family? She and Tilly had two boys, one of whom had passed, so she had her grandson living with her.

"She wasn't right for you," she repeated. Her hand continued its sweep, up and down. "Any woman oblivious enough to put you through hell for years, never knowing how you cared about her, would never be good enough. Willa though?" She paused then looked at him, her smile returning. "She traveled out of her way to look you up, spent hours in a situation that made her nervous as hell. She was totally aware of how everyone around her looked up to you, and made sure to behave in a way that would reflect well on you. A woman like that, who knows about your life and cares enough to protect you in whatever way she could? That woman...she'd be a match for you."

Leaning over, he kissed her on the cheek then tilted his head down, no longer seeing the grass between his boots, but hazel eyes lifted to his.

***

He stood in the lot near her little car, watching as students left the building and headed towards the line of buses waiting at the curb. He saw a small hand lift in a brief wave to him and recognized Jim, the foster kid from the apartment above Willa's. He raised his hand in return and watched the little man jump up the steep bus steps two at a time. A moment later, he saw the face framed in a window and then realized the boy was pointing towards the building.

Mason turned and went motionless, taking in the sight of her walking towards him. He saw the smile curving her lips and felt a tearing in his chest. *Fuck, she's so goddamned beautiful*, he thought and stood waiting for her. When she reached him, she didn't stop walking until they were nearly chest-to-chest. He lifted one hand and curved it around her waist, tugging her closer as he tilted his head to brush his mouth across her lips. He felt her hand curl around his and she gave him a squeeze. "*Hola*," she said. "*Como estas?*"

He nodded twice, brushing another kiss across her mouth. "*Bien*," he said. "*Muy bien, mi corazon.*"

She pulled back, wrinkling her nose at him. "Yeah," she said, "hello and how are ya...that's about all I got."

He laughed, lifting his head and seeing the kid's face still in the bus window as it pulled away, attentively watching him and Willa. "Wanna ride?" He asked the question even as he handed her helmet over.

"With you?" she asked teasingly, and he growled at her.

"Babe, you riding on anybody else's bike? Just gonna tell you once," he rested his forehead against hers, "ain't gonna happen 'less you want said man dead."

"Jealous?" She flipped the question out while her fingers worked on the helmet strap, sure movements testifying to the number of times she had ridden astride behind him over these last few weeks.

"Fuck yeah," he growled, nipping at her lips. "Mine," he said in a deep voice, loving the way she shivered when his tone hit her. Stroking his palms down her shoulders to her bare arms, he felt his muscles tense at the thought of another man with his hands on her. "My woman." He stepped backwards, tugging her with him to the bike parked next to her car. They settled on the leather seat, slightly heated by the sun, and he started the engine, weaving their way out of the lot, leaning hard as he pulled onto the street.

An hour later, he steered into the lot of a diner and they stood, climbing off the bike. Willa groaned, rubbing her ass with both hands. "God," she said, "my ass is numb."

Mason tipped his head back, laughing hard, and she looked at him with a scowl. Reaching out, he grabbed her hand and pulled her towards the diner, saying as they walked, "I'll tell you a story about Slate and Bear over supper." He wanted her to get all the jokes, wanted her to fit in better and better each time she was around his Rebels. Knowing she had repeated what Bear had often said during his first long run with Slate would be just the first of many insights into the life. He glanced back at her laughing face, their fingers wrapped around each other. *Owned*, he thought and smiled, knowing it was true.

After they ate, at her direction, he took them to a skate park and was amazed at the number of kids she knew there. More than half of the boys brave enough to come up and say hello offered her their board, with a tentative variation of, "If you're lookin' to rip, Miz Shipman."

Mason quirked an eyebrow at her and she laughed quietly, ducking her head. "Look at me, Willa," he ordered, and her chin immediately raised, gaze locking on his. "You skateboard?" She lifted one shoulder and tilted her head, shrugging. "I wanna see this," he said then repeated it, somewhat differently, "I seriously wanna see this."

Without looking away from him, she raised her voice and yelled, "Need a board. Gonna get some kinda gnarly up in here."

Three boys headed their way, and she pointed at one of them, who immediately grinned his smugness at being selected while the others stopped in place, a defeated slump to their shoulders. The young man picked for the task glanced at Mason, but his focus was fully on Willa as he approached.

With a quickly muttered, "Thanks," she accepted the skateboard from the boy and stepped away to set it in place on the lip of the cement ramp, putting a foot on it. She yelled, "Dropping" as she pushed off and down into the swirling mass of skateboarders...backwards. "What the fuck?" Mason gritted out, gaze glued to her as the boy laughed.

"She's fine." He heard words that were supposed to be reassuring, but uttered by a kid who was hardly old enough to shave, talking about his woman who was right now riding blindly into danger, those words were far less so than the kid intended. The boy continued, "She's goofy-footed, but Miz Shipman can fucking rip. Watch this; she's gonna do a Madolly off that hip. Watch this...look at this; she bustin' big time, man." There was a pause as they watched Willa do a jump, and the boy covered his mouth with one hand, scarcely hiding a broad grin as he bent double with a laugh. He rose on his toes, yelling, "Rip it, Ship-it." To Mason, he said, "Relax, old timer. She hardly ever slams, dude. This is her norm loc for sessions. She knows the glide. There's a lotta footage of her. You should check out the boards, scan her freeze frames. She bustin' alla time." Mason didn't understand a lot of what the kid spouted, but what sang out loud and clear was his admiration and affection for Willa.

He held his breath, watching for the next five minutes as she wove and rode between the crowds. She skillfully found lines to follow between the people and skateboards, leading her to places she could swoop and jump, expertly ride the edge of a ramp, do intricate footwork on the board...all without falling, stumbling, or running into anyone.

When she returned to his side, panting, a broad smile firmly in place, he reached out, pulled her into his arms, and kissed her. He threaded fingers into her hair and tugged her head back, possessively covering her mouth with his, licking along the seam of her lips, demanding access to her mouth. When he broke away, they were both breathing heavily, and he rested his forehead against hers, eyes closed. He felt her move, and pulled back to see she was holding the board out to one side, her eyes still firmly closed. Mason caught the kid's grin when he relieved her of the skateboard, and then her arm was wrapped tightly around Mason's waist, her face buried in his chest. "You liked it?" He could barely hear her over the music piping into the park, the noise the boards made rolling across the joints between the slabs of cement, or the cries of excitement at a trick mastered. One arm possessively around her shoulder, he turned them towards the exit.

In the relative quiet of the parking lot, he leaned against the seat of his bike, pulling her to stand in between his legs. "Yeah. Fuck yeah, I liked it." He put his arms around her, holding her close. "What does goofy-footed mean?"

She laughed, turning her face to rest her cheek against his chest. "According to the guys, I skate with the wrong foot out front. It's simply how I learned, how I skate." With another laugh, she said, "Always puttin' my goofy foot forward's my motto in life."

My woman is full of surprises, he thought. With the sounds of the skate park as background, they were both silent as he held her for a long time until his phone buzzed in his pocket for the fifth or sixth time and she asked him, "You gonna answer your phone?"

"Probably should," he responded but didn't move, content just to hold her for a time.

29. Balance lost

As he turned the bike's front wheel towards Fort Wayne for the third time in as many days, Mason thought about why he was headed down this time. He had been there only last night, hadn't been home more than a few hours before he got the call. Nothing was making sense, and this kind of shit made him crazy. *More Insane than normal*, he thought with a snort.

He could nearly hear his father in his head, remembering sitting on the stoop listening to him talk about mining and how a miner would decide to attack a seam once the company gave the go-ahead. *Start from where you are and plot out where you needa be, and then follow that path like a taut line through water. Methodical and easy-handed, only thing what helps make an old miner.* Pale light shown high in the eastern sky, and he shuddered at the chill winding its way down his spine.

Utah. That was the biggest question mark, since he knew where the string wound up on his end, but he needed to trace it back to the beginning. Birdy, who had been a brother for a few years now, had betrayed them. He had been a gypsy from a club out in Utah, added to their ranks after given high praise when Red had called his old president. The man had hung through a short prospect period, more to make sure everyone fit than anything else, since he had references and was already in the life.

He was a good enough member, worked hard and was respectful to officers, but the man had a serious hard-on for non-members, hangarounds. Mason had seen his attitude raise its head on more than one occasion, but couldn't figure out what it could have to do with this present situation.

Mason downshifted to idle through a tollbooth, tossing his coins and waiting for the arm to lift before he gunned the engine again. Hangarounds. Why would the man have gotten down to business with Manzino's sister? What did he have to do with the drug dealer? Some kind of association seemed to be an ironclad assumption, since Slate said they picked him up in one of the bitch's meth-cooking locations.

Did Birdy have anything to do with Gunny's disappearance? According to Hoss, nothing was out of place, merely Gunny and Sharon gone. But the minute they told him the man's dogs were in a cage in the basement, Mason had known it was not a voluntary absence. Even before they discovered the bodies in the bedroom, Mason had known. He doted on those dogs, called them his pups, and he would have never left them to starve in a locked, dark room.

Utah. His mind kept circling back around to that topic, and then he had a thought. Pressing on the earpiece he put in before getting on the bike, he said, "Dial Watcher's cell."

"Mason, motherfucker, what's this I hear about you taking an old lady?" Watcher sounded like he had been up for hours, not likely just woken at four in the morning.

"Deacon." With one word, he felt the coldness radiating from the phone. Deacon had an association with Diamante, had been behind the near takeover Watcher had struggled through recently, and Mason's friend was hell-bent to get his hands on the old man.

"I'm listening."

"He have anything up in Utah? I got more shit here than I know what to do with, and I keep circling back to Deacon, because there isn't a better solution." He gunned the engine on his bike, relishing the way it leaped underneath him. Yesterday, Gunny had made him a present of the bike. *Jesus, fuck, that had only been yesterday?*

The Vincent Black Shadow was a rare and sought-after motorcycle, and he knew he would never be able to pay Gunny back, but once he saw the bike, he hadn't been able to tell the man no. For one, it had meant a fuckton to his brother that he accept the gift; the emotion had been shared plainly as Gunny talked through things. But, for the honest truth, Mason had wanted the bike as soon as the cover drifted to the floor, exposing the black and chrome monster.

"Nothing in Utah I know of, why? Tell me what's going on, brother." He knew Watcher would do anything he could to help, if only by listening to Mason talk things through.

"Birdy came to me by way of Provo. Chief stood for him." Chief was the president of the Legends club based out of Provo, Utah, and he had vouched for Birdy. "Had good reports all around and patched him in a while back." *Give or take his shit with hangarounds, everything had been okay.* "Few months ago, he petitioned me for a move to the Fort. Didn't really give a reason, but I didn't identify any problems. We still needed good brothers there after the shit we had with the chapter before Slate took it on." Mason struggled to remember Birdy's reasoning, but couldn't. *But, there'd been something...*

"He transferred down not long before the shit with Devil's Sins finally circled the drain." Watcher made a noise, but Mason kept talking. "Now, he's fucked up one side and down the other. He's been fucking a dope dealer's sister, fucking Manzino's goddamned sister. The same fucking dealer who rode in tight on the edges of our territory when

Bingo was president, and Birdy was helping her cook meth in my fucking town while wearing my fucking patch. And Gunny's gone—"

Watcher interrupted, "The fuck you mean, gone?"

"I mean fucking gone, but everything at his house is buttoned up like he's on a fucking vacation. Except he left bodies behind, four of them. One of them fucked in a way that means he spent time and effort dealing that death. Still could be a vacation, except the only ripple, and for me it's a fucking big one, is his dogs were left caged in the basement. He didn't show for work, no call-no show, and his pups were caged." Mason took a breath.

"His old lady had some shit in her past; he's been looking into some of it. She worked at Shinedown in Kentucky before making her way to Indiana." Watcher took in a breath, and Mason heard it over the roar of the wind. "Fucking yeah, Shooter's joint. Watcher, man, something is fucked and I can't put my goddamned finger on it."

"I feel ya, brother. You headed to the Fort now?" Watcher was doing something, and Mason listened as a woman's voice faded out on that end of the call.

"Yeah, should be there in about three." Mason swept the bike to the shoulder of the road, passing trucks creating a roadblock, watching as the three semis wide across the highway receded quickly in his mirrors. *Motherfuckers.* He glanced at the speedometer sitting steadily at one hundred, and he rolled the throttle.

"Lemme make a few calls. Some of my boys will still be up." There was humor in Watcher's voice and Mason laughed.

"You mean the bastards who haven't got a warm and willing to go home to." He looked at the speedo again, hovering at one hundred ten now, and rolled the throttle a little more, tightening his thighs around the fuel tank.

"And we circle back around to the first question I had in this convo. I heard through the grapevine you're sporting tail when you go to the Fort." Over the whine of the wind in his ears Mason made out the sputter and gurgle of a coffeemaker and laughed.

"You making coffee, motherfucker?"

"Answer the fucking question, old man," Watcher shot back.

"Yeah, there's a gal I've been seeing." Mason winced when he said those minimizing words, because it didn't come close to how it felt when he was lying next to Willa.

"But not the princess, right?" Those words had less power than they would have a year ago, and Mason found himself answering readily.

"Nope, not Mica. This is a gal in Fort Wayne. Her folks were in an RC, and she's a little kooky." He knew he was grinning and didn't care.

"The one you brought to the wedding?" Watcher was only asking for confirmation, because, like everyone important to Mason, he made sure the man met Willa.

"Yeah, the one who was at the wedding with me."

"Goddamn, she was pretty. Why's she settling for an ugly fucker like you?" He heard the teasing and didn't care.

"No fucking idea, but I'm all kinds of glad she is." And, he was. Every day he didn't keep company with her was hard, but when he could hold her, everything seemed easy. He'd finally found his easy, his soft, and it was wrapped up in the skin and bones of a beautiful woman who seemed to fit him in every way he had ever imagined.

"Good for you, Mason. You deserve the shine, man." His voice changed and he said, "Let me make some calls. I'll catch you in a couple hours. Let me know if you need anything else, man."

"Yep." He crouched low over the tank and rolled the throttle open a little more as he disconnected the call.

***

"Pick up the goddamned phone," Goose yelled through the clubhouse at no one in particular, and Mason shook his head. They were waiting for Slate, Bear, and Jase, now known as Captain, to come up from the room in the basement, where they were questioning Birdy. "Pick up the phone, Prez."

Mason jerked and looked, but Slate wasn't visible, so he reached out and took the phone off the wall. "What?"

"Mason." It was Gunny's voice, and with one word, he conveyed he had been to hell and back.

"Where are you, man?" No time for more questions, those could come later. If they could rescue their brother, they would, just needed a location.

"Diner at I-69 and Highway 224. We're safe." With those few words, the band around Mason's chest eased.

"On our way, brother. This your phone?" He made a mental note of the number.

"Naw, a nice lady at the register loaned me hers. We'll be waiting, brother."

Mason stood as the call disconnected and yelled, already walking towards the outside door, "Got Gunny. Get me a goddamned cage, right the fuck now!"

Twenty minutes later, they pulled up in front of the only diner at the highway intersection in Markle. Mason stepped out of the van, shading his eyes with the flat of his hand to detect a jerky wave from inside the building. He had communicated to his men that Gunny had said 'we' when he spoke, so they were hoping to find his woman with him, but the members, including Tug, all felt it could be a trap, demanding to escort him in force. Given how things were in the club right now, he could understand how they could think that way, but he knew Gunny. Knew his brother would have given him a head's up if things weren't right. Because of that, what he expected to find inside the diner were his brother and his brother's old lady, nothing more, nothing less. *We're safe*.

With that bone-deep trust, he strode into the diner as if he owned the fucking world and had the right to be any-fucking-where he pleased, because all was right in his goddamned fucking world. Sometimes, presentation was everything.

***

Thirty minutes later, and they were back at the clubhouse, back on familiar ground and behind reinforced walls. Safe. Gunny said he wanted to limit the people who knew everything he had to say, so Mason only called Slate and Bear into the office. They already knew Sharon's ex-husband was one of the men in Gunny's house, because his had been one of the bodies left behind. That was the sum total of all they knew.

Gunny told them this had to do with him asking around about Shooter and Judge; it seemed his questions had stirred up a hornet's nest. *Two days*, Mason snorted. Two days since he pulled together all his officers who mattered and told them about the connections stringing back and forth between him and Shooter, him and Judge…him and Eddie. There was so much uncertainty. So many goddamned unknowns right now, and Mason was getting sick and tired of feeling pushed into decisions where he didn't have any real control, nudged along from bumper to bumper as if he were a pinball, getting knocked into obstacles and traps by events moving too fast to see.

Now, he sat alone at the bar in the clubhouse, staring at himself in the mirror, trying to organize everything in his mind. Idly, he thought, *Not bad-looking*. His jaw was wide, and he guessed it looked strong. Not what he would call dreamy, even if it was what Willa had said. He still had a full head of hair, but his eyes were tired. Reaching up, he flipped his wraparound sunglasses off the top of his head and onto his face. *Problem solved*, he thought with a silent laugh.

Captain walked up and Mason eyed him. Tonight had been a harsh introduction to the darkest secrets the club ever kept, and from what Bear and Slate told him, Jase had stepped right the fuck up and taken care of business. He knew the decision would not have been an easy one. It would be an anchor on the man from here forward. Mason had a sudden flashing thought about where Jase might be right this minute if he hadn't pursued the man for the club, but then shook it off. Coulda, woulda, shoulda never got anybody anywhere.

"You doin' good?" Better than leaving an open-ended question, or asking with a waffling 'okay,' he always liked to feed words into men's mouths that meant something.

"Yeah, Prez. I'm good." Jase looked exhausted, and Mason made a show of looking him up and down, wincing inwardly when he saw the red stains on his boots.

"You look like hell, man," he said good-naturedly.

"Not every day, thank God. Just tonight, right?" Jase rubbed a hand across the back of his neck, pulling at the muscles there. "Listen, I'm not looking for absolution, but we did the right thing, eh?"

Mason laughed harshly. "Your Alberta is showing, man." That drew a grin to Jase's face for a moment, and he watched as it faded away. "Yeah, from everything you all reported, this was the only outcome. You did the right thing. The man knew what he was doing. He planned this, plotted to betray the club. Had a hard-on for your old lady, because she was doing her job. He knew his play when he patched in. If anything, the cost is on me for not catching on sooner."

Jase shook his head, denying Mason's responsibility. "There's no likely way you could have. Hell, I've known Birdy for a long time. He taught me how to ride a motorcycle. Until we were downstairs, and we'd taken away all options allowing his lie, he didn't show his true colors. Wasn't until he didn't have anywhere else to go, no other plays, that he finally gave us the truth." He sighed and spoke in a low voice, "He threatened DeeDee, Mason. I couldn't get around it. Not DeeDee, no way."

Nodding, Mason said, "I know. I heard, Captain. You know you couldn't leave him breathing, right?"

"Logically, I know. But, it all seems surreal right now. It felt right in the moment, but who am I to make that decision? How dare I take some man's life in my hands—"

Mason reached out, interrupting him by putting a hard hand on Jase's shoulder and tugging him closer. "Because he threatened your own. Your woman, your club, your brothers—he threatened what was yours, and we can't stand back and let that slide, man. We protect our own, and you did. You protected us all with your willingness to take the burden on yourself."

"We—" Mason swept his hand out, but kept his eyes locked on Jase's "—thank you. I don't know the cost to you for tonight's work, but I can imagine. I know what the cost was to me, the first time." He shook Jase with the hold he still had on his shoulder. "Listen to me, Jase. Nelson Mandela said something in a letter he wrote from prison. 'When a man has done what he considers to be his duty to his people…he can rest in peace.' So, I thank you for taking that duty on. For keeping my cousin safe. For keeping my club whole. Rest easy, my brother."

Nodding slowly, Jase reached up, gripping Mason's shoulder in a similar hold before stepping back. "Gonna go hold my woman for a while." Mason simply looked at him as he turned to walk away, but his back was straighter, his head held higher. Watching him, Mason clung to his hope that tonight wouldn't break a good man who had done hard work for the right reasons.

30. Look again

Mason was beginning to back the Vincent onto the walkway when he caught sight of the boy sitting on the step in front of Willa's door. Putting down the kickstand and killing the engine, he watched the kid in the mirror as he pulled off his gloves, tucking them into the bag on the side of the bike. Glancing around, he verified her little car was in the lot, and wondered why the boy was sitting outside.

Remembering how skittish the kid had been, Mason kept himself from looking directly at him as he got off the bike and turned towards her door. Stopping several feet from the boy, who stared down at the toes of his scuffed sneakers, he stood and waited quietly. After a couple of seconds, he heard the softly spoken, "She's not answering her door."

"Did you knock?" Mason still didn't look directly at him, but saw the nod. "Lemme try," he said, stepping around the boy and tugging on the screen door to find it latched. That was odd, because it was the kind of door without a key; the lock was a slider on the inside.

"Door's locked, too," the boy offered.

"I caught that." If it was locked, then she should be inside, should have answered the door for the kid. He noted, not for the first time, this door was not particularly sturdy, and he knew he could easily twist the knob and break it. That would piss Willa off if she were here, though, so he stalled the thought, saying, "Let me try a loud knock." Pulling back his hand, he hammered on the metal frame of the door, knowing the sound would echo inside the apartment.

"Her car's locked, too..." There was a hesitation, but then the boy continued, "...but the window in the kitchen isn't."

Mason had held still, listening hard, but hadn't heard anything from inside yet, so he pulled back his fist and hammered harder and longer. "You go inside?" He asked this like he was asking if the sky was blue, because he suspected the boy had slipped through the window once he found it open.

"Yeah, she ain't inside." Mason turned and sat on the step next to the boy.

"Her stuff all inside?" Car here, outside door locked, no Willa. A chill crept into his belly, pulling his balls up tight against his body. Where could she be?

"Yeah. Even her purse and computer." He cut his eyes up to look at Mason, seeming to know the import of this, because Willa never went anywhere without a tablet or computer. She said she never knew when she would need to reboot the school district's systems or work on something, but Mason thought it was mostly because she liked the tech.

"You checked all the rooms?" His hands itched to snatch that door open and go inside, searching for himself.

"Yeah. Closets too." Mason felt the hot gaze, and he turned to find the boy glaring at him. "You told me you had this."

Mason drew in a breath. "I do. I'll get things sorted, son." He pulled out his phone, dialing Willa's number, and squeezed his eyes shut tightly when he heard her phone ringing from inside the empty apartment. "I need to get inside. Think you could open the door for me?" Before he even finished the sentence, the boy was up and running around the side of the apartment, the worn soles on his ratty sneakers slapping along the walkway. By the time Mason stood, he heard the inside door rattling, the chain being taken off, and then it opened and the boy opened the outer door. He stepped onto the sidewalk and looked up at Mason with a nod, holding the door until Mason reached out to grip it, and then he trotted up the stairs to the foster family's apartment.

Mason went inside, senses on full alert to find...nothing. It seemed everything was in order and looked as if Willa could step out of the bathroom or any other room at any moment. Standing in the doorway, he swept his gaze across the room side-to-side, seeing pillows and blanket neatly folded at the end of the couch, no empty bottles or glasses sitting around. He made a mental note to check the kitchen sink and the dishwasher. Her purse and laptop bag were standing at the end of the couch where she always dropped them.

The landline phone rang and he looked that direction, moving closer to listen as the ringing ceased and there was a beep. "Miss Shipman, this is the second day you've missed work. It's not like you not to call, so I hope everything's okay." It was a woman's voice on the phone, and Mason assumed it was the school calling. "Willa," she paused. "Call me and let me know you're okay." There was another beep and then silence.

Two days. The timing seemed too coincidental to be anything other than connected. Inside chain on the door, outside door locked from inside. No Willa. He pulled out his phone, wincing as he heard a sleepy female voice in the background when Gunny answered with a groggy, "'Lo?"

"Gunny." He took a breath; had to before he could continue. "Willa's missing." He didn't waste time with pleasantries, even knowing the man couldn't have been asleep more than a couple hours. Just saying the words hit him like a gut punch. He hadn't even allowed himself to think the words until they were out of his mouth. Willa was missing. Missing. Two days.

There was a rustling and then, *"Fuck."* Instantly sounding alert, he knew Gunny was dressing as they talked, and he silently thanked his friend for his willing and immediate response. Then his brother gave him everything with, "I'm in the wind, brother. I can be there in ten." A pause, then, "Where are you?"

"At her place, I'll text you the address, but I don't know what we'll find here." He looked around, realizing he hadn't even gone through the entire apartment yet. "Give me a couple minutes to finish looking around." The call disconnected and he stared at her purse for a moment more, and then dialed Slate.

Nothing. A fat bucket of nothing was what the rest of the apartment turned up.

Nothing on the nightstand, the bed wasn't disturbed. He couldn't say for sure if any clothes were missing, but he didn't think so. There was nothing in the sink. Some food in the refrigerator, but nothing had gone bad, so as the call from her work indicated, she couldn't have been gone long. The log of recent calls on her cell consisted of ones from him and the school. He talked to Myron and booted up her computer at his request, and they found she had last been on it yesterday morning, which tightened the timeline a little.

By the time Slate and Gunny rode up, he had kicked off all the standard processes the club had for rolling on something like this. She didn't have any enemies, and he knew it was only her association with him that seemed to hold any elements of risk, which likely meant whatever happened to her was on him, set squarely at his door. And that 'whatever' could be any of a dozen different things. Shit relating to Birdy, Manzino, disgruntled ex-Rebels, holdout Devil's Sins, Demon's brother and his new club, the Diamante...the list went on and fucking on. Enemies out past the fucking horizon, where the earth curved and monsters lived.

The more they didn't find, the tighter he curbed his reactions. Fumbling for self-control, he felt an ache take up residence in his jaw and hands from the tightly clenched positions in which they remained. He couldn't let himself fear for her, couldn't allow doubt to creep in, because every eye was trained on him. He had done this to her, brought this on her with his interest, and every man saw themselves and the ones they loved walking the same narrow blade. His reaction exuded calmness and strength, giving lie to the quivering fear lodged in his chest, clogging every breath with bitter terror.

He planted his feet and stood in her kitchen as the gathering of bikers grew and overflowed the apartment throughout the day. Men coming to him in waves over the hours to tell him they had nothing.

That bucket of nothing grew and grew.

None of her neighbors had seen anything. When he asked to talk to the boy, the family upstairs looked at him oddly and said yeah, they had foster kids, but no kids named Jim. When he asked to speak to any boys they had, the woman glanced around him at the bikers at his back and shook her head, slowly closing the door. Nothing about this made sense; he couldn't find the lead to follow. Nothing to take him to her, nothing to bring her back to him. Not a fucking thing. Nothing.

Then he got the call from Myron. He had spent the day digging through her accounts, through her electronic activities, monitoring everything Willa had online. He had found something, but the no-nonsense tone in his voice said Mason wasn't going to like it, and he was right.

She had terminated the lease on the apartment, turned off her utilities, and called a moving company. The van and men would be in within two days to pack up all her stuff and put it into storage.

Wherever she had gone, she wasn't planning to come back soon, if at all. Gone.

He gazed around the room, seeing the pained looks of sympathy from the Rebels who stayed all day. Mason didn't know what to do with the feeling coiled in his chest, because only once before had he ever felt so bereft and abandoned. Surrounded by his brothers, men he trusted with his life, for the first time since he was eight-years-old, he felt alone.

She was gone. He had nothing.

***

"Myron, check again, man," he said gruffly. "Something doesn't fucking add up." It was the next day, and they had both been at this nonstop since Myron got to Fort Wayne while Mason was still at Willa's apartment, refusing to believe the information provided. Denying she was gone.

With a sigh, Myron bent over his keyboard, tapping in a series of letters and numbers, accessing a national database that would provide him further access to personal information. "Okay, boss. What am I looking for this go-around?" They had conducted countless searches already, using facts and information Mason knew about Willa.

"Recent jobs filled for which she'd be a fit. It'd have to be the elementary or high school level; she doesn't have the degree for a secondary school job. Unless it was private, then all bets are off, so we won't consider that yet. Look at jobs filled within the last two weeks." Mason scrubbed across his jaw with the palm of his hand, feeling the rasping scratch of a heavy five o'clock shadow.

Minutes later, the printer made a racket and spit out two pieces of paper. Mason grabbed them and looked them over, not seeing her name or a version of her name that would indicate she was working but trying to hide. "Nothing," he spit out, knowing Myron already knew it. "Look at her parents. I want accounts and...fuck, the phone would take too long. Just get me accounts. Call whoever can help; pull in whatever markers you need."

"Mason—" Myron started to say something, but then shut up when he saw the look on Mason's face. "Yeah, boss."

Same routine with the printer. Same result. "Fuck," he ground out, slamming his palm against the wall. "Why would she leave like this?"

Myron shook his head, leaning back from the computer. "I'm less certain she left. For anyone expecting to work and live, there are always droppings left behind, but I can't find anything, boss. If she did leave, then she's damn good if she can cover her tracks like this."

Tracks. In his mind, Mason saw the small footprints she had left behind at the campgrounds where Slate's wedding had been. There were larger footprints all over, of course, confusing the trail, but he would recognize her footprints if he saw them again. Tracks. *Trace it back*, he thought. *There's something here. Follow the line through the water.*

"Birdy. Manzino's sister." He tipped his head, staring at the expanse of floor between his toes and Myron's feet, his gaze sweeping back and forth while he turned things over in his head. "Manzino never raised his head. He left no trace, telling Slate through safe channels how his sister and Birdy had gone off on their own. Making their own path, laying their own tracks. The meth house was running utilities off the place next door. Who owns the place? Not the meth house, that was a city property, abandoned. Who owned the place they were running electricity from?"

Myron's fingers flew across the keyboard. "Hmm. Gimme a sec." He typed in a few additional pieces of information, and then clicked through a series of screens. "Local church."

"Fuck." Tipping his head back, he stared at the ceiling. "Did Gunny get you an address for the location he and his old lady were held at?" Myron nodded. "Who owns that?" More tapping. "Manzino."

There it was. "Fuck." Mason gently pounded the back of his head against the wall. "Manzino's sister traps a brother, and then Manzino is connected in the shit that went down with Gunny. How about Elkins? Any idea how he got latched onto the Diamante crew out of Lexington?" As soon as Gunny had said the name Fury during the debriefing, Mason knew who they were dealing with. Ex-military and hard as nails, the man was known for his cool head, and his club name was an antonym, because he never lost his temper.

"I couldn't find anything on Elkins, boss, not to connect him with Diamante." The look on Myron's face was apologetic, but Mason couldn't fault his efforts.

"Maybe there's nothing to find. Hell, if she's been taken, and my gut says she has been, it could be a dozen different people." He sighed. "My own fucking fault, man. I left her unprotected. I've been spending a lot of time with her over the past few weeks. I should have put our brothers on her. Hell, I jumped straight up Slate's ass not long ago because I accused him of leaving Willa exposed, but then I go and do the same fucking thing." He sucked in a deep breath. "But I can't believe she'd just leave. She wouldn't do that." Shaking his head, he closed his eyes tightly. *Not to me.* "Look again."

31. Here be monsters

"Mason, I need your help." He heard Mica's voice on the phone and looked at it in surprise. She hadn't called him in weeks, not since the last time he had to turn down babysitting Jon for club business, back before Eddie was taken. He would have far rather been babysitting than listening to Bones argue with Chismoso, president of the Chicago chapter of the Diamantes, but he couldn't tell her that.

"Whatcha need, darlin'?" She sucked in a quick breath at his question.

"Babe." She responded with a single word, and he frowned.

"Yeah? Mica, whatcha need?" Now he was confused, which didn't take a lot these days, since he wasn't sleeping. *Goddamn, fucking women*.

"I'm not darlin', Mason. I'm babe." Her tone was snippy and he consciously decided to let this go, and instead, he would push her to figure out what the fuck had her dialing his number in the first place. He had nearly lost touch with his patience in the past few days, circling around Willa's disappearance again and again, exhausting himself in trying to dissect their last few conversations, their last time together.

"You said you needed my help?" He waited, and then heard a pounding on his front door. "Hold on a sec, honey."

He pulled the door open to find her standing there in a sweatshirt and jeans, the phone still to her ear. Tucking his phone into the pocket of his jeans, he grinned, reaching out to pull her in for a hug, realizing as he wrapped his arms around her that he hadn't held her like this since her wedding. "Mica," he rubbed his cheek up and down on hers, "it's fucking good to see you."

"Well, you'd see me more often if you'd talk to me," she muttered, and he laughed.

"I'm talking to you now, ain't I?" Pulling back, he kept an arm around her shoulders and turned them both towards the kitchen. "What's got you over in this neck of the woods?"

"Dropping Jon off with Molly. She's going to watch him for a couple of days." He couldn't miss the tensing of her muscles. This was not a happy topic for her, and he wondered if it tied into whatever kind of help she thought she needed.

"You got shit going on for a few days? It surprises me, you dropping him off like that. Hell woman, you can't be away from your boy for an hour without shaking in your boots and being all weepy about it. So tell me...what kind of shit you got going on that you need my help with?" He parked her in a chair at the table, turned to the coffeemaker, and set it up for a cup. Then, he paused and looked back, holding up a mug as he asked, "Same as always?"

She nodded absently then smiled at him when he brought the cup to the table, losing the smile to a frown when he reached back to pull a beer from the refrigerator for himself. "It's early, Mason," she said, eying the beer.

"Late for me," he said, spinning the top from the bottle with the side of his hand. He took a long drink, watching her fiddle with the cup in front of her, studiously not looking at him. "Tell me," was all he said, and her eyes shot to meet his, a familiar little line forming between her brows as she frowned at him.

"You always do that, you know?" Shaking her head, she said, "Daniel's retired. You heard the news, right?" He nodded; it would have been hard to miss the media frenzy when the owner and franchise forward of the Mallets had called it quits on the world of hockey. "He's not doing well with retirement." She snorted and then said, "Understatement. He's doing incredibly poorly with retirement. I need you to help me figure out what to do."

"Mica," he said, surprised. "Daniel and I aren't best buds." They were friendly, yes, but friends would be pushing the description significantly. There was too much between them for that, mostly wrapped up in the woman who sat at the table with him now. "I don't know how I can help him if his friends can't."

"You made it so Jase had something when he quit." She said this with quiet hope, and he suddenly knew where this was going.

"It's not the same, honey. Not even close to the same. Jase had a stake in the club long before I patched his ass in." Which was true, the man had chased DeeDee for months, bought a bike from Road Runner, and learned how to ride it just to impress her. Then he helped out with the club in Fort Wayne for a time before he and DeeDee ever made things formal between them, which was long before he was made official in the club. When he retired from hockey, he took a position working for the club and then opened a facility introducing at-risk kids to the joys of hockey.

"Daniel doesn't have anything other than Jackson's in common with me and mine." And her, but he wouldn't be the one saying those words. The single conversation they had about her status with the club still rubbed even after more than two years, ending as it had with him walking out of her house and her affections, leaving Daniel standing in his place.

Her frown deepened, and she looked down at the coffee in her mug. "Well then, I don't know what to do."

"Tell me what's going on, okay? Let's start there." He should be able to discern a pattern; it was one of the things he used to think he was good at, after all. His mind flipped to Willa, and he remembered a conversation with Eddie a couple days ago when she had vigorously agreed with him that leaving like this, out of the blue, was not something Willa would ever do.

She might be kooky, but she was considerate. She would have put in notice at work and emailed or called her friends. The kicker was no matter how busy Eddie was with Bear and the kids, the Willa they both knew would have at least talked to her best friend. But right now, not even her folks seemed to know where she was. There had been no demands, no news, and no rumors. Off the map, hell, she had gone off the reservation.

Something in that bucket of nothing wasn't right; he hadn't been able to find it yet and he didn't have any corners left to look in. There was nothing at all to grab ahold of where Willa's disappearance was concerned. It was why he had come back to Chicago, because after canceling her moving service and picking up the lease on her place, he spent hours sitting in the dark in her apartment. He knew his fixated behavior became less productive by the day, and while there he couldn't keep his mind from doggedly circling the problem again and again. Here, at least, he could attempt to keep himself busy with work.

"He gets up and works out, just like before. Then he goes into the office, like before. But he won't watch the team practice. He's willing to sit in the box during games, but even then he stays well away from the glass, like he's putting as much space between him and the ice as he can." She sighed, pushing her hair away from her face with her fingers.

"He won't talk to me, Mason. And except for when I was stupid, we've always talked, ever since that first night we spent together in Milwaukee."

He nodded and waited. She looked at him and blushed and he winced inwardly, thinking he probably knew what else had changed in their relationship. "He won't sleep with me," she said bravely then cut her gaze to the table.

Thinking again of Willa, he asked, "You mean *sleep* sleep, right?"

She nodded and whispered painfully, "We're no longer intimate."

"How long did he think about walking away before he pulled the trigger?" He knew Jase had struggled with the idea for months, but it was after being severely injured during the season and laid up for weeks. Forced off the ice, he could recognize the end of his physical game wasn't far in the future. He was also planning for retirement even before Mason stuck his finger too far in the mix. Had gone back to school for a degree, something he sidestepped earlier to focus on his athletic career, but Mason knew Daniel already had that piece bagged.

"It seemed he simply got up one day and was done. I'm sure it had been on his mind, and I don't care that he quit...I like it better, in fact. I hated the way he'd get beaten up every single game. Coming home with bruises, cuts...the stitches were the worst." She ducked her head, looking into her cup. "I know it's a physical sport, but the evidence was there after every shift, every game."

"Did he quit for himself, or for you?" He hadn't read anything about injuries in the past season, neither career ending nor minor, which was one of the reasons Daniel's retirement had come as such a surprise to the hockey world.

"I think for me." Spoken in a guilty whisper, she said the words without raising her head.

If Daniel had quit because she hated the game, then he was going to resent her for taking it away from him. Even if he didn't want to believe it of himself, there would be some level of bitterness, no doubt. Mason stilled, the thought flitting through his head that if she and Daniel were no longer together, could it...would it open the door for him again? He followed the thought, finding a surprising anguish in realizing if he did open that door, it would firmly close the one leading to Willa in its wake...and he wouldn't survive the loss. "I'll always love you," he said without thinking, snapping his mouth shut after the words had already escaped into the still air of the kitchen.

She snorted indelicately. "Yeah? And?"

"Nothing, just seeing how it sounded out loud." He shook his head. "I will, you know. But let me talk to Daniel, figure out what's going on in his head."

"I love you, too, Mason." She smiled up at him, cupping a hand around the nearly empty mug of coffee. "I always will." She pushed back from the table. "And now, I have to head to the airport."

"Airport? Where ya headed, hon?" For some reason, he had thought her leaving Jon for a few days was about this concern about Daniel.

"Provo. I've got a new business account and they want me to do a presentation at the home offices there. Jess was supposed to go with me, but she had to bail a half-hour ago because Brandy's sick." Moving around the table, she leaned on his shoulders, pressing against his back and wrapping her arms around his neck. "Daniel's at home, but with work and everything, it's easier to have Molly keep Jon." She hugged him, noisily kissing the side of his face. "Muuwah. Call me if you figure anything out?"

"You got it, Mica," he said, turning his head to kiss her cheek in return. "Safe travels."

"Shiny side up," she agreed, laughing, and walked towards the door.

He reached down, gently touching the lump through the fabric of his jeans, then threaded his hand into his pocket and pulled it out. The piece of glass lay in his palm, beautifully polished by the abrasive splendor of the ocean until it shone like a gem. He had kept it all these years, and it never failed to bring back the magnificence of that day, the freedom he felt standing on the beach, tasting salt on the wind. The color matched Mica's eyes, and until today, it had lifted him up to look at the sea glass, to know he held it in his hand. Now, instead of sea-green eyes, he saw hazel ones, and heard the ghost of a giggle in the house she had never visited.

***

"Are you even open yet?" Daniel asked, glancing around as he walked into Jackson's.

"Nope," Mason said, pushing a beer across the bar top. "Sit your ass down."

He watched Daniel as he looked around the bar again; they were the only ones here and would be for a couple of hours. Mason strolled over and used the key hanging from under the handle to lock the door, turning back to find a grin on Daniel's face. "What, motherfucker?"

"Nothing. Just reminded me of one other time you met me here before opening hours." After a second, the grin on Daniel's face fell away as Mason watched, stone-faced. He remembered that day, too. It had been the real start of him backing away from Mica, letting Daniel have room to take her.

I'm just a poor wayfaring stranger

"Yeah, I recall the day," he finally acknowledged with a sigh. "Fuck. This chat is about Mica, too."

"She's in Provo," Daniel said helpfully, running a hand through his hair.

"Yeah. I know." Walking back behind the bar, he picked up his beer, draining it and throwing it with more force than necessary into the trashcan, shattering the bottle. "She came to speak to me this morning."

"Okay. Let me have it. What's up, Mason?" Daniel hadn't taken a drink of his beer yet, and now he pushed it a couple inches away, keeping his eyes on Mason's face.

"Why'd you quit hockey?" This seemed the safest topic to lead with, a fuckton better than asking him why he had quit fucking Mica, the woman whose bed they had in common.

Puzzled, Daniel tilted his head and looked at Mason. "That's why you called me here? My retirement decision?" His head moved side-to-side twice, and then he dipped his chin, but kept his gaze locked on Mason's eyes. "Because it was time."

"You played well last season. What changed?" Mason didn't read any avoidance in his physical reaction, other than the unconscious emotional denial of the headshake.

"I'm old for hockey, man. Every year, I got beat up worse and worse, and it took longer and I had to work harder to come back. My recovery time at the end of the season had elongated to an unreasonable arc before I could even think about rebuilding and conditioning. At some point, the effort doesn't equal reward, and I'd nearly gotten to that place." Reaching out, he picked up the bottle of beer and looked at it, eventually setting it back down untasted. "In the end, I was...tired."

"Had you thought about retiring for long before you announced it?" He still wasn't reading anything off in Daniel's responses, which puzzled him.

"Only for years, Mason. Every season, I analyzed things like my speed on the blades, the accuracy of my shots, ability to read opponents...the tapes showed I had slowed down a lot over the past couple of years. I couldn't keep up with the kids coming up out of juniors any more. During recruiting last year, I had a chance to look closely at the crop of bantams and midgets we'll be facing in only a couple of years and...got tired. I'm fucking old, man. Old for hockey, like I said." Daniel cleared his throat and picked the beer up, taking a sip.

"Got plans for after?" Mason didn't touch the old comment. He would circle back around to that last, knowing the fifteen years between Daniel and Mica was more of an age difference than he had with her by three years, but he had never felt old. "The trucking business runs itself, has for years. Hell, you set it up that way, and there's no way you'd take it back from J.J. now, not with him getting serious about Molly. So what plans do you have? Gonna stay owner of the Mallets?"

"I've had offers for the team," Daniel said cagily, and then he sighed. "Yeah, I'll keep the Mallets. I can't imagine not owning them after all this time. You're right about the transportation company, too. I just...don't entirely know what to do with myself." He laughed and took a deep drink from his beer, and Mason could watch the tension uncoiling inside the man by a little. "At this time of year, I should be living, eating, and breathing hockey, but that's gone now."

Nodding, Mason leaned back. "I can see how it would sting. If something happened and I wasn't where I am, I can't imagine what I'd do." He rubbed his chin slowly, thinking. "Have you talked to Captain at all, man?" At Daniel's quizzical look, he laughed and revised, "Jase?"

"No, I didn't want to bother him. I knew he had a lot going on with DeeDee and the grandbabies, his foundation...hell, the Rebels." Picking at the bottle label with one fingertip, he stared down at the bar top. "He was pretty lucky to have such a sweet setup when he quit playing."

"Wasn't without hardship for him," Mason said, surprised the two men hadn't talked yet, given how close they seemed in the past. "He'd already given up a fuckton of money to trade to Fort Wayne, and then when he only played a year, he lost the second-year bonus. They do okay; he's got a good salary with his position in Mason Corp., plus DeeDee's still working, but I think it helped they consolidated households, too."

Daniel laughed. "Wasn't talking about money."

"Naw, didn't truly think you were." Mason frowned at him. "But, there's a lot the same between the two of you. The job keeps him busy, like you being GM for the Mallets. Family, I believe we can draw some comparisons between you, Mica, and Jon, with him and his little crew. He's stepping up to take care of Bingo and his crew of kids, too, which is a hell of a lot of work and a big commitment." There was a muffled thump against the outside door and he swiveled to look, frowning, but turned back to the bar when it didn't repeat. "I think, out of all that, what's kept the bounce in his step is the foundation. He knew he had to maintain a foothold in hockey. The sport had been too big a piece of his life for him to walk away. Is that what you're feeling?"

"I miss it, man. I miss the nerves before a game, the desire to best the other team...other players. There's a lot of satisfaction in pitting yourself against the elite in the game and coming out on top." Daniel laughed, and then picked at the beer label again. "Not to boast, but I was pretty good."

"I know you were. The last couple of years you were top of your game. All the stories marked your skill. Your game had matured enough to make you steady, and you have so much damn talent you could skate circles around half the yahoos who took the ice against you." Mason grinned. "A joy to watch, which was why the asses were filling the seats. So take what you had going and make it more."

"What did I have going other than playing? 'Make it more.' What does that mean?" Daniel turned to look at him.

"I know you ran training for the team, not your coach, some because you were captain, but mostly because you liked it, right?" Mason leaned back in his chair again. He thought he had something here; it felt like a solid tug right on the end of a line. Daniel nodded. "Was it the knowledge transfer, teaching, that did it for you?"

Shaking his head, Daniel said, "No. It was more watching people get better because I pushed them to polish what they already knew."

"So skill reinforcement and conditioning?" Mason nodded slowly. "There's a market for those skills, and not only for hockey. But in the world of hockey, hell man, Chicago has a wealth of opportunities. Look at all the pro and semi-pro teams we have here. Fuck, Daniel, you own your facility. You could literally write your own goddamn check."

"What, like take mediocre players and make them a smidge better? Backslapping the wannabes?" Daniel sneered and laughed.

"No, be particular. Make yourself a scarce commodity. Take great players and make them exceptional." Laughing, Mason cuffed him on the shoulder. "I know you'd pay for that when you were playing, if it were available. Someone to make you focus on what you were doing right but not flawlessly, and then help you perfect that skill."

Shrugging, Daniel nodded. "Yeah. But, those kinds of services exist on all levels. You look at the peewees and there're camps galore, because, for every parent who oversees their kids' day-to-day training, there are a dozen coaches who are better. Then in midgets and juniors, players attend camps and one-on-ones, because there you have access to training talent you wouldn't have elsewhere. Even with pros, some teams have assistants for nearly everything." He paused, and then reflectively said, "But not all teams. And, you're right, Chicago is a well-placed city for something like that." His shoulders bunched and stretched, and Mason saw him chewing on the inside of his cheek. "Trainer. How the hell do you recognize and see things like that, man?"

Laughing, Mason stood and gathered their empty bottles, moving behind the bar to place them gently in the trashcan. "Sometimes it simply takes seeing things from the outside to gain clarity." He paused, thinking about Eddie's call again. Email. They had looked at Willa's phone, but he hadn't asked Myron to check her outgoing email. At least it was somewhere to start again. "Sometimes you need someone to point out the obvious." He grabbed his cut, settling it on his shoulders. "I gotta scoot, man. Lock up after yourself?"

With a wave, Daniel laughed. "Sure thing, Mason."

He glanced down as he opened the door and froze. The source of the thump he had heard was a bundle of red fabric tossed at the bar's entrance. Looking around, he didn't note anything out of place, no suspicious people, and no idling cars at the curb. Squatting down, he set about picking apart the layers, holding his breath as the red rubbed off onto his fingers in sticky swaths of color. Inside the parcel, which he realized looked exactly like the sweatshirt Mica had been wearing only that morning, was a human hand, feminine, nails raggedly bitten, but stunningly graceful, even in dismemberment.

32. **Utah**

"Prez, I'm telling you that hand does not belong to Mica or Willa." Myron scowled, looking up at Mason with a cautious expression. Something was coming Myron knew he wouldn't like. "But the prints are in the system." He paused. "Boss, it belongs to Sosa."

Mason leaned his head back against the wall with a thump, hearing Daniel sobbing in relief nearby. His own terror hadn't eased, because this was too much. For this to be going down only hours after seeing her for the first time in weeks, the timing screamed at him, and his brain was countering with a list of everyone else who mattered to him, all the people who could be targets for no reason other than association with him. Willa, Chase, DeeDee, Bethy—Bethany, who he still hadn't connected with after several attempts over three weeks—Molly, who had both her son and Mica's in her little house, only protected by a loving man in a wheelchair. The list in his mind grew and grew, faces flickering past as fast as telephone poles on an under-traveled straightaway drag race. *Fuck.* He had to dial it back, ask the questions, find the scope. "Do we know if the shirt is Mica's?"

"No way of telling quickly." Myron shook his head. "The brand is right, but it's a popular one. Her plane is still in the air, but I didn't find any exceptions filed for the passenger list. And there would have been if she hadn't shown up, since she checked in electronically before leaving home."

Tapping his earpiece, Mason called Slate. "Hoss fill you in?" He heard a grunt, so he continued, "Lock the club down, Slate. Bring in all the families; make sure everyone is fucking accounted for...no...wait, man. Hold. Gimme a sec."

His mind was racing, and he teased along the edge of something. Shooter's long plays. Twelve years for Chase, nearly ten for Eddie. Judge was his kid, learned at his daddy's knee. Long plays—big plays. Shooter always liked the big show, made certain he had an audience for his business, especially whenever it involved revenge.

What act would hold the most horror for a hit against a club? Retaliation for the death of his birthright would have to be big, showy, make a dramatic statement to everyone. Long plays...he could have been planning for a long time and had the timeline moved up because of what happened in Cali. The terror of Oklahoma City...long plays.

Mica and Sosa weren't club; they were...families. "Get Deke in the room, brother. Bring him in the office. Get him on the phone right fucking now."

Less than a minute later, he heard a new voice in the background, and then a slam as the door closed. "Deke, call your brother. Have him bring a bomb squad and run through the clubhouse. We ain't got anything there that would trigger their shit, so no worries. You...I want all of you out of the clubhouse by the time I hang up. Get people moving, Slate." There were shocked indrawn breaths from the men standing around him, but he ignored them, still thinking.

"Bear's house. Park some of the families there until you get the clubhouse cleared. Just fucking be careful, brothers. This shit isn't lining up with anything we've had to deal with before." He paused, and then took a moment to steady his voice before asking, "Where's Chase?"

Standing motionless, he let the wall at his back support him, his own legs weak from fear, waiting...expecting the worst, that his boy was missing, too.

"In the main room here with Tug and Maggie." Slate's voice rang with confidence and surety, which was fucking good to hear.

I'm just a-going over home

"Okay, that's good. Okay." He sagged a little, relief rolling through him. "I'm going to have Digger put together a couple of travel options for us. I'm thinking Duck, Tater, Hoss." He knew they would understand his shorthand speak about heading to wherever they decided was the most likely place for Mica to have been taken, if she wasn't on the plane about to descend into Provo.

Provo. Provo, Utah. Birdy had come from Provo. Watcher said there were rumors about Deacon being there. Was it coincidence?

"Gunny, Bones, and Watcher." Slate said the names as if they would make sense to Mason, but he had gotten lost in his head thinking about Utah, so he stayed silent, waiting for the man to fill in the blanks. When his friend spoke, he was reminded that Slate had good instincts, too. "Take Bones with you, brother. I'll bring Gunny and call Watch, he'll meet you wherever, and I'm guessing that wherever is gonna be in Utah."

33. Broken

Judge sat in the chair, watching the women through the glass. He kept them in separate enclosures, wanting to passively manage them as much as he could without having to put his hands on them. Not because he didn't want to touch—he would fucking enjoy touching—but he didn't trust his own control if he had to manhandle any of them again. He wanted to touch them too much, at least one of them.

He looked and watched, evaluating the women individually. His uncle certainly didn't seem to have a type, because other than the varying shades of dark hair, the women were as different as could be. Thin, curvy. Trashy, classy. Smart, stupid. Fearless, scared. Alive—he glanced at the room at the end of the hall, the only glass door without light behind it—dead.

He stared longest at the only one of which he had personal knowledge. *Willa*. He had known her for a couple of years. He always liked that she was never afraid of him. For as long as he had been around her, she had given him grief, always handing him attitude, but never fear. He enjoyed that, the feeling of normal surrounding him whenever she was around. He didn't have a lot of normal in his life, ever.

She had been around other bikers, strong men, but he had always been stronger and she noticed. They had a connection; he knew it to be true, even if he never moved on it. *I didn't touch, but I looked, yeah*, he thought. She was his fucking sister's best friend...but he fucking looked. Looked long and often, sometimes from goddamned close at hand, too, because Willa never locked her doors.

At one point in time, she had been the highlight of his stint in purgatory, until the night Mason showed up and she caught his notice. He had belittled Judge that night, ordered him around, too, and his own father—his president—hadn't blinked at anything Mason had barked. And, Willa had noticed. Of course she had. How could she not? His humiliation on public display like that.

He snarled silently, his memories a loop of that night, hearing Mason's voice chastising him for daring to ask a fucking question.

The mental images paused as she shifted from the mattress-covered bedframe to the floor, and he winced when she shivered, hating to think she was uncomfortable. Leaning her shoulders against the wall, it looked like she had her eyes closed, but he knew she would be listening and thinking, trying to figure out where she was and who had her, working things out in her head. "So smart," he whispered.

He turned, looking into the room two doors down. Princess. Having had to put up with so much shit about the Rebels' fucking princess, when he first saw her, it had been damned anticlimactic. He expected so much...more. Especially given the state she kept Mason tied up in for so long. She was pretty, but awfully damn weak from what he could tell. A typical woman, she seemed to know her place and was happy to stay in it. House mouse, weak and compliant. She was no Willa; that was for damn sure.

In the center room, though...this one he found even more interesting than the princess, because he knew practically nothing about her. He had heard nothing about her, ever. A blank page tucked into an unwritten part of Mason's history. When Manzino had fronted him the info and he checked things out, sure enough, she had a connection with the man, but no one knew exactly what it was. How they fit together was hard to determine. Bethany Taylor was pretty, but her life in Nashville was so far away from club life she could be on a different fucking planet.

Willa, though, she was an enigma. A beautiful conundrum and mystery. He ran his hands through his hair, pushing it back from his face, feeling it slide stickily through his fingers. "So fucking smart," he whispered again.

She could recite the lines from a dozen different movies they had watched together. He knew she could; he had heard her dialogue commentary a thousand times, laughing at her humor, wiping her tears as she cried, holding her when she was afraid. Those were the best times, when it was just them, no club, when he could relax and simply be Luke. He ground his teeth. Eddie had been there too, but it had always been him and Willa. "Me and Willa." Glancing down then back up at her door, he took a deep breath. "Me and my girl."

Glancing down at his phone, he decided he would wait another five minutes. Five more minutes and he was going to make the call he had been dying to make. He had wanted to tell Mason everything for so long. Wanted him to know Judge was family, because once he knew about their connection, he would change his tune. They would be able to put everything behind them, concentrate on the future.

He knew Deacon would be pleased, too. Even before he knew how deep their connection ran, Luke had listened to every Mason story the old man had. He believed Deacon had long ago forgiven his protégé for the betrayal and defection, so bringing Mason back to the fold now would make his mentor happy. Their mentor, he guessed, since Mason had been first to sit at Deacon's side.

He glanced at the phone, seeing the numbers had advanced until there were only three minutes to wait. His knee jittered wildly up and down, a match to the thoughts ricocheting in his head. Only three minutes. Still three minutes. He tipped his head, considering. Mason might not believe him, might not believe he could deliver. By now, he should have gotten the package, though. That should have been enough to get his attention and let him know they weren't playing kiddy games.

He looked down the way towards the dark door. Sosa had been a favorite whore, at least for his father. Before reporting to the River Riders in Indiana, before his banishment, Luke spent time in Kentucky setting up shit for her and her kid.

He focused on the dark door, again hearing the rasping grind of the handsaw as hard pulls on the handle wedged the sharp blade between delicate bones in her wrist. He smirked now, thinking of the jokes he had flippantly recited for the silent woman, her fucking mouth quiet for what he suspected was the first time in her entire fucking life. Muttering softly, he repeated his favorites. "Want to give me a hand, bitch?" Laughing softly, he asked, "Did you hear the one about the blind hooker?" He grunted, and then continued with a lopsided and jeering grin, "You have to hand it to her." He snorted, and said, "I crack me up."

Her kid. Mason's kid. He knew it was Mason's kid before Mason even knew about him, but hadn't known the kid was his cousin at the time. Looking at the kid lately, it was amazing he hadn't seen it, because it was so clear now. Last year, they had even been the perfect ages, Chase fifteen and Luke thirty, like half and half. Halfsies.

When he saw the kid at the clubhouse in Fort Wayne, he had to make sure the boy wouldn't tell anyone about their...past association. He rubbed his knuckles absently. The kid had learned a few moves, but he hadn't come close to besting Luke. Securing his silence had been easier than expected; all he had to do was threaten the ugly little dark-skinned bitch the kid was drooling after.

He glanced at Willa's door again and whispered to himself, "So fucking pretty."

The alarm on his phone startled him and he looked down at the display. "Time's up, cuz," he whispered, dialing the number burned into his memory.

Waiting for Mason to answer the phone was hard; he listened to ringing that seemed to go on forever. When it transferred to voicemail, he nearly lost it, fists clenched, and screaming so loudly the women in the rooms all came alert, the soundproofing not enough to suppress his anger and disappointment as he disconnected. Seeing them move in unconsciously synchronized movements, he had a thought.

Before he could stop himself, he walked around the edge of the room and yanked open the door to Mica's cell. True to form, she screamed briefly and backed up. Moving as far away from him as she could, she pressed herself flat against the back wall of the small room. He had gotten the idea for the rooms from Demon, when he visited the Sins' clubhouse several years ago. The man had himself a pretty redhead at the time, and with only a little room to move, the woman paced day in and day out. Even with her eyes blinded by rags tied around her head, she walked the edges of the room in which he kept her.

Lips trembling, Mica whispered, "Please. What do you want?"

He gripped his crotch, thrusting his hips towards her. "Wanna fuck. You up for it, bitch?" Intentionally crude, he wanted to gauge her response and was disappointed. Her only reaction was to shake harder, turning her gaze to the floor. "Well?"

"No." The word was so faint he wouldn't have heard it if he hadn't been focused on her.

"Okay." He shrugged as if it didn't matter to him, stepping back and closing the door. He retreated across the room, staying out of Willa's sight. Propping his ass back on the stool there, he watched as Mica continued to stare at the floor, not even acknowledging he had left her alone. "Bitch. Stupid fucking bitch. Princess, my sweet ass."

Without letting himself look at the clock, he dialed Mason's phone again. This time he was less reactive when it went to voicemail, and he hissed a one-word message that simply said, "Yes." It would be enough to make the man wonder and think, might be sufficient to make him understand. Yes, he had the women at his mercy. Yes, he was blood. Yes, he would kill for Mason, faithful to family. Yes, he would kill Mason if that were the way things went down. *Yes.*

He walked to the wall with the doors, covering his face as he walked in front of the glass, twisting the one-way knob on each and leaving them all slightly ajar before retreating once again to his stool. Seated within the shadows, he monitored the three women's responses as they individually contemplated the change in their status. He studied how they pondered the variation in routine. Each different. Watched as they thought about whether or how to explore, weighing the chances of taking advantage of the apparent promise of freedom. Bethany had been his captive the longest, and he had been busy getting everything in place, leaving her alone for days at a time. He thought this sudden opening of her door would scream 'trap' to her, even more so than the others.

Not surprised when Willa was the first to push the door open wide, he watched as her eyes scanned the area. Her body locked in place, on guard as her gaze snapped back to where he sat. He knew she could detect his presence in the shadows, but probably wouldn't be able to recognize him. At a noise beside her, she startled, whirling away from him, and laid eyes on Mica.

Chicago, he thought. He should call them by their cities. The distance would undoubtedly help him later, because he had nearly loved Willa, but fucking hated Fort Wayne.

Fort Wayne and Chicago looked at each other, and he could visualize the wheels whirring around in Will—Fort Wayne's head as she struggled to understand. Then Nashville pushed her door open, exiting so she stood between the two women who knew each other, however casually. Then he was surprised once again.

"Bethy," Fort Wayne breathed, while Chicago looked between the two women, confused. Nashville nodded and made a gesture with her hands, causing Fort Wayne to continue. "I'm Willa, Mason's girlfriend. You're his sister, Bethany."

Even as rage washed over him at her self-proclaimed title, he could see the moment realization hit Chicago that there were portions of his life Mason had never shared with her. The difference between the relationships was hard to misinterpret, one at arms-length on a pedestal and one a fully embraced partnership. He raised an eyebrow in surprise at not only the real identity of the woman, but also how close Mason had let his Willa. "But he shared with you, didn't he Wills? Big, fucking chunks. He let you right the fuck in, didn't he?"

With abrupt, jerky movements, she twisted around to look in his direction. Clearly recognizing his voice, he saw stark shock and disbelief on her face. Her voice tremulous, she questioned, "Judge?" Then, more incredulously, she asked in a louder voice, "Luke?"

Fuck, he thought. Remaining seated on the stool, he stayed silent, not wanting to confirm her suspicions, wondering what she would do. Would she fear him, or come to him for comfort?

Stepping protectively between him and the other two women, she faced him, head held high, anger now the dominant emotion on her features. "You know, I've been going over things in my head. Over and over. I told myself they all had to be wrong. Not Luke, he was one of the good guys, so they had to be wrong. Because surely I couldn't have misread you like that. They had to have it wrong, but they didn't. They weren't mistaken, were they? You actually did it, didn't you? What they said? You did all of that to Eddie."

He was taken aback, because she sounded so...disappointed. In him? She was disappointed in *him*? He had made sure she was safe, watched over her, discouraged Shooter when he wanted Willa brought with Eddie to San Diego as leverage to guarantee his bitch sister's compliance. "I made sure you were safe, dammit."

"Am I safe now?" Her eyes darted around the room then back to him. "Am I? Where are we, Luke?" Her breath was coming faster now, and she sounded panicky. "Where are we?"

"You're safe, Willa. Promise." He frowned, because she was shaking her head at him. "*You* are, honey," he said, putting subtle emphasis on the single word. Glancing behind her, he tried to smile, but knew if she caught sight of his face it would come across more like a grimace. "Not sure about the other two."

"Luke," she whispered his name, taking a step back as the other women moved together. "Where are we? Why are we here...how?" There was a frown on her face and he wrinkled his nose, knowing she was probably running scenarios through her head. So methodical. So smart, she would put things together, probably faster than he wanted. "How did I get here? Last thing I remember is standing in my bedroom. I was getting ready for work...Luke?"

"Mason told you to lock your doors, *babe*." She blanched and took another step backwards, her shoulders bumping into Chicago and Nashville. "Maybe you shoulda listened to...what did you call him? Your boyfriend? That's a pretty domesticated title for the man, dontcha think?"

"So, what...I'm supposed to believe you broke into my apartment and...kidnapped me? Like you did Eddie? Did you drug me, too?" Her voice rose with every word until she was shouting at him by the end. He shook his head at her and made a tsking sound.

"Had to do something to get you on the truck, didn't I?"

"Why?" she asked, and he laughed.

She needs to shut the fuck up, he thought, standing and walking across the room towards the gathering of women. *The fucking bitch is disappointed in me?* Fort Wayne stepped out to meet him, her hand raised in a placating manner. "Nope. Time to make me happy is past, honey," he said, reaching out to drag her closer.

Hand curved around her throat, he held her in front of him, pressing hard against her so she could feel the heat and firmness of his erection against her crotch. He tightened his hold on her, thumb digging into the flesh under her jaw as he waggled the gun at the two women standing near their open doors. "Go inside now. Be good little sheep." He laughed, then snarled at Willa when she flinched from his grip. "Be still and quiet, Willa. Shut the fuck up already. I only want some time." *With you*, he thought, but didn't say. She had been an island of sanity when things had been at their most difficult, and he wanted it back. Wanted her to be his center again. *Goddamn Eddie, always fucking shit up*, he thought, anger welling and rising inside him. Even when she wasn't here, she fucked shit up.

"I said," he roared without warning, drawing a short scream from Mica. "Get. The fuck. Back in. Your goddamned rooms." That got them moving, and he stood, watching them move backwards, eyes on him and Fort Wayne. He waited impatiently, ignoring the scratching of fingernails on his hand and arm. Waited until the soft snick of two locks slipping into place reached him before he shifted his gaze, looking her in the face. Taking in the silent struggle on her purpling features, he loosened his hold marginally, supporting her weight as she gasped and coughed, sucking in great draughts of air.

He pulled her close, reaching out to wipe the spittle from her chin with his sleeve, and she flinched away from his touch. He gripped her cheek, pulling her face back toward him, snarling at her and tightening his grip on her throat when she again tried to turn her face away. "What the fuck? Huh? What the fuck you going to do now, Willa? You not even going to look at me now?" He rapped the side of her head with the barrel of the gun, watching as pain chased the fear from her face for a moment. "Look. At. Me. *Look* at me, dammit. At *me*."

Lips trembling, she complied and he smiled. "Better, hon. Much better." Still gripping her throat, he pushed her backward towards her room and felt her relax minutely under his hand. She seemed to think she was headed back to safety—well, he could keep that lie going for a bit. "Back to your room, little sheepie," he said, watching her eyes roll back and forth as she tried to keep track of where they were in the open space. He kept his gaze locked on her as they walked into the small room, recognizing the contradiction of their movements, with her stumbling backwards and him striding confidently forwards. He was rewarded with the sight of her eyes widening when the door swung shut behind them, locking him in with her. "My favorite little sheepie."

Giving her a shove, he grunted and felt his cock swell as he watched her tits bounce when she hit the bed on her back, elbows out to break her fall. She slid her gaze back and forth between him and the door then back again, even as she raised one hand to her throat, gingerly rubbing the darkening marks his fingers had left there.

He smirked. There was no way for her to know about the fob remote in his pocket. He had been careful to only open the doors by hand, so, for her, this would look like he sacrificed his own freedom to be here with her.

Negligently waving the gun in her direction, in an offhand tone of voice, he said, "Lose the clothes, hon." It gave him a thrill of pleasure to watch the fear fan to life in her face. He had always enjoyed feeding off the terror of others and told himself this was no different. Even if he knew her...perhaps *because* they had been friends, he could feel the rawness of her fear, smell the scent of despair on the air...savor the taste of her dread. When she didn't move, staying locked down inside herself, he drew in a deep breath and screamed at her, "I said lose the fucking clothes, bitch."

She scuttled backwards on the bed until her shoulders hit the wall, pushing up to a seated position, eyes still locked on him. "Luke," she breathed, staring at him. "Don't do this. You don't have to do this. Please."

"Know what I'll do, Willa?" He asked the question casually, almost conversationally, frowning when she didn't respond. "I'll do whatever the fuck I want to do. For once, this is about what I want. Me." She shook her head and he waved the gun, bracing for the noise as he pulled the trigger, firing a round into the ceiling above her. She screamed, falling back against the wall, hands covering her ears. Over the ringing in his own ears, he could hear the other two women screaming too, calling out her name. "Because I hold the fucking power." He shook his head. "Now lose the goddamned clothes."

Bottom lip clenched between her teeth, she moved then, pulling up the tail of her shirt, tugging it over her head. He laughed, because there was another shirt underneath that one. "Keep going, keep going. I wanna see some boobs, little sheepie." She swallowed and removed it, revealing a white sports bra. "Nice. But Eddie was always the practical one," he commented, reaching down to tug on the head of his hardening cock, pulling it into a more comfortable position in his pants. "You were fancy," he murmured, tugging his cock again, watching her move on the bed.

"Except that night at the Riders' clubhouse, you dressed extra pretty for him, didn't you? Extra fancy? Eye-fucked him right in front of me. Until then, you were extra cute. Daddy even warned you off him, and you still creamed your fucking panties thinking about his dick." Nearly as an afterthought, he unfastened his belt and pants, pulling his cock out and stroking it tip-to-root, fingers circling the base like a ring as he gripped himself tightly.

Stepping closer, he ordered her, "Touch me," and sighed when she shook her head, turning her face to the side. "Fucking shit, honey. Don't make things worse. Don't make me hurt you," he muttered, reaching out to grab her hand, bringing it to his crotch. He used his hand to wrap around hers, forcing her palm against his hard length, his fingers threading through hers as he stroked himself up and down using her hand.

"Mmmm," he hummed, pressing down harder on their joined caress. "Feels nice. You feel how I want to fuck you? Wanted you for a while now. Coulda had you so many times. You wanted it, I could see. You eye-fucked me, too. That night at the bar north of town, you were nearly creaming your pants waiting for me, and riding my bike had you fucking squirming. Legs wrapped around me, twisting on the leather seat. I could smell you when you climbed off, you know. It wouldn't have even taken a hot breath to make you come. If it hadn't been for having to find goddamned fucking Eddie, I'd have had you that night, drunk or not. But, nope, I had to find her. Had to make sure Daddy's little girl was safe. Little sheepie." He forced her hand down to the root, tightening their combined grip hard around his cock. "Mmmm. Feels nice, don't it, Willa? Knowing I want to fuck you like this?"

Stepping back, he said, "Take off your pants now," laughing when she shook her head in refusal of the demand. Keeping his gaze on her face, he reached into the front pocket of his sagging pants, pulling out his pocketknife. With a flip of his wrist, he bared the blade, grinning as she flinched at the noise, her eyes flying open and then widening in alarm at him standing in front of her holding both a gun and a knife.

Slowly...deliberately...he leaned in and trailed the tip of the blade up her cheek to the edge of her eye then across her temple to her hairline, and back down to her ear. Not cutting her, simply...threatening until she was frozen in place like a deer staring down a car, afraid to even breathe. Distinctly, with pauses between his words, he repeated, "I said. Pants. Now."

She held her head still, the tip of the blade indenting her cheek as she reached her hands down. Pushing at the elastic waistband of her sweatpants, she awkwardly lifted herself to shift them past the curves of her ass. He stepped back, idly noting the other women had stopped screaming as he watched her drop the discarded sweats onto the floor. That left her dressed in panties and bra, and he raked her frame with his gaze. "Are you a sheep or a deer, Willa?" He paused a beat and then shrugged when she didn't answer. "Actually, it don't matter much. Gonna fuck you like a bitch."

He settled next to her, putting the gun and knife on the floor within easy reach. The next minutes were filled with her cries of pain and sadness, little bursts of breath as she fruitlessly repeated, "No," over and again. Afterward, Judge felt some compassion for the loss of friendship he assumed she suffered, and he stroked her shoulder slowly, watching as tears darkened the hair at her temples, her eyes clenched tightly closed. He sighed, relaxing into the bed and his last thought before falling asleep was how beautiful she was, even broken.

34. Passing time

Mason was running alongside the building, bent over low, staying out of sight of any observers who might be looking out the widely spaced windows. He glanced up at the dark clouds, swollen and ominous, heavy with unshed rain, scudding across the sky, running before the storm. In the distance, he heard a rhythmic thudding noise, the sound bouncing off the trees encircling the clearing in which the building sat. They were deep in the forest here, the only access roads narrow, rutted gravel tracks. They had left their trucks more than a mile up the road, not wanting any alerting noise.

Gun in hand, he paused at the corner to chance a quick glance around the blinding obstacle before continuing on his path, ensuring there were no surprises awaiting him or his men. Hesitating a second when he saw the door swing open and closed in the rising wind, he watched it slam back into the doorframe before slowly swinging open again. With the door open, he could now hear a counterpoint to the bangs, a weak sounding crash that repeated. *There's got to be an interior door*, he thought.

He looked back, seeing his brothers at his back. He was filled with a sudden, overwhelming pride to know that for every man with him today, another dozen had petitioned to come, ready to lay down their life for Mica.

When he reached the doorway, he allowed the swing of the door to finish its arc, thudding closed then open before he caught the edge and slipped inside. His eyes quickly adjusted to the dim lighting as he scanned the room, seeing only a desk and chair. He then focused on the row of glass-fronted doors in the wall opposite, glimpsing movement in the one on the left, the only one with the door firmly closed.

His eyes widened when he heard a far off screech and recognized the form behind the door, face pressed tightly against the glass. Lips pulled back from his teeth, mouth gaping open in what looked to be a furious scream was Judge. Without speaking, he directed his men to check the other rooms, but kept his gaze fixed on the man, who now stood facing the blood-smeared glass of the door. He rattled the door in its frame by hitting it repeatedly, alternating between closed and bloody fists, and his reddened, open palms. Methodically, Mason visually cataloged Judge's condition: knuckles bleeding and broken from hitting the door, lip and cheek swollen from an altercation, what looked like gore from gunshot wounds in his upper thigh and shoulder.

Without turning, he asked, "Anything? Y'all find any keys?" Hearing a tense chorus of "No," from a half-dozen throats, he nodded. "Bones, close the outside door, would ya? I want to say hello to my nephew." Taking several strides forward, he reached out and twisted the doorknob, stepping back as it slowly swung open. "Come on out, boy," he called, watching through the glass as Judge stared at him.

Lips pressed tightly together and slowly shaking his head back and forth, Judge took one then two steps backward, the backs of his knees hitting the edge of the mattress. He glanced down then back up with a look of raw terror on his face, and Mason felt a frisson of fear shiver down his spine. Something about the bed had the man spooked.

Looking down, he saw a scrap of fabric twisted in the sheet and froze. The small woman's shirt was out of place here, this far into the woods, in a room only occupied by Judge. He looked at it again and Mason choked, his throat closing off entirely when he realized he knew that shirt. *Oh, God*. He had last seen it weeks ago, in a bedroom far east of where they stood now. *No*. Had watched, laughing while it fluttered to the floor when jokingly thrown at him. *Not Mica*. The recognition blindsided him. *My Willa*.

Silently, he stared at the shirt for several long minutes, taking in and absorbing all the implications. *She hadn't left him*.

When he twisted his neck, bringing his chin up and raising his gaze to meet Judge's again, he knew the man saw his own death staring at him. Mason worked to clamp a lid on the rage building inside him, jaw clenched so tightly he wondered for a moment if it would fuse in place. Swallowing the bile rising in his throat, threatening to burn his voice even rawer than the ferocious screams he fought to keep inside, he waited until he thought he could control himself before uttering a word.

"Boy," he said in a guttural, commanding voice. "What did you do?"

Without speaking, Judge merely shook his head back and forth, and then, pursing his lips, mouthed the word, "No." Fear rolled off the man like a wave, so thick and dark Mason could practically taste it on the air, heavy and dense. Willa's shirt; his terror when he looked at the bed; the remote location; his wounds. *Fuck*. Trying desperately to hold himself together, Mason felt lightheaded when he considered the associations and what they likely meant. *My Willa*.

"Prez." This curtly spoken word came from behind and startled him, because he had mislaid the knowledge for a moment that he and Judge weren't alone here. He twisted around to see Duck pointing to the top of the desk. There was a large pocketknife laid neatly alongside a 9mm Glock, magazine ejected and the gun locked open. He walked over, and when he leaned in to look closely, he saw bloody flecks speckled across the barrel of the weapon, blowback from firing too close to a living target.

It felt as if smothering cotton were wrapped around all his senses, keeping everything happening at a far remove. Like walking through water, the currents of anger and fear pulled him this way and that. *Her shirt. Willa.*

He glanced up and caught Duck's gaze, seeing the slight nod that indicated he too believed the wounds Judge bore were from this weapon. Someone had used it to shoot Judge then abandoned the gun, leaving sure protection behind as they fled the building. *That bed. Willa.*

Hands steady, unshaking, Mason picked up the knife and flipped it open, relieved to see it at least was clean, free of any blood. He remembered plucking Jackson's open pocketknife from his lax hand, the blades in the same pristine condition. *Willa had been here.*

"Prez." He heard his title again, this time called from a room two doors beyond Judge. Four rooms, one occupant. *That goddamned fucking bed.*

His gaze skipped past the room his nephew stood in when he saw Watcher's head duck out and back in as soon as he realized he had Mason's attention. *Ten days. She's been gone for ten days.*

Standing in the doorway, he looked inside at the body of Carrie Sosa lying on a narrow bed, limbs carefully arranged. She was cold and gray, the abruptly terminated stump of her wrist covered with the edge of a sheet. Even with the covering pulled across, it still couldn't hide the hard use the woman had taken. Myron had already told them she was dead before the hand was removed, and now Mason saw the cause of death in the angle of her neck.

Mason considered for a moment how he was going to tell Chase about his mother then set it aside for a different time. *Ten days.*

For now, there was enough of a cluster to manage given the fact Mica wasn't here, but Judge was...and there had been occupants of the other rooms, who were also missing. *Willa. Judge looking down at the bed, a dangerous horror swamping his face.*

Another quietly spoken "Prez," called Mason back to the main room, where he stared in confusion at Bones. His friend had opened a door in the wall on the other side of the desk and stood in the doorway, the features of his face drawn into anguished lines. Mason walked towards him, intending to pass through into a room that looked to be filled with computers and technical equipment, but Bones didn't move. Standing in the way, he just stared at Mason then looked over to where Judge still stood, waiting silently in the small room. The grief-stricken look on Bones' face changed to rage and then flashed past that emotion to hatred. "Mason...that *pinche cabron* needs to die," he said vehemently, his accent thick in his voice.

Mason heard a soft gasping noise from inside the room and again tried to move past Bones, but an arm shot out across the opening, halting his progress. "My friend, this is something filled with pain, and a thing with which you do not need to be acquainted. Not firsthand. Just believe what he has done cannot be forgiven. *No puede ser perdonado. Amigo*, do not press me. Not on this." His voice lowered, became more impassioned, and he leaned closer to Mason before he said, "But know if you are unable to kill your blood, this is a time where I will gladly take the burden from you." That soft noise came again, followed by what sounded like a word, and Bones stiffened, eyes closing in what looked like sorrow before they flew open again, his gaze locking with Mason's. "Gladly."

"What did he do?" Mason asked the question quietly, and then the small shirt twisted in the sheets flashed through his mind and he sucked in a hard breath, because without a doubt, he already knew. *Ten days.* "Willa?" Seeking confirmation, but praying Bones would deny the proof he had seen, Mason said her name like a question. Bones nodded, his face twisting, watching as Mason shuddered helplessly, filled with a blend of fear...and wrath. *My Willa.*

As Mason moved again to stare through the open door at Judge, Bones called out from behind him. "Hoss." Vaguely, he listened to parts of a hurried conversation, turning to face his men when he overheard a name he didn't expect. He saw Hoss walk outside, closely followed by Gunny and Tater. Bones swung back to look at him, holding his gaze for a long minute before inclining his head. Hoss had gone hunting, and Mason knew he would find the ones who had fled the building. He would find them and bring them back, one way or another.

Without a word, Mason reached out and picked up the gun, hands automatically working to release the action, slipping the clip back into place, instinctively familiar with the movements needed to lever the slide to place a bullet in the chamber. When he looked up, at first he was startled, because he thought Judge had gotten out, escaped past them somehow. Then he realized the man had lowered himself to his knees, balled fists resting on his thighs. Head bowed, his face was relaxed for the first time Mason had ever seen. He was...waiting.

Mason didn't make him wait long.

35. Redemption

He was standing outside the building when he saw the initial flash of movement through the trees. Mason could not have said when he recognized everyone, but for the rest of his life, he remembered clearly the first moment he saw Willa's face. Dirty and bruised, stumbling and unshod, she still looked breathtaking to him. He watched the sun and shadows take turns flashing across her face, light and darkness first illuminating her fear, then hiding her courage, until there was only sunshine. Glancing up, he saw the dark clouds from before had vanished, leaving behind a brilliant blue sky.

There were other figures walking beside and behind her; he saw Mica, and then Bethany, step out into the sunlight, and watched as Willa reached back to stroke her hand along Mica's arm in encouragement. For him, the men who surrounded them were background noise, leaving him confident the women were safe, but not competing to draw his attention from Willa.

When she saw him, her reaction made his heart clench, because after jerking convulsively, she looked down, avoiding his gaze. He had made assumptions as to what Bones had seen on the video playing in the tech room, and her response confirmed his worst suspicions. She pretended to watch her footing, staring at the ground in a move he recognized as nervous distress, and he knew this would be something they would have to address. In time. Not right now, but in time, they would work together to settle her fears. He never considered anything else, because she was his. Assessing her movements, he saw she was hurting, and had to hold back a howl of anger at how ill-used she had been by his...family. His blood.

Instead, he stood solid and calm, and waited, letting her walk towards him. Confident, accepting... secure in wanting her. Needing her. Ten days he had been without her, but it had to be her decision to come to him. He felt his heart begin to pound, fearing rejection when he held out his arms, lowering his chin and silently pleading with her to let him in. And she did, sprinting the last thirty feet and plastering herself against him with a soft cry, and in return, he wrapped himself around her, holding on tight.

Mason bent his head, and when he placed his mouth alongside her ear, the only word he could utter was her name. "Willa." She nodded silently, and after a moment, he promised her something he hoped was now the truth. "You're safe, babe."

There was a tug on his hand and, without lifting his head, he unwound an arm from Willa, reaching out to scoop his little sister in close, holding her tight, too. Bethy put out a hand behind her, tugging Mica into the group as she and Willa enfolded her with their arms. There was no crying, even though it was clear the women had all shed tears at some point, the stark tracks through the dirt on their faces attesting to that.

Hoss said, "Prez," and Mason shook his head. Whatever the man wanted to say could wait; he would give the women this time. He needed this time. Ten days of not knowing, of fearing, of doubting. *Willa.*

I'm just a poor wayfaring stranger

Eventually, when he could make himself turn loose of Willa, he led the group around the outside of the building to the lot where Duck had parked their trucks. He was unwilling to take them back into the room that had been a source of torment and fear for all of them.

Tater had been a medic in the army and checked them over, everyone but Willa, because she wouldn't let him touch her. When the man gently pushed it, she began trembling, and Mason sent him away with a sharp gesture, gathering her to his chest as he sat on the tailgate of one of the trucks.

Bones came out with a box of equipment, and when he tersely stated, "Video," Mason waved at him, not giving the first fuck about that shit. Willa was in his arms. *Ten days.* Bones placed the box in one of the trucks and came over to stand near Mason, waiting quietly and watching as Willa slowly dropped off to sleep. Softly, he said, "She will be okay, my friend. If she did not trust you beyond all men, she would not have left herself vulnerable in this fashion." He gestured to her, dozing with her head on his shoulder.

Mason nodded, his arms tightening around her for a moment, and then he forced himself to relax. "I did this," he said quietly, shaking his head when Bones made to argue. "No, Bones. You know it. I did this. I did. This was my shit, and I didn't fucking clear it." He looked down at her, his breath coming fast and hard. "Every fucking time I turn around, I drop someone else in the shit. Every few days, it seems like. Slate and Ruby, on me. Bear in Des Moines, on me. Eddie, my blood...on me. Even fucking Winger and Lockee, on me, because of blood."

He felt hollow inside. Dragging his gaze up, he looked Bones in the face. "All of this. Today's entire play, on me." Looking back down, he stroked a gentle fingertip across Willa's throat, tracing the bruises there and along her jaw. Quietly, he said, "Her last week and a half, on me." Sighing, he closed his eyes. "Ten days, Bones. He had her for ten days. How the fuck can I accept her trust? How can I do that, when I know I have never kept anyone safe. My boy's mother, dead in that fucking place, but fuck...she was used seventeen years ago...by my blood. The same blood who orchestrated this entire fucking play."

Watcher walked up. He had evidently caught the last bit of their conversation, because he was shaking his head. "Mason, what the fuck are you talking about?" Willa stirred and Mason scowled at the man, soothing her with slow, gentle touches.

In a quieter tone, Watcher repeated the question. "What the fuck are you talking about? There isn't anything that's happened here your fault."

He denied it flatly, saying, "Slate and Ruby, Ruby's stint with the Sins...on me. Bones, do you remember when you got smacked, argued with the bat?" He waited for a nod, and then continued, "I found out about Sins being behind your beating and about Chase, same day. Wanna take bets on what I followed up on? Sure as fuck wasn't the Sins, man. If I followed that line through the water and dealt with the shit, Ruby would never have gone with Demon...she'd be unbroken."

Watcher laughed loudly, startling Willa awake briefly, and he smiled at the glimpse of her hazel eyes through the rifts of hair covering her face. When she settled again, he transferred his smile to Mason, saying, "You wanting to be the be-all, know-all now? Check this...if Ruby hadn't gone with Demon, well then Slate would have never found her, because she wouldn't have been where she was, when she was. You take away one fucking thing that happened—it changes everything. You lose all the good from the present if you start fucking with the past, man. I count today a win, man. Three good women, safe and healthy. All going home to people who love them."

Mason reached up, trailing the backs of his fingers down Willa's arm. "Eddie, Judge, Shooter...they're my family. This is all on me." He remembered the first night he ever saw her, how he had been willing to issue a challenge to Judge for her. *Shoulda killed the fucker that night*, he thought then remembered Shooter's face as he impassively watched

Ripper die, lying on a dirty bedroom floor. *Shoulda killed the father, and then the son*.

A voice from behind him drew his attention. Twisting, he looked to find Mica standing there, a sad look on her face. "Mason, you gonna listen to me?"

"Probably not, Mica." He numbly watched as she winced then looked away from her and back down at the woman in his arms. Ten days with that motherfucker, and her all bruised to hell and back. Trembling and avoiding touches from any man but him, he knew Judge had used her as hard as Sosa. *Ten days*.

"Well, I want you to at least pretend to try and listen to me. You remember Ray Nelms?" His head came up and he looked at her, unsettled, because of course he remembered Nelms. Her personal nightmare, who he had finally taken care of...but only after the man had wounded her, again. On his watch, she had been hurt. He nodded and she smiled, glancing across the lot. "Remember when I first found out about Duck? You brought him to Wisconsin to Darlene's house, and the big guy and I had a chat." He nodded again.

"Did he ever tell you what we talked about?" She cocked her head to one side, waiting for his response. Silently, he shook his head.

Taking a deep breath, she said, "He wanted to own what had happened...from Ray. You know my family, my history. Mason, you know everything about what's happened to me from birth to now, as well as I do. There was something I knew, which he hadn't yet learned. What I told Reuben...Duck, was one of the things I learned early on is you don't get to pick your family. You just don't. That's an association we get locked into without our consent. Part is luck—some kids get the good parents; some of us got the shitty ones. Our families. Because we don't get to choose. There's nothing we did to deserve them, so we don't have to be held accountable for something because of them. We...are not...our families."

Gazing at Mason, she stepped forward and reached out to cup a palm over his cheek, smiling sweetly at him. "Our friends and the ones we surround ourselves with...that's the piece we have to take responsibility for. You totally can tell a lot about someone by who they have in their pocket, in their circle. Especially when the crap hits the fan." She looked around, smiling at Watcher and Bones, watching Bethy standing nearby, chatting with Hoss and Tater. Duck had walked up and Mica moved close to him, slipping her arm around his waist. "I'm not responsible for what my father did. I don't have to hold that; it's not mine. Duck wasn't responsible for Ray. You'd never tell him it was his burden to carry, would you?"

Mason shook his head, the corner of his mouth curling up. He knew the argument she was making, and she kinda had him against the wall with this one.

Reacting to his half-smile, she mock-growled. "Shaddup, you. I'm not done yet." She grinned at him, the humor feeling somehow out of place here, when he knew there were two bodies only a few yards away, both connected to him. "Mason." She sighed, allowing Duck to place her in front of him, his arms crossing protectively over her belly and chest. "I'm gonna tell you this one time. You trackin'?" Her using his words like that pulled a genuine smile from him, and she beamed back. "You don't get to be mean to my friend. Mason's my friend, and he's not at fault in this. It's not his fault I was nabbed, or that Bethy was brought here from Nashville."

She looked down at the sleeping woman in his arms...his woman. Softly, she said, "You didn't cause what happened to Willa. Everything Luke did was his decision, not yours." Her voice hardened in a way he had never heard from her. "Today, he reaped the consequences of those decisions, didn't he?" Mason nodded.

She touched his cheek again, pulling back to cup her hand over Duck's arm, holding his wrist. "Then he owned those decisions, didn't he?" He nodded again, waiting. "So...let him own it. It was his, not yours. Let it go, Mason." She shrugged. "I want to go home. I want to see my husband and my boy. Take me home?" He slowly dipped his head again, at a loss for words at the wisdom she had shared.

***

On the plane ride back, Bethany filled him in on everything that happened. She had been working at the recording studio when the electricity went out. The next thing she remembered was being thrown over someone's shoulder and hauled into the small room, which would become her home for three weeks. Carrie Sosa was next and, true to form, she had raised hell at Judge every chance she got. He would leave and be gone for a few days, and when he got back, she would light into him, provoking him. One day, he disappeared into Carrie's room, and when he came back out, everything was quiet. That was about a week after he had shown up with Willa.

"It wasn't until he brought Mica in yesterday that things changed." She pushed her hair away from her forehead tiredly, curling her legs into the seat and wrapping her arms around her knees. "He let us all out, let everyone recognize each other."

"Who did he think you were?" Mason reached out a hand, trailing his fingers through Bethy's hair, hand shaking with the thought she almost wasn't here for him to hold. Things could have gone so differently. One bit of information mislaid, one assumption gotten wrong, and everything could have gone sideways.

"He knew my name, but since it's not Mason, it wasn't until Willa recognized me that he knew who I was." She shrugged. "He was talking to himself a couple times and seemed to be reciting the names of people who were important to you, so it didn't dawn on me he wouldn't know until he was surprised there at the end."

"That was near the end?" He reached into his pocket and pulled out the sea glass, running it through his fingers as he so often did, the unconscious movements coming fluidly, effortlessly.

"Yeah. He called Willa over to him, and when she wouldn't go…he went to her." She shuddered. "He started choking her. Told us to go back to our rooms like we were children. Then they walked towards her room—"

Mason interrupted, "She walked with him?" He glanced over to his other side where Willa slept, slumped against him.

"More like he pushed her backwards and she couldn't hardly keep her feet underneath her." Bethany straightened in her seat, glaring fiercely at him, protective of her newfound friend. "She saved us, Davy. Saved us." He nodded and she subsided, somewhat mollified. "There was a gunshot, and I thought he'd killed her." She curled her arms a little tighter around her knees. "I was so scared. Then, after a while…there was shouting and more gunshots, and then she was opening my door and we got Mica out. And then we just left." She looked down at her bare feet, cut and bruised. "Not thinking clearly, because there we were, three unarmed, barefoot women running into the woods like the devil himself was chasing us."

"Did she say…has she said anything about what happened?" He would be talking to Willa as soon as they had privacy, but the more he knew upfront, the better off everyone would be.

"She said he hurt her and then went to sleep. So she took his gun and then, when he woke up, she tried to get him to open the door and he laughed. So she shot his arm." She shook her head. "She said she shot him, but she talked about it like she was buying milk. No big deal, just another day at the office, kind of, 'oh hey, by the way, I shot a guy today'…but you could tell it *was* a big deal. I guess she'd known him at some point. He got up, and she shot his leg. He had some kind of remote entry thing. Used it to unlock the door and she took it, and then shut him right up in the same room. Locked him in. She's pretty amazing, Davy."

He nodded, thinking about his Willa having to make a choice to hurt Luke. Knowing how hard it would be for her. It would not be something she could sweep under the rug and ignore. *Ten days.* "Then she got you?" His eyes scanned Bethy's face, trying to determine how upset she was by everything, watching as she shivered with remembered terror again.

"Yeah, she got me out, and she stood staring at him for the longest time. Watching while he threw himself at the window, trying to get out, kind of like how we'd all probably done when he first shut us up in there. She put her hand on the glass and he got really still. That part was super spooky. He went to put his hand up to match hers and she jerked away, and then she turned around as if nothing had happened and we got Mica out. She put the gun and the knife on the table and we booked it as fast as we could out of there." She pushed at her hair again. "I want to go home, Davy. When can I go back?"

"Soon," he said, leaning over to kiss the side of her head softly.

"What I don't get is why he brought Carrie and Mica." She frowned up at him. "If he had known who I was, it would make more sense. I'd understand me and Willa, because, well"—she gestured to herself—"sister and"—she gestured to Willa—"girlfriend. But why the other two?"

"Mica's been important to me for a long time," he said softly, his gaze going to where she sat several seats away, staring out a window of the plane. "A long time. Since the day I met her." He shook himself, pulling his thoughts back to the present, and looked down at the glass still in his hand, pushing it deep into his pocket. "Carrie was my boy's mother." He hadn't thought about his words before they came out and was startled by Bethy's reaction.

"What? Your...boy? You have a boy? Davis Mason, you have a son?" Her voice was so loud it startled Willa awake and drew Mica's attention, along with the focus of his brothers. "I have a nephew?"

"Well, yeah. I've been meaning to tell you—"

"You've been...meaning to tell me?" If anything, her voice was even louder. "How long have you known about this boy? Does the child have a name, or do you call him Boy? Like the cat you once named Kitty? Boy?"

Frowning, he patted the air, making a 'cool it' motion with his hand, reaching the other one around Willa's shoulders, tugging her to him. She was trying to pull back, leaning away from him, and he didn't want to give her any room. "Hey, babe," he said, looking down at her and smiling, but she was frowning up at him. He felt a hard elbow poke his ribs on the other side and swung back to look at Bethy with a scowl.

"Well? Tell me now, it's as good a time as any," she prompted. "I'm a captive audience." Even as she quipped, he saw a wave of fear cross her features at her words and knew his sister would have fears to work through in the coming weeks and months, sorrowful she had this weight to bear, but pleased as fuck she was here to have to deal. He would just have to hang closer, make certain all was well with her. The friendship she seemed to have with Willa would help, he hoped.

"Chase, his name is Chase. I haven't known about him that long. Carrie kept him a secret until Watcher," he nodded at the man seated down the plane, "found out about him and told me." Watcher was grinning widely, his gaze going back and forth between Mason and Bethy.

"Chase Mason," she mused with a smile. "How old is he?"

"He's sixteen now." He wasn't prepared for the return of the loud screech, and he glared at his sister.

"Sixteen? I have a sixteen-year-old nephew?" Shaking her head, she reached out and playfully slapped at Mason's shoulder. "When did you find out?"

He tilted his chin down. The elapsed time was going to cause a repeat of the noise and violence; he just knew it would. "You wanna meet him?" He offered this, hoping it would gloss over her unanswered question.

"Well, duh." She snorted a laugh. "Aunt Bethy," she considered, "I kinda like it. What does he think about having an aunt?"

"He doesn't know about you," he said quietly. "Things were fucked up with Sosa."

She seemed to turn the information over in her head and then nodded. "Poor guy, and now you'll have to tell him his mother is dead." Tilting her head a little to one side, she looked over at Watcher and said, "I always knew you were a keeper, Michael Otey. Glad you located him, and more than glad you got him to Davy. How long ago did you find him?"

Fuck, he thought, seeing Watcher's eyes light up as he prepared to throw Mason under the Bethany-bus bearing down on them. "Oh, hard to remember. About four years ago? Does that sound right, Mason?"

Dropping his head into his hand, he listened to his sister's scolding with a smile, because at least she was still here to harass him.

***

Deacon stood and watched as the dying flames cast light and shadow across the trees. *All my plans, torn to absolute shit*, he thought, not reacting as part of the building collapsed in on itself. A cloud of smoke and sparks rose into the night sky, burnt, curling pieces of paper drifting down around him like dark, bitter snow. "Goddamned fucking Mason." Muttering, he turned to walk through the trees back to his bike.

He shook his head at his companion, who softly asked, "Fuck. The boy, too?" At Deacon's nod, he raised a hand and rubbed at his forehead. "Dammit, I liked Luke." Sighing, he asked, "What's next?"

Deacon shook his head at Morgan, not responding. This had been a well-planned play; it had been expensive and hard to set up, but it wasn't his only one, not by a long shot.

36. Restoring family

"Carrie's dead?" Chase asked in a flat tone, and Mason winced but nodded, holding the boy's gaze with his own. "Did she OD?" This was asked in such a matter-of-fact tone it broke his composure, and he scrubbed his palm across his jaw.

"No, she was killed by Judge," he admitted, watching as Chase's eyes widened. He was smart, and not three minutes ago, Mason had told him Eddie was his cousin. He knew the boy would make the leap.

"But Judge is...was your nephew." His Adam's apple bobbed as he swallowed. "Did she know he was your...was our..." Here, he paused and took a breath, and Mason interrupted, wanting to help.

"Yeah, she knew him." He stopped, because Chase was shaking his head.

"No, I know she knew him. He helped set up an apartment one time when Carrie was too dusted and we got evicted." He thudded a closed fist on the table between them. "He knew her, knew she was my mom. Why did he kill her? What did she do?"

Fuck. That meant Judge had gotten close to his boy before he even knew about him, which was a terrifying thought, given how things had shaken out. *We never actually talked about her after she dropped him off*, he realized with a frown, wondering at how quickly Chase had gone to this being Carrie's fault. *Kind of how everyone always expected the worst of Shooter, and he is happy to oblige,* he thought, then shook himself. "I don't think he meant to kill her. It looked to be quick, Chase. She probably never knew what happened."

Sniffing, Chase was taking little sips of air through his nose, his shoulders jerking. When he lifted a single index finger to press against his eyebrow, Mason saw his hands had started shaking. He got up from behind the desk and moved to where his son was sitting, pushing him over on the couch with his hip, settling in beside him. Wrapping his arms around Chase, he didn't say anything for a long time, just pulled his boy against his shoulder. He rested a palm on the back of Chase's head and listened as his son cried for his mother.

"I'm glad she didn't OD," Chase said finally, in a small voice sounding much younger than his sixteen years.

"Me, too," Mason agreed, sighing and resting his cheek on the top of Chase's head. "Me too, son."

Pulling back, Chase looked up into Mason's face, and with a start, he realized there wasn't as much of a height difference as there had been not even three months ago. "What happens to me now? Do I have to go…is there anything I need to take care of?"

Tugging his son to his side again, Mason shook his head, letting the boy rest against him. "Nope, I got this, Chase." And he did; well, Myron did. Caroline Sosa's death certificate would read death by traumatic dismemberment in a single car accident. What little possessions she had, her miserable grasping family had already buzzarded over, and when Deke came back from Kentucky, all he had were baby pictures of Chase.

Mason had looked through those books, grudgingly put together by Carrie's mother, and had watched as a joyful baby turned shy toddler then sullen child. The pictures ended when Chase looked to be about eight or nine, and he wondered what that said about Carrie. The woman who would tell her twelve-year-old son to call her by her first name, because she thought she was too young to have a child so old. She probably quit taking pictures, because they were a reminder of time marching inexorably on, regardless of her wishes.

"You want to do anything? Want to call Benny and Lucia to come over?" He knew Chase had been spending a lot of time with them, both at Bear's home and at the studio Slate had built for Benny in his house.

"I'll call Ben later," Chase said, his voice muffled by Mason's shoulder. "Can I just stay here with you tonight?" There was a pause, and he tentatively added, "Dad."

Mason nodded, frowning, glad he had this next thing already set up, because, much as he wanted to hear it, the boy never called him by that name, so Chase dragging it out now spoke to the depth of his need for family right now. "I'll go you one better," he said, sitting back a little, letting Chase move away, because he wanted to watch his face. "Myron rented us a house here in town, got us some furniture. Why don't we go check it out?" The shock on his son's face shouldn't have hurt, but damned if it didn't. *Did he think he could avoid me forever?*

"But you live in Chicago," Chase said.

Mason grinned. "And now Fort Wayne. I can't be here all the time, since there's too much work with the various chapters all over the states, but as national president, I can pretty much pick which chapter to settle with. I'll always be from the mother chapter, a founder from Chicago, but I can settle here." He shrugged, looking at Chase from the corner of his eye. "Seemed to me you were putting down roots here finally, and I want to be where you are, son." The look of disbelief cut a little, but the follow-up smile helped soothe the sting.

"Means Tug won't have a chaperone anymore," Chase said cryptically, and Mason grinned.

"Man can stand on his own feet, I suspect." His smile fell away, and he looked at his son. "You gonna be okay?"

"Yeah." Chase sighed. "She's been leaving me since I was about five, Dad. Haven't seen her for more than a year. It's simply...final this time." The title came more naturally this time, but the rest of the words had Mason thinking back and he realized it had been that long since Carrie dropped Chase on him.

Startled, he wondered...had he missed the...with a heavy sigh of relief, he remembered the date and matched it up with the paper in his head, the one from the folder the Chicago policeman handed him all those years ago. "Your birthday is next week, isn't it?"

With a broad grin, Chase raised his grey eyes, meeting Mason's gaze. "Yeah." He smiled shyly. "You remembered."

Pulling him in for a hard hug, Mason stood and grabbed Chase's hand, dragging him to his feet. "Of course I did. I'm your dad."

***

They were settled in the apartment later that evening, litter from their unplanned pizza party cluttering the dining room table, when the doorbell rang. Mason sighed and said, "I'm too fucking full, boy. Go get the door."

With a laugh, Chase got up, slapping the bottom of Mason's socked feet where they were propped on the coffee table. "Tired, old man?"

"Fuck yeah. Tired and full, now go get the door, son." He smiled, because he had never had this with Chase before, and he found he kind of liked it. It felt...like having a home. He looked around, once again reminding himself he needed to thank Myron. The man seemed to have the touch when it came to living arrangements, and he had matched this one really well. The downstairs was sizable, living room and den sharing space with the kitchen, so most of the area was a big, open L-shape filled with couches and chairs. There were three wall-mounted flat screen TVs downstairs, and a cooking range in the kitchen over which he knew Road Runner would drool.

Upstairs was expansive, too, with two suites and four additional bedrooms. Security was tight, he had a three-car garage to park cages and scoots in. Hell, the pantry had even been stocked when they rolled up to the door tonight; the pizza was only because Mason was too fucking tired to cook.

There were noises from the entryway and he frowned, trying to pick individual voices from the cacophony. Groaning, he recognized one of the people, closing his eyes. "I didn't tell him yet," he yelled, knowing his words would at least draw the drama farther into the house. *No reason for the neighbors to hate us on the first night.*

"Well, he knows now," Bethy said tartly, standing in the doorway with her arm slung around Chase's neck. Transferring her attention back to her nephew, she told him, "I totally want you to call me Aunt Bethy. I'm pretty geeked about all this, Chase. You look so much like your daddy it's uncanny." She sucked in an excited breath, and then said loudly, "Oh! You need to come to Nashville and stay with me for at least a month this summer. Maybe two!" Mason saw the terror-widened look in Chase's eyes and laughed.

"He can, but only if he wants to, Bethy." He stretched out his arms, motioning her over, and said, "Come here, baby sis. Let me hug on you." She kept her elbow firmly around Chase's neck, tugging him across the room with her, him bent absurdly far down so her arm would reach. Mason waited until they were within range then he exploded from the couch, catching her around the waist to pull her away from Chase. He tossed her on the sofa, crouching in an exaggerated wrestling stance, waiting on her response. "Run, boy. I got this. Save yourownself," he stage-whispered to Chase, startling a laugh out of him.

"You think I'm kidding?" he said normally, standing upright. "She's got deadly tickling fingers, son. I've abided the brunt of them many ti—"

True to form, the moment his attention was elsewhere, she launched herself at him from the top of the couch, her trilling cry loud in the room. "*Fuck*," he grunted, catching her. "You're too big for this, Bethy. We ain't kids anymore." He dropped her back onto the couch as laughter rang through the room and he turned, realizing for the first time she hadn't come alone. Willa, Tug, and Maggie stood in the entryway behind him, and he had barely opened his mouth to greet them when he felt the first digs of her manicured fingers into his side.

37. Consumed

Mason pushed back from the small desk and drew a trembling hand across his face, scrubbing hard, trying to erase visions of what he had seen on the video he made himself watch. He found he had to know, had told her honestly this week the not knowing was its own kind of hell. Positioned on the edge of the bed where she couldn't see the screen, Willa took her hands from her ears and sat quietly, waiting for his response. Her request wasn't unreasonable, but the fact she had to utter the words destroyed him.

"Make it have never happened."

That was her first wish, the real one. The wish screaming of truth. When he hadn't responded, she held out her hand, palm up in supplication. She leaned forward, the look on her face shattering him with the belief he could fix it, change it, that he could unbreak her.

"Then, make me forget."

He closed the laptop and leaned forward; taking her hand in his, he placed an open-mouthed kiss against the fleshy part of her palm. He laid another at the base of her thumb, followed by a quick bite savage enough to pull a gasp from her. Yet another soft kiss, and another across her palm, the tip of his tongue trailing along her lifeline. With every wordless press of his skin on hers, he told her none of it mattered, nothing changed inside him. She was his.

Rising from the chair, he took the single step to cross the space separating them, and sank to his knees at her feet. He turned her hand over, kissing across her knuckles, dragging the back of her hand along his jaw, feeling his short beard rubbing against her soft skin.

Turning her hand back over, he nuzzled the inside of her wrist, trailing more hard, wet kisses up the inner bend of her arm, nibbling and gently biting her bicep. With hands and mouth, he touched every inch of skin as he moved. Raising his head, he looked into her tear-filled hazel eyes, pleased to recognize the heat of passion soaring over remembered fear, and watched as a shiver of eager anticipation shook her frame.

"As I can, babe. Every touch, every finger he laid on you, replaced by mine." He ran his tongue across his bottom lip, watching as her eyes followed its path, her tongue unconsciously sliding out to echo his movement. "Every place he took you, we go farther, harder. I didn't keep you safe, but I can goddamned well do this."

Touching her, kissing her, tasting her, all of this had aroused him; she was as addictive as ever. He wondered if showing her his desire would bring her to dark memories, because of what he had both heard and seen on the tape. Then, he rightly judged not showing her would erode her confidence, so he pulled her hand to cover his erection, groaning when she fondled him through this jeans.

"His touch on you is gone, babe. This is just you and me now. And, know this to be true, Willa. God, I want you...hell, I need you more than I thought was possible. Want you more than I know what to do with. All the time, you fill my thoughts. I told you once I'd fill you up with fire for me, consume you...I was wrong, babe. I'm the one consumed. By you, for you...with you. I love you, Willa Grace. Always will." With those words, he settled his mouth over hers, kissing her hard until they were both breathless.

***

Mason lay on his couch holding Willa in his arms, her hip and body wedged between him and the back of the sofa. He didn't want her alone, didn't like it, because the few times she wound up on her own were hard for her. She never wanted to talk about it, but simply by looking at her face he could recognize how deep inside herself she withdrew. He and Eddie traded off times spent with her, and so far, they had been able to arrange their schedules so she was hardly ever without company.

She seemed to long for his touch as much as he craved hers, so he held her as much as he could. Organizing things with Jase and Myron, he put off club business again and again to remain at her side. Stroking her, trailing his hands on her skin, anchoring her into the present. Now he came alert when she jerked and jolted, muscles all over her body tensing, and then she said, "No." Just the one single word uttered in sleep, the sound filled with remembered pain and shame.

Recalling the way she had always slept in fits and starts, tossing and turning, you would think the stillness of her body during sleep now should have seemed deeper, more restful. Better than before Judge stole her away, before he took her from her apartment. Mason knew as often as she had woken or partially woken from sleep in those days, every time she closed her eyes again it was with a mind at peace, allowing her body real rest.

Now, she woke just as often, but when she did, she would be frozen with fear, limbs drawn tight in response to dreamtime happenings, pulled deep inside her memories. Which meant she couldn't rest, not really. Her sleep was easier if he was there to hold her, and so like tonight, he spent as much time as possible wrapped protectively around her. "No," she whispered again, panting breaths hitching painfully as the single syllable stuttered from her lips. Soothing her, palms running over her back and arms, he held her, his eyes wide open, staring into the dark. *I didn't keep her safe*, he thought, his arms tightening in response to his self-recrimination, *but I can goddamn well help her sleep.*

***

Mason heard the loud pipes and squeezed his eyes shut. *Why did I agree to the truck again? Oh yeah, because Chase was seventeen, irresponsible, and did not need a bike. So, we got a truck instead.* Then the boy had gone and talked to Bear, and Bear had turned traitor, giving the little shit free work. Now the kid had a beautiful truck, but his pipes...Mason could do without those, except on a bike. He looked down, fingering the small patch on one edge of his cut and grinning, 'Loud pipes save lives.' He knew his attitude was out of sync with his own life's experiences, but he didn't give a fuck.

He opened the refrigerator, pulled out a cold six-pack of pop, set it on the countertop alongside a bag of chips, and waited, knowing the kitchen would be the first place the boys came. "Bethany," he called up the stairs. "They're here." She had come back to Fort Wayne and was staying with them this week.

Chase had been hot to have his aunt meet Ben Jones, the person he dubbed his musical mentor. Mason grinned when he remembered how comically Bear's face had fallen at Chase's statement, and laughed aloud when he recalled how the boy had backpedaled, loyally trying hard to ease the sting until he realized Bear was jacking with him.

Willa had gone back to work today and wanted to stay at her apartment tonight, telling both him and Eddie she needed to get back to her regular schedule. Which meant, with Bethy here, he would stay home, surrounded by family...and she would be alone. That shit didn't sit well with him, but he knew from talking to Gunny he had to let her take back the power in her own life, painful as it would be to watch.

Chase walked in, followed by Benny and Lucia, the intrepid trio who seemed to always be joined at the hip these days. Since Ben had begun to teach Chase to play, they had spent hours upon hours working up a set Ben was happy with, and one Chase could master.

From the other side of the room, his sister gasped. "Ho-ly shit, I know Chase said it was Ben Jones, but I don't think I put it together until just now." She looked down at her clothes and scowled at Mason, loudly whispering, "This is your fault. All your fault. I don't know how, but it is."

"What?" he asked, laughing at the look on her face.

"Do you know who *he* is?" She indicated Benny with her finger, unsuccessfully trying to hide the gesture behind her other hand as Ben looked on with a broad grin.

"Uh, yeah. The baby brother of one of my Rebels." He frowned at her; it could be this was a delayed reaction to the kidnapping. *I should call Gunny*, he thought, reaching into his pocket for his phone, when she responded.

"Well duh, but do you know *who he is*? This is Ben Jones, lead singer and guitarist for *Occupy Yourself*, only one of the most successful indie bands in the past five years." She ticked off her fingers, flipping them up in sequence as she said, "They've played the Engine Line, sold out the Braiding Ball, and the House of Indie Rock." She pointed to her blouse. "And I have spaghetti sauce on my shirt." Reaching out to slap his shoulder, she said, "See? Your fault."

"Sis, only one of those sounds like a club, so I'm still not..." She wasn't looking at him anymore; chin lifted confidently, she strode across the kitchen with her hand outstretched.

"Mr. Jones, it's a real pleasure to meet you. I'm Bethany Taylor..." She used the name she had taken when she married away from Mandy Holler and then corrected herself for this audience, tacking on her maiden name. "...Mason, a talent scout for Iron Indian Records." Ben reached out and shook her hand, flashing the kind of smile at her normally reserved for fans; Slate called it his rock star grin.

"Ms. Taylor-Mason, please call me Benny." He elbowed Chase in the side. "Little dude, you lose points for not telling me your aunt is hot."

"But I gain points, because I remembered this." Chase reached into the bag Lucia had on her shoulder, digging around as he ignored the look she was giving Ben. "One demo CD, coming up." He handed it to Bethy and Mason laughed as her eyes grew wide, and then she smoothed her features out before responding.

"I'll have to determine if I can clear some time on my schedule to give it a listen, Mr. Mason." She reached out and ruffled Chase's hair then looked over at Ben, saying in a less formal voice, "Seriously, if you are looking for a label, I can guarantee you an audition."

Tilting his head, Ben asked her, "How can you guarantee an audition if your label hasn't listened to the demo."

"Because I'm pretty sure 'my label' has already heard this in rehearsals." She laughed and stuck her tongue out at Mason. "After all, your rhythm guitarist is living with him."

38. The cost

She entered the bar cautiously, stepping inside and scanning her surroundings before dropping her hand and allowing the door to close behind her. Walking across the quiet room, she stood beside the table for a minute, staring unblinkingly at him. He looked into those grey eyes, so like his own, and waited patiently. He found himself willing to give her whatever kind of time she needed in order to come to grips with their connection.

After a long sixty seconds, she moved, reaching out and adjusting a chair at the table to put her across from him, but without having any doors at her back. The entire journey, her steely grey gaze never broke from his. In the past, he had noted intimidation came naturally to her. But, only at certain times and in certain company—for instance, she had never seemed one to back down from even the most alpha of men, which made her an excellent match for Bear. *She is her father's daughter, after all*, he thought.

Mason had mentally gone over the potential outcomes of this meeting a dozen times in the past week, and had picked up the phone to cancel the meet nearly as many times. Frustrated by his own uncharacteristic reticence, he had finally allowed the call to ring through, determined to hash things out over the phone, but then he heard her voice. His number must have been in her contacts, because instead of hello, she answered with a guarded question. "Mason? What can I help you with?" He took a breath and confirmed their meeting before hanging up, leaving her sounding confused.

As Eddie settled into her seat, he flicked a finger at Merry, who nodded in response, even as he felt her eyes boring into him. The woman had known him for more than twenty-five years; he would not expect her to miss the physical similarities between the young woman seated at the table and him. She would have enough restraint to wait until after Eddie was gone to ask her questions; at least, he hoped she would.

As prearranged, she brought over a beer and a mug of apple juice, wordlessly setting them on the table between them before turning to leave. Eddie broke their gaze then, glancing up at Merry and thanking her. With a gentle look on her face, Merry said, "No trouble at all, little miss." The use of the sweet pet name made Eddie smile, and that loosened Mason's muscles somewhat. Merry retreated behind the bar, and Mason knew he couldn't stall much longer.

Might as well dive right in, he thought. "Do you know who I am?" He asked the question expecting a headshake in response, and was surprised when she opened her mouth instead.

"Shooter always said you were one of the most dangerous men he had ever met. Davis Mason, national president for the Rebels. I know you've known him a long time. But, you've known Bear for a long time, too, and he thinks the world of you. For me, his opinion counts for far more than Shooter's ever could, which is why I was willing to meet you here today." She eyed the mug and then asked, "What did you get me?"

"Apple juice." Seeing the surprise on her face, he laughed. "No tequila, unless I'm wrong about something."

With another wary look, she shook her head. "You're not wrong." Frowning, she asked, "How did you know? I only told Bear two days ago."

He smiled. "Got a call, honey."

A bright smile flashed across her face, but it was quickly gone as she considered him. "Bear doesn't know I'm here."

"Yes, he does," he responded, which brought a frown to her features. "Don't be pissed off at him. If my woman were carrying my child and heading out of town on short notice, I'd call in my brothers, too. I told him you were only coming up so we could talk." Bear already knew about the family association, and had become one of the biggest pain in the asses, because he thought Eddie should have known months ago. "But back to my question, Eddie. Beyond my name, do you know anything about me?"

"Not really," she admitted, and he smiled.

"Okay then. Story time." Sighing, he reached out and grabbed the bottle, but didn't pick it up. "I grew up in Kentucky. My family was religious and we lived up on a mountain, away from most folks. Daddy worked the mines until a seam fire closed them. Then he turned to preachin', but not a kind most folks recognize as such. It was a hard life, Eddie. My mama was a mystery to me for a long time. When I was little, she went missing for years, and then came back for a few months before leaving again. I never saw her again. I was eight."

He took a drink now, but kept his eyes on her face. "I was sixteen when I found out what happened to her. I'd gotten out of Mandy Holler in Kentucky and moved to Chicago, was patching into the Rebel Fiends. Your dad was already a member, and that's how I met him. Soon as I said my name, he locked on me, and it wasn't but a couple of days later I found out why. The reason Mama left was because Justice Morgan took her. Three times he had her, two times he took her. He had her before I was born, and then when I was four years old, he took her back.

Then the last time when I was eight. On Shooter's side of things, his mother went missing, too. When he was nine, she left and was gone for not quite five years. Then for a final time, she was missing for a few months when he was about seventeen."

As he talked, he had watched as recognition rolled across her face, and now he nodded. "Yeah. Mama was his mother, too. John and I are brothers...well, half-brothers. Our raisings were different; we lived in different worlds until I found him in Chicago."

"You and Shooter are brothers?" Her mouth was tight and she shook her head disbelievingly. "Jesus, Mason. That's hard to wrap my head around. Why wouldn't he have said anything to me?" She eyed him, frowning. "Why wouldn't you? We've been part of the same extended MC family now for a while, so why keep it a secret?" Tilting her head, she took a breath and then slowly asked, "And why tell me now?"

"Good questions, Eddie." He led with praise, because the topics he had to cover today were hard, and she would need to know he had always been proud of her. "You always ask good questions. Like I said, we're half-brothers. I met your granddad, Morgan, only a few times, but he and my first club's president were thick as thieves, which is why Shooter was here when I came to Chicago. Kind of like how Judge patched into the Fort Wayne club for a while, learning from a mentor."

He twisted the bottle between his hands, fingers plucking at the label. "Morgan didn't want you or Judge knowing you had family beyond California. I never knew the why of it, but I was young and didn't give a shit either way, so I just went with it. I suspect Shooter was the same; after all, it wasn't like we were planning a fucking family reunion."

"Okay, but why tell me now?" she repeated her question, and he nodded.

"I need you to know what happened in Utah," he said and saw her go ashen. Anyone associated with the club knew some hard shit went down, but they were keeping the specifics restricted to inner circle members only. Even with him and Eddie swapping off taking care of her, he still didn't think Willa was talking about what happened yet, except to him. She would have a general idea, but wouldn't actually *know*. Nodding, he said, "Yeah. Hard shit for just apple juice." With a snort, he shifted in his seat. "Then, in the end, I get to tell you about some good that came out of everything. We'll hold it in front of us. That'll be our carrot."

Leaning back into the seat, he folded his arms across his chest. "Which means we get to start with the stick." He stared at her, proud she wasn't shying from his gaze. "Judge was fucked up; we both know that. Man who does what he did to his own sister, he's fucked up beyond where there ain't no understanding. You survived, which is good, but not without scars. Scars the result of wounds caused by your own blood. I got scars like those, too. When you and your mom were missing, Shooter came to Chicago. He'd always been hard to control. There were countless times when he'd fuck up club business simply by opening his fucking mouth. When he first headed back to Cali, you were young still when he went home. But even after he returned to the Outriders, he'd come back to visit." He shrugged. "Then you and your mom were gone."

"One of those visits, he seemed to go a little crazy. Attacked a brother, but it wasn't clear who'd provoked the fight. When Ripper—that's the brother he was fighting with—started choking the life out of him, I reacted without thinking. One of the few times in my life when thought didn't precede action. Put Ripper in the ground to save him. Choosing blood over my brother and best friend."

She was listening intently and, when he paused, she sat back in the chair but kept her gaze fixed on him.

"Money came up missing. Fifty large." He scoffed. "All signs pointed to me like a fucking roadmap. It would be years before I knew for sure who'd stolen the money and put those signs in place. I was in Cali when

I found out it was Shooter, but Morgan told me he'd take care of it, so I let it lie, left to go home. Stopped in Kentucky." He scrubbed at his face with his hand.

"I have Shooter to thank for Chase. He paid Carrie Sosa, a skank from home, to drug me. I'm not sure if the intent was for her to get pregnant, but it was a total fucking mess. Then it was twelve years before I found out I had a son. Years Shooter stole from me that I'll never get back with my boy. Seems every shit thing that's happened to me or my club can be laid at Shooter's feet.

"Fuck, Eddie. Even Bear's been manipulated by him. Judge was the carjacker that caused Rob Crew to become Bear in the first place, and then Shooter was behind the fucking beating Bear took in Des Moines, also via Judge. Then you being taken, hell you know how that went down better than the rest of us. Also Judge. Then Willa." She sucked in a breath. This would be the first she had confirmation about Judge's involvement in the kidnapping of her best friend.

"Judge was at the compound in Utah when we got there. Willa got out, got the other two women out. Sosa was already dead by then, but the motherfucker had cut off her fucking hand and sent it to me, special delivery. I was about out of my mind until Myron could tell me for sure it wasn't Willa's." He saw tears gathering in her eyes and shook his head.

"Hard as fuck to hear, I know. Eddie, if this gets too much, you tell me and we take a break, okay, honey? Bear's in the back if you want him." Her eyes widened, and he gave her a sad smile and nodded. "Yeah, his condition on the meet was that he be in the building. You want him, you tell me." At her silent nod, he gave a chin lift to Merry, who reached over and pounded on the door behind the bar. Within seconds, it was open, and Bear was striding across the room to kneel at Eddie's side.

"My heart, are you okay?" He ignored Mason, which was fine by him. At Eddie's nod, he circled her shoulders with his arms, pulling her head to his chest. They remained like that for a few minutes then she moved and Bear pulled back, turning to look at Mason. "You got much more, Prez?"

"Yeah." He swallowed, reaching out to put his hands around the barely tasted beer. "Utah. Utah was fucking hard. Part of it is Willa's story to tell, only if she wants...but, you need to know he hurt her. He took and hurt my woman. That is shit that cannot be forgiven. Ain't no marker can cover the pain dealt out to her. Your brother was a man in the end, accepting his death with courage."

"You killed him? You did for him?" He could hear the tears in her voice, and she turned her head to press into Bear's neck, muffling the rest of her words. "Luke is dead?"

"Yeah, sweetheart. He knew what he was doing, knew what he'd done. It was a calculated play on Judge's part, and I still don't know for sure if Shooter knew anything about it, but Judge worked his play end to motherfucking end." It was becoming difficult to restrain himself, because the idea of Judge's hands on Willa drove him insane and it was all he could do to not pound on the table in an effort to make this woman understand. "There was no other acceptable response to what he'd done. None. He was my responsibility, his blood my cost."

"Did he know who you were?" This was an interesting question, and one for which he didn't have a definite answer.

"I think so, but I'm not certain. Some of the things he said to Willa and Bethany led me to believe he did, but I don't think it was knowledge he'd held for long." He paused, because she was frowning.

"Bethany?" She shook her head. "I thought he had taken Mica."

"He did, but Bethany Mason from Nashville was the first one he locked up, and then Chase's mother." At the mention of Bethy's last name, Eddie's eyes grew round and large, but Mason ignored the response for now. "Willa was next, and finally Mica. He had her only a couple days before we found his ass."

"Four women? He kidnaped four women. Two of them with children?" Now she was getting pissed at Judge again, and he hoped she could hold onto part of that anger, because it would help get her through the grief.

"Yeah. That's the hard part. Your brother's death, at my hands. I'll be flying out to visit Shooter tomorrow, because he deserves to hear it from my mouth, like you have. Eddie, I won't say I'm sorry—"

She interrupted him, "No, you're right; Judge would have known the cost of his actions. All his life, he has always pushed and pushed, but then he'll simply sit back and take whatever punishment Da—Shooter deals out. I don't expect an apology." She paused for a minute and then looked up at Bear. "Baby, don't hate me," she said, and he jerked in surprise as she turned back to face Mason. "I'm glad to know I don't have to worry. That my kids don't have to worry. I think there was a time when Luke was...salvageable. By the time Mama died, it seemed his path was pretty set. I loved him, but I hated him, too. I'm not sorry he's dead. I'm not glad—don't get me wrong—but I'm not sorry. I wish I had been able to help him more. It seems like Shooter was always pushing him aside for me. I'm sure it didn't help anything."

Mason nodded slowly, thinking she was something else, Shooter's girl. Looking past her pain and exposing the painful practicality of dealing with unstable family, saying things society would be horrified at, but he understood. "I get you, Eddie. Cause and effect are clear, and they should leave no room for blame, but goddamn if regret can't pitch a tent anywhere. Luke's raising is on Shooter, not you, so don't you try to own any of that. Judge's actions were his own, not yours, so again, don't try and take it on yourself." He heard Mica in his words and smiled, and then, taking a breath, continued, "So like I said, that was the hard. Now for the easy."

He smiled at her and stretched out his hand across the tabletop. "Eddie Crew, I'd like you to meet your uncle, Davis Mason." She grinned and grabbed his hand, wrapping her fingers around his and holding on tightly. "You have an aunt, too. Bethany, my baby sister. She lives in Nashville and can't wait to meet you." She made a noise and he paused, but she nodded for him to go on. "You already know Chase, my boy. He's your blood, too. He's excited for you to meet Bethy, and was even more excited to know you two are cousins."

"I like Chase. He's been around the house a lot, working with Benny and Luce. They're rehearsing for shows, and he's helping out with some guitar tech stuff." She smiled and turned her head to look up at Bear. "There's always more room, right?"

Bear nodded and smiled. "Always more room for love."

Mason squeezed her hand, pulling her attention back to him. "Got one more thing, Eddie. When Judge first moved to Fort Wayne, he hooked up with a gal, got her pregnant." At her gasp of shock, he nodded. "Yeah, need you to listen quiet for a minute, because these things are twisted a little." He waited for her acknowledgement, and then continued, "The woman died when the boy was about five. His sister was in the wreck that took Winger and Lockee from us. She and her mom died on the same day, leaving the boy alone. Jonny, the boy's name is John Justice Morgan, hit the system and wound up being shifted from family to family. Not long ago, he lived upstairs from Willa, and I got to meet him."

"I remember him," she cried. "Sweet but shy, Wills feeds him all the time."

"Yeah, she did. You know DeeDee and I are cousins, right? Makes her your cousin, too." She nodded and he smiled. "She always wanted a big passel of kids, happiest whenever her house is full to overflowing. Jase found out about the boy; I don't know for sure how. Now they are moving down the path to adopting Jonny. Luke's boy, your nephew."

"Wow." That was all she said, but the single word spoke volumes.

Nodding, Mason said, "Yeah, wow."

"So you're my uncle. My husband's president is my uncle. The man my best friend is in love with is my father's brother. I have an aunt, a nephew, and two cousins I didn't know about." She waved her hand in front of her face. "Wow. Just letting it soak in a little." She smiled at him and leaned into Bear. "So you're this little one's great uncle?" The hand not clasping his dropped to her lap, palm covering her belly protectively.

"Yeah." He held up the bottle of beer and motioned to Merry, shaking it gently and saying, "Skunky and warm." Turning back to Eddie, without considering the uncertainty his words revealed, he asked, "You think Willa loves me?"

There was a light smack to the back of his head and he grinned up at Merry. "Don't be stupid, Davy. It's not a pretty look for you."

***

He stood in her kitchen, gaze tracking her movements. She traveled between the refrigerator and cabinet a dozen times. Each trip, she retrieved a single ingredient and added it to the dish then returning it to its original location, studying the instruction card again before getting the next item. He kept his face carefully calm, brow relaxed and smooth. This wasn't how Willa cooked; she was methodical in her work, but one of her favorite things was chaos where she lived, so this carefully organized and maintained order was foreign, a new change, and one he didn't like.

She wasn't talking either, hadn't said an unprompted word other than her initial hello. And, it hadn't escaped his notice she had been too busy to kiss him properly, only giving him a peck on the lips when he arrived. That wasn't his Willa, the woman who had boldly given him her number in the middle of a biker clubhouse, ignoring the aftermath of uninvited visitors barging in. His Willa had a hard time keeping her hands off him, nothing overtly sexual, no more than constant, glancing touches…and he had been the recipient of none of those tonight.

He shifted his weight and didn't miss the stutter in her movements when he did. *Fuck.* She was tracking him out of the corner of her eye, and if he wasn't wrong, and he knew he wasn't, she was nearly ready to run right now. From him. *From me.* When he got here about forty-five minutes ago, her doors were secured, every lock engaged, and he waited for several minutes on the doorstep. It was a long time before he heard her inside, moving the chain, unbolting the latch, turning the deadbolt. He wondered now if she had been watching through the peephole, trying to decide if he was worth the effort of allowing inside.

Looking around, he saw differences in her living space, too. Gone were the splatters of paint she claimed as art, the cheap, mass-produced frames mounted to every surface, each holding papers given to her by the kids from school. In their place were large, wide-matted, placid landscapes taking up broad, orderly swaths of wall space. Her clothing choices had changed, too, with matching colors and entirely covered skin. It looked as if she was remaking herself into a bland version of Willa, one without anything remarkable to draw attention.

Since Utah, in the weeks since he brought her home, they had struggled through periods of time when she became distant, detached, but this felt different. The reason he insisted on dinner here tonight was because last weekend he waited for an hour at a restaurant, only to find out she was 'out of town' at a conference. He was still splitting his time between Chicago and Fort Wayne and wasn't able to be here as much as he wanted, but when he was here, he wanted to be with her. Ditching him, and he didn't believe her excuses anymore, wasn't going to fly, because he had promised her they would work through this together. *Enough is enough*, he decided, straightening, and his heart clenched when she cringed, her shoulders rounding down, making herself a smaller target.

"Babe," he called softly, not wanting to startle her any more than he already had. She glanced over her shoulder and he saw the wet shine of tears on her cheeks.

"Sorry. Won't be long now," she said. "So sorry, I'm slow."

"Babe," he said again and took a step towards her, watching as her back stiffened, her hands freezing in place, gripping the edge of the countertop. He took another slow stride. "Don't worry about supper." Her shoulders hitched and he knew it was with a silent sob. "I don't come here for the food." He took another measured pace. "I'm here, because of you." He was within arm's reach of her now, his hands hovering an inch over her shoulders. "Babe," he said quietly, his mouth beside her head as he settled his palms on her, pulling her to him. "I'm here, because of you," he repeated, looking into the mixing bowl in front of her with a frown.

"Good," she said on a sob, and he turned her around, still looking down into the bowl over her shoulder. "Because I don't know what I'm doing." He stroked down one arm with his palm, gently gripping her wrist and slowly bringing it up around his neck. "I don't know anything anymore, Mason," she cried as he performed the same actions with her other arm, lifting and smoothly draping it around his neck too.

"You know plenty, baby doll. Let's go have a chat," he whispered, swaying her back and forth a second before he picked her up, cradling her to his chest.

Seated on her bed, back against the headboard, he held her in his lap, patiently staying in that position until she finally seemed to run out of tears. She hiccupped herself into silence, having said only a handful of intelligible words during the whole time. He caught his name, Eddie's name, and once…Luke. Mason hadn't tried to soothe her, simply held her as she cried herself out. He hadn't told her it would be okay, hadn't told her she should give it time. He offered no empty platitudes, certain in his knowledge that her confidence in him was already gone. There was no call to give her any reason to think he was stupid, too.

"I get it," he said finally. "You can't trust me." When she made a quarrelsome noise, he shook his head. "Shut that shit. It was my blood, my club, Willa. Sure as anything, it was associating with me that put you at risk."

He held her, not giving an inch when she tried to squirm out of his arms. Firmly, he told her, "I said shut that shit, Willa. Hold the fuck still." She froze, and then while he waited quietly, she slowly calmed. The long muscles in her arms and legs relaxed as her breath evened out. "Don't matter to me. Because I love you."

She wiggled again, and he growled, "You want a spanking, you contrary woman?" Her head turned back and forth on his chest then, after a few seconds, she gave a small nod and he laughed quietly, lips pressed together in a private smile. "There you are, Willa Grace. I've been looking for you." Sighing, he loosened his grip slightly and she tugged at his arm, silently asking for a return of his protective and possessive hold, and he gladly complied. *Anything you need, babe*, he thought, loving the feel of her in his arms. *Mine.*

"I'm not ever letting you go." He voiced this warning seriously, resting his chin on top of her head. "I can't, not and stay sane, babe. I need you, can't imagine my life without you. You haven't met belligerent yet, because I'll fight you every fucking step of the way if you try to get shut of me."

"I don't want—" she started, but he interrupted.

"You did tonight." Tipping his head, he kissed her cheek. "You wanted clear shut of me tonight. Way I've lived, I've had a lifetime of study on how to read people, and you wanted me out of your space in the worst way. Clear as fucking day, baby doll."

"Idontwannafeelthatway," she said quickly, running her words together, her shoulders hitching again. He waited, heard her swallow, and then, pain threading through her voice, she said, "I want to go back to before. Before my apartment wasn't safe. Before my life was torn up. Before my boyfriend had to watch a video of me being raped." She covered her mouth with one palm, having found more tears somewhere, she jerked and shuddered with the efforts of holding everything inside. Her voice dropped, becoming nearly inaudible as she said, "I want to go back."

"Can't," he said, shrugging.

"But I want to," she whispered. "I want to go back to maccy cheese, and laughter, back to when you wanted me."

He forced himself to breathe slowly and evenly, trying not to let her know how bad that hurt. When he finally thought he could respond without roaring, he said, "Like I said, can't do any of that. But you got some things wrong, babe." Twisting to one side, arms still around her as he pulled her ass off his lap, he settled her on the bed next to his hips so he could watch her face. "Your apartment is safe. I got good locks in place, and a linked up security system you use. Safe as toads, as DeeDee's fond of saying. If this place doesn't feel safe, we'll find you an apartment or house that does. You feel safe at my place, you move in. We find where you can be comfortable, and we build from there, babe.

"Tore up, yeah, your life has been fucked over; no hiding from it. By someone you trusted, because of someone you let in your life. Tore up, because of me. And, I saw what I saw. It is what it is. That doesn't define my feelings for you, though. It is what it is, Willa. I saw it. I heard it. But, that's all I have from it. I didn't have to live through it. You did.

"Can't go back, so we gotta move forward. We can do maccy cheese, easy breezy." He offered her a short-lived smile, tilting her chin up so she would look him in the eyes, because the next part was the most important. "Laughter is still inside you. Just gotta let it out. Set it free.

Find the door it's hiding behind and set it free. We can find that door together, set the sound of joy free in you again. Let me help you find it, babe. Because the other thing you got totally bass-ackwards wrong is thinking I'm past wanting you. I breathe air in, I want you.

He took a shuddering breath, letting her see the desperate desire on his face as he said, "I want you. Fuck yeah, I do." He saw her pupils dilate in response and took an easier breath. "And us? We're going to be all right, Willa, and that's not me blowing smoke up your ass. I breathe, I think, I exist...because I want you. Nothing changed there, except me trying to give you a chance to settle yourself, I see now I shoulda held back on."

She stared at him, her eyes flickering back and forth, gauging the sincerity of his words and actions, and then he saw the smallest crinkle at the corners of her lids. In a scolding tone, he asked, "You laughing at me, Willa?" She shook her head, but those tiny crinkles turned into larger ones, and she pressed her lips together, her shoulders beginning to shake. "Yes, you are. You're laughing at me. What are you thinking, woman?"

Throwing her head back, she gave a single bark of laughter, but it was more than he had from her in weeks and he was willing to take it. He would fucking take it all day long. Looking at him, she smiled, shaking her head. Wiping her nose with the back of her hand, she said, "Safe as toads? That's a weird saying."

He nodded, reaching over for a tissue and handing it to her, saying with a grin, "Clean that nose up, Willa. It's snot funny." When she finished laughing again, he settled her, letting her lean into his side. "It's a Kentucky saying I remember from my aunt." From her stillness, he knew she was listening carefully, like she always had when he talked about anything in his past, drinking up all the knowledge she could about him. Wanting to know everything. "When there was a storm brewing, she'd make sure us kids were tucked up in bed, telling us we were exactly like the toads snuggled under logs. We were safe as the toads, regardless of the weather."

"That was DeeDee's mom?" she asked, and he nodded.

"Yeah. My own mother was MIA most of my life. Aunt Barbra was all the soft I had for a long time. Pa made sure we had the basics, but she kept track of important things like birthdays. Safe as toads," he repeated and smiled. "A lot of our life there in the holler was hard; the mines were greedy for men, the land holding selfishly to its treasures, the precious black blood in her veins. I've got some pictures that show how it was, raw and real. There was this photographer who came through the holler not long before I left. Myron tracked him down years ago, got me some prints. William Gedney. If you want to understand Kentucky through my eyes, look at his pictures sometime. It was dirty and miserable, hard and hateful.

"But there was beauty there, too. In the songs and language. In the people and their love for each other and the land. I remember my aunt, how hard the life made her. Remember her making decisions between buying seed to grow food, and buying food for eating now. Watching her husband and sons take that damn elevator down into the ground, knowing every single time could be the last, their bodies left behind as too unsafe to retrieve. Then, I think about my mother, and how soft my memories of her are, how sweet she seemed, compared to her sister." He shrugged. "I wonder if she had it easier." He looked down at Willa, seeing her gaze attentively fixed on his face.

"Then I realize I know she didn't, because the last clear memory I have of her is pain. It's of her missing John so badly she was willing to risk a beating to share knowledge of him with me. I know she had to miss me and Bethy the same, no matter how comfortable her life was out there in California. Her death was hard. Harder than Aunt Barbra's, that's for sure. Club wars are as deadly as the mines ever thought to be." He shrugged, and smiled for a moment when he realized her hands had been moving on his arm, fingers twining with his as Willa stroked his skin. Touching him.

"Life goes on. I left the holler at sixteen, hardly ever looked back, except to make things better for the family as I could. I found out John did the same, once he learned where Mama came back to when she left them. He bought businesses and hired family. Hid those ties as deep as he could, because he had anger in him too. And that's something he didn't bury deep enough, so it fucking seeped."

He stared at the wall, his mouth moving without any filters tonight, his mind on her touches and caresses, so like her unconscious actions from before. Before Utah. "His shit seeped and seeped, poisoning his son. Judge learned anger and betrayal at his father's side, saw his sister accepted for what she was, the preferred child—while he was used for the jobs that couldn't be trusted to anyone else. But his hate, that vile poison? The shit what tracks right back to Shooter and his hatred and anger? It tracks back farther even, to his old man, Morgan. The man who set all this in motion. His hate seeped down until it got all over you, babe. Do I wish I could change the past? Hell yeah, I'd spare you all of this if I could only turn back the clock."

He reached up, cupping her chin in his hand, tilting her head up to capture her mouth with his in a hard, possessive kiss, stroking into her mouth with his tongue, tasting the tears on her lips. "I can't, babe. It's as set in stone as Gedney's black and white pictures. You can't change it once the paper is fixed. You can alter the look of it, overexpose, double expose, strip out the shadows, but the base is still there. The original's still embedded in the bones of the photo." He kissed her again and then whispered against her mouth, "We can find our way together. I know we can. We will, babe. You are strong, and I make you stronger. Come with me, and let's find a path we can agree on, move forward. Let me help you find your door to laughter, to passion, to life...to love."

She tipped her head back, and he felt the moment when she gave herself over, surrendering to him entirely, trusting he would be there to catch her. Easing her down on the bed, he leaned over her, kissing his way along her cheek and jaw, his hand settling on her stomach, feeling her skin twitch and tremble, fear blooming under his touch.

They had made love since it happened, but it had been too long, and he had given her enough room in her head that now she had a fence to get over, it seemed. He nuzzled along her neck, nipping and kissing his way down then slowly back up, taking her mouth in another hard kiss, his tongue stroking hers, drawing a gasp from her when he gently bit her lip.

"I want you, Willa." He said this firmly, settling his chest on her torso, using his weight to anchor her in the moment. Slipping his leg between hers, he pulled his knee up, pushing hard on her core, feeling her lift up to grind her hips on him. Without giving her a chance to think, he kissed her again, slipping his hand into her still buttoned jeans, feeling her belly hollow under his touch, and then his fingers were on her pussy.

He didn't tease her, wanted her to feel good fast, to know how much he wanted her, how hard it was to hold back. He pushed farther, sliding first one finger then a second deep inside her, rubbing her clit with his thumb, thrumming back and forth over the tight bundle of nerves. He felt her hand leave his neck and a fluttering along his arm, and then the constriction of her jeans released and he could move his hand more readily. Her hips pushed up again, legs opening, and he thrust his tongue deep into her mouth, sweeping against hers while he fucked her with his fingers, capturing her moans in his mouth.

Shifting his hip, he pinned her to the bed and said, "Be still. Let me get you off, babe."

With a catch in her breath, she whispered, "But I want to move."

"I know you do. But be still for me, just trust me." He bit her bottom lip, tugging on it as he ground his palm into her pussy. "Let me get you there," he said, and she made a noise he took as agreement, bending his head to nip her breast through her shirt. When he felt her hands on his cock through his jeans, he moved his hips back and lifted his head, pausing all movement. "No, Willa. This is for you."

He nuzzled between her breasts, using his teeth to drag the top of her shirt down. He kissed the skin he exposed, taking in as much as he could, sucking hard as he increased the pace of his hand and fingers. Feeling her pussy tighten and release, she was hoarsely calling his name, and he pushed a third finger in, going deep and holding there, fluttering his fingertips while maintaining a steady, fast stroke across her clit with his thumb.

"Kiss me," she begged, and he lifted his face, letting her lead the way for a moment then crushing her mouth beneath his, nearly coming in his pants, because feeling her clench around his fingers was so good. She tasted so good...felt so good. He slowed the kiss, stroking between her folds deliberately, gently, waiting for her heart rate to settle back down, her breathing to even out. Drawing back, he looked down into her face, seeing a soft smile there, and he said, "Hey, babe. Love looks good on you," realizing her eyes were echoing the emotion.

Leaning down, he kissed her again, rubbing his cheek along hers. "Wanna fuck you now, all right?" She made a humming noise deep in her throat, and her head moved alongside his, her nod slow and sure.

He sat up, reaching to push her pants down, leaning past her hips to pull them off her legs, taking her panties and socks at the same time. He turned and said, "Lift," as he pulled up the hem of her shirt, and she obediently raised her arms. True to her nature, she had something like four shirts on, but no bra, and he grinned at her, stripping them off all at one time.

He stood, watching as she settled on the bed, seeing how she kept her eyes on him while he took off his cut. Then her eyes widened as he reached behind his head, gripping the collar of his shirt and pulling it over his head. "That's so sexy," she whispered, and he laughed.

Unfastening his jeans, he pushed them down his thighs, bending over to remove his boots and socks. "Taking off my shirt is sexy? Damn woman, I'm sexy every day then."

"Yes. Oh yes, you are," she muttered, turning on her side and tucking a palm under her cheek. "You want covers, Mason?"

"Fuck no. I want to lay eyes on every beautiful inch of you. Remember how addicted I am to your skin? No covers, no clothes, the only thing over you is going to be me, baby doll." He put a knee to the bed, and then paused, because she had a frightened look on her face. Reaching out, he cupped her cheek in his hand. "Willa, what is it?" Lying down beside her, he settled in, keeping his hand on her, using his fingers to sweep her hair back from her face.

"I'm scared," she said this in a hoarse whisper, and he heard the tears that threatened to climb to the surface again.

"Of me, babe? I'd never hurt you," he reassured her, tracing her cheek with his thumb.

"We've used protection every time," she said, and he was confused. He hummed and nodded, keeping his gaze on her face, trying to read her intent, then shook his head. He thought he knew where she was going with this, but would wait on her so he would be sure.

"Not the last time, babe. You rode me bare," he said, and her eyes widened. "Every touch, replaced by mine. Remember?"

She nodded and sighed, her voice hitching as she said, "I got a blood test…after." Keeping his face immobile, he nodded again. He knew that, had taken her to the doctor and held her hand during the examination. Had laughed when she couldn't look as they drew his blood, and then wiped the sweat from her face when they stuck the needle in her arm. "There was one thing they meant to test for, but I didn't want to know. I'm scared." She took a deep breath. "There was no bad stuff, which was good."

"I'm clean. You're clean. That's all good, Willa." He stroked her cheek. "Babe, I'm not trackin'. You gotta spell things out for me. Why are you scared?" He watched as she closed her eyes and swallowed.

"I'm late." Those two whispered words dropped into the silence of the room like rocks in a pond, and it took every bit of self-restraint he had to keep his breathing slow, to not rail at the injustice of what had been done to her. For a moment, he saw Ruby, bent double in a ditch, and then Molly, seated in J.J.'s lap, holding her newborn infant as he slept. Two similar situations, with incomparable outcomes, and he knew which one he wanted for them right now. He kept his hand moving on her face, trailing his fingers down her throat to her chest, cupping and plumping her breast, tweaking her nipple between finger and thumb.

"You want it?" he asked.

Her eyes flew open, gaze intently fixed on him. He leaned in, lifting her breast to his mouth, sucking hard on her peaked nipple as he shifted and moved forward. He aligned their bodies so he could press his thigh between her legs, rubbing and pushing until she tilted her knee up, opening to him.

"I don't not want it," she said then shook her head. "That sounded stupid."

"Not stupid," he murmured against her skin. "Confused, but not stupid. You are far from that, baby doll. Smartest woman I know."

"I'm not even sure," she whispered. "I might not be. Stress and all that." He nipped at the side of her breast and her breath caught in her throat with passion, not tears. "If I am, I can't think of anything but keeping it."

"Then we keep it," he said calmly, trailing his lips up her chest to her throat, where he dragged his teeth on his way back to her lips.

"We?" The single word question spoke of all her worst fears and explained so much of her behavior tonight.

Against her lips, he whispered, "We." He kissed her thoroughly...until she was moving on his leg and greedily running her hands over his shoulders and arms. "Plus, there's an excellent bonus," he said with a smile, and she tilted her head, lifting one eyebrow in a question. "No more condoms for this cocky bastard." He leaned down, rolling her onto her back and kissing her hard, moving between her legs and sliding in slowly. Placing his mouth next to her ear, he whispered, "Because if you aren't now, you will be soon, babe. Can't wait to share this with you. However things shake out."

Seating his cock deep inside her, he reared up on his arms, lifting his chest off her, watching the expressions chasing across her face as he thrust hard. "Love you, babe," he said, kissing her palm as, fingers tracing his skin, it slipped past his face, nipping at her thumb when it came close to his mouth.

Much later, they were walking back to the kitchen, moving slowly, stopping every few paces so he could kiss her again. She wrinkled her nose. "What is that smell?"

"Whatever you were cooking tonight," he said, and she laughed, looking over into the bowl and picking up the spoon to stir the gloppy mixture. "What the hell were you cooking, Willa?"

She laughed again. "No freaking idea. It looks like there's wine, cabbage, and three kinds of candy, mostly."

He stroked her hair, closing his eyes.

"Sounds perfect."

**

"My heart." He heard Bear's guarded words and knew Eddie had to be chomping at the bit to get inside the house. Mason stepped around the front fork of his Vincent, meeting them beside their SUV. He gave Bear a chin lift and pulled Eddie in for a hard hug.

She looked around then asked, "Where's Wills?"

He shook his head. "She wanted to give you a chance to meet him without her...hold on, let me get this right...'stealing all your golden thunder with her awesome maccy cheese goodness.' That sounds about right." He paused a beat, trying to decide if he should say anything, then with a grin left the news for Willa to pass along when she was ready.

Bear was watching him intently, and then he tilted his head and said, "Prez has a secret."

"Shut the fuck up," he said, gently pushing Eddie back into his friend. "Keep your old lady off me, man. Don't need no mauling today."

"You have a secret, and it's to do with Willa." Tilting his head the other direction, he looked at Mason and then must have recognized the growing lack of tolerance, because instead of pursuing that line of questioning, he quickly shook his head and said, "Let's go inside."

"One second, man." He turned to Eddie, marveling again that he was looking into eyes exactly like the ones he saw in the mirror any time he cared enough to look. Shaking his head, he said, "Need you to hear me. You trackin'?" This would set the stage for Willa's news, if it turned out to be Judge's baby instead of his.

"I got you, Prez," she said, and he knew she understood the import of what he was about to say.

"DeeDee's sick with thinking you want the boy. You need to understand—" He stopped, because she was already shaking her head.

"I've seen him, remember? I know him. I know I'm going to love him, but she and Jase are his family in the ways that matter now. If he wants to know about his dad someday, I'll talk to DeeDee, find out how much she wants him to know. She shouldn't be afraid, Mason. If anything, the boy'll have too much family. Between Lucia and our boys, Slate's kids, the tribe they've got with Bingo," she spread her palm over her belly, "and any new additions."

Shaking her head, she said, "If he didn't have Jase and DeeDee, then yes, in a heartbeat. I'd have him out of foster care and in my home." She took Bear's hand in hers, and he watched their fingers fit together comfortably, saw Bear's lips stretch in a loving smile. Clearly, he had found his way past the demons that had chased him as long as Mason had known the man. "Our home."

"I just want to meet him now, with the knowledge of who he is." She looked past him and waved, calling, "We're on our way, DeeDee." Looking back at Mason, she said, "I got you," and he nodded, stepping back and out of the way, turning to follow them up the walk.

39. Love

Standing in their bedroom at the apartment, he looked at the woman in his arms. Willa had moved in with him and Chase, settling into their lives as if she had always been there. He glanced in the adjoining bathroom and saw the sack from the pharmacy still on the countertop. Sighing with frustration, he knew she hadn't opened it yet. "Babe," he scolded, frowning at her. "Will you just go pee on the stick already?"

She shook her head firmly, sniffing loudly.

He tried to hide his twitching lips, but she saw and her face fell, a look of hurt closing in on her features. "Don't laugh at me," she said, pouting a little.

Now he couldn't help it; he smiled openly, leaning in to kiss her hard, possessing her mouth. "What are you afraid of now, Willa?"

"What if I'm not?" This was near a whisper, her voice breathy with anxiety.

He shrugged, knowing if she was pregnant, she was afraid of what came next. Telling people, explaining the timing, if his real reaction didn't match his stated intention...so many things for her to fear. He also knew if she hadn't caught, it would be a blow of a different kind, still hurtful, still tender, because he told her he wanted this with her. She was coming back around into her own, but he suspected she was going to always be changed, altered by what happened in Utah. By Judge.

Gone was the woman who feared nothing, because she expected the best out of people. The woman unafraid to sit her ass on a stool in a biker bar in Chicago, stalking a man she had only met a couple of times. The friend who gave freely, unselfishly, all the while greedy for returned affection and love. Judge had taken those from her. In their place, he had given her fear and distrust, caused her to send sidelong glances at people she met in the street, and dredged up a need for scrutiny of folks she knew. Beyond all that, at the core of everything was what he had taken from her, the ability to trust herself.

Over the past weeks, Mason had been able to give laughter back to her, and helped regrow her confidence in him, but he knew the greater world was scary now, where it had never been before. She didn't seem to have the coping skills most people developed over time, emotional calluses made when reality fell short of expectations and you got screwed over. She had never needed them, because, before Judge, she only had good in her life. He could give her a few more hours, or days. Or hell, weeks, if that's what it took. She held the rest of his life in her heart; he would gladly wait forever for her.

"Then don't pee on the stick." Reaching down, he took her hand in his, threading their fingers together as he folded it against his chest, holding it to his heart. "Knowing today versus tomorrow, or even next week won't change anything either way. Let it go, babe. Life happens, so just let it go."

***

"See what I mean?" He asked the question softly, resting his chin on the top of her head. She had tired of playing in the waves and come back to wedge herself between his thighs, leaning against his chest.

"Yeah," she said, assuming the same reverent tone. "It's peaceful."

They were on an extended road trip, and together had explored a variety of landmarks and attractions. He was completely unsurprised when she demanded they stop and visit the world's largest ketchup bottle, and then was bemused when she had an intense argument with the man selling tickets about the correct spelling: catsup versus ketchup.

Since the moment months ago when he realized what Willa meant to him, he had wanted to bring her here. Wanted to show her this piece of earth that had embedded itself into his mind in a way that meant he could pull it out anytime he needed, and it would soothe him. As she did. Today, and every day, he was amazed at how profoundly transformed he was by her presence. She was his future.

She never failed to surprise him, and he loved that about her, exactly as he loved so many other things. He smiled, kissing the top of her head as he thought about the surprise he had planned for her. This had seemed a likely location for it, and once they were here, he knew it was perfect. Turning his head, he looked up the beach to where that long-ago family had waited for their boy to return to them, trusting he would. "What do you think about Garrett?" He fingered the lump in his pocket, remembering the awe in the boy's voice as he talked about the chunk of sea glass.

"Ohh, that's a good name. You should tell Bear you thought of a boy's name. I believe he's running the betting pool." She snorted a laugh, and then covered her nose with her hand, laughing loudly. "We don't even know yet. How could he know before we even know?" She twisted around, looking at him accusingly. "You said something to him, didn't you?"

"Nope, he's just one of the folks who pay attention." He trailed a fingertip along her jaw then gripped her chin in his hand. Lifting her face, he kissed her softly, lovingly, and then turned her face back to the ocean. "Watch the waves, babe. They're amazing."

"Like Slate and Gunny," she said, nodding.

He slid his hand down, possessively cupping his palm around the column of her neck. He could feel her heartbeat through his fingertips, strong and steady. "Amazing?" He was surprised; he didn't know she liked the two men so much. He frowned, remembering a story Gunny had told on more than one occasion about caging her into a booth at Marie's so she couldn't interrupt one of Bear and Eddie's first romantic interludes. According to him, she had stayed pissed off at him for a long time.

"No, goober. They watch. All the time, everyone. I've decided if I'm around them, or you...or Bear, I don't have to worry as much. I can follow your lead." Yawning, she stretched her arms out in front, winding her fingers together and flipping her hands into and against her chest, her fingers moving to stroke the backs of his hand where he held her. "And the waves are amazing, and amazingly sleep-inducing."

Pulling his hand away, she flipped to her knees between his legs, leaning in for a brief lip touch, and then climbed to her feet. Wobbly in the shifting sand for a moment before he reached up to steady her, she squeezed his fingers in silent thanks. Shading her eyes with the edge of her hand, she looked up the bank behind him and said, "Bathroom break. I'll be right back."

"Want me to come with?" he asked casually, knowing she still struggled with strange situations, but she shook her head.

"I think I can walk a hundred feet by myself, Mason." Wrinkling her nose at him, she repeated, "I'll be right back." He watched her striding away through the sand as she struggled a little as it shifted away from the pressure of her feet. She climbed the little dune and made it to the walkway, waving at him before disappearing into the building there. He turned and faced the ocean again, watching the steady advancement of the waves rolling through the water.

True to her word, a few minutes later, she was wedging herself back between his thighs and he grinned, wrapping an arm around her and kissing the side of her head. Pointing up the beach, he indicated a group of teenagers who had appeared right before she returned. They were all crouched on the sand, huddled around pieces of equipment they were assembling into something large and colorful. "I think they're going to fly kites. Isn't that the coolest thing?" She pressed something into his hand and he looked down, seeing a white plastic object.

"Babe," he said softly. "You ready?"

"Hold off until after they launch the kites; I want to wait and find out which color flies first." She shivered, and he wrapped his arms around her, marveling at her strength. *My Willa*, he thought, tightening his arms. *My life*.

He watched as two boys gripped the outer edges of a huge, green fabric wing, while another boy stepped backwards, his mouth moving as he counted off the paces so he would know how much line he had free. At his nod, the other two boys tossed the structure into the air and Mason held his breath when the wind caught it, taking it up, the kite racing quickly into the sky, arcing overhead. The sunlight shining through the fabric gave it a shimmering look, the bright sea glass green nearly blinding as they watched it soar.

While she was still gazing up, he pried the cover off the test with one hand, grinning to see a huge pink plus sign. "Love you, Willa Grace. We agree; we both like the name Garrett. What if our baby's a girl?" She twisted in his arms, and he was silently relieved to witness a look that held only pleasure and anticipation on her face.

"It's a yes?" She whispered the question, holding her breath until he nodded. On an outrush of air, eyes wide with excitement, she asked, her voice shaking, "We'll figure it out, right?" He nodded again, leaning in to kiss her, and then faced her forward again, and together they watched the kite chase the sun.

40. Friends, family...enemies

Looking around the bar at his brothers, Mason was filled with pride as he viewed the comfortably affluent members of the club sitting at the tables and booths of Jackson's. It had long been his desire every member have the opportunity to make the most of their talents, become successful in whatever way that mattered to them. Who would have thought a boy raised in a family compound in backwoods Kentucky—ruled by the fundamentalist patriarch of the family, where individual success had never been encouraged—would come to this? He had grown up with hunger and exhaustion as constant companions, and for decades had found himself perpetually angry at the world and his family.

Mason leaned forward, propping his elbows on the table, and muttered to himself, "No longer dirt-floor poor." He knew if he stepped outside, there would be more than a million dollars' worth of rolling steel in the parking lot in the form of motorcycles. He also knew the prosperity his brothers enjoyed was a direct result of *his* planning and discipline. As long as he could keep the chapters and members in line, keep them satisfied without becoming complacent, everyone profited. *Remember, boy, pride goeth before a fall*, he heard his father's voice and was startled for a moment then realized it was a memory.

I'm just a poor wayfaring stranger

He shook his head at the memories, quickly followed by an unwelcome one of Deacon. Because, unlike his predecessor, he had always cared more about his brothers than himself, ensuring they were taken care of before anything came to him. Even if it meant he had to dress up in monkey suits and meet with investors and bankers on a regular basis, or sit on the fucking Chicago City Council.

Few of his brothers knew he had a business degree, and fewer still knew the full breadth of the assets Mason Corporation held in trust for all. Security and stability in all their lives was a critical need for him. Mason was determined never again to feel the sting of poverty or hunger. Now, as ever throughout his life, he was willing to do whatever was necessary to make certain he had both the power and money to provide for everyone he loved.

He looked across to see Willa perched on a barstool, head thrown back, laughing at something Merry had said. It had been a good few months since their trip out west. He had come home with a deep, rich appreciation for Willa, and was still in awe of her strength. Watching her regain her joy, her laughter, was worth every moment he spent coaxing it out of her, sweet-talking her out of the dark place she had retreated to after Utah.

California had been the turning point. Sitting on the beach between his legs, she had learned she could trust him, which meant she could trust herself. He had matched words to actions that day, holding and supporting her without caring who had fathered the babe she carried in her belly. Then, he matched words and deeds again when he asked her for a gift, freely given—a title, like president, he would gladly bear for the rest of his life.

My wife. She turned sideways, and his gaze greedily raked over her swollen belly, watching as her hand dropped to rub gently along her side. *Mine. My always.*

***

The man's thoughts twisted and twined, watching her, a certain satisfaction in knowing she couldn't see him. As she tugged futilely on the doorknob again, he laughed quietly and reached out, using his middle finger to thump loudly on the glass separating them. She jumped backwards, her blonde hair swirling around her frightened face. The contrast between her dark coloring and light hair was mesmerizing, and over the past week he had found himself standing for long hours watching her through the mirror. He was pleased she only jumped, but hadn't shrieked or screamed, which earned her points for bravery. From her escape attempts, he already knew she wasn't stupid. Brave, smart, and beautiful. He admired her.

As he stared at her, evaluating both her condition and state of mind, he knew from the tension and strain evident in her features she had to be right on the edge. He suspected he had nearly held her long enough now; she should soon be ready for him to ask his questions and expect honest answers in return.

He could already recognize how she wanted to tell him, was eager to explain away her father's behaviors, and truly needed him to understand why the Southern Soldiers hated him. And, she would talk, no doubt. They would have a conversation. It might be a bit...one-sided at first. But she *would* talk.

Then, the minute he held the information he sought, he would be in the wind. Gone and away, long vanished before anyone found the girl or her beautiful bones. Because someone somewhere was already calling out his name.

***

Mason lay behind her on the bed, his body curved to fit against hers, sharing his warmth with her in the early morning chill. Her mumbled words were hard to hear, but he eventually understood she was talking to him in her sleep. "I won't stop. I'm gonna fight, Mason. I promise. I know you're coming. I've known from the first minute I saw you that you'll always come for me."

She was quiet a moment then whispered in a sleep-slurred voice, "Your eyes...so beautiful. You are so beautiful. You always see...everything. Give me confidence no matter. I love you." She sighed, shifting in the bed, pressed to him tightly.

Yesterday, he had introduced her to Tilly, sitting on the blanket beside the granite headstone, which, over the years, he had visited too many times to count. Seated there, bracketed by two of the women he loved most in the world, he told her the story of how a good man, a beloved husband and father, lost his life, because Mason had failed. Merry had listened to his version a thousand times, and he knew what she would say at the end. What she always said these days, telling him she didn't hate him and hoped he didn't either.

Willa stared at him the entire time he spoke, her face closed off, unreadable.

When he came to the end, winding down to silence, they sat there side-by-side for a moment. Then, she threaded her fingers through his, bringing the back of his hand to her lips, pressing a kiss onto the flesh there. "You did good, Mason," she whispered, and he drew a breath in shock. Snorting a laugh, she told him, "As controlling as you like to be, those two men were on a collision course that had nothing to do with you. I'm sorry, but your brother is flatout butthole crazy. I think you know he is, and probably knew it back then, too. So you couldn't control his actions, and it was his actions that caused Tilly to do what he did. His actions that caused this beautiful woman to lose her husband." She leaned over, reaching a hand out to grasp Merry's, then she tilted her chin up, looking into his face. "But you cared enough to preserve the two things he loved. His wife, who you kept safe, and to this day protect and love, and his bar, which you renamed to wipe out the memory of yet another act by that crazy man."

Pulling him back to the present, she sighed again and stretched, moving heavily, rolling half onto her back and leaning against his muscular frame. He pressed his face into the crook of her neck, breathing in the scent of her as his hand curved over her hip, spreading possessively across her belly. His child. Regardless of parentage, this was his child. Smiling when he felt the soft thud and pressure outwards from her stomach, he gently rubbed, feeling another thud against his hand.

She shifted and made a noise, coming partially awake, and he whispered, "Shhhh. My boy and I are communing." He stroked his palm across her belly, trailing his fingers over the curves, sliding his palm up and down her side as he said, "Garrett Davis Mason, son, you need to go back to sleep and let your momma get some rest. We have plans for tomorrow." He felt the same thud and push, the heel of the child's foot unerringly locating his hand and making itself firmly known.

***

Watcher looked at his phone again, waiting for the fucking thing to ring. "Juanita, tell me again why our girl needed to live on campus, when we live in the same fucking town where she's going to school?" There was a noise from the kitchen and he shook his head. "Her apartment mate, is that even the right word? Roommate I get, but fucking apartment mate? Anyway, the gal called and left a message. Know anything?"

His wife leaned out and shook her head, pointing to the phone she was holding, and motioned him to come to her. "Is that her?" She shook her head, passing the phone to him wordlessly.

He had a sinking feeling in the pit of his stomach and gingerly took the phone as if it were a Gila monster about to bite. "Yeah?"

He got no further than that before the voice on the phone said, "Estavez needs to talk to you, amigo. Un momento."

"Let me speak to him then," he barked, and his wife covered her mouth with her hand. "What the fuck is up? I'm waiting for a call here."

"Watcher, my friend," he heard the smooth voice of the Macho's president and shook his head.

"Estavez, what do you need?" That sick feeling in his belly wouldn't go away and he waited.

"Lalo," he said, and Watcher's hand tightened on the phone.

"Yeah?" He gritted his teeth. "What about Lalo?"

"Has your daughter." With three words, his world came to a crashing, screeching halt, and the only word he could utter was a plea.

"Where?"

***

"Promise you won't be mad?" Chase asked, and Mason stopped and looked back at him, trailing behind as they walked up to the clubhouse.

"Can't promise if I don't know the topic, son, so...no." He turned to face Chase, marveling that every time he had the opportunity to stand near the boy he noticed he had grown taller and broader than before.

"It's about the club." Chase reached up, raking his hair back off his forehead.

"Let's pull up a bench," Mason said, steering the boy around the corner of the clubhouse, where picnic tables waited for the next family party. "Sit." He pointed, and once Chase had parked his ass, said, "Talk."

"If I didn't want to patch in right away, would you be mad?" His boy wouldn't even look him in the eye. How the fuck had he gotten things so wrong?

Sitting beside Chase, he gripped his son's shoulder and shook him gently. "Fuck no, I won't be mad. Remember, it was me who told you that waiting was better. Need to know for sure it's a fit, son."

"And if it isn't ever a fit?" Chase whispered the words, cutting his gaze up to his father's face.

"Then it isn't." Mason shrugged. "That it? The big question you wanted me to bring you here to ask? I thought you might be going to wish for a bike from Gunny for your next birthday," he said and laughed.

"That would be sweet." Chase grinned, the stiffness falling from his muscles.

"Fuck no, ain't happening. Let's get inside, find out what's going on. Willa wants us home for lunch. I told her it was a maybe, but you know she's cooking anyway." He stood, stretching, and dug in his pocket when he heard his phone. With a smile on his face, he answered, "Watch, man. How you doin'?"

***

Waking her abruptly, the dogs started going off, noisy barking filling the night. She lay there for a minute, waiting as they barked themselves out, becoming embarrassed as dogs will when they've sounded an alert for no reason. The barking trailed off until a final flurry of yaps came, again drawing her attention outside. Throwing back the comforter and sheet, she slid out of bed, standing beside it in a polka-dotted, oversized shirt, already rumpled from the brief hour she had been asleep. Squinting around the small room, she took in the familiar silhouettes of the piles of books and CDs stored on every empty surface, comforted her favorite escapes were only an arm's length away.

Sidling up to the narrow window, cautious now, as she might not have been before, she reached out a small hand to pull back one side of the curtain, letting in weak light from the aged security lights. Stiffening, her gaze locked on the outline of a big man leaning nonchalantly against a truck parked across the street. He looked up, presumably at the movement in the window, and lifted one hand lazily, giving her a two-fingered wave before climbing into the cab of the truck. Frozen in place, she flattened a palm against the cold windowpane and listened as the truck coughed and then started, roaring and growling. Bethany watched as her brother slowly pulled away, driving down the quiet, residential Nashville street.

She turned to climb back into bed, her foot kicking a chair leg and she stumbled, reaching out to catch her balance. Looking down at the demo CD in her hand, she smiled, putting it in her bag for tomorrow.

THE END (of this story)

THANK YOU FOR READING *MASON*!

Thank you for reading *Mason*, book #6 in the **Rebel Wayfarers MC** series. Davis Mason came to visit along with Mica in the earliest rendition of our Rebel family, and the man has clearly been prepared to go the distance. Not only is he in every story and has influenced each character in profound ways, he still populates my dreams with frequency. Expect to hear more from him in future books beginning with *Hoss*, next book in the series, available now.

MASON'S PLAYLIST

I put together YouTube playlists of music both mentioned in the book, and used during writing and editing. Want a peek into the mind of me? Be sure of your decision, it's not always normal here!

Mason's playlist: bit.ly/mason-playlist

ABOUT THE AUTHOR

Raised in the south, MariaLisa learned about the magic of books at an early age. Every summer, she would spend hours in the local library, devouring books of every genre. Self-described as a book-a-holic, she says "I've always loved to read, but then I discovered writing, and found I adored that, too. For reading...if nothing else is available, I've been known to read the back of the cereal box."

Also by MariaLisa deMora

Alace Sweets

A dark thriller, this book is not a light read. Filled with edge-of-your-seat suspense, this intense story commands the reader's attention as it drives towards the explosive ending. Alace Sweets is a vigilante serial killer, with everything that implies and is sure to trip all your triggers. Be ready.

At seventeen, Alace Sweets turned a corner in her life, taking the wrong shortcut home from school.

Resisting the harsh knowledge her attackers will never be made to pay for their actions, Alace takes a stand. Justice must be served, and if fate's scales are out of balance, she's determined to set things right as best she can.

When the laws of men fail, the rules of Alace prevail.

5-Star Reviews for Alace Sweets

"deMora has a superb story-line and exceptional character development. All of her characters have such depth that will intrigue the reader..."
~Turning Another Page

"Hot, sweet, dark thriller."
~Beth D

"It will keep you on the edge of your seat and give you chills."
~Escape Reality Book Blog

"Disturbing, haunting, sickly; yet hot, sexy and heart racing!"
~Amanda L

"From the first page [deMora] pulls you into the world she has created and you do not even try to escape..."
~Little Shop of Readers Blog

"A must read for all those dark, gritty romance fans out there."
~Sweet & Spicy Reads

"You will find yourself so drawn into the story that the outside world is blocked out and your locking the doors and turning on all the lights."
~Danena F

"Don't judge me for bonding with a vigilante serial killer, she's more than what she does."
~iScream Books

"Thrilling...chilling...full of suspense, nail biting edge of your seat excitement."
~Tracey H

"Every time MariaLisa deMora picks up her pen (or opens her computer), she creates characters you want to believe in."
~Gail S

"Intriguing dark storyline, beautiful love story and nail-biting conclusion, what more could a reader ask for?"
~Manda M

"This book takes you a dark and twisted ride that is gripping..."
~Renee Entress' Blog

"This book is dark and gritty and I literally had to take a day off from reading it because it's that intense."
~My Girlfriend's Couch

"This is my favourite book so far from this author ... I recommend this book if you enjoy dark romantic thrillers."
~Cheekypee Reads and Reviews

"There's not enough stars to give this book and 5 just doesn't really do it justice!"
~DeLane C

"I couldn't put this book down from page one! Tried to stop & go to bed but couldn't sleep thinking about Alace and got up & finished the book."
~Debbie M

"MariaLisa DeMora, wordsmith that she is, made this a story of the enlightenment of a woman and finding love in a life where she has had none."
~Kat W

"Whatever deep dark trench [deMora] pulled a character like Alace from should be revisited again and often."
~Confessions of a Serial Reader

ADDITIONAL SERIES AND BOOKS

Please note that books in a series frequently feature characters from additional books within that series. If series books are read out of order, readers will twig to spoilers for the other books, so going back to read the skipped titles won't have the same angsty reveals.

Rebel Wayfarers MC series:

Mica, #1
A Sweet & Merry Christmas, short story #1.5
Slate, #2
Bear, #3
Jase, #4
Gunny, #5
Mason, #6
Hoss, #7
Harddrive Holidays, short story #7.5
Duck, #8
Biker Chick Campout, short story #8.5
Watcher, #9

A Kiss to Keep You, novella #9.25
Gun Totin' Annie, short story #9.5
Secret Santa, short story #9.75
Bones, #10
Gunny's Pups, novella #10.25
Never Settle, short story #10.5
Not Even A Mouse, short story #10.75
Fury, #11
Christmas Doings, #11.25
Gypsy's Lady, #11.5
Cassie, #12
Road Runner's Ride, novella #12.5

Occupy Yourself band series:

Born Into Trouble, #1
Grace In Motion, #2 (TBD)
What They Say, #3 (TBD)

Neither This, Nor That series:

This Is the Route Of Twisted Pain, #1
Treading the Traitor's Path: Out Bad, #2
Trapped by Fate on Reckless Roads, #3 (TBD)

Other Books:

With My Whole Heart
Alace Sweets
Hard Focus

More information available at mldemora.com.

www.ingramcontent.com/pod-product-compliance
Lightning Source LLC
Chambersburg PA
CBHW071642260626
47170CB00001B/202